THE

RETREAT

Earth was ruined. Humankind destroyed. Or so they were told. . .

www.kellystclare.com

✳

THE RETREAT

Kelly St. Clare

- The After Trilogy, Book 1 -

Praise for The Retreat:

"superbly written"
- Readers' Favorite ★★★★★

"part fantasy, part sci-fi, and all cosmic-chemistry"
- Amy's Bookshelf Reviews ★★★★★

"all I can say is WOW!"
- Taking It One Book at a Time ★★★★★

"I had very high expectations for this one and I'm happy to say that the book met them all and more."
- Bookaholic ★★★★★

"I can't start talking about this or I won't stop. This is a must read!"
- Amazon Reviewer ★★★★★

BOOKS BY KELLY ST. CLARE

The Tainted Accords:
Fantasy of Frost
Fantasy of Flight
Fantasy of Fire
Fantasy of Freedom

The Tainted Accords Novellas:
Sin
Olandon (2017)
Rhone (2018)
Shard (2018)

The After Trilogy:
The Retreat
The Return

THE RETREAT

To following your dreams, even if they are a world away.

THE RETREAT

Acknowledgements

I slid my foot farther over the science fiction threshold for this novel, a little dubious about just how much research it was going to require. To my surprise, I've loved every second of it—learning about space, global warming, even the physics. My high-school teachers would fall down dead if they knew.

But my study could only take me so far before I required the help of people significantly more intelligent than myself. To Declan, who corrected my use of inertia, and to Bianca and Anna, my environmental scientists, a large high-five for the lot of you. Thank you for taking the time to give The Retreat a touch of authenticity. My beta readers: Barbara, Michelle, Hayley, and Kayla. You are all authors I respect, and it was an honour to have your feedback on this novel. I can assure you, the snakes are now venomous, not poisonous.

The polish-and-shine crew has been just as amazing in this series.

To Tracey at Soxsational Cover Art for the gorgeous cover. To Robin for her copy-editing skills. And to Melissa Scott, my content editor, who does a fabulous job taking out my italicised and capitalised words that I always try to sneak in.

I would like specifically mention my friends and family, who have accepted my absence from many social gatherings. For my readers who are familiar with The Tainted Accords, you'll know I've written this book and the fourth in my other series at the same time. The support and understanding from you all during my Octopus Author phase was noted. And much appreciated. Pizza's on me!

To my husband, Scott. I doubt anyone will ever know how much you ground me, providing the utmost support with your unwavering presence. We've been married for a year now and so far I haven't regretted it.

My readers—you're a gorgeous lot. The release of this book marks the two-year anniversary of the first moment I sat down to pen *Fantasy of Frost*. It amazes me that so much time has flown by. I can close my eyes and remember releasing my debut novel as though it were yesterday. Your messages never fail to put a big ol' smile on my face. And I truly enjoy getting to know you through social media.

Happy reading,

Kelly St. Clare

The first genetically enhanced humans were cultivated, and the original four thousand left Earth in the year 2050, in what is historically known as **The Retreat.**

THE RETREAT

PROLOGUE

Had they really just been celebrating mere minutes ago? Romy heard the cries of her knot as they were battered relentlessly.

She was going to die. Her knot was going to die.

Metal screeched and the heat was intense as their craft continued to burn. She could feel the heat even through the padding of her suit. Romy pushed back, gripping her harness tightly as she turned her head away from the scorching fire outside.

The keening of buckling alloy was unbearable, overriding all except the peeling heat. Romy was going to melt alive. Eyes streaming, she squinted through the tiniest of gaps in the flames.

Earth.

Her breath caught as she saw it, truly saw it for the first time. How beautiful their world was. The swirl of blues and greens.

All of this could have been theirs, in time.

The battler let out a splintered scream and all the air was crushed from her as she was hurled to one side. A network of cracks splintered the visor of her helmet with the immense pressure. Her head throbbed, a sharpness stinging at her right temple.

Black edged her vision. Where were the others?

Romy was at the mercy of the descent with no idea of up or down. Her world was blistering pain; her orientation shredded, her calm obliterated. Tears streamed from her eyes until what remained of her sight was blurred beyond use.

Soon it would be over.

THE RETREAT

.

CHAPTER ONE

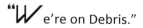"We're on Debris."

Romy looked up from her nano to meet the ever-cheerful face of Thrym, one of her knot mates. His finger was pointing, a bit unnecessarily, out the window, at outer space.

Unobtainable Earth was a bright beacon of blues and greens in the distance. That wasn't what Thrym was talking about, however. He was referring to the debris littering the area where their space station coasted in Earth's orbit.

"*Really*. Again? We were on it two days ago." Elara threw herself back onto the narrow white bunk, one of five beds in the bare white unit.

Five bunks for the five members of their team. The room possessed all essentials, few inessentials, and was identical to the hundred other units on board which housed the other teams.

"Yes, really," he replied. "Last night's battle left a whole heap of junk. It's clean or collide."

Romy knew about the small skirmish with the Critamal that Thrym spoke of. Unfortunately, it only took one exploding spacecraft to provide Knot 27 with days of clean-up. And because all space stations sat right where the debris liked to gather, four hundred kilometres above Earth's sea level, Thrym was right: it was clean or collide.

Elara sat up, slouching dramatically. Her brown hair was short and choppy, and a few adorable freckles dotted her nose. Soft hazel eyes blazed from her delicately featured face. "I know, but can't someone else do it?" She snapped . . . the delicate part was misleading.

The pixie-like girl was the laziest person Romy knew. Elara must be what humans were like 150 years ago. Ironic, considering the space soldier's genetic engineering was supposed to eliminate faults such as fear, idleness, and curiosity. Somehow the scientists must have screwed it up in Elara's case because she possessed laziness in copious amounts.

Thrym glanced Romy's way, his blue eyes dancing from beneath his professional mask. If Romy didn't know to look, his amusement would've passed unseen.

"ETA for the first of it to arrive is thirty-four minutes. We need to move," he said.

"I'll alert Deimos and Phobos," Romy replied.

She lifted her wristwatch and pushed the square button on the side three times. Scrolling through the locations stored on the device, Romy selected "Earth Dock" to send an urgent alert to the entire team to gather there. Elara and Thrym silenced their own beeping devices without looking.

Wordlessly, the three began preparations.

Romy tied back her chin-length white-blonde hair as best as she could—though it was almost certain the fine strands would escape within minutes. She reached for her spandex suit next. Each space soldier was trained to get the orange spandex ventilation garments on in sixty-five seconds. Elara took three minutes on average. According to Deimos, her fastest time was 153 seconds.

The entrance to their tight quarters swept upwards at their approach and the trio began to move at a fast clip down the clinical white, pressurised hallways of their home: Orbito One.

There were eight orbitos in total. Each identical. Each containing five hundred active life forms. And each equipped for efficient space survival. Clothing came vacuumed-sealed, the food dehydrated. You remained clean. You remained healthy. You did not waste resources.

Each orbito was a flawless operation at all times.

It was how things had to be.

Orbito One was the first of its kind, built onto the historical International Space Station left over from pre-global-warming. The ISS was the oldest reminder of what life had been in the past. Romy believed it was this relic—her closest link to the ground—that triggered her passion for Earth's history. Sparked the uncontrollable urge to learn all she could about their lost home.

Romy, daydreaming just for a change, walked into Thrym, who'd stopped in front of her.

"Sorry," she mouthed, earning a fleeting wink from the man and even a rare smile, which showed bright white against his black skin.

With Thrym, you usually had to watch his blue eyes for information. He didn't show much. Perhaps it was due to being the most serious and focused of their group. Romy smiled; she could always rely on Thrym to have his dark hair shaved to regulation and his possessions neatly stored in his small personal compartments.

"Knot 27, reporting for Debris," Elara stated as a red light scanned the trio.

"Wait!" A thin shout echoed behind them.

Romy grinned as Deimos and Phobos hurtled into sight. Running was strictly prohibited, everywhere, at all times—not that it ever stopped the twins.

They didn't really look alike, aside from their startling green eyes, but everyone called them "the twins" because the pair was rarely apart. Their wavy, shoulder-length hair reminded Romy of pictures of the surfers she'd read about, from a time when humans would stand up on streamlined boards in the ocean for fun. Needless to say, the length of Deimos's black hair and Phobos's dark blond hair was in violation of the chin-length maximum—another rule they somehow evaded. All space soldiers were attractive, a vanity of the Orbitos' creators, but the twins were drop-dead gorgeous. No doubt, this helped the pair escape punishment time and again. Romy could attest to their effect, having been on the receiving end of their innocent green gaze on several occasions.

Their entire knot was scanned anew in front of the Earth Dock entrance.

A clinical voice replied, "Authorised." The voice sounded like that no matter who replied from the control deck.

"Oh goody," Deimos replied.

Phobos tied back his blond hair. "I keep hoping one day they'll say 'access denied', but it never happens."

Romy's four knot mates were the closest thing to a family she'd ever had—or would have in this life cycle.

The term "knot" described five human-sized tanks, filled with amniotic gel, and gathered in a bunch. Each tank held one soldier. The other four pods you were grouped with, held your future team members. A jumble of tubes and cables connected each cluster of pods to various medi-tech at its centre. At the heart of each space station was a locked room dedicated to rows and rows of these developing knots.

Once harvested from these cultivation tanks at age twelve—which ensured mental and physical maturity—a knot trained together in space warfare as cadets, and then worked together until age thirty-five. Life in space was hard and it was thought that beyond thirty-five, the reflexes slowed and deteriorating general health impacted performance. This was the cycle of a genetically enhanced space soldier. If your knot was lucky, you were all recycled at your expiry date; if your knot was unlucky, you were all killed in battle and immediately replaced. It was important that the number of active soldiers remained constant. The total of 4000 was constantly replenished from the hundreds of knots cooking in the tanks at any one time.

She wondered if she'd been part of the same knot before, in another cycle. Their bond sure felt that way. But Romy knew the geneticists liked to try different personality combinations in order to find the 'ultimate team'. She hoped Knot 27 would stay together until the return to Earth— though the wish was neither likely, nor in her control.

Thrym and Romy prepared two of the debris pods for launch while the twins changed from fatigues to orange spandex. The one thing Romy liked about debris clean-up was that the chore didn't necessitate space suits. Sure, there were emergency suits in the pod—making the ventilation spandex space suit underclothes necessary—but no one ever had to actually use them.

Debris duty was the most menial task you could get in this life, the bottom of the heap. Just below kitchen duty. And high command didn't take too kindly to the quirks of Romy's team. Elara was lazy, the twins were trouble, and Romy had her head in the stars. Thrym was focused, but he still ranked fun alongside duty just like the rest of them. It was not an ideal quality in a space soldier. Seeing as knot demotion was the only real form of punishment aboard the orbitos, Knot 27 found themselves as the lowest of the low.

Not that it bothered Romy to be poorly ranked.

The small, circular pods sat half in and half out of the outer wall of the Earth dock. The dock was situated on the outer wall of the orbito, facing their ruined world. The white alloy exterior of the pods was completely smooth and round. Romy entered a quick code, hardly looking at the screen, and in response, the pod's uninterrupted surface fractured with a hiss, retracting into a circular entrance.

"You coming with me?" Thrym asked her.

Romy glanced back. "I'd better go with Elara or nothing will get done. You take the twins." She shot him an evil smile, leaning back to snatch up Elara's arm.

Phobos was speaking as Romy sealed their pod behind Elara. "Thrym, poor dude, how do you always get stuck with us?"

The two girls giggled as they buckled themselves into their usual seats: Elara in the pilot's seat, and Romy on docking controls. The interior was as white and bland as the exterior—even for a spaceship. Each pod was uniform, with four bucket seats, the minimum of pilot controls, docking controls—for catching the debris—and a compartment under their feet with emergency gear.

The girls had done this a hundred times over the twelve years they'd been alive. At twenty-four years old, Romy found it easy to slip into the task automatically, no matter who she worked with from their knot. The movements of the others were as familiar to her as her own.

"Pressurising pod." Elara's voice crackled through Romy's headset. It was hard to hear out in space once the thrusters and stabilisers were going. Even with noise-cancelling tech.

Above Romy, rows of buttons and panels flickered to life, throwing neon blue light through the craft. Most of their two-year cadet training was spent learning what each of these did. Romy reached up for the left-most switch. "Shutting off vents. Initiating Terminal Launch sequence."

She watched as Elara tested the thrusters. "Programmed manoeuvres clear," Elara confirmed. "Open valve."

Romy sighed, looking at her watch. She hoped they were back in time for the lecture this evening. It was one of her favourites. "Valve opened," She called. The familiar sound of liquid hydrogen and oxygen flowing into the pumps gave a subtle hiss.

Romy smiled as Elara hissed along with the gases, for as long as her breath allowed. Every time.

Her friend reached overhead. "I'm sure we'll be back in time for the lecture, Ro."

Elara could read Romy like a nanopad.

"I know. It's just it's my favourite: the first introduction."

A typical debris shift usually lasted two hours, but if the space junk concentration was at hazardous levels, the group stayed longer. At max, ten hours. Knot 27 had only had to do the ten-hour shift once, after a two-week battle with the Poachers when they were just fifteen. She *should* be back in time. But you never knew what you'd find out here.

Elara hid a small smile. "Launching in T-minus ten, nine, eight, seven—I don't know why you go anyway; you probably have it memorised—three, two, one."

They drifted away from Orbito One for fifty metres, entering space, their playground.

"All right, where's the damn debris?" Elara grumbled.

The girls looked up at the circular screen in front of them. It provided a 360-degree view of the surrounding space. The pod system identified foreign objects approaching their station.

"Incoming," Romy said, initiating the docks as she spoke. "Closest point of contact at Grid G90 in thirty seconds."

"Jeez, a little notice would be nice." Elara fired the right thrusters. The acceleration slammed the girls sideways in their harnesses. Romy winced as the strap pressed into her side. She shouldn't celebrate not wearing space suits on debris duty; they provided more padding than the orange spandex.

"You wimps need to hurry up; we've already hooked five." Deimos's voice flooded their system.

"Poacher poop," Elara swore.

Debris clean-up was a simple matter of approaching the debris and pulling it into the pod. Most of it was fleck-size, like dust, although some debris could be as large as a shoe. There had been a mass effort to clean Earth's orbit before the launch of the orbitos in 2050. Debris the size of a pin could cause sizeable damage to the stations. Cracked windows had been a common occurrence in the first ten years of space life, though less common now—even with regular battles against the Critamal.

Sometimes Romy wondered if the Critamal's plan was to kill them by littering their orbit. Errant debris wasn't a problem the alien species had to contend with, since their position was farther away from Earth's atmosphere.

Romy concentrated on operating the docking station as Elara came alongside the debris. Debris travelled at around 8.05 kilometres per second. They'd approach anything less than ten. The approach was a crucial step and not as easy as the other soldiers thought. If Elara and Romy tried to intercept the debris head on, it would simply tear through the craft, its force increased by the pod's opposing force. When Thrym got down about Knot 27's low status, she was quick to remind him of that fact.

The pod still jerked violently when it came into contact with the debris.

Elara held out her hand and Romy met it in a celebratory fist-pump.

"Seven down," Phobos's voice came through their headsets.

"You're gonna need that head start," Romy replied calmly.

"Did you guys hear that? Romy just schmack-talked. We're shaking in our space shoes." Their snorting could be heard in the background.

What did the twins usually say back to these kinds of things? Romy racked her brain for an insult. She was distracted by Elara mouthing words in her direction.

"You . . . better . . . be!" Romy read Elara's mouth, grinning in success.

Her friend just rolled her eyes in exasperation.

Phobos snorted. "Need to work on those lip-reading skills, Ro."

The knot worked steadily for the next three hours, falling into silence, apart from the competitive tally each pod kept. Their games helped alleviate the tedium of the task.

"What the hell are they doing?" Elara leaned forwards to look out the window.

Romy turned and peered into empty space, jerking back as the other pod whirled across the window in front of her. Romy laughed as Phobos and Deimos waved, floating upside-down inside the spiralling craft.

"Who's driving?" Romy pushed her white-blonde hair behind one ear.

"I couldn't see Thrym at all."

"Poor Thrym."

Elara cackled. "You'd think he'd know better than to turn his back on those two by now."

The girls were first to make it back to Earth Dock. Romy dragged their bag of space junk to the weaponry chute where it would be reused as projectile missiles in the battlers. She listened to the bellowed shouts of Thrym as the boys' pod docked. The pod entrance retracted and she saw that the twins stood in front of him looking suitably chastised—apart from the unconcealed grins on their faces. It was the eyes. How did they do it?

"They tied me up with their socks!" Thrym shook his head, gaze flat.

Romy did her best not to laugh at his exasperation. Elara didn't hold back, and her laughter didn't abate in the slightest under the full force of Thrym's glare.

He whirled on the twins, holding their socks high. "These. Are now mine."

The smirks on the twins' faces disappeared. Romy whistled low. She didn't blame them. You only received one pair of socks per month. Pulling down the top of his suit, Thrym shoved the twins' socks inside before storming out of the docks.

Deimos draped his arm around his twin's shoulders. "Pho, we might have annoyed our brother," he pondered.

Romy swore Phobos's eyes sparkled with unshed tears. Perhaps Thrym was overly harsh.

The light-coloured twin shook his head in stunned bewilderment. "I believe you might be right, Dei."

CHAPTER TWO

"*W*ater vapour was the biggest secondary contributor to the global warming effect." The lecturer cut off as Romy slipped into the room.

She stood to attention, arm raised in salute. "My apologies for interrupting, Vice-commander Warner."

It wasn't unusual for someone in high command to teach these lessons. With the small population on board the eight stations, most had more than one role.

"Take your seat, Soldier Rosemary."

Romy saluted, wincing at the use of her given name. She quickly took the closest seat, ignoring the whispers behind her.

"We were discussing the Critamal," he said for her benefit. "Cadet Icarus, please continue."

A boy recited in a calm voice, "NASA first became aware of the Critamal in 2050, after global warming had already damaged Earth beyond human repair. The life forms aboard the orbitos were intended to incubate until Earth became inhabitable once more, but in actuality they were forced to become soldiers—to protect Earth from the Critamal."

Romy raised her eyebrows. The cadet was good. Usually, they fumbled through everything. It was unsettling, the influx of information when you were first removed from your cultivation tank.

These lectures were for the fresh cadets, but Romy could hear the same material fifty times—she probably had—and still want to hear it again. The current information about what was happening on Earth was limited. It arrived in a slow trickle as only a tiny portion of their force could be spared from station duties for research. And so Romy enjoyed sitting in here. It made her feel like there was at least a *bit* of progress.

Earth's people were no more. Earth as it had been was gone—no matter how similar the Earth of today looked from the orbito windows. The Earth humans took nature for granted, and two industrial revolutions caused the greenhouse gas levels to rise so dramatically, the damage couldn't be reversed.

The good news? Their home would one day be inhabitable again. In approximately 850 years. For now, it was a waiting game. Or should have been, if the current conditions on Earth didn't present the perfect habitat for the Critamal.

"Global warming is like having a jacket on that you can't take off. Heat can get in, but can't get out," came another boy's wobbled answer.

Romy's heart gave a pang at the twelve-year-old's uncertainty. He was so fresh, he probably still had the amniotic gel gunk from the tanks up his nose. Before you had time to get it out you were thrown into warfare training, and then rushed into battle. At that point there were only four pathways available to you: get blown to smithereens in battle and never see Earth; survive an explosion and be taken hostage by the Critamal; survive an explosion and be saved by the Orbitos as the sole survivor of your knot, minus your sanity—which was worse than death in Romy's opinion; or, if you were lucky, you might just reach the ripe age of thirty-five, where you would re-enter the cultivation tanks, have your genetics upgraded, undergo a memory wipe, and emerge ready for another round two years later.

Like most soldiers, Romy was grateful for the memory wipe—or the "merciful wipe". To live in this life for a thousand years was no life at all. To remember it all—every battle, every bit of space junk, and every dead comrade while Earth was dangled before you year after year after year—*that* would be more than she could bear.

In the 150 years since the orbitos were initially launched, Romy might have lived four or five times. And one day, if she was luckier than she had any reason to be, she would plant both feet on her homeland and all the debris clean-up, the repeated life cycles, and the gel gunk from the tanks would have been worth it.

Staying alive was a daily lottery.

"Correct. Can anyone name the major greenhouse gases?"

"Water vapour," a girl answered.

Romy listed off the others in her mind, listening with half an ear to the hesitant stream of answers. What would it have been like? Earth. Having actual dirt under your feet. Clouds above you, instead of far below you. And animals. Romy longed to see a real-life animal—if there were any left.

Earth was a shiny bauble dangling just out of reach. A beautiful, untouchable swirl of greens and blues. If she could ever hate anyone, it would be her ancestors for selfishly throwing away their home.

The lecturer's next words caught Romy's attention. "As you know, select teams are sent to collect any materials we might be in deficit of. They also monitor Earth's progress. What are some of their findings?"

The cadets looked blankly at each other. Romy caught the questioning glance of the lecturer.

"That the effect of global warming is more catastrophic than any of the forecasts predicted," she offered.

Vice-commander Warner nodded for her to continue.

"One in ten species were predicted to fall extinct, but it is guesstimated three in five are no longer. While it was predicted that one-twelfth of humankind would perish, in actuality, half died from global-warming related causes . . . ."

". . . while the other half killed each other in the anarchy before The Retreat," the vice-commander finished for her.

Romy sagged as the attention moved from her.

Who could say? Maybe the Earth humans deserved what they got? Or they never lived long enough to learn the harsh lesson that, at the end of the day, nature would always have the last laugh.

A flurry of movement startled Romy from her daydream. The lecture was over and the cadets were milling about the classroom.

She exited behind a knot of cadets, spotting Thrym standing at ease in the shining white hall. He held two sets of sneakers. The cadets scuttled past him, staring in awe. Romy had to admit he *did* look the part of "saviour of the world". It was accompanied by a familiar twang of guilt.

Thrym was desperate for a higher ranking. He definitely drew the short straw when they were handing out knots.

Their watches beeped in unison. Neither of them bothered to check the alert, dismissing it with a wave before pivoting in the direction of the health centre. Twice-daily exercise was mandatory to maintain the space soldiers' bone density and cardiovascular health.

It was Romy's favourite time of the day.

"The twins just earned us extra duties. Kitchen clean-up for two months." Thrym sighed.

Romy stared at her friend in disbelief. She had to tilt her head slightly back to meet his gaze. Each of the space soldiers were around six-foot. It would have made more sense to be shorter in a space ship. But all of their genetics were designed for an eventual return to a hostile Earth, so tall they had to be.

"I don't even want to know what they did. Why does command always punish *all* of us?" she asked.

Romy and Thrym both knew the answer. Orbito One command was aware that Deimos and Phobos really only answered to three people:

their knot. Very occasionally the twins listened to the commander. Usually in the wake of having done something wrong.

"I think they hope the rest of us will get annoyed and pull them into line."

Romy smiled. "Pull Dei and Pho into line. . . ."

Thrym's blue eyes lit up. "I know." The light faded slightly and she knew he was thinking about their knot status being stuck at the bottom for the next two months. They'd been there for the better part of twelve years, but he never stopped trying to better their ranking. If it were based on his efforts alone, they'd be at the top. Alas, the sucky attitude of the others counted for more.

She dropped her gaze, and they walked silently into the gym.

Elara and the twins were already pounding away on the treadmills. The health centre had a long, narrow gymnasium filled with treadmills and weights. This was also where space soldiers came to be hooked to the medi-tech if they were sick or wounded.

Romy giggled at the large frown marring Elara's face as she forced her legs to move. She struggled at the lowest speed allowed. At zero incline. You'd think after twice a day for twelve years, she'd get over her aversion to exercise, Romy thought.

Romy pulled on her exercise sneakers. The soldiers received one set of sneakers each year for exercise. Romy's had holes all through them, and she had another three months to go. Elara would swap with her soon— her sneakers remained pristine from minimal use.

Jumping on the treadmill, Romy bent to pick up the two bungee cords attached to the machine and pulled them up, muscles straining with the strong tension. She clicked the tensioned cords onto her belt either side of her hips, and her knees immediately bent with the extra weight.

The entire ship was locked in place with Quantum Levitation, suspending them in Earth's orbit with semi-normal gravity levels, but the additional weight through her legs during the run helped mimic the conditions on Earth's surface.

Romy settled in to her rhythmic thud on the moving belt beneath her. She found the high-pitched whirring of the exercise machine to be soothing.

Their genetic enhancements went a long way to reduce the adverse effects of life in space, but bone softening and muscle deterioration were major health risks. All orbito personal were susceptible to a range of cardiovascular, eye, and immune system weaknesses as well.

"Increase speed to fifteen kilometres per hour," she said.

Despite the semi-gravity conditions on board, and their superior genetics, none of the space soldiers would live long without the nanotech. Both the nanotech in the walls of the space station, and within each soldier. This technology continually repaired the orbito walls to reduce radiation leaks, and also regenerated tissue affected by the small amount of radiation that found its way inside.

There were other perks to the nanotech. Non-life-threatening injuries such as broken bones and torn ligaments healed rapidly. And the nanotech could help delay death from more dire wounds, making it more likely you'd reach proper care in time. It wouldn't help if a missile hit you, but it was an important part of sustaining life here.

Romy relished the burn in her muscles as the speed adjusted to her order. Not that she'd ever tell anyone, not even her knot, but Romy liked to pretend she was running on Earth. Was the ground softer than the treadmill she pounded on right now? Would tree branches and leaves be in her way? She could imagine ducking and dodging as she ran. Her heart squeezed. How incredible it would be to run in a real-life forest.

"Increase speed to eighteen kilometres per hour."

If she was on Earth there wouldn't be any tension cords holding her back. Romy would fly. Like the birds she read about on her nanopad.

"Romy. *Romy.* Romy!"

Romy was wrenched from her jungle run to find an amused Knot 27 waiting for her by the door. Another knot had arrived and were elbowing each other, smirks on their faces. Deimos grinned at them and their smirks disappeared. No one wanted to be on the twins' list.

"Sorry," she puffed. "Stop treadmill." The machine came to a gradual halt.

Thrym handed her a small towel, and she nodded her thanks, gasping for air, her mind still down on Earth.

"Dinnertime!" Deimos and Phobos shouted in unison as they left. Though not as vocal, Elara was hot on their heels as the knot walk-jogged down the hallway. It was their knot's compromise speed.

"Do you think they've forgotten we're on kitchen duty after?" Thrym asked.

Elara pretended to think. "Do you think the other knots have forgotten that their underwear is now three sizes too small?"

Romy groaned. "How did they manage that?"

Thrym flashed his white teeth in a full grin.

The Rec was the largest room on the station. It could fit all five hundred members if needed, which only happened during rare assemblies. Any announcement from the control deck could be heard throughout Orbito One, negating the need for such a large gathering place, but the original designers had wanted a social area.

There were a lot of soldiers present tonight, many more than usual.

The still-sweating group got in the massive queue for food.

"What's it gonna be?" asked Elara, her voice tight with excitement. "Dehydrated potatoes?"

"I wish!" Deimos said darkly. "It's probably that buckwheat stuff."

The knot pulled similar faces at that.

A whisper rumbled down the line. The only thing better than guessing the menu was deciding whether the rumours from the front of the line were true.

Romy heard the whisper of "chocolate cake" from three rows ahead.

"Lie!" Romy cried. "The only time they give us chocolate cake is on Retreat Remembrance Day."

"Or when officials visit," Phobos said.

"Hey, look," Thrym whispered in Romy's ear.

Romy glanced over her shoulder. Four women and three men in black fatigues had entered the Rec and were moving to the front of the line. One of the men was Commander Cronus of Orbito One. He was smiling kindly at a knot, clapping one of the space soldiers on the back.

Only the orbito commanders wore black. All others wore white fatigues when off duty.

Each orbito contained a transmission platform for communication between the eight stations. But only two stations could be linked at one time, so the command officials often travelled to the other orbitos. It wasn't unusual to see them together, just rare to see so many in one place simultaneously. Usually the commanders split in half to congregate at Orbito One and Orbito Three—whichever was closer—to discuss strategy against the Critamal.

"Buttholes," muttered Elara. The rest of the knot looked at her askance.

"What?" she said. "I'm hungry! And they're pushing in."

"It *is* chocolate cake!" Thrym said as they reached the food ten minutes later. His face remained still, aside from his eyes, which closed in bliss.

The knot grabbed their meals, Deimos and Phobos somehow wheedling extra dessert.

The meal was one of the better ones: dried beef, mashed potato and beans, *and* dessert. The commander was either putting on a show or had bad news. The knot whittled away at their food until only the extra chocolate cake in front of Phobos and Deimos remained.

"So. . . ," Elara drawled out. She looked around their knot and back at the cake.

"So what, Ellie dear?" Deimos asked after she completed the cycle twice.

"You know what." She shot him a withering glare. "You gonna share that?" Her fists clenched on the table.

Deimos draped an arm around Phobos. Two pairs of green eyes watched the other three members of their knot. "Pho, what say you? Should we, who employed our full charm to yield this cake, simply share it with our knot?"

Romy looked into their green eyes and softened. They had worked hard for it.

"Should you, who earned us kitchen duties for two months, shut up and give us some?" Thrym retorted.

Romy snapped out of her stupor as Deimos and Phobos scrutinised him across the table.

"Fair point." Deimos nodded.

After a lengthy discussion of how best to complete the task, Deimos grabbed a knife and cut the square into five parts. Elara, Thrym and Deimos grabbed the three largest pieces. Two remained, one just a little wider than the other.

Phobos winked at Romy and took the smaller of the two.

Dessert was usually once every two weeks, and was usually a dried fruit salad—not that she minded that either. But chocolate cake was chocolate cake. She consumed it with relish.

"Uh-oh, everyone be cool," whispered Phobos.

Romy interpreted Thrym's loud exhale to mean trouble was headed their way.

An angry voice whipped overhead. "Which one of you took my dessert?"

Daniel. Romy groaned inwardly. Daniel belonged to Knot 76, one of the highest in rank. Knots weren't ranked in numerical order. Entire knots were lost in battle and this created gaps in the lineup. Of course, these holes were continuously filled with cadets.

But despite rank not being in numerical order, everyone knew who the top space soldiers were. . .

. . . and everyone knew who was at the bottom.

Daniel was also a first-class poacherknob. Genetic enhancement hadn't solved that.

"Danny, how are you? That red flush on your neck brings out your square jawline; you should do it more often," Phobos said.

"Now, now. The poor man only wants his dessert." Deimos spoke over Daniel's outraged splutters.

"In that case, we regret to inform you that we do not have your dessert," Phobos announced happily.

"People saw the server give you two." The bulging man was barely able to speak the words from between his gritted teeth.

Phobos gestured to the table. "Do you see an extra plate?" The sixth dessert plate was gone.

"I know you had it," Daniel hissed. "Why the bottom scum should even get dessert in the first place is beyond me. They should leave it to the real men who go out there and kill the poachers."

The soldiers seated around their knot went quiet.

A stab of anger pricked Romy, and she felt her hands clench in response. So what if they did the menial tasks? Someone had to do them.

"And women," Deimos added cheerfully.

Daniel stopped halfway through his next rant. "W-what?"

"Well, you said, 'They should leave it to the real men to kill the Critamal.'" Deimos stood. "But the women kill just as many," he shouted. "Am I right, sistahs?"

His shouts triggered a chorus of approval from the women. Even with the twins destroying their underwear, the women still liked Deimos better than Daniel.

The soldier from Knot 76 scowled at the twins before storming off.

The sight of Elara's cheeks puffed out in supressed laughter set Romy off, and soon the entire knot was doubled over. There's no way Daniel wouldn't hear it, and that, perhaps, was the point. They were the lowest in rank, poorly motivated space soldiers who held having a good time in greater priority than being punctual, tidy, and professional, but they could pretend they didn't care.

"Attention." Commander Cronus's voice rang through the room.

The whole room stood in salute in one movement, excluding the other orbito commanders.

"At ease."

The soldiers resumed their seats.

"Our scouts have reported today that the Critamal are showing signs of mobilising," he announced.

Romy, along with likely everyone else there, thought, *So what?*

The poachers mobilised every other day. Then the Orbitos defended, or attacked. The Critamal *could* blow up the stations, but in the time it took for their bombs to travel to the orbitos, retaliation bombs could be fired. Their technology and weapons were eerily similar, causing a stalemate that would likely last until Earth was inhabitable again. It was a deadly game and she couldn't imagine it ending.

Unless more Critamal ships arrived. That was always a threat, and one that would tip the exact balance in favour of the Critamal.

"At this stage, they appear to be mobilising *all units*." His voice echoed down throughout the room.

She sat up straight, listening closely. That didn't happen every day.

"*All* units?" came Elara's incredulous whisper.

"It could be a bluff," Thrym added.

Cronus surveyed them with a calmness Romy had always respected. "All units are on standby until the threat is contained."

Romy glanced at Thrym. It was lucky they'd cleared the orbit of debris today, or standby would be a moot point for their team. More often than not, Knot 27 was still expected to go out and pick up the junk despite lockdown alert.

"Spacewalks and external duties are suspended until further notice." The commander looked over the rec room with dark, wrinkled eyes.

Those in the topmost positions were permitted an extended lifespan because they didn't go into battle. The commander was over *fifty*. The same rules for health and fitness applied, regardless of his position, so he was fit. But he couldn't completely erase the signs of age. And the uncommon sight of the age lines never failed to amaze her.

Romy felt sorry for High Command.

Sure, they got an extended life. But each of them had to go on living. This could be the second or third time command had watched Romy's life span. They had to endure the endless cycle: cultivation tank, grow, learn, recycle. Over and over again. What a lonely existence. It was no wonder the commanders were all so close. She didn't envy them for a second.

"Dismissed," Commander Cronus called, sitting back down.

Knot 27 remained seated while the rest of the room filed back to their quarters or internal duties.

"Guess we might get a chance at the action." Thrym broke the silence, voice tense.

His excitement was contagious. Romy grinned along with him, while the twins ignored the others to practice their handshake, and Elara looked inconvenienced by life.

Standby would be a nice break from routine. They were only called to battle maybe once a month, where other knots with higher ranking were called twice a week. More often than not, standby didn't eventuate to actual fighting for Knot 27. There were far more false alarms. Still, standby was a little thrilling and it was nice to see Thrym so excited at the prospect of getting noticed.

The room was mostly empty now, though the seven commanders remained at their table, heads bent together.

"I can't wait to bond with you guys over dishwashing," Phobos said.

Romy and the others groaned at the reminder. It looked like the stack of resources on her nano would remain unread for the next two months.

CH/\PTER THREE

*H*er *life was privileged. She was gifted life, to protect, to serve. To serve, to fight. To protect, protect, protect.*

Rough hands shook her. "Romy! Wake up!"

Romy jerked away, breath catching when she found Deimos a bare inch from her. Someone else was screaming. No . . . not screaming—the sirens were wailing. *All knots are on standby!*

"Hurry—even Elara's nearly ready." Deimos blew in her face.

Romy flew into action. Elbowing the panel containing her clothing, she dragged out the orange spandex suit and pulled it up with deft hands.

"Don't forget diapers!" yelled Thrym.

"Are you serious?" Phobos shouted. "I hate those things."

"Fine, pee your space suit after six hours."

Romy groaned and caught the white, puffy nappy tossed her way by Thrym. She hated them too, but the thought of her own pee circulating around her spacesuit was worse.

"We are never talking about this. Ever!" Elara complained, turning away to put hers on.

"Come *on*. All the good crafts will be gone," Deimos complained from the entrance.

There were only ninety operating battle crafts on each orbito, and not all of them were made in this century. When there were large battles like this, instead of fear of dying—which the soldiers genetically couldn't feel anyway—there was a desperation to get the best vehicle. If you got a bad battler, *that* was when you were more likely to get blasted apart by the Critamal before your expiry date. Goodbye recycling. Goodbye return to Earth.

"Ready!" Romy dodged Elara's flying limbs to stand next to the black-haired Deimos.

"Incredible," Thrym said as he and Phobos joined them. "Elara was first awake and is still last."

Knot 27 set off at a fast clip down the passageway to the moon dock station.

There were 450 active soldiers on board Orbito One at all times. The remaining fifty personnel included the newest batch of forty cadets who were in warfare training, priming to slip into position of "space soldier" at any time. Then there were ten officials, including the commander and vice-commander, who stayed on board to direct the battle. This number didn't include the hundreds of baby space soldiers ripening in the cultivation tanks in the heart of the station.

The hallways were empty. They were definitely last.

"Where are we in orbit?" she called to Thrym.

He studied his watch briefly, expression tight. "Five minutes until spotlight."

It took ninety-two minutes for the stations to orbit Earth. Spotlight was code for the position closest to the Critamal's mothership. Once Orbito One reached spotlight, they would deploy their battlers and Orbito One would continue its orbit around Earth. It would take a further eleven and a half minutes for the next orbito to rotate into spotlight after them and deploy the second wave of battlers.

The moon dock—the dock on the poachers' side—was wide open; the knots already there were moving in orderly, precise fashion.

"Wait here, I'll get a craft," Thrym ordered. He had to yell over the flurry.

"If we get a bad one, it's your fault." Phobos glared at Elara.

"Shut up, meteor face."

"Shh, Thrym's coming back," Romy said.

"We're one of the last to leave," Thrym said dejectedly. "Eighty-four crafts have already been prepped."

Deimos snorted.

They had six crafts to choose from. The odds of doing well in battle with such a craft were low.

The knot wove through the moon dock, piling into a battler right down at the end.

"Mighty Mercury, will this thing hold together?" Phobos asked.

Romy read the manufacture information engraved on the inside of the door. "Made in China, 2045."

"Are you freakin' kidding me?" Elara screeched. "It was made on *Earth*?"

"Just get into your suits." Thrym groaned, his patience in tatters.

Romy never understood why they had to get into their space suits for battle. The logic of it made sense; if you had to evacuate your battler, then you'd be able to survive in space. But barely anyone survived evacuation into a battlefield, and if you did there was a fifty-fifty chance you'd get picked up by the Critamal. The black, scaly creatures with the beady yellow eyes weren't known for their gentle side.

Suited up, Romy strapped herself behind a gun. She grinned, gripping the dual handles with relish. At least the artillery on the battler was up-to-date.

The twins followed suit, sitting behind the remaining two guns. There was a gun on each side, and one at the back. Thrym acted as co-pilot and manned the missiles at the front beside Elara—their pilot. Romy felt secure in the knowledge that if they died, it wouldn't be because her knot member crashed.

"Pressurising Battler 56," Elara shouted.

"Shutting off vents."

"Initiating Terminal Launch sequence."

"Guns functional."

"Open valve."

"Ah, screw it," grumbled Elara. "I'm just going."

Romy was thrown to the back of her seat, head rattling in her helmet. Thrym's voice crackled through her earpiece, shouting at Elara for incorrect deployment.

It always took Romy a minute to get her bearings with the speed these crafts put out. This particular battler made her feel like she'd shake apart before they even reached the battle.

A high whining followed by a disjointed voice rang in her ears. "Battler 56, this is Control Deck. Assistance required at H8." The voice cut out.

"Roger that, Control," Elara responded, poking her tongue out at Thrym. "Everyone ready?"

"Elara, I can assure you that if *you're* ready, the rest of us were probably ready ten minutes ago," Phobos said. Romy laughed, peering out of her window as they approached the front line.

The battle was in full swing, with their forces concentrated in a semi-circle facing the Critamal. The Orbitos battle crafts were grey and sleek, and the fleet of Orbito One attacked the Critamal in two rotating waves. You fired, you circled to the back, you fired, you circled to the back.

Debris was everywhere. Grey alloy, as well as the dark green of the Critamal battlecrafts. There were already casualties on both sides.

Elara dodged a ruined ship, slamming everyone to the right. "You know what, Phobos? I'm gonna make sure I crash on your side. See how ready you are for that."

Battle was an odd thing. Jokes were funnier, pain was more acute, and you were so aware of everything; your head was constantly turning, every flash drawing your fidgeting attention.

"Approaching H8, ETA: nine seconds. Guns ready," Thrym chimed.

Romy knocked back the safeties and tilted her head to the right—she swore she shot better this way. Her chest rose and fell in even breaths as she eyed the chunky, ugly enemy crafts.

Oddly, Romy didn't really blame the Critamal for trying to invade Earth. It wasn't like the Orbitos owned the planet. Did it mean she wanted the aliens to have it? Comets, no. At the same time, she couldn't blame them. Killing the Critamal was just a job to be done. *Protect Earth: Kill the Critamal.*

She supposed she should feel bitter because the poachers annihilated so many of the knots. However, the space soldiers killed just as many of the Critamal kind. Time had proven that neither side would lose from lack of number. While the Orbitos' four-thousand-strong force was continually replenished from the cultivation tanks, the Critamal bred at astonishing rates.

Again, Romy put the blame for the death, like most other things, on the shoulders of their ancestors. If they hadn't ruined Earth, it wouldn't have attracted the Critamal.

"Battle concentrated to our lower right quadrant," Deimos reported.

"Preparing to fire." Romy's fingers strained as she held the tension in the trigger for just the right moment.

A poacher ship came into range; she followed it until the green craft lurched upwards, exposing the underbelly of the ship. She squeezed the trigger and a red laser shot from their battler in response.

The enemy ship exploded into unrecognisable debris as her laser connected with the fuel cylinders on the underbelly of the craft. The fuel cells were Romy's favourite targets. "Hit," she cheered.

"You'll be cleaning up debris and yellow poacher guts tomorrow, Ro. Ever think about that?" Deimos cackled.

Romy pulled a face. Though the exterior of the Critamal was a hard black shell, their insides were gooey and yellow. The worst was their brains—huge bulbous organs that held together far too well after the body was destroyed. The skulls she'd seen in cadet training were as hard as steel, so that came as no surprise. The Critamal had no mouth, ears, or nose; they seemed to communicate telepathically, at least from what the Orbitos' scientists could glean from study of their remains. The poachers did possess beady yellow eyes, however, which gave Romy the hand sweats.

"Preparing to fire," she said again.

"Initiating evasive manoeuvres," Elara responded calmly. Romy released the trigger and clicked on one safety, grabbing the straps of her harness.

Elara's evasive manoeuvres were killer.

One of the Orbito battlers exploded in front of Romy, victim to the white fire of the Critamal. Sadness weighed her stomach as she farewelled five of their crew who would never see Earth.

The battlefield was overrun with poacher fire. Flashes of white filled the gaps between debris, and the constant ebb and flow of their battlers. Romy twisted and saw their battle lines were broken. More white fire than red. Not a good sign.

What had broken through their lines?

"Lordy lordy, I hate it when she does this!" Deimos squealed as Elara flipped the battler in a sideways spiral.

Romy focused on a panel above her head so she wouldn't get sick. Elara's insane laughter screeched through her earpiece. The combination was unsettling.

"Launching missile one," Thrym said. "That should scare them off."

There was a brief pause as Thrym fired. None of their ammunition was explosive. Explosions and spacecraft didn't mix well. Instead, the battler missiles were actually the debris they collected, shot at rapid speed. Romy heard the whir of the stabilising engines behind her as they strained to counteract the force of the missile. She was surprised they even worked on this battler.

"Nope, they're still coming."

"Very helpful, Pho. Thank you," Thrym shot back.

"No probs."

"Guys," Elara squeaked. "I have six Critamal ships up my butt."

A white flash seared past Romy's window as their battler looped backwards in stomach-lurching suddenness. It continued for a few minutes, battering and rattling them until they didn't know which way was up. Elara was trying to shake their six tails.

The craft stabilised.

After the disorienting flight, Romy had no idea where they were. "Current position?" she gasped. She was determined not to lose last night's chocolate cake.

"Uh . . . K4," Elara said quietly.

K4 was the part of the battle grid directly at the heart of enemy territory!

"K4?!" Deimos shouted.

Romy lifted her head. Her eyes grew wide as she stared through the window at a hundred or more Critamal crafts. Most were rotating in waves to meet the rest of the Orbito force, oblivious to the enemy ship in their midst. However, no sooner had Romy made this observation than the Critamal noticed Knot 27's presence. She threw off her safeties as five Critamal crafts swung towards her.

"I've got five," Romy said.

"Three," Deimos spoke.

"One," Phobos finished. "Oh, wait. Make that six."

Elara slammed them into evasive manoeuvres as a wave of Critamal fire shot towards them.

They weren't supposed to feel fear. But fear wasn't just a single gene you could just delete, no matter the advancements in genetics. And Romy knew, as her palms grew slick with sweat, that her body was feeling fear despite her mind remaining unresponsive to it.

"What the hell are we doing in K4?" Thrym demanded.

"I got turned around," Elara said, as though it was the most obvious answer in the galaxy.

"Opening fire," Romy said, helmet rattling with the zipping motion. She heard her words echoed by Thrym, Deimos, and Phobos. None of their comrades would be this deep in poacher territory. Knot 27 were on their own.

Perspiration ran down Romy's face as she fired on everything within sight. The Critamal swooped and angled their crafts to evade her fire, well seasoned in space battle.

"Shoulda let Thrym drive," Deimos muttered.

Romy's breath caught as her fire connected with the underbelly of one of the evil-looking crafts.

"Hit!" she shouted. There was no break in the rapid staccato noise coming from the underside of their battler.

Poacher crafts were everywhere. Possibly the only thing working in Knot 27's favour was there were so many Critamal crafts, their enemy risked shooting their own ships by firing upon the space soldiers. The white Critamal fire still seemed to flash in blinding waves as Elara threw them side to side.

"Uh, guys?" Phobos said. "We seem to have the company of one rather large battleship."

"How big?" Deimos asked.

"Like . . . I would say one of its guns is the size of our entire battler."

"That's pretty big."

"Yep," Phobos said, creating a popping sound on the "p."

The gigantic craft rose into view on Romy's side as Knot 27's battler spiralled past, and if she was unsure before about fear's effects, she wasn't now. For a stretched second, she forgot she held a gun, forgot she should breathe. She just froze, staring at her death in the form of a gigantic metallic spacecraft, unable to even blink. It was goliath, bigger than any other poacher craft by twenty times. Nearly a quarter the size of the Critamal's mothership!

The shouting within their battler brought her back to the present.

"Don't you think I'm *trying* to get out, Phobos?" Elara screamed.

Romy swallowed and stared down at her gun as she was thrown backwards and forwards by Elara's piloting. Her hands were shaking so hard, she couldn't maintain her grip on the weapon.

This must be why the poachers chose to mobilise their entire force! She observed the craft as closely as she could while being tossed around. The ship manoeuvred smoothly despite its size. And the guns. . . . Romy's mouth dried. A single hit from those guns and Knot 27 was dead.

Romy's tone was grim. "We need to take it out. Or this battle is only ending one way."

Elara grunted, voice strained as she did everything possible to keep the knot alive. "Underside?"

Deimos hummed in doubt. "I would usually say yes, but the poachers aren't stupid. I think they would have hidden the fuel cells elsewhere."

"I second that." Romy broke from her shock. "There's no way this new craft will have the same weaknesses." Her chest rose and fell faster than it ever had.

There were at least ten smaller poacher crafts hot on their trail. Romy had no idea how Elara was evading so many.

"Should we focus on the thrusters, then? There's always rocket fuel there," Phobos added.

It was also one of the best-protected places of any craft. No one fired there expecting to get an actual hit. It was a desperate suggestion, worthy of their predicament.

Romy readjusted her grip on the dual triggers, grimacing at the slick sweat inside her suit gloves. "I think we'd have a better chance shooting underneath the cockpit. If we take out their stabilisers, it will buy time."

"You got it, Ro," Phobos said.

If Elara was the best pilot in their knot, Romy was the best gun. Romy liked to think that if rank was decided on battle skill alone, their knot might fare a bit better.

"Roger that, honey," Deimos added.

She glanced over her shoulder at him. He was sitting unusually still in front of the gun. It wasn't just her body that was experiencing fear, then.

"Drop us, Ellie," Thrym ordered.

Unfortunately, they were already upside-down when Elara obeyed, and Romy's stomach rose into her throat. She hardly noticed it as she screamed, "Fire!"

She didn't know if she was the only one shouting, or if everyone screamed at the same time. Knot 27 threw a wall of explosive power at the underside of the poacher craft.

Romy struggled to retain her sense of direction as Elara threw them in stupefying twists and spirals.

How many poacher ships were in pursuit? It would only take one laser strike in the right place for their craft to become an inferno.

Someone in their craft was crying, "Die!" at the top of their lungs. And Romy was afraid it was more likely to be them dying than the Critamal.

Knot 27 had agreed at fifteen years old that they'd rather die than be taken hostage. The Critamal's hostages were never returned alive. And never in one piece—a string of pieces would be a more accurate description. But the worst thing was that their comrades' eyes had always turned yellow—the same beady yellow as the Critamal's eyes.

No one knew what interrogation by the Critamal involved. And it wasn't worth finding out.

Romy kept up a steady wave of bullets until Thrym called a halt. Romy's plan hadn't worked. The control panels were strongly reinforced.

"Why isn't it working?" Thrym's voice rose above the din.

Romy swallowed repeatedly as they swung and lurched through space. She could only glimpse the smallest bit of red fire and grey battlers in the distance. Their force. Too far away.

Phobos was gagging behind her from the relentless dodging.

"Is it me, or is the fat ship keeping us on one side?" Deimos asked, unaffected by the motion.

Romy studied the ship, lips pressed in a grim line. "No idea." She fired at three Critamal ships in her sight. They were relentless! No matter that Elara was keeping them alive, she just couldn't shake them from Knot 27's tail.

"Let's see." Elara dipped, slamming on the thrusters, spiralling atop the massive craft and to the other side.

The ship starboarded away.

"I think you're on to something, Dei," Thrym said, voice tight with excitement. "Do the same manoeuvre, but this time we open fire across the port side."

This time Elara swooped along the underside of the ship. It was a dangerous move. That's where the poacher's guns were located. But it was also an unexpected move.

When you're up to your neck in poacher poop, the unexpected is your best chance, Romy thought.

As their tiny craft rose in line with the colossal battleship, Romy tensed her body, hovering her thumbs over the triggers. She tilted her head to the right, waiting, *waiting*.

The scream to fire echoed in her ear. Without blinking she directed her weapon across the port side of the poacher's ship.

Her sense of hearing was useless in the booming uproar of fire. Romy pivoted the gun on its axis, giving the enemy everything she had. Their battler jerked backwards as one of Thrym's missiles bulleted towards the back end of the craft.

Elara spiralled them underneath the massive ship once more, and for the longest second in Romy's short life, she stared straight into the mouth of a gun—one hundred times her size.

And then Thrym's missile connected.

The dark space was lit with the initial explosion. It was large enough that their stabilisers couldn't counteract the entirety of the force. They were flung backwards, along with dozens of smaller poacher crafts. Groaning, Romy craned her head to watch as secondary explosions erupted all along the port side of the ship.

The roar of the explosion was followed by an eerie silence, as though a blanket had been thrown over Romy's senses. And in that black hole, her insides quaked at what she knew was coming.

"Get us out of here!" she screamed, slamming her safeties on.

Elara dropped the battler in a violent uncontrolled loop as the biggest explosion Romy had ever seen blotted the expanse of space in a wall of white and red.

The rocketing force slammed her against her harness as a hundred thousand wreckage meteors whizzed in all directions like shooting stars. If not for the suit, her entire chest would be cut to bits from the harness.

She couldn't contain her screams as they zigzagged. Nausea threatened to best her. In those few moments she wouldn't have known if there was a Critamal sitting right next to her. Her ears were roaring, her eyes still blinded by the flash.

"We're nearly there." Elara's voice crackled in her ear.

The silence in the cockpit spoke louder than words. Something nearly tangible—fear, she supposed, saturated the small atmosphere of the ship.

Romy didn't dare open her eyes.

Until. . . .

"Stabilising now." Elara sighed the beautiful words. "E2." *Safety*.

Her sound of relief was echoed by the rest of the knot. E2 was directly in front of Orbito One.

Romy's mouth dried in disbelief as she looked back at the wreckage back in K4. Fragments littered the battleground. Not only had they destroyed the colossal battleship, but the resulting explosion seemed to have eradicated a fair number of the Critamal's smaller crafts as well.

There was a goliath hole in the poachers' defence!

"Do you see that?" she whispered.

Knot 27 watched from relative safety, listening as new orders fired through the orbitos' communication system. A third of their force was ordered to launch an attack on the breeched defences of the Critamal. Out to her left, Romy could see the forces from Orbito Eight streaking through space to help them.

"Did we just do that?" Deimos broke the silence.

Phobos replied in the same awe-filled voice, "We must have."

The tell-tale high whining filled their helmets. "Knot 27, this is Commander Cronus. Excellent job, soldiers. Return to battle docks immediately."

"Roger that, sir," Thrym whispered, clicking off communication.

"We did it," he said into the silence.

A lump formed in Romy's throat at the yearning in his voice. This was what he'd been waiting for. This was what Thrym deserved. Knot 27 would be promoted for sure.

"We're going up, guys and gals," Thrym shouted. He leaned over Elara and gave a single strong burst of the thrusters towards the landing docks.

Cheering filled the cockpit and Romy leaned back in her seat, laughing until tears streamed down her cheeks, fogging up her helmet. Part of her knew it was a reaction from the shock and adrenaline of battle, but part of it was real.

Maybe a promotion wouldn't be so bad!

Phobos was dancing in his seat, arms raised overhead.

He lowered them as a beeping noise cut through the craft.

"Turn that racket off," joked Deimos.

Elara was pushing at the flashing dashboard. "If I knew what it was, I would," she replied.

Romy's chest tightened. "You don't know what it is?" That was a first. She gripped the gun without thinking.

Elara threw a glare at her while reaching for a switch. "What did I just—"

"Thruster failure. Thruster failure. Thruster failure." The computer's clinical tones blared in their ears.

Romy caught Elara's alarmed look as she turned to face forwards again, flicking switches in a frenzy. A second beeping noise added to the first. Then a third, and a fourth. There was a high whining in their helmets, telling Romy that Command was attempting to communicate, but she couldn't understand the disjointed message from their station.

Elara and Thrym were desperately working at the controls, while Romy and the others could only watch their frantic movements in horror with one eye and the Orbito One station with the other.

They approached the station with no control, no thrusters. Battlers were returning from battle, docking on the white stretched cylinder of the orbito.

It was the only home she'd ever known.

Romy blinked in disbelief as they rolled beneath Orbito One and past it. As she watched, the station became smaller and smaller.

"No, no, no!" Elara cried. "The thrusters won't turn on!" She was jabbing buttons and flicking switches in a blur of her suited hands.

They needed to go back!

Phobos was trying his best to calm her. "It's okay, Ellie. We'll just orbit until we get picked up."

But Romy was busy watching their declining altitude towards Earth. The battler would only stay in orbit above a certain height. Thrym's last action with the thrusters was to jet them downwards. Given enough distance they would eventually lose the added velocity and get caught up in orbit. But. . . .

"What's the lowest height we can go to before we exit orbit and plummet to Earth?" Romy whispered, not daring to take her eyes off the altitude gauge—currently showing *248 kilometres*.

"One hundred sixty kilometres, and then air resistance will override orbital velocity," Phobos replied, tone grim. He was already following Romy's thought process.

"And then?"

"Then we get pulled into Earth's atmosphere, possibly disintegrate, and die," he finished.

"That's what I was afraid of." She swallowed a dry lump in her throat. "Thrym, what's our velocity?"

He didn't have to reply because everyone was looking through the window and knew the battler was moving fast. Too fast.

"One hundred ninety five kilometres," Deimos said. "We ain't stopping in time, guys. Let's run Earth Protocol. Wait, is this thing even capable of entering the atmospheric layer?"

"Yes," responded Elara instantly. "We're equipped with parachutes. But we sustained enough damage to cause thruster failure. I don't know what other damages we might have incurred. If there is any external damage to the wings, gas could make its way in. . . ."

"And?" he asked.

"And we die," she shouted into our helmets. "What do *you* think, Deimos? How am I supposed to do any damn protocol with a broken ship? We're supposed to contact the Orbitos and, and then coast along in orbit until we're picked up." She muttered her way through the protocol. "And if we fall, then we . . . we drop any extra load."

"Please don't throw me out," Deimos begged.

". . . brace and open the chutes before landing, using the landing engines to do the rest," Elara declared triumphantly. She stared at the controls for a few seconds. "We don't have any landing engines!"

Phobos attempted to soothe her from his position behind Romy.

She ignored them, unable to take her eyes from panel above her. *172 kilometres.* She was frozen, unable to take her gaze from the gauge, barely able to breathe as various forces decided their fate—to die, or to live.

"Velocity is dropping fast." Thrym flicked a series of switches. "We just need one damn thruster to work."

"I've tried everything I can think of." Elara fell into a panic.

Not a good sign, Romy thought.

Thrym and Elara's arms were a blur in Romy's peripherals. But even she couldn't look away from the gauge.

168.

"We're nearly coasting." Elara's voice broke. "Come *on.*"

They just had to lose the extra velocity. Then they would survive. Orbit would save them.

163.

Romy didn't want to watch anymore. She squeezed her eyes shut. There were still eleven more years in her lifespan! She'd nearly died once today already; twice wasn't fair.

"We've lost the extra velocity," came Thrym's quiet voice.

They had? Romy's wrenched open her eyes and peered at the gauge. Her heart sank. *158 kilometres.*

"Just too late," she responded in a hollow voice.

It began as a small pull in Romy's abdomen. But the immediate follow-up was exponential as gravity rapidly took hold faster than her mind could comprehend. Soon, it wasn't just that they were dropping; it was like a gigantic hand was throwing them to the ground.

"Two lousy kilometres. Someone must hate us," Deimos shouted over the groan of their craft.

"Earth Protocol!" Phobos called.

Their voices cut in and out, distorted in the hammering and wild descent. Knot 27 hurtled towards Earth.

Still they picked up speed. Romy's mouth was bone-dry, her eyes wide as the battler rolled over endlessly, disorientating the knot inside. They were still in the black of space, but she could see the whites and greys of clouds below. How many times had she stared at them from the orbito's windows?

"I'm getting rid of the guns!" Elara shouted. Romy was thrown from side to side as the floor of the battler vibrated beneath her feet. With a groan, the three guns disengaged from the craft, one after the other. Head knocking in her helmet, she stared outside as they entered into the clouds.

Earth loomed before them. And there was no doubt that Romy was about to get her dearest wish.

It wasn't supposed to happen like this.

Romy's heart thundered in her ears. She squeezed her eyes shut. All of their training was based on surviving in *space*. She gasped for air.

"Honey. You need to breathe," Deimos called to her.

She obeyed and drew a long deep breath through her nose. Upon doing so, she opened her eyes the slightest crack.

There was fire outside her window, a bare two metres from her face.

"Fire!" she screamed.

Elara's voice was tight with focus. "I think that's normal. From the friction."

Romy didn't care what anyone said; you couldn't be sitting inside an object writhing in flame and think the situation was *normal.*

Had they really just been celebrating mere minutes ago? Romy heard the cries of her knot as they were battered relentlessly.

She was going to die. Her knot was going to die.

Metal screeched and the heat was intense as their craft continued to burn. She could feel the heat even through the padding of her suit. Romy pushed back, gripping her harness tightly as she turned her head away from the scorching fire outside. Her eyes met Thrym's, and held. The only serenity in the urgent chaos assaulting them on all sides—his blue eyes.

As they said their silent goodbye, her heart broke into a million pieces.

The keening of buckling alloy was unbearable, overriding all except the peeling heat. Romy was going to melt alive. Eyes streaming, she squinted through the tiniest of gaps in the flames.

Earth.

Her breath caught as she saw it, truly saw it for the first time. How beautiful their world was. The swirl of blues and greens.

All of this could have been theirs, in time.

But life on the orbitos was a daily lottery, after all.

The battler let out a splintered scream and all the air was crushed from her as she was hurled to one side. A network of cracks splintered the visor of her helmet with the immense pressure. Her head throbbed, a sharpness stinging at her right temple.

Black edged her vision.

Where were the others? She hadn't told them how much she loved them.

Romy was at the mercy of the descent with no idea of up or down. Her world was blistering pain; her orientation shredded, her calm obliterated. Tears streamed from her eyes until what remained of her sight was blurred beyond use.

Soon it would be over.

And then, as her awareness of the anarchy around her faded to the background, Romy smiled, remembering her knot. Who she had loved from the beginning.

CH∧PTER FOUR

The first sound Romy remembered after cultivation was that of the watery gel from the tanks dripping from her body to the white floor of the spaceship. In her memories it was a soft trickling; a pattering as it hit the floor. Not at all like the hissing, sparking noise assaulting her senses now.

She must still have memories from the last life cycle.

Though . . . she couldn't recall feeling pain the last time she woke. And right now, her entire being was in agony. Her right ankle in particular was an inferno.

Her sense of smell made her aware that not all was well. Not *what* she could smell; rather, that she could smell at all. It took several days of sneezing to remove the gel gunk from your sinuses after the tank.

But she could smell—smoke and fuel.

Blinking several times, the first thing Romy saw was red. Blood coated the inside of her very cracked helmet—her own blood. The cracks must not be allowing Earth's air in, or Romy would already be dead.

There was only a small section clear enough to see through.

Head spinning, Romy peered through the clean patch.

And saw . . . *green.*

She gasped at the sight and shut her eyes briefly before redoubling her efforts to focus her vision.

Yellowed grass. And trees! Dirt. They were basic words Romy had learned from her nanopad, but never believed she would use.

She groaned as her head throbbed viciously.

The destroyed Critamal battle craft, the failed thrusters, the lost altitude. Their battler had been hurtling towards the ground. She didn't dare believe they'd survived.

But there was no other explanation. Romy's mouth dried. Knot 27 was on Earth.

Her knot!

"Hello?" she called, wincing at a flash of pain through her skull. "Dei? Pho?" They'd been closest to her on the battler.

There was no reply. Why weren't any of them speaking?

Romy gasped—they were injured. *Maybe dead*. Rational thought flew from her mind as terror took its place. Her knot. She had to get to them! Romy thrashed against her constraints.

She couldn't be alone! They couldn't be dead. She screamed, throwing herself around in an effort to escape, despite the pain warning her to stop.

Finally, panting from exhaustion, she admitted defeat.

Romy twisted as far as possible in her seat, squinting through the small blood-free patch of helmet as hope and dread warred for top spot. She froze, stomach lurching at what lay behind her.

It turned out there was a good reason why the others weren't responding. If Romy *had* to guess, she'd say it was because most of the ship seemed to have disappeared. The next few moments rendered her incapable of thought, but eventually she decided on relief. Her knot had landed somewhere else. They weren't dead.

They weren't dead.

Romy's side of the battler must have torn away during landing. Only a few shredding battler walls remained. It was as though her side of the ship had been ripped off like a chunk of bread from a loaf.

The floor underneath her was gone, leaving her legs dangling. Romy herself was suspended by the harness, which dug into her torso. It was the only thing keeping her from falling three metres to the dry grass.

The bottom part of her battler segment had embedded itself into the ground on an angle. Romy's end of the segment was immobilised in the air, forty-five degrees to the surface. She looked to have landed at the edge of a grassy clearing. Or maybe a forest, she amended, judging by the multitudes of trees before her.

Behind her, the ripped walls were flayed wide open, smoking, sparking, and hissing.

She took in the vast splash of colours before her with unseeing eyes. She was on Earth. Hanging above real ground.

Quite alone. And if her knot hadn't . . . survived . . . she was quite possibly the only person, or being, on the planet. A numbness set in so deep that Romy could no longer feel the harness. Her head drooped as she struggled to regain her calm. She had to find her friends. That was an absolute. They were alive. She had to believe it was true.

She waited, willing her shaking hands to still until eventually they obeyed.

Inhaling sharply, Romy looked around once more.

The question was: How far did her section of the craft land from the others?

If it were a matter of hours, that would be okay, but anything more and she would require food and water. A post-global-warming Earth meant the food and water here wasn't safe. The yellowed plant life confirmed that. The battler held supplies, but did she have any in her part? And how much oxygen was in her suit? Romy's heart began to quicken once more, and she forced the unfamiliar fear away.

First priority was getting to the ground. Under normal conditions she would take the chance and jump the three metres, but the injury to her ankle and the extent of the damage to her head caused Romy to hesitate. If only she could take her suit helmet off . . . but the air conditions had to be terrible. She wouldn't last five seconds.

No, she decided. She'd pull herself up onto the back of her seat and see if there was an easier way out from the back of the smoking wreckage.

She sighed in weary exhaustion, not sure she had the strength to move a single finger. But that wouldn't help her friends.

Romy released one half of her harness. Holding tightly to the strap, she released the second half of the harness—

Something gave. Not the harness, but whatever it was attached to, or attached *with*. For a moment Romy thought she might be able to salvage the tatters of her plan and still climb up. Until, with a loud ripping, the harness tore free from the rest of the chair.

It only took seconds to remember where she was when she woke this time.

The white-hot pain in her ankle helped.

Romy lay flat on her back, staring up at the remnants of the battler.

It took longer to realise the cracks in the visor of her helmet were larger. A hole the size of her thumbnail was directly in front of her mouth. Her eyes widened, though she lay unable to move.

She'd been breathing the air since she fell unconscious! And there was nothing she could do.

Would she feel it? Death? Or would she just slowly succumb to the lack of oxygen in the air?

Romy waited.

And waited.

Five minutes later, she sat up. She was very much alive—with very little idea as to why. She knew in the beginning that humans took a while to succumb to poor air quality. But Romy assumed the situation to be much worse in the current time.

As in, immediate-death-upon-breathing worse. Clearly, she was mistaken—and so were the researchers.

Her death was set in stone now, regardless. . . .

Screw it, Romy thought; the suit was coming off.

Taking a firm grip, she twisted one glove clockwise and shook it off, repeating the process on the other side. It was glorious to stretch her fingers. She groaned with the pleasure of it. A faint tickling sensation danced along the back of her hand. Romy yelped, swatting at the digits to dislodge whatever caused the feeling. The tickling faded, and she raised both hands to her face. Was it acid vapours?

She shrieked as the feeling started once again, worse than before! But there was nothing on her hands.

The answer came as soon as she let the panic go and glanced at the yellowed bush. The trees were swaying.

A *breeze*, she sighed. What an idiot. A small wind. Something they didn't have in space. Of course, it was just a breeze. A hysterical giggle left her mouth, and she clamped down on the sound.

Every interlocked panel she removed took a huge weight off her shoulders—literally. But at the same time every action was harder here with the force of Earth's gravity. Romy knew it was only a difference of 20 per cent compared to the orbitos, but it made everything more difficult, on top of being injured, panicked, and dehydrated.

She took a deep breath and searched for the calm she was engineered to possess. Her mission was to find her friends or die trying. Her chest rose and fell evenly once more.

Romy took off the whole spacesuit, including the boots, and sat in the orange ventilation garment. Leaning forwards, she ripped a hole in the end of the orange booty encasing her right foot and rolled the spandex up, staring at her very unpleasant-looking ankle. Her head already felt much better thanks to her nanotech. However, a few prods and attempts to move the foot told her the ankle was broken. A break was better than a ligament, but it would still take at least a week for her nanos to repair the damage. She needed a crutch and a splint.

A medical kit would be ideal to compress the joint. She eyed the battler.

Wait. What was she thinking? A week? A human couldn't survive on Earth for a week. Romy laid back down to contemplate her next step, tired beyond belief.

At least she had a diaper on.

The sun was so bright she raised a hand to shield her eyes. Comets, it was hot. Sweat trickled down her temple just from lying there. She wondered where she was.

Romy rolled on her side and stood, careful to rest her whole weight on her left side. The trees had long limbs, which could form a makeshift crutch. She recalled that wood was a popular material from Old Earth. It always seemed odd to Romy, to cut down the very plants that gave you oxygen. Just another thing about Earth humans she'd never understand.

Hopping with some difficulty, she entered the tree line. One type of tree seemed more common than the rest. Its trunk was a greyish-white, the leaves a pale green. It made sense that the acidic water would cause changes in the plants, though not all seemed to be affected. Many showed patches of greenery amidst the pale yellow. She had no idea what it meant. Phobos was the one with the interest in agriculture and botany.

Tree limbs were strewn everywhere. And now that she was closer, Romy noticed a glorious smell—it was sharp and cleared her head. It came from the grey-white trees.

Romy reached down for a branch.

A sudden burst of movement from under her hand sent her reeling to the ground with a choked scream.

She pushed to stand on her good foot just in time to see a long, thin *something* sprinting off into the bush. No, it hadn't sprinted—it slithered. A shudder vibrated through her. If that species had survived or evolved through global warming it was probably dangerous and very tough. And the slithering creature blended with the tree limbs as if it *were* one— she'd have to be careful.

In no time Romy had two crutches and a splint. With nothing to strap the splint to her leg within easy range, she made do with what she had. Romy had shoved the thin pieces of wood inside the skin-tight ventilation suit, on either side of her injured ankle. It would do until she got to better supplies.

Able to mobilise, she checked off mentally. Now to search her part of the battler.

When she hopped back to the ruined piece of the ship, she marvelled for the first time that their knot had survived the crash. The craft was shredded. Was it luck, or excellent design?

The battler was much easier to get into from the back. Romy pulled herself up over the serrated side, avoiding the curled pieces of aluminium. Adding a laceration to her list of injuries would be the last thing she needed.

The battler was a mess.

Romy had never seen a true mess. Even the knots where they were developed, with the jumble of tubes, tanks, and wires, were a *systematic* mess, all attached to medi-tech in the centre.

This was a chaotic mess.

It was strange, but she didn't have a clue where to begin. What did you do with a mess? Even the orbito kitchens were ordered.

She frowned. Finding water had been her secondary plan. She'd start there.

Romy headed for the emergency food panels, picking her way over with painful hops on her crutch. Her section of the wreckage only held one of the emergency panels. The door sat wide open. Abandoning any logical order, she searched on hands and knees and found—to her heartfelt relief— the medical kit, water, and some dehydrated fruit lodged beneath the remains of the docking clamp. It was more than Romy had hoped for.

Back out on the grass, she took two small sips of warm water. Bafflement edged her thoughts as she wondered why she wasn't already dead. Not that she was complaining. Was it her nanotech? Or was the strange smell from the trees cleaning the air?

She pushed that aside for now. The thought was immaterial when her knot was out there, possibly injured. All she could bear thinking about was that the others were alive and together. Her mind wasn't capable of processing any other outcome of the crash. And that was why she was up and gathering supplies. Otherwise, she would be incapable of moving,

Romy would find her knot no matter how long it took. Or until she died from breathing the air. Or drinking acidic water. Or as the victim of slithering post-global-warming creatures.

She could spread the food from the battler across several days if she needed to. Despite her knowledge of Earth's history, she knew precious little about survival here—and no one knew what was safe to eat here *now*. The research teams didn't waste time with analysing food. Not when the Orbitos were yet to secure an inhabitable Earth. Who knew what was safe for consumption now, a century and a half after The Retreat.

The surrounding area was mostly flat. Sparse bush covered everything else, a mixture of the pleasant-smelling trees, dry leaves, and shrubs. The sun was overhead, and Romy knew this meant it was the middle of the day. In the distance sat a small rise, the highest ground she could see. The air rippled in the distance, making it impossible to tell how far away the hill was.

After an internal debate, Romy returned to the craft. She cut away a portion of parachute and fashioned a knife from a sharp bit of wreckage, using a strip of parachute for the handle. Take *that*, slithering creature!

She almost cried when she found more water, though no food—hopefully the others had plenty on their side.

And after further debate, Romy cut a large length of extra parachute for shelter and warmth—life in space had taught her it could go from blazing to freezing in an instant.

Fashioning straps from the chute rope, she hoisted the makeshift bundle filled with her knife, food and water, and parachute shelter onto her back and picked up her crutch. Romy paused under the shadow of the still hissing and sparking battler.

What if the others came here while she was gone?

A thinly veiled panic churned just beneath the surface, despite her soldier calm. What if she never saw her knot again? What if everyone was dead? She dashed away the sweat dripping from her forehead. Surrendering to despair would only waste time and energy, she scolded herself.

Another couple of trips to the tree line and back were all it took to make an arrow made of branches pointing in the direction of the hill. If the others entered the battler—which they would if they found the wreckage—there was no chance the knot would miss the arrow upon coming back out. Or Romy's space boots, removed and strategically placed next to it.

Romy had to believe that if she didn't find them, her knot would find her.

Her choices were few.

Sit and die.

Or move and live.

CH/\PTER FIVE

From Romy's vantage point in the wreckage, the dry bush had appeared sparse, but upon entering, the growth became so dense she couldn't tell if she were moving in the straight line she'd set for herself. A nagging self-doubt plagued her—a fear that every step she took might move her *away* from her friends.

Romy knew she could be thousands of kilometres away from her knot.

She couldn't stop thinking about how it was her piece of the wreckage that possessed the parachute. Did the battler have more than one parachute? And there was also the fire outside the craft, let alone the fact the ship tore to smithereens somewhere during the crash landing.

She took one unsatisfying mouthful of water to quell the scratchy thirst in her throat. The sun was lower in the sky, and the temperature steadily dropped. She welcomed the reprieve from the beating heat. Progress was slow. Her palms, though used to gripping guns and cleaning, were covered in blisters from the crutches. Her ankle had settled into a deep burning ache, which throbbed with every jarring hop.

The sun dipped just below the trees when the ground beneath Romy's feet began to slope upwards. Startled from her mechanical motion, she peered through the trees and saw she'd reached the bottom of a hill; whether it was the one she'd aimed for was another question.

Indecision tugged at her. It was dark. Her day's adventures included: a crash landing from space, a head injury and broken ankle, a long fall from the battler, and several hours of painful walking plagued with heartache. Her body and mind needed rest.

Though loathe to sleep on the ground with the slithering creatures, she just didn't have the energy to climb a tree with her injured ankle. Propping her crutches in a triangle against a tree, she draped the length of parachute over the sticks and dragged herself in, making sure to tuck the material under her legs. Her ankle was soon elevated on her makeshift pack and the throbbing lessened immediately. Romy studied the inside of her shelter and retrieved her knife, cutting three small holes from the top so air could circulate.

For the past hours since the crash, Romy had pushed through her bone-deep exhaustion. It wouldn't be denied any longer.

* * *

Something cold dripped on Romy's forehead. She blinked through sleep-crusted eyes, ready to glare at Phobos. Instead, she stared at the condensation gathered on the inside of the parachute. And then she remembered.

A rhythmic creaking noise called from outside her tent, faint and not alarming—some post-global-warming insect, most likely. Blinking away the blurriness of an exhausted sleep, Romy pulled herself up and began inventory. Her ankle felt substantially better. The swelling had already lessened. The blisters on her palms and walking leg had healed in the night—*Thank you, nanobytes*, she thought.

She packed up her shelter, ate two slices of dried fruit, took three sips of water, and started up the hill.

Not long into her hike, she decided to dub the hill "Mount Death." If Knot 27 were the only humans on Earth, she could name it anything she damn well liked, and Mount Death seemed fitting. The blisters of the day before came back twofold, and every bone and muscle in her body begged her to rest.

She'd rest when she found her friends. Honestly, she'd half expected to die in her sleep. The research team had reported Earth wasn't safe. And Romy believed them, so if she wasn't going to drop-dead, it was likely she would slowly succumb to cancer, sickness, or infection.

It didn't matter. Thrym would know what to do. She just had to find him.

Romy paused for rest while the sun was highest, taking two more sips of water. A quarter of her water was now gone, but her thirst nearly overwhelmed her.

The sensation was hard to put into words, but the air seemed wet. It was like breathing with your face buried in a pillow.

In the last half hour the hill had started to plateau. The trees began to thin as the top of Mount Death flattened. Soon only shrubs and boulders remained, making it a great deal easier to hop.

This was it. Soon she might not be alone anymore.

Romy hopped to the bottom of a large boulder and dropped her parachute pack and crutches with a clatter. Using a succession of smaller rocks as footholds, Romy made it high enough that she was able to reach for the smooth top of the large boulder and drag herself up, wincing as her ankle shot pain to her hip.

She made it—eventually—breathing hard on all fours. Her knot could be at the bottom of the hill. With a deep breath she rose to her knees and looked over Earth.

There was so much to look at, her eyes couldn't focus on just one sight. The beauty before her stole all thought from her mind. The vision was so breath-taking Romy decided that, if she died, this vision might just have made everything in the last two days worth it.

Earth. An oasis. *Her* home. She could feel it. This was where she belonged.

Romy twisted in a full circle on her knees.

She spotted the area she'd hopped from. A thin trail of smoke wound up above the tree line from the wreckage of the battler. Having located her starting point, she then began to turn in a circle, slowly scanning.

She did this three times.

And three times the result was the same.

Nothing.

No other smoke trails. No wreckage. No visible sign her friends were anywhere close by.

She sighed. Had she really expected it to be so easy?

At least there were a few signs of water. She noted the largest body, far in the distance; it must have been an ocean as she couldn't see the end of it. The last book she'd read was a fascinating tale about a man lost at sea for over a month.

Another body, smaller, lay off to the far right—a lake.

And the final visible water source—a river—twisted through the wilderness to the ocean.

So there was plenty of undrinkable water around. But the real question was, did she return to her wreckage, knowing it was her best chance of recovery by the Orbitos. . . .

. . . or. . . .

Romy studied the river once more.

If she went straight down and to her right, she would intercept it. It would lead her to the ocean. Maybe if Romy was drawn there, then her friends would be, too. Her training told her the decision made no logical sense. But with nothing else to go on. . . .

She left a second large arrow, made of dead tree limbs, on the top of the hill, pointing in the direction of the sea. It made her feel better to leave a trace of her passing.

Romy's second night on Earth was spent somewhere on the side of Mount Death.

By the next morning, half of her water was gone and so was a quarter of her food. Without the exhaustion of the previous night to drag her under, every single scratch and snuffle in the night had woken her. There were animals out there—a lot of them. And if Romy wasn't mistaken, some of them were large.

Today she was able to touch her foot to the ground for short periods. It was a good sign. She wanted to throw her crutches in the fiery abysses of hell. How humans used to do this for the months it took to heal a bone was beyond her. She loved her nanotech.

The sun was still low in the sky when a new sound interrupted the silence of the bush.

Romy crouched beside a tree, trying to dissect the low-pitched rushing noise. She edged closer, pausing behind trees as she drew close. What *was* it? It sounded like. . . .

Romy dragged her hands over her weary face when she realised. Streaming water. It was the sound of the taps in Knot 27's quarters, multiplied by two or three thousand.

Five minutes later she was standing on the bank of her first river. The pool in front of her was calm, though rapids ran into it from above. It stretched several metres across, and disappeared farther down around a bend.

Romy had a problem.

Her water would only last another two days.

You can breathe the air . . . maybe you can drink the water, too.

Romy exhaled slowly, pushing her smoky, unwashed hair behind her ears. Sweat trickled down her spine, and she looked at the cool surface of the river in yearning. She wanted to dub the water "River Glory." But she decided to wait and see if the water would kill her. No one liked a misleading name.

She crouched by the water's edge.

Acid water. Normal water had a pH of 7—neutral. The water on board Orbito One was between 8 and 9—slightly alkaline to help reduce the effect of stomach acid. The last recorded pH of fresh water gave a reading of 6.05—acidic. Not healthy. Its effects on the human body: vomiting, diarrhoea, eye and skin reactions, and seizures.

Romy picked her way over to the nearby plant life. The long leaves drooped over into the river. There was no colour bleaching, but the leaves were already a sickly yellow so that didn't mean much.

There was only one way to find out.

She dipped one finger in the water and when it didn't instantly burn her, she counted for three minutes. Romy pulled her finger out and waited a further five minutes. No discomfort. The water wasn't acidic enough to cause pain—a good sign.

But did it make the water safe? Romy tapped a finger against the side of her knee.

She wouldn't last long without topping up her water supplies. If she died, she wouldn't find her friends. And her friends might be in dire need of her help.

She had to take the risk.

It probably would have made sense for Romy to mix the questionable river water with the water she carried with her to dilute any harmful effects. But she didn't want to waste a drop of the water she knew was safe.

Romy decided to try a small sample. She scooped water into her hands, peering down at it before taking the plunge.

The water hurt her teeth. It was cool and . . . sweet. She'd never tasted anything so amazing!

If this was what acidic was like, it wasn't so bad. Romy made herself stop after a few mouthfuls—more than she'd initially intended to drink.

She paced up and down beside the calm pool as she waited to see if she'd become sick. As the minutes went by, she began to wonder if the water *was* safe. Romy knew that some areas of the world—the low-lying countries like Brazil and Mexico—were more severely affected than others. Maybe this part of the Earth wasn't as bad to begin with? It could've been missed by the research teams. There were only three teams, after all. And they had a whole planet to cover.

If the water was safe—and if she could find her knot and somehow contact the Orbitos. . . . What news! And maybe, *maybe*, the other soldiers could all come down. Imagine the fun their knot would have around here once they reunited. Knot 27—on planet Earth. It was her greatest dream come true.

By dusk, she still hadn't experienced any ill effects.

Romy took two sips from her own water anyway before setting up her little tent some way back from the riverbank.

Of more concern were the layers of smoky grime covering her body. The hand exposed to the river remained unblemished and free of irritation. Romy peeled off her orange ventilation suit and dipped it in the river. She scrubbed the material against itself in an effort to dislodge some of the dirt. The result wasn't too shabby. The river bubbled enticingly as she draped the spandex garment over a wiry shrub.

Romy had a strong desire to jump into the river herself. Removing her underwear, she scrubbed both pieces and used them as a sponge to wash the rest of her body.

Rinsing her underwear once more, she put the wet undergarments back on, leaving the orange garment to dry over the shrub.

Her hair. The strands, usually silken, were limp with sweat and dust. Romy couldn't swim and it looked too deep to touch the bottom. But she could still dip her head in. Wait until Deimos heard what she'd done! Romy chuckled thinking of his reaction.

The spot she'd selected was deep and still. The river itself seemed to have quietened alongside the dying light. She leaned forwards on her hands and knees, staring down into the water. If she was braver, she'd jump in—then Deimos would really lose it.

Romy hummed to herself as she brought her head closer to the water.

Her nose breeched the frigid surface.

Water exploded in every direction, the river erupting into a furious white torrent.

Romy toppled back in a mass of flying limbs, too shocked to cry out.

Before she had time to process what had happened, a *monster* scaled the riverbank.

A long-muzzled and scaly monster. Romy screamed, scrambling back until she hit the trunk of a tree, pain shooting through her ankle.

Calm down and think, Rosemary.

The water animal had a long, thick body atop short, thin arms and legs. It was designed for water . . . surely she could outrun it.

Romy slowly stood in careful increments, trying to hush her gasping breath. Climbing the tree was her best option.

But her assumption about the animal's speed was wrong.

In a thrash of movement, the sharp-toothed creature burst forwards, lashing across the ground—jaws wide, and slitted, red eyes trained directly on her. Romy grappled behind her for any hold on the tree.

She covered her face with an arm, mouth opened to scream.

Crack!

The sound echoed through the bush.

The monster skidded half a metre to her feet and collapsed.

Romy shook from head to toe, limping out of its path as quickly as she could. Staring back, she wondered why it fell. Was it dead?

The beast was going to eat her, until that cracking sound happened. Did its tiny limbs break underneath it?

The monster remained still.

Summoning her courage, Romy crept to the side of the immobile river creature and inspected it. Blood flowed from its head in a steady trickle. Her stomach rolled at the sight and her eyes widened in shock. It was dead. There was a hole in its flat head.

There was no sound in space that the human ear could hear. Aside from the staccato sound of lasers and debris missiles leaving the battler, Romy had never heard the echo of a fired gun.

But someone had shot the river animal. With a gun. An *Earth* gun.

A soft snap from behind caught her attention. In her fascination with the scene she'd forgotten one thing: A gun didn't fire itself.

She remained bent close to the monster, but all her senses were trained on the foreign noise.

There was something else she'd missed, though:

The creature wasn't dead.

The animal rolled grotesquely, bursting upwards. Romy flung herself out of its trajectory. She was too close. The monster turned its head and she watched in horror as ten-centimetre teeth descended.

A man burst from the bush and threw his weight on top of the thrashing animal. Her first feeling was relief that the Orbitos had found her.

The man was trying to pin the writhing beast to the ground.

And that's when she noticed he wasn't wearing an Orbito uniform.

Earth human.

Romy left everything, half hopping, quarter sprinting, and the rest limping, in a random direction. *The first half of the population died. The second half murdered each other.* The tall man wasn't encumbered like she was with her half-healed ankle. She only had until he dealt with the injured animal to escape.

A second *crack* echoed through the bush and Romy paused, holding her breath, straining for any hint of his next move.

It wasn't subtle.

The man's large body crashed through the bush towards Romy, whipping her into action. She looked around frantically. With a weak ankle, it took a full precious minute to climb far enough up a tree that she was above eye-level.

The crashing stopped.

Bark grazed at her ivory skin, but she worked through the pain, quietly dragging herself farther up.

The bush was still. She had no idea where the man hid, and knew that the lack of sound was a bad thing. Every night since the crash, the creaking insect had starting singing at sunset. It wasn't singing now.

She lodged herself in a straddling position over a broad branch, facing the tree's trunk. She hugged the trunk and worked to calm her breathing, ears straining. It would be a perfect time for her knot to appear. With guns. Phobos could take the strange man down. Romy recalled the man's size against the animal.

Better have Deimos help, too, just to be sure.

Romy pressed her shaking hands against the tree. The man was close. She knew this as surely as her own name.

There was no way Romy was climbing down.

CHAPTER SIX

Romy winced at the pain in her neck as she straightened from hugging the tree. She'd spent the night up there, wedged in the fork between the trunk and a thick branch. It was now dawn and her butt was numb in the worst possible way.

Retrieving her belongings was out of the question. If she were hunting someone and couldn't find them, that was where she'd wait. She didn't relish the thought of travelling in her underwear, but surely she could find some kind of shelter at night.

She probably should have slipped off in the night, but the engulfing quiet put her off. Now there was more noise to cover her descent.

Romy gingerly tested a lower branch, slipping down onto it when it proved sturdy. In this fashion, she slid down the tree, forcing her stiff joints into action.

The tree took just as much skin off on the way down as it had on the way up.

She paused at the base of the tree, listening.

Nothing. Romy put a slight weight on her ankle and winced. Last night's dash through the forest had set back her healing.

A warm body slid behind her as she made to turn. In an instant, one muscled arm clamped around her waist. She sucked in a terrified breath. He was too close to elbow, and her injured ankle couldn't hold enough weight for her to kick out. Romy whipped both arms up above her and encircled his neck, intending to bend over far enough to break his hold.

Her plan backfired.

Using his other hand, the man took control of *both* her hands, encasing them in an iron clasp. Romy struggled against him, arms lifted awkwardly, forced to rise on her tip-toes from the pain in her wrists.

A voice rumbled in her ear. "I'm not going to hurt you."

The Earth human spoke! "Get off me," she ordered.

The man tightened his grip. "No."

He spoke English. She was in an English-speaking country.

"Release me if you mean no harm." She pulled at his grip.

"Why would I?" came the infuriating answer. "You'll run."

Oddly, his reply only served to sear away her galloping fear. Romy let her entire body go slack. "Well, who are you, then?"

The man's chest vibrated behind her. Was he . . . laughing at her? She threw her head back and caught him in the face. It didn't crunch as she'd intended, but it was satisfying.

. . . Until she found herself flat on her back.

He straddled her hips, and no matter how she writhed, it was impossible to free herself. The man just watched her, in slight amusement.

Realising she wasn't going anywhere, Romy gave up her struggle and took a good look at her attacker.

The tall man was tan with jet-black hair and the most incredible grey eyes. He was older than her, but just by a few years.

Her stomach flipped. The acid water. Was it finally taking effect?

"Who are you? Why are you here?"

"Saving you from a crocodile. Would have thought that obvious. What kind of fool washes without checking the water first?"

Romy gulped at the reminder while trying to process what he'd just said. "Crocodile?"

The man observed her, grey eyes turned flinty and hard. And the way he was staring while *continuing* to pin her down was really getting on her nerves.

She broke the quiet. "You didn't tell me who you are. Are you an . . . Earth human?" Romy ground the words out.

His expression smoothed. "I crashed here five years ago."

The air left Romy's lungs. "W-what?"

He *was* from the Orbitos. That made her feel a lot better.

The man nodded. "Crashed. Been by myself."

Five years by himself? No wonder he was looking at her like she was some kind of strange experiment. He was bound to be a little rough around the edges if he'd lost his knot.

"For five years?" she repeated. "I take it you couldn't get in touch with the Orbitos?" She frowned at the black singlet that hugged his chest tightly. His pants were also black, with pockets down the sides. "How are you still alive?"

He shrugged. "No idea. Just am."

Romy rolled her eyes. *Well, that was helpful*, she thought. "Where is your uniform?"

He snorted. "You expect me to wear it for five years?"

She clamped her mouth shut so no more stupid questions came out.

"I'm going to let you up," he grunted. "I'd rather not have to track you down again—which I will if you bolt. There are all sorts of dangerous animals and plants out there. You're not safe. Understood?"

Romy thought about it and nodded. He rose in one swift motion and she clambered to her feet.

"My name is Atlas," he said, his back to her. "What's yours?"

She took her time answering, still trying to piece everything together. He'd been here for five years. This place could support human life. *How do the Orbitos not know about this?*

"Romy." She hated how her voice shook.

The man, Atlas, pulled her supplies and another pack—which clearly belonged to him—from the shrubs at the base of her tree. He'd returned to the riverbank and then crept up on her. How did he sneak up on her? She could've sworn she hadn't fallen asleep.

He frowned and looked down at her pack in his hands. "That's not an Orbito name. Unless they've moved away from historical names."

"They haven't," she said. "My full name is Rosemary." She noticed she was fidgeting with her hair, and dropped the limp strands.

He smiled a curious half-smile. "Rosemary was draped around the neck of Aphrodite when she arose from the ocean."

Romy gave him a doubtful glance. "It's also used in cooking."

She smiled a moment later when the man gave a larger quirk of his lips.

"And Atlas was forced to carry heaven on his shoulders as punishment." She was sorry for the words when his face hardened.

He brushed both hands on his sides as he stood straight and regarded her before finally saying, "It's also a book of maps."

She nodded warily, questioning his sudden change in emotion. *Five years*, she reminded herself. He tossed Romy her belongings.

She dug out her orange suit. A night in underwear was acutely uncomfortable without protection from the tree bark. If she did run again, it would be while fully clothed.

"What happened?" he asked in a low voice. He opened his pack and passed her some slightly pink meat. It looked tough.

Romy stared at the foreign food in her hand and glanced away.

She ignored his question and asked her own. "How did you find me?"

He bit into his own food—whatever it was.

"You ask a lot of questions for a space soldier who shouldn't possess curiosity."

Romy blushed. "Can you blame me?"

He studied her, swallowing. "You know what kind of noise a battler makes when it enters Earth's orbit and crashes to the ground?"

"Because I've spent so much time on Earth?" Romy rolled her eyes.

The man's eyes flashed with laughter. "Neither did I until I saw your craft streaking through the sky yesterday."

Her heart jumped into her throat, and she drew closer towards Atlas without thinking, gripping his hand. "Did you see where the rest of the ship landed?" She leaped to her feet, ready to go right then and there. "What luck that you found me! I had no idea where to start searching," she babbled happily. Her knot! He could help her find them.

"No."

"How long do you. . . ?" Romy trailed off as she looked into the man's grey eyes again. They had the experiment look again.

"No," he repeated.

Romy's mouth dried, and as elated as she'd been seconds before, she now felt close to vomiting. Her head throbbed painfully. "No, what?" she managed to get out through the tightness in her throat.

"I only saw the one. I assumed they were with you. . . ."

He assumed that the rest of her knot was with her. And that she was the sole survivor.

How far could the eye see in the sky above? *Thousands of kilometres.* A gasp sounded in her ears and she knew it came from her mouth.

It could take her years of travelling to find her knot.

Despair built inside of her, overwhelming everything else. "I crash landed with my . . . my knot," she said through numb lips, staring down at her hands in an attempt not to cry. "My part of the ship was torn off sometime during landing, I think. I lost consciousness partway down. I'm trying to find their part of the wreckage. But I haven't found a clue yet. I, I was heading in the direction of the ocean next." A tear leaked out and she dashed it away before Atlas noticed.

"It's as good a place as any," he said quietly.

Romy held up the dried meat—anything to change the subject. "What is this?" It seemed almost like chicken.

"Kangaroo."

"We're in Australia?" Romy's mouth dropped in surprise.

"Queensland, Australia," he clarified. He gave her a sideways look. "How do you know what a kangaroo is, but not a crocodile?"

Romy frantically reviewed what little she knew of Australia. Big and dry. Nothing that could help her find her friends.

She waved a hand when she noticed Atlas waiting for an answer. "Oh, I only know a few animals; kangaroos, koalas, pandas, kittens, lemurs—and a couple others."

His lips quirked again. "You're only interested in cute animals."

Annoyance bubbled within her. "No, I'm not. I like tigers, and pygmy hippos. Hippos were one of the most dangerous animals in Africa." This time she was sure he was holding back laughter. His lips were pursed. Who did that for any other reason?

Romy narrowed her eyes, daring him to laugh. "And how do you know this is Queensland, Australia?"

He picked up his pack, shouldering it. "Because I'm an Atlas."

He made for the edge of the clearing, looking back when she didn't follow. "Come on. Let's go to the ocean."

There was something off about the black-haired man's reaction to her. Was he just close-mouthed and unused to talking? He just seemed so comfortable here. And so knowledgeable. How had he survived so long on his own? Romy frowned.

After five years alone, she wondered, shouldn't he be ecstatic to find another human? Shouldn't he have asked if she'd been able to contact the Orbitos? Romy glanced around. Atlas was on Earth; he had lived here for years. It was every space soldier's dream.

Maybe he was worried she would contact the Orbitos. Maybe he thought he'd be forced to return. Which was ridiculous. The Orbitos would leap at the chance to reinstate human life on Earth.

Romy threw her bundle over her shoulder and decided to walk with the man for now.

He hadn't hurt her, aside from trapping her while they talked. And he'd saved her from the crocodile.

He might be the only other human left on Earth.

She'd follow him.

Really, she had no other choice.

Because she didn't want to be alone.

* * *

Atlas made very little conversation, though his grey eyes followed Romy's progress at all times—much to her discomfort.

On the odd occasion Atlas did speak, it was to drag her away from a poisonous plant or point out things to avoid. She learned that the slithering creature was called a snake. The name was vaguely familiar.

She'd grown quiet when he told her most were venomous, many fatally so.

Actually, the man made it sound like every single thing in Australia was designed to kill you.

"If it's so dangerous, then how have you survived so long?" Romy was getting annoyed at how surprised he was that she'd survived for three days.

He didn't answer—just for something new.

"Don't touch or eat this plant," he instructed, pushing it back out of her path with a stick. "It's a black bean."

She sidestepped around it, now walking on her injured ankle.

"Worse than nightshade?" she asked.

He shook his head. "Can't say I've tried either."

Romy giggled and though Atlas's eyes still faced forwards, she thought they softened.

"How are you still so . . . okay?" he asked. It was the first sign of hesitancy she'd seen in the Orbito soldier.

Her smile faded, knowing what he spoke of. Every soldier knew what happened to those who lost their team. In fact, most knot survivors were transferred to Orbito Four for "special treatment," which was a nice way of saying most survivors went crazy. The genetic engineers held the survivors there until the soldiers' expiration dates to study the phenomenon. And then, upon expiry the survivors were recycled into a new knot. The thought of Knot 27 dying. . . .

She shuddered, studying the dusty red ground.

"They're not dead," she grated out. "My knot is still alive."

He glanced back at her and lifted a dark brow. "Odds are, they're dead."

No! Romy's vision blurred, and she stumbled over her crutch. Her breath came in gasps, out of control. Like some kind of panic attack. Their faces flashed in front of her: Elara, Deimos, Phobos, and Thrym. Her Thrym. She clutched her stomach with one hand, choking on fear.

Hands pulled her back up. "Hey," Atlas murmured. "Hey, it's okay. I'm sure we'll find them. They're all right." He gripped her arms. "Shh, Rosemary. They're all right."

Her cloudy vision receded somewhat with his reassurances. She concentrated on the confident set of his face and nodded once she felt calm. She shook her head, wondering what came over her. Probably her reaction had been building inside since the crash. She'd never experienced anything like it before.

He gave her arms a final squeeze and he turned away, face smooth.

Romy stood to move after him, unable to shake off an uncomfortable weight churning in the pit of her stomach.

She pulled up short, staring at Atlas's back.

"They're alright," he'd said. . . .

And he'd sounded so sure.

Atlas turned, waiting for Romy beside a large tree. She tripped after him.

Were his words just an empty reassurance, she wondered.

Or did Atlas know more than he was letting on?

* * *

The smell of the air changed the next day.

Romy inhaled, assessing the smell. "Are we close now?"

She quite liked it—but not as much as she liked the grey-white trees she now knew were eucalyptus trees, thanks to Atlas. He'd even crushed a leaf in his hands and rubbed the smell on her wrists so she could experience the scent all day.

"We are." He brushed the remains of his breakfast from his unusual trousers.

She stared at the eucalyptus trees. "Why did this tree turn grey with global warming while the others have gone yellow?"

His nose scrunched in confusion.

"The acid in the water?" she asked slowly.

His expression cleared and he coughed into his hand.

She eyed him in suspicion. He was doing the pursed lip thing again.

"It's summer, Rosemary. The plants are yellow because they're dry. And to my knowledge, eucalyptus trees have always been this colour."

She tilted her head, even as her pulse began to rise. "How long has the water been safe?"

"At least five years," he replied seriously.

"But if the water is safe in Australia, wouldn't it be safe elsewhere?" she asked quietly.

He didn't reply.

Romy studied him more closely than she had since their first meeting.

"You're tall," she observed.

Atlas had that look in his eye that told Romy he was contemplating her intelligence. She threw him a withering glare. "I *mean*, you're taller than any other soldier I've seen. I'm five foot eleven. My knot mates are six-foot, at the most." She folded her arms. "You must have had a bit of trouble getting around your station."

"I did," he grunted. She could hear the annoyance in his voice. The ceilings were only six foot three inches. It would've sucked poacher poop stooping down the halls every day.

"I guess you would've needed a bigger bed," Romy noted.

He appraised her with an amused look. "Thinking about me in bed?"

His question had an undercurrent she didn't understand; his eyes were saying something his mouth wasn't.

She narrowed her eyes. "I'm thinking about your feet sticking off the end of the bunk." *And wondering why you're taller than any space soldier I've ever met.*

Atlas laughed and offered her a hand to stand, pulling her up with a quick jerk. His gaze trailed downwards and a low humming sound came from his throat.

"Have I got something on my face?" she asked as he continued to stare.

He flashed a smile. Not answering. *Again.*

"You didn't eat any milky mangrove by accident?" she teased.

"That doesn't cause fatigue—it causes blistering and blindness."

"My mistake," she said demurely. She returned his questioning gaze with innocent eyes.

He turned his head to the right. "We can camp here tonight."

It was still light. "There are still hours of daylight left." She frowned up at him.

Was it just the sunlight, or was there a twinge of sorrow in his eyes?

Romy took the plunge.

"Look, Atlas . . . if you don't want to return to the Orbitos, I understand. Earth is beautiful. I just think that the other soldiers deserve to know there's a place we can return to. And that . . . if the research teams have been lying to us, then the High Command needs to be told."

There was too much here that didn't add up. There was an entire country safe for colonisation. How was it that the Orbitos didn't know?

His head snapped up.

She pushed her palms out in front of her, not liking the stone-like quality his eyes held. "But I don't have to mention I met you. I'll only tell them about us—I mean, my friends and I. My knot."

A loaded moment passed as he surveyed her and she tried to decipher him.

Atlas shifted his gaze to look behind her.

He's lonely. The unbidden thought sprang from nowhere. Yet, he didn't seem eager for company.

Atlas was a mystery Romy couldn't solve. She lowered her palms. "Look, you stay here if you want. But I'm not stopping until nightfall."

She strode forwards a few metres to make her point and glanced back casually—as if her stomach weren't twisting at the thought of being alone again. "You coming?" she asked.

Romy soldiered on without waiting for his reply, straight-backed. Even so, her ears were strained behind her, and her speed was deliberately slow.

She ignored the relieved buckling of her legs, moments later, at the sound of his following footsteps.

* * *

Atlas steadfastly refused to let her see the ocean before morning. He didn't give her a reason not to. But maybe the ocean sucked you in at night, or crocodiles swarmed the beach. The book of the man lost at sea loomed in her mind. Romy only conceded because she wouldn't be able to search for Knot 27 with the light gone. She didn't want to miss them out of stupidity.

For now, she was happy to play in the sand. Romy knew she was greatly amusing the large man across from her, but he didn't say anything or openly laugh. The LI-924 silica tiles on their ships, heat regulators capable of withstanding great changes in temperature, were made from sand— obviously a very different type of sand.

"What will you do if you can't find your friends?" Atlas asked.

Romy blinked at the sand running between her fingers. "I *will* find my knot. They're alive."

"What if you find the wreckage and they're all dead?" he asked softly.

For a few moments a weight compressed her chest so fully, no air was able to enter her lungs. *Why does he keep saying these things?*

"Shush, Rosemary. Breathe." Atlas's warm hand circled her back.

Her heart broke. That was what Deimos said before they crashed. She couldn't stand it anymore.

She whirled on him. "Do you know, Atlas? Have you seen them? Is that why you keep saying such horrible things? Are they all—?" Romy couldn't say it.

Her anger morphed into hopeless tears, and she gulped large mouthfuls of air as sobs wracked her body.

He pulled her close. "Stop. No, I haven't seen anything. It's *okay*."

She tried to pull away. "Then why do you sound so sure they're gone?"

He pulled her back, despite her resistance. "I'm not sure," he whispered. "I'm not sure about anything."

She softened against him, and Atlas drew her closer still, holding her tight. Damn him for being warm. His embrace was the most comforting thing she'd experienced since the orbitos. It made her realise she was craving the touch of other humans. Not a day went by on the space station where she didn't receive a hug from one of her knot mates.

Was it possible to be too tired to feel anything? If so, Romy was. She whispered, "Why are we still alive?" to no one in particular.

They were simple words to use for all she wanted to know.

Why could they breathe?

Why could they eat and drink?

How was it Atlas had lived for five years?

He rubbed her arm. "I'm . . . I'm not sure."

And why was Atlas lying to her?

* * *

"Rosemary. . . ," a hoarse voice whispered in her ear.

She stretched her arms above her head and rubbed her face. "Hmm?"

"Come with me."

She was dragged upwards before she could voice her protests.

Eyes barely open, Romy stumbled through the sand after Atlas, grateful her foot was 90 per cent healed. Hopping along on crutches would be impossible on this terrain.

Atlas directed her to a log facing the ocean. "Sit here. Watch."

"But I want to put my feet in the ocean," she whined. She sounded like Elara. It was early.

He pushed her back onto the log. "Stay. You won't regret it. Then you can play in the water all you want."

Romy huffed. "That's not what I was going to do. I wanted to test if it was acidic."

"Sure you did."

She shivered and scooted closer to Atlas's side. Romy leaned in when he didn't move, grateful for his body heat. Sudden curiosity took over her, and she tilted her face up to smell him. There was no reason why. It wasn't something she'd ever wanted to do before—to anyone. Atlas froze.

Romy's cheeks reddened. "Uh, you smell like Eucalyptus," she explained, peeking up at him.

His face was smooth as he held her gaze, eyes masked.

Why did she just do that?

He broke off their stare to face the ocean. "Here it is," he breathed.

She sat up. What was here? She followed his awed stare across the water. Romy couldn't help her intake of breath. Without conscious thought, she lunged to her feet and took two faltering steps towards the water.

It was beautiful.

The ocean lapped gently, creating a line of white where the liquid tripped over itself to land on the sand. Tears pricked the corners of her eyes. The surface of the water was uninterrupted and as smooth as glass. But where a moment ago the world was dark, it was now a myriad of colours. Oranges, violets, greys, and all shades between could be seen in the painting before her.

The lower of the clouds appeared almost purple in hue, while the sun threw its powerful light over the sea, basking it in yellows and reds.

It was the most magnificent sight she would ever see.

"It's. . ." she started. Romy turned to Atlas, who had moved and now stood beside her.

"Glorious?" he supplied.

Romy nodded thoughtfully. It was, and more. "Inspiring," she decided.

"It is," he replied after a few beats.

She looked at him questioningly, and he gestured to the water with a smirk. "Weren't you going to do an acid test?"

"Are there any crocodiles in there?"

"If there are, I'll save you, I promise." He winked at her.

Romy punched him lightly and ran to the water. Just one toe.

The air whooshed out of her as Atlas seized her from behind and tossed her into the surf.

She'd never been submerged in water. The experience was terrifying. She glared at him, emerging from the water in a spluttering and coughing explosion of spray.

Atlas was bent doubled in laughter. And she crept up on him, wondering how best to submerge him. But in the next breath, it was like someone sucked all the laughter from him.

Atlas pulled Romy out of the water, all humour gone from his face.

"Atlas, stop. What are you doing?" she gasped.

"Romy!" came a familiar shout.

Romy froze in the ankle-deep water. She knew that voice. Her muscles locked, telling her not to look because what if he wasn't there? She would break into a million pieces if she turned and the beach was empty. For all that she had held together until now, she would fall apart, never to be whole again if she were only imagining the sound.

"Romy!"

Her eyes flew up to Atlas's.

"Romy!"

Atlas was glaring over her shoulder. The voice was real?

The voice was real!

Still half-disbelieving, she spun to find the beach *wasn't* empty.

Romy knew his dark skin and athletic form better than her own reflection.

Thrym was sprinting down the beach towards her.

"Thrym," Romy whispered.

Forgetting her mostly healed ankle, she let go of Atlas's hand and took off, water flying everywhere in her splashing steps.

"Thrym!" she screamed. Romy tore through the sand, running to him, only seeing *him.*

He reached for Romy and swung her high. The weight threw them both to the sand, and the pair rose to their knees, clutching at each other, making desperate, furtive touches to reassure themselves the other was there.

Romy could barely see him through her thick tears. Both trembled.

"Thrym," she choked.

He held her to his chest, rocking her. "I can't believe I found you. Romy, I thought. . . ."

"The others?" she asked fearfully, holding him at arm's distance.

"Deimos, Phobos, and Elara are alive," he said.

The dam inside her broke. Romy covered her face with both hands and cried as though her heart were breaking.

Thrym stroked her hair. "They're all alive."

But his tone was off.

Romy lowered her hands.

"What does that mean?" she asked quietly.

"Deimos is badly hurt. His nanobytes aren't healing him." Thrym couldn't meet her eyes. He choked, "Ro, I'm not sure he has much longer."

Romy was on her feet. "We have to go quickly. Atlas might be able to help." She looked behind her, stomach dropping when she found the beach empty. Where was he?

"The man you were with?" Thrym asked curiously, but she wasn't listening. She pulled Thrym with her, back to their camp.

Atlas was still there, packing his things. He looked up as she slowed her pace.

"I turned around, and you w-weren't there," she stuttered.

"I thought I should pack up." He sounded tense. Something was wrong.

She began to pack up her own shelter. "Our knot mate is very sick. He needs help." She paused, waiting for him to reassure her. When it didn't come, she muttered, "The others are alive."

Atlas nodded. He was either unsurprised or didn't care.

"You should go and be with them," he said.

Romy paused her packing and settled back on her heels. "You're not coming?"

Cloud-grey eyes studied her. It might be her imagination, but she no longer thought them hard, even if she couldn't understand why he was acting so strangely.

His eyes flickered over her shoulder.

"No. I'm not," he said, hefting his pack into position.

She'd just found her friends. Romy should be ecstatic, not crushed. She studied the set of his jaw and wondered how it was he'd been laughing just ten minutes before.

"How will I find you?" she asked calmly. Thrym came forwards to stand by her side. She ignored him for the time being.

Atlas rose, extending his palm. In the middle sat a single eucalyptus leaf.

"Goodbye, Rosemary," he said.

She took the leaf and he turned away. Her mind raced over their conversation.

"Atlas," she called. "You haven't told me how to find you."

He didn't answer or slow as he strode back in the direction they'd come from.

Romy started after him. But a hand latched on to her wrist. With a start, she remembered Thrym's presence.

"Romy, leave him," Thrym said. "He looks dangerous. And we need to go. Dei needs us."

She was torn and couldn't believe it. Deimos was *family*. But the thought of never seeing Atlas again was somehow unbearable.

Romy lifted the leaf to her nose and inhaled the sharp clearness it brought.

She turned her back on the bush. "Lead the way."

CHAPTER SEVEN

"Elara and I have been taking a different direction each day to find you. We're not far away. I'd only just left," Thrym explained as they ran down the beach. Running in sand was a lot different to running on a treadmill. Her calf muscles were on fire.

"What happened to you guys?" she panted. She'd filled him in on what happened to her already.

"Elara and I were the only ones who didn't lose consciousness during re-entry," he puffed. "She deployed the parachutes and said we were slowing down. That everything seemed as all right as it could be."

"Then?" Romy prodded.

The pair reached a stretch of rock pools.

Thrym picked his way across, Romy following in his footsteps.

"Then the ship tore in two. There was no warning—your part just disappeared." His voice was shaking. "I've never felt so crazy in my life. We were strapped to our chairs and couldn't even see where you'd gone. It was terrible.

Romy squeezed his arm.

He smiled down at her. "The parachutes did their job, but three of them were ripped away with you, leaving us with only one. We wouldn't have survived if we hadn't crashed into the ocean."

Romy shook her head. "Why didn't you drown?"

Thrym gave her a tight smile. "We had our suits on, remember? We had oxygen."

"Of course," she echoed softly.

"We had to go back for Deimos. He was stuck between his seat and the wall of the craft. It wasn't easy. We've tried to strip the battler of everything useful. But we've run out of oxygen."

If Thrym said it wasn't easy, it must have been horrific.

They rounded the corner and Romy felt her legs give way for a second.

And then she was leaving Thrym in her dust as she flew towards Phobos, who stood at the edge of the tree line.

Phobos turned at her pounding footsteps and she only caught his widened eyes before she wrapped herself around him. She held on, determined to never let go of her friends again.

"Romy," he said, disbelief colouring his voice. He squeezed her arms as though checking she were real. "You're alive?"

"I am." She choked on a sob. "Are you?"

"Still figuring it out," he said truthfully, resting his head atop of hers. "My little Romy is alive."

"I'm here. And you're here. And I love you." Romy kissed his cheek. "Please take me to Deimos."

A shadow flickered across his eyes. A foreign expression for him.

She didn't even want to ask. "He's not. . . ?"

"Not yet."

She shivered at the despair in his voice. Phobos had given up hope.

The shelter the rest of her knot had erected was much larger and more permanent than her own tent. They had salvaged large pieces of aluminium and even four seats from the battler, now decorating the rudimentary home. It was no parachute on sticks.

A rattling sound drew her attention to one corner. Thrym was leaning over someone. *Deimos!* She rushed across the shelter and sank to her knees beside him.

She gasped, pressing a hand to her mouth as nausea threatened to overwhelm her at the sight of her frail knot mate. His skin was stark white, utterly devoid of blood. Deimos lay as still as death. Other than the shuddering rise of his chest, there was little sign that he was alive.

"What's his injury?" she whispered.

"A jagged piece of wreckage stabbed him in the side on landing. It's definitely injured his lungs, but we don't know the severity." Each soldier possessed decent medical training for small wounds, and Thrym was fairly knowledgeable, always having held a stronger interest in this area than the others.

Romy stood angrily. "Why aren't his nanos working?"

Phobos slumped visibly. "You know they only work to a certain severity, Ro."

She refused to believe Deimos was going to die. "What have you tried?"

"We wash the wound daily, but we're running low on water."

"I know where a river is."

"Romy. . . ."

"It's not harmful. I've been drinking it for the last four days. And . . . Atlas has lived here for five years."

Phobos and Thrym both turned to her, jaws dropped.

She nodded and spread her arms wide and spun in a slow circle.

"The man you were with appeared healthy, too," Thrym mused. "I assumed the ocean water didn't affect us because we had the suits on. Are you sure you're okay? I'll check you after Deimos."

Usually Romy would poke fun at his overprotective tendencies. But just hearing his voice, she didn't have the courage to because at any second it could all be ripped away.

"Wait, wait, wait. What man?" Phobos looked between them. "There's someone else here on Earth?"

Romy dropped her pack against the tent wall, averting her face. "Yes, but he's gone now."

* * *

As the wind began to steadily rise, Elara returned.

She sprinted to where Romy still kept vigil at Deimos's side. The girls embraced, resting their foreheads together and exchanging stories in hushed voices.

Elara sagged in her arms. It was strange; when Romy had imagined this moment, she'd been the one leaning on Elara. Romy tightened her hold on the pixie-featured girl.

"Is he okay?" Romy asked.

Elara cast a worried glance at Phobos, whispering. "His breathing seems worse."

Thrym eyed the sides of the shelter with distrust. "Phobos, come help me outside. The wind is growing stronger."

Phobos knelt beside Deimos, his head bent. Romy didn't know if he'd heard Thrym at all.

"I'll come," she said softly.

Phobos and Deimos were closest to each other. This was terrible for her, but even worse for Phobos.

She circled the shelter with Thrym, wiping at the sweat dripping from her chin. The air had grown thick with water.

The buckling of the aluminium and the howling of the air was loud enough that Thrym had to raise his voice to be heard. "I think if we stack everything against the wall on the inside, at least the walls won't cave in during the night."

Romy nodded in agreement. The main danger was the sharp aluminium hitting them. "Let's place some wooden bracers on either side and set them into the sand," she shouted back.

She peeked up at the sky and hoped it would be enough. The ugly bruised clouds were a radical change from the calm serenity Atlas had shown her this morning. Her stomach twisted. Why was he so set on leaving? He'd been alone for five years. She'd told him she wouldn't tell the Orbitos about him. Didn't he trust her?

The convenience of their exit point on the beach, five minutes from her knot, hadn't escaped her notice for a second. Atlas had known her knot was there. But then, why lead her to them when he so obviously wanted to be alone?

She recalled the loneliness in his eyes and rubbed her forehead. Stupid man made no sense, she thought. And what did she care? Odds were she'd never see him again. Her eyes burned as the wind whipped around her face.

"You gonna help?"

Romy started and flashed Thrym an apologetic smile.

They began searching for sturdy limbs to fortify their holding.

"So what was with that guy?" Thrym asked after a while. "When did he crash here?"

She looked up. "How did you know he crashed here?"

Thrym shrugged. "He looked like a soldier. And, well, he would have to be one of us, wouldn't he?"

She pressed her lips together, unwilling to share information about Atlas without his permission. "You don't think it's strange that we're able to breathe? And drink the water here?"

Thrym thought about it. "There are only three teams. They've probably just missed it."

She'd thought so, too. But Atlas had been here five years. . . .

Romy didn't know what to think.

She frowned at the ground.

"Romy," Thrym started. She turned at the hitch in his soothing voice.

"You should just be careful if he comes back. I didn't like the way he looked at you."

She studied her knot mate. "Like what?"

Thrym shook his head, frowning. "I don't know. It just made me angry."

Romy looked down at her hand as a splash of rain appeared on the same palm, which earlier held a eucalyptus leaf. "I don't think he's coming back."

Thrym cupped the side of her face with a gentle hand. "It's about to start raining. Let's get inside."

Romy tilted her head back to stare up at the sky and the angry clouds wrung out their water from far above her. It was breathtaking.

She untangled her arm from Thrym's and stood in front of the shelter, letting the rain wash over her skin. The raindrops were warm and refreshing. She pulled her fingers through her hair, letting the water run through.

"Romy, get inside, you'll get soaked," Elara shouted. "Trust me, it's cool the first time—until you have to sleep in wet clothes."

Romy stayed where she was for another minute, riveted by the sight, and then ducked inside.

* * *

Romy was glad she'd listened to Elara. The rain showed no signs of abating over the next two days. Their flimsy shelter threatened to collapse upon them every second as the wind battered the structure from all sides. Elara said it was a superstorm, a result of global warming forcing too much energy into the weather systems. It was like five pre-global-warming storms put together.

Deimos somehow clung to life, his nanotech doing everything it could to tether him to this world. But his breathing had turned from rattling to stuttering that morning and he hadn't regained consciousness at all since she'd found the knot.

Phobos spent most of the time staring at his dark-haired counterpart. He hardly spoke, didn't sleep—just stared at the struggling body of his brother. It was the best and worst part of belonging to a knot. Living together was joy, but for one part to be ripped away was torture. Romy herself felt like her insides were being cut into shreds. And she wasn't sure Phobos could make it without his twin.

"If Elara hadn't flown into K4 we would have never crashed." Phobos's voice was hoarse from disuse. "Deimos wouldn't be lying here like this."

It was the first time he'd spoken in two days.

Romy shared an uncertain look with Thrym. Phobos was upset and lashing out. But she caught a glimpse of the distraught expression on Elara's face and couldn't let it slide.

"We can't think that way, Pho," she said quietly. "We were one of the last knots to get to the docks. We got the worst ship."

"Because of Elara," he said bitterly.

It was true, Elara always took the longest to prepare, but. . . .

Thrym shook his head. "We're in a crappy situation. It's not fair to point fingers. If we thought that way then it could be said that the blame is on you and Deimos. If you hadn't landed us kitchen duty, we wouldn't have been so tired and would have been more likely to wake at the first alarm. Maybe it's Deimos's fault he's here like this."

Phobos fixed Thrym with a murderous stare. "Did you just blame Dei for his own *death*?" he shouted, eyes red with lack of sleep.

Thrym held up his hands, coming to his feet. "No, I was just illustrating the futility of thinking that way."

Phobos leapt up and took a single step in the other man's direction. "How about I illustrate the futility with my foot up your arse."

Romy winced, quickly rising in a hurry to stretch out her arms between them. "Wait! Just sit down and we'll talk about it. Everyone's upset."

"Get out of the way, Romy. This is overdue. He's not thinking straight," Thrym ordered.

Romy looked at Elara as the young woman stood, tears streaming down her face in a steady torrent. "It *is* my fault. All of this," she sobbed.

There was a mighty roar and Phobos bore down on Thrym in the tight space. Thrym pushed Romy to the sand. Elara screamed and rushed in to grab Phobos's swinging arm, but he knocked her back, causing her to trip over a propped branch.

Romy watched the scene from the ground in disbelief. They'd never fought like this in their lives.

She started as hands gripped her waist and lifted her up. She looked over her shoulder and up.

Atlas. Her mouth formed the word.

Atlas peered down at her for a beat, checking she was okay, and then strode into the middle of the tent.

"Stop. Now," he commanded.

Romy's chin all but dropped to the sand when it worked. Even Elara stopped crying. Thrym was the least affected, probably because he'd seen Atlas before.

Her knot stared at the stranger in their tent. All she could feel was overwhelming relief he was here. He'd followed them after all.

Atlas crossed the shelter and dropped to his knees beside Deimos, picking up a limp wrist. He checked the wound with his other hand. The grimace told Romy all she needed to know.

"We'll have to work fast," he said.

Romy approached behind him. "You can save him?"

He tilted his head to her. "We'll try."

"We?" she echoed. But Atlas didn't comment further, instead putting his thumb and little finger to his mouth to let out a shrill whistle.

Five men entered the tent, all in funny green-patched clothes and helmets. All of them with Earth guns.

"What's going on?" Thrym boomed.

Romy backed up.

Who were these men? There were too many of them to be the rest of Atlas's knot. And he'd said his knot was dead . . . didn't he? Were there *two* other knots here?

Something wasn't right.

The group approached Deimos, ignoring Thrym's angry question.

"Atlas, what's happening? What are you going to do to Deimos?" she asked quietly.

"Stand aside. We need to act quickly," he replied, signalling his men.

The air already had her overheated, but Romy felt her body temperature rise that little bit more. She turned around and flung her arms out, stopping the five men in their tracks.

She faced Atlas, anger coursing through her. Because she was sure when she was spilling out her life story to him on the walk to the beach, he never once mentioned five other men.

His face remained impassive as she glared up at him.

"I *said*, what are you going to do with Deimos?" she demanded.

Romy hated that her anger made him laugh. Not laugh outright, but he was doing that pursing lips thing again. Deimos shivered violently behind him and Atlas's expression grew grave.

"He doesn't have time for us to talk. You should all come. Only grab what you need—we have supplies at camp."

Romy looked from the mysterious man's sincere expression and met the gazes of her knot. Thrym nodded at her and she understood he was passing the decision to her.

She knew Atlas the best of any of them. But she hardly knew Atlas *before* this moment—Romy looked at the other men behind her—and now she knew him even less. She thought they'd forged some kind of bond, a camaraderie forced upon them by their situation: two people possibly alone on Earth. Apparently not.

He'd disappeared without any explanation back at the beach. The most horrible feeling was building inside because *nothing* was as it was supposed to be. On Earth, with Atlas, with Knot 27—nothing.

Did Romy trust the grey-eyed mysterious man with her knot? Deimos's breathe gurgled, and her heart stopped until he resumed his stuttering efforts to survive.

Deimos would die if they stayed. But if they went with Atlas, Deimos might live. Put like that, it was the easiest choice she'd ever made.

Romy stepped aside and let the five men rush forwards.

Atlas met her eyes and she avoided his gaze, preferring to watch the ministrations of the men transferring Deimos onto a stretcher. The extra heat flushing her face had not dissipated in the slightest, and she knew it wouldn't until she knew what the hell was going on.

No matter what he'd done since they'd met, she knew Atlas had been lying to her the whole time.

CHAPTER EIGHT

The men swept Deimos out on a stretcher.

Romy left everything behind and followed.

The others scrambled to collect food and water, not willing to leave it behind and place sole trust in the men who had barged into their midst.

She just wanted to make sure they wouldn't disappear with her brother.

The rain fell in thick sheets. The five men carrying Deimos were a blur only a short distance ahead. Wet strands of hair clumped around her face. She held one arm over her eyes, jogging to catch up. The roar of the rain was unbelievable, almost frightening. Or maybe it was the situation. She caught fragments of conversation as the five men shouted to each other.

The men rounded a large tree and Romy slowed to a stop. She watched numbly as Deimos was carefully loaded into what could only be. . . .

. . . an automobile.

Two of them.

A low voice spoke in her ear. "It's a vehicle."

Romy spun to face Atlas, heart beating fast. She looked back to the car. Her head was spinning as she attempted to comprehend all the impossibilities of the last few days. "But all automobiles were seized in 2047," she whispered. In a desperate attempt to change the fate of the planet, the government bodies had systematically confiscated all vehicles. It was just before society erupted into anarchy. She rubbed her forehead. In that moment, she just wanted to go back to reading about Earth on her nano in her room on Orbito One.

It was too much.

Hands gripped her shoulders. Atlas dipped his head near hers. Romy avoided his gaze, closing her eyes to conceal her burning tears.

"I promise you," he said, "I will explain what I can, soon. But right now, I need you to get in the car. You're the only one who is keeping it together right now. I need you to lead your friends."

This was keeping it together?

"Deimos needs help. Now." He brushed his thumbs along her upper arm in a soothing gesture. "Can you do that, soldier?"

Romy studied his face. The situation was quickly spiralling into something she couldn't cope with. There was an overwhelming temptation to stick to what she knew—her knot—and deny that everything else was happening.

"I need you to do this," he said.

She looked away and nodded, Deimos once again influencing her decision. Atlas hesitated before dropping his hands.

He shouted to the men, wiping the rain from his eyes, and made for the second car.

The rest of her knot crowded around Romy, each of them attempting and failing to find some small protection from the rain. Romy had once read the phrase "soaked to the bone". She remembered laughing, thinking it a cute remnant of Earth.

Romy had never before been so completely drenched that it sucked the life from her.

Thrym hovered to her left. Elara had taken hold of her hand on the other side. Atlas was right. Romy was in no way calm, but her friends were falling apart. She stood tall, aiming for nonchalance, hoping her knot would take comfort from it.

One of the unknown men approached their group and herded them to the second car. The back panel sat open and Romy took the lead, pulling herself into the vehicle.

The interior was pristine. The seats were black. It was . . . confined. Hoping she hadn't made the biggest mistake of her life, Romy moved into the farthest seat. She sighed at the reprieve from the beating rain. Not that sitting in her soaked clothing was comfortable, either.

"What is this?" breathed Elara.

Thrym and Phobos stared in awe as they took their seats in the back cabin. "An automobile," Romy answered calmly.

The armed man snorted. "It's the best carbon-neutral ranger there is, sweetheart."

"It's electric?" Romy asked, surprised.

The man burst out laughing. "Electric?" he scoffed. "I think my great-gran had one of those."

Phobos hummed in disbelief as the man left, slamming the back door, causing the entire craft to shake almost as much her insides.

"That's impossible." He faced Romy, water dripping from his shoulder-length blond hair. "Isn't it?"

The others waited, staring at her. Out of all of them, she knew the most about Earth. Carbon-neutral economies and technology had held her interest for several years. The carbon-neutral campaign had gained wide popularity in the 2020s. If the campaign had commenced a single decade earlier, *maybe* Earth could have survived. Romy slowly nodded. A carbon-neutral way of travelling was possible.

But if the vehicle wasn't electric. . . .

What fooled the world into a false sense of security was the twenty-five-year delay between what they were doing, and the effect it had on Earth.

The humans saw all the pollution, but couldn't see immediate consequences. It made ignoring the problem too easy. Unfortunately, when it became clear that the end of the world was approaching, all funding was pulled from carbon-neutral and pushed into nanotechnology and The Retreat.

The last available cars had been electric. If research had ground to a halt in 2040 like she was always led to believe, and Earth-dwelling humans had perished by 2060 . . . then how the hell, a century and a half later, was there *better* technology?

A sick feeling had churned inside her since Atlas barged into the shelter with the other men.

Romy wanted to scream. But she couldn't because her knot was currently watching her. They only remained calm because they thought she knew what was happening.

Romy had to keep it together.

"It has to be powered from nuclear fusion." She shrugged as if it were no big deal. Nothing could be further from the truth.

Thrym's face twisted. "Was that around before The Retreat?"

"Yes." She didn't add the fact it had only been used in military transportations, such as submarines. Or that nuclear reactors small enough to power a car, while not killing the driver with radiation, had been at least another decade from perfection. Even then it would have had to go through rigorous testing before public use.

The churning in her stomach worsened but the others accepted her lie without batting an eyelid.

A thought—a terrible thought—had occurred to Romy. One so twisted it couldn't possibly be true. So perverse she felt ashamed to think it, let alone give it voice.

Something was going on. Knot 27 was out of their depth. Romy pressed her lips together in determination. Atlas promised he'd explain. There had to be a clear, concise, logical justification for why there was human life, for why the knot was still alive, and why they were sitting *in a damn nuclear powered carbon-neutral vehicle.*

"Where did they take Dei?" Phobos asked, pushing his head against the window.

She slowly inhaled and hoped Elara didn't hear the shake in her breath. "They drove him off already. I think they needed to get him to help straightaway."

"They have medical?" Thrym asked, just as Elara asked, "Will he be okay?"

Romy wrapped an arm around the slightly smaller woman. "I don't know." She had no idea what they were walking into. However, if they'd stayed on the beach, Deimos's death would have been assured. "But this is Dei's best chance."

"It *is* my fault," Elara whispered, so quietly Romy hardly caught the words.

Romy didn't think she was meant to hear it, so she laid a gentle kiss on her sister's head and held her tightly as the vehicle lurched forwards.

* * *

Romy's head lolled to the side, startling her from sleep. She was in a small, dark box.

Heart racing, her eyes fell on the sleeping forms of Elara, Phobos, and Thrym, and she recalled where they were: a vehicle.

Romy tried to focus her blurred recollection of the last . . . few hours?

The vehicle had maintained a slow lurch through heavy sludge for most of the day as far as they'd been able to guess. They drove for so long, the rain finally stopped.

But they were no longer moving. So where were they? The twisted thought from earlier came back in force. It was clear that the situation on Earth was nothing like they'd been told. She could only think of so many excuses before she had to look the truth in the eye. During the drive she'd given it serious consideration. Now the questions were who, and why. Who was covering up the fact that there was still human life on Earth? Had these people survived through generations of global warming? Or were the Orbitos reintroducing the soldiers in secret?

Romy looked through the window beside her, trying to see out. They were parked in some kind of shelter. She had to crane her neck to see the ceiling. It appeared much sturdier than their beach shelter. The metal sides were smooth and bolted together.

But it looked nothing like the Earth houses she'd seen on her nano. A shiver worked its way through her. Her instincts screamed that she should remain alert. Who could say whether the Earth humans were really here to help, or not? If this was all a cover-up, Knot 27 could have followed Atlas and his men into a trap.

She untangled herself from Elara and leaned across to the window beside Thrym and Phobos, confirming their car was the only object in the high-roofed building.

A prickling tickled the back of her neck.

Where was Deimos?

Not wishing to cause undue alarm, Romy quietly squeezed through the jumbled legs of her friends and tried the handle.

She breathed a sigh of relief when the door swung open. If the Earth-dwellers—or crash survivors—meant them harm, surely the vehicle would be locked. She eased the door open, just enough to slip out, before resting the door so it appeared closed to the casual observer. Her chest rose and fell in even beats.

A panel on the side of the building was illuminated with daylight.

Romy approached with soft steps, one ear listening behind her for any signs of the knot waking. She felt across the panel.

Where was the handle?

Romy swallowed back her misgivings, recalling the nuclear fusion automobile. Maybe this held more advanced technology.

"Open panel," she stated clearly.

When this didn't work she tried "Open door", "Requesting exit", and "Let me the hell out", to no success.

Crouching down, Romy felt her way along the panel on her hands and knees. She was grimy, tired, and hungry, and wasn't used to being in charge. Space soldiers were made to follow, not to lead and ask questions. At this point a memory wipe sounded like a good time. Falling asleep to wake with no memory of any of this would be a blessing. The image of the sun rising over the ocean stirred before her eyes and she blinked it away. *Well, maybe not.* She gazed down at the door and discovered a slim metal handle along the smooth surface.

Moving into a squat, she gripped the handle with both hands and heaved up with all her strength. The door whipped around in a coil at the top with a *bang!* Romy winced at the crashing sound, even as she raised a hand to protect her eyes against the glaring light.

It turned out that door wasn't locked either. . . .

Eyes watering, Romy stepped out of the empty building and into the light. The sun was barely in the sky, signalling early morning.

When her vision cleared, she gaped at the sight before her.

There was a clearing in the bush, and it was full of low wooden buildings. The . . . camp, she realised, was longer than it was wide. She could see that only five or six of the low buildings were dotted across, while she could not see the end of the shelters to her left or right.

The dirt under her feet was a ruddy red-brown, and the few parked vehicles were that same khaki colour that the men who took Deimos had worn. Her orange suit stood out against the neutral landscape.

The odd village seemed to merge with the bush. If she had walked fifty metres either side of it, Romy couldn't be sure she would have spotted it.

A shiver ran up her spine as she scouted the area for life.

Romy took a few steps forwards and scanned once again. There would be a guard of some description watching them if Atlas meant to harm the knot, though no one had come running when she'd flung open the panel.

Nothing disturbed the still morning.

A few hundred metres to her right was a cluster of buildings. They were the tallest Romy could see in the camp.

She took off at a fast clip towards them. Was this an old township? It didn't *look* hundreds of years old. And she knew that wooden buildings were rare in the twenty-first century. Romy glanced back and saw a clear trail of her footsteps extending from the building she'd left.

"The doors were unlocked," she reminded herself before abandoning any attempt to sneak her way through the village.

The red dirt clung to her ventilation suit as her steps disturbed the smooth surface, adding to her general grime.

As she walked through the camp, the houses remained quiet. Empty, for all she knew. But the window coverings were lowered against the rays of the morning sun.

And the homes looked too . . . pristine to be empty. But if the low houses were full. . . .

What were the odds that every single battler that had ever crashed on Earth ended up in this exact place?

The dead weight in her stomach grew heavier.

Romy scouted ahead, creeping towards the taller buildings. There were three of them, arranged in a semi-circle with the tallest in the middle. All were much larger than any of the homes she'd passed thus far.

A flickering caught her eye. To her right was some kind of pixelated black and white hologram. It rose up from a small black box bolted into the ground. The pictures on it were rotating, like a slide-show; pictures of families laughing, of the young helping the elderly, and of children holding hands. Romy blinked in alarm as a message flashed across in large letters, 'Take Less Than You Need'. The images the projection showed were happy, but for some reason it felt sinister. What was the projection for? And what did the message mean?

She tore her eyes from the hologram and looked up at the building she'd stopped in front of—the tallest one, in the middle. There was something about it which gave her pause. It felt like a point of no return. What would she do once she reached them? Look in the windows? Open a door? Or should she retreat—with a little more knowledge—until Atlas revealed his true motives?

Romy never got a chance to make that decision.

A siren blared overhead. All around her. Romy brought her hands up, spinning around to locate the alarm.

The sound came from speakers under the roof hangings.

Someone must have seen her!

Still covering her ears, Romy froze as a middle-aged woman exited one of the wooden homes. The sirens cut off abruptly. In the lack of sound Romy heard the thunderous thudding of her heart. The woman hadn't seen her yet, occupied with carrying a basket of clothing.

Not breaking her gaze from the approaching Earth human, Romy edged backwards. She never should have left cover, she realised.

She was in plain sight, dead-centre in the clearing.

The woman glanced up. Romy stilled and saw her do the same, surprise etched upon her weathered face.

For a long drawn out second neither moved. But Romy couldn't help feeling the dark-haired older woman was having the exact same reaction as she—utter confusion.

She dropped her basket suddenly, jaw dropping open.

Romy tensed to run.

She could outdistance the woman. She would go back to her friends and—

Her frantic plans fell flat as the crucial piece of the puzzle she'd been missing finally revealed itself.

Atlas has Deimos. That was why the doors were unlocked. *That* was why everything was too easy. They had her friend. Atlas knew she wouldn't leave without her knot mate!

Romy shuffled one foot back as the woman took a step forwards.

The expression in her eyes was unnerving. It was as if she'd seen something impossible. Her demeanour was . . . strange. It raised the hairs on the back of Romy's neck.

She was so focused on the woman that it took the slamming of several doors to alert her to the presence of others.

She broke away from the woman's intense stare and looked to the right, jumping at how many people had appeared in the short time.

She whirled at a scraping behind her. More of them! Romy stumbled away—back towards the foreboding buildings. But the buildings were no longer there. Gone was the flashing hologram projection. There were only people. Too many people! All staring. All with the same dumbfounded expression on their faces.

Why were they looking at her like that?

Romy turned back to the woman and screamed upon discovering her much closer than anticipated. Romy stood motionless, taking in the woman's shining tears. The unfamiliar grey streaks threading her hair.

She stretched a wrinkled hand towards Romy. Romy drew her shoulder back so the fingers didn't connect. The woman kept her arm reached out as Romy jerked back.

The old Earth-human eyes were wide, as if with fever. And finally she spoke, the sound crackling and low.

"Thank you for your sacrifice."

CHAPTER NINE

Romy processed the word "sacrifice" through numbed senses.

It was like the browned, reverential group had been waiting for a cue. They started shuffling forwards. Romy searched for a weapon—something to protect herself. But what was the point? She was trained in *space warfare*. She shot guns and picked up debris; she didn't fight with her fists!

And then a firm body was at her back.

Romy shrieked and threw her hands at her attacker's face. But then one strong arm was about her waist and the other was clamped across her chest, pinning her flailing arms.

She couldn't get away!

Tilting her head back, Romy stared up. Her wide-eyed panic instantly recognised the grey eyes above her. She glared at Atlas. Had this been his plan the whole time?

To lead Knot 27 into a trap?

Romy summoned every insult available to her and prepared to unleash them. She couldn't move, but she was damned if she'd be dragged to her death in silence! What was he going to do to her? What was she being sacrificed for?

"Romy!"

She looked towards the scream, heart sinking as she sighted the rest of her knot racing towards her. *No!*

"Run!" The scream ripped from her throat. Romy wrenched aside to dislodge the iron arms around her. But it was just as futile as the first time they'd met.

How had he fooled her so completely?

Her friends weren't running. They were fighting their way towards her, she realised. She silently begged them to go the other way; to escape.

The large presence behind her sighed, snapping orders to someone out of sight.

"Restrain them. Now," he said.

"Don't hurt them," she pleaded. "Please, Atlas. Please don't harm my knot."

Atlas spun her to face him, gripping her firmly. An unfathomable expression bore into her as she felt a stabbing pinch at the side of her neck. Romy blinked slowly, not looking away from the traitor in front of her as her head began to droop.

Her last thought was to wonder how she'd ever thought his hard eyes were gentle.

* * *

Heated voices drew Romy from troubled dreams.

"How much did you give her?" a low voice growled.

Romy's eyebrows drew together as her head swam. She groaned and cracked her eyes open.

Before her was a sight too confusing to deal with. She closed her eyes again.

She listened as Thrym spoke. "She just takes a little longer to get up. It will be worse because you knocked her out."

What?

Romy shot up, instantly regretting the speed as her head spun wildly.

"The situation was out of control. You were supposed to stay put until I had a chance to brief you."

She turned to the speaker. Atlas. Romy struggled to remove herself from the blankets as the bent woman's voice floated through her mind: *sacrifice.*

"Rosemary. Stop," Atlas commanded.

"Do *not* call me that." She shot him a withering glare, ignoring him and standing anyway. "You traitor."

There were two exits, and fewer people here. Only her knot, Atlas, and one other young man in a lab coat. He looked like the doctors on Orbito One.

"Give me a chance to—"

Romy ignored his request. Her knot could overcome both of the other men. She looked to her friends to give a signal to attack.

And stopped in her tracks.

Because in her half-awake state she hadn't truly assessed the situation.

The others were unrestrained and . . . calm for the first time in days. Elara was leaning against a wall, arms crossed over her chest. Thrym was bleeding from a cut on his head, but his tension came from his concern for Romy. And Phobos . . . he didn't look like anything was wrong with him at all. They looked at *her* with concern.

92

Her voice cracked. "Thrym, what's going on?"

Sympathy burnt in Thrym's gaze as he stepped forwards and took her into his arms. He spoke, matter-of-fact, as always. "We don't know. But we've been assured of our safety."

He looked at Atlas. And she knew that Thrym wasn't fooled either.

"I'm so sorry I led you into this. But Deimos. . . ." The rest of her words were lost as the lump in her throat rose into tears.

"Shush, Romy. Whatever this is, it isn't your fault," Thrym soothed.

He was just being nice, she thought. She didn't deserve his unwavering support. The Commander of Orbito One himself could say it and Romy still wouldn't believe it was true.

"Why do I feel so weird?" She spoke quietly. The room was spinning, and she clung to Thrym, swaying on her feet.

Atlas approached and Romy swatted his helping hands away. She'd rather fall to the ground.

After a few dizzy beats, the room began to right itself. She glared up at the man in front of her.

Her first lesson on Earth: Don't trust anyone.

"I trusted you." The accusation in the sentence was clear. She had trusted him. Trusted him with herself. But more than that, she had trusted him enough that she'd placed Deimos's life in his hands.

"I was letting you rest," he replied softly. "I haven't had a chance to speak to the settlement about your presence." His tone grated. "Now you've created a mess that I will need to fix."

Romy's eyes widened incredulously, mouth dropping open.

Atlas fixed his gaze on the doctor. "*Someone* was meant to be watching the shed."

The doctor, who looked little more than five years older than herself, shrugged. "You gotta go when you gotta go."

Elara pushed off the wall. "Well, I, for one, would really like to know *what the hell is going on*. Now," she snapped. Phobos stepped beside her, supporting her without words.

All four of them turned the heaviness of their stares on the man who had the answers.

Atlas surveyed the group, unfazed, and clasped his hands behind his back. It was a soldier's pose. That was what didn't make sense. If he was from Earth, why did he stand like a soldier? How did he know so much about the Orbitos? And if he *was* from the Orbitos, what was happening? Why were there so many people here? Had the humans survived after all?

And why did he not tell her this? Why did he lie?

Romy stood, fist clenched at her sides. She'd never been so angry, nor felt so violent in her life. "Tell us."

Atlas stopped before her.

"Why did the woman call me a 'sacrifice'?"

A smile cracked on his face. Romy blinked at him. That wasn't the reaction she was expecting. A wheezing noise came from behind Atlas.

She peered past Atlas and saw the doctor had his fist shoved in his mouth and was . . . crying. Tears streamed from his eyes. She shared a baffled look with Phobos.

Atlas smoothed the smirk from his face with one hand and rubbed the back of his head. The wheezing continued behind him.

"I can see how Meredith's words could be construed that way," Atlas started.

The wheezing behind him turned to howling laughter.

Atlas coughed and glanced back. "Houston, give us a moment."

"S-sure."

The doctor left them through one of the nearby exits. They listened to his laughter recede down the hall.

"Follow me," Atlas commanded.

He didn't wait to see if they would follow. It was almost exactly like the first time he'd said the words to her. He was arrogant enough to expect her knot would just stand and shadow him. And Elara and Phobos did.

She looked to Thrym, who stared back at her. Steel passed between them. There were only four people she trusted in the world, and Thrym she trusted more than any other.

"There's only one way we're getting information," he muttered.

Romy sighed and trailed after her friends.

Atlas didn't take them far. Not even out of the building. Romy assumed they were in one of the important buildings.

They crossed down a hallway to a room full of tables and benches. All of the furniture faced the front, kind of like a more informal orbito lecture theatre. He waved the four space soldiers to the front row, not making any move to sit himself.

Atlas ignored Romy's friends for the most part, watching her closely. And Romy had absolutely no idea what he was searching for. She couldn't glean anything from his body language at all.

She found her voice when he looked at Thrym, who entered behind her. "What happened out there? Why did the woman call me a sacrifice?"

Atlas leaned forwards and gave her a flat look. Romy imagined he might sigh if the situation wasn't so tense.

"First, you need to be aware I can't tell you everything. I must seek clearance from my superiors. The information is classified," he started. His eyes flashed as he said the words.

"That's poacher poop!" Romy spat out. "We deserve to know everything."

"And yet you can't. Because the knowledge will force you all into a certain life. One you won't understand the consequences of right now."

"How are there humans living on Earth?" Phobos demanded.

Atlas didn't seem the least bit phased by Phobos's outburst. He stared at the knot dispassionately.

"No more lies." Romy implored him with her eyes to tell them something.

Indecision marred his face.

"Atlas," she said softly. "We need a reason to trust you."

She needed a reason to trust him.

Resolve lit his dark eyes and Atlas spoke as if the words were being dragged from his mouth. "When Meredith thanked you for your sacrifice, she was thanking you because, to her, to everyone here, you *have* made a sacrifice."

Romy stared at Atlas, not understanding.

He closed his eyes briefly. It was nothing really, just a long blink. But Romy noticed nevertheless.

"You choose to live on the orbitos, protecting Earth," he said finally.

"Choose to?" Elara echoed.

Thrym rose to his feet. "It's not a choice," he said slowly. "We must protect Earth until we can return. Once it is safe for human life. . . ." Thrym trailed off, having seen the contradicting evidence since setting foot on land.

The truth was clear in Atlas's stone-grey eyes.

It was like someone had let go of a stretched rubber band in her mind. Pain stabbed at Romy's temples. The terrible thought she'd had the day before. . . .

"It's a lie," Romy said hoarsely. "The orbitos . . . everything . . . it's all a lie."

Elara gasped and rocketed from her chair. Phobos and Thrym were yelling at Atlas, demanding answers. Romy covered her ears, trying to process it all, wishing one of her other theories had been right instead.

Any theory would have been better. That life on Earth had continued somehow, and the Orbitos were unaware because of lost communication. That a few of the knots had deserted to live down here. That Atlas was telling the truth at the beginning. That the researchers were lying to High Command. She would have preferred any of those to what Atlas had just confirmed.

Never once had she suspected her entire existence was based on a lie.

"Did global warming even happen?" she choked. The others turned to her, but she couldn't peel her eyes from Atlas.

The man, Houston, had re-joined them at some point. The doctor nodded at Atlas and stood against the only exit. Romy wasn't sure if that was a purposeful move, or not.

Atlas turned his attention back to her knot. "You must promise to never repeat what I tell you. No one, other than Houston, myself, and a few select others know what I'm about to impart. Do you understand? You do not speak of it to anyone outside this room. Better if you don't speak of it ever again."

Romy nodded along with the others. But something in one, or all, of their expressions didn't satisfy Atlas.

He approached, dark hair flopping forwards as he loomed over the knot. Romy shivered at the cruelty on his face.

Every inch of his face was carved from rock, inflexible and sincere. "I don't threaten idly. If any of you speaks of this, your entire knot will die, including your friend who is currently recovering. And not by my hand." He waited and then added, "And don't forget, I didn't have to tell you anything."

She could tell the others' reactions were as mixed as her own. In one sentence he had given them hope and crushed them with fear.

"We understand you completely," Romy said coolly.

"Good." He met her angry gaze with unflinching calm. "It would be a shame for Deimos to be killed when he's just reclaimed his life."

He studied the wall behind them. "There are three things you need to know. One, global warming has come and gone and humankind survived it."

Air left Romy's body in a whoosh. He'd said it so casually. Without care or warning. Every breath she'd *breathed*, global warming hadn't just existed. It had been fact. It was the sole foundation for all they did. Their ancestors had ruined the world. They'd learned too late. The lessons, the history, the nano-libraries full of material. It wasn't possible for everything she knew to be fabricated. . . .

Before Romy had absorbed the first point, Atlas moved on to the next.

"Secondly, you were all made for one reason only: to protect Earth from the Critamal, because no one else could or wanted to do it at the time."

A pained moan came from Elara's direction.

"Thirdly, everyone on Earth thinks you're fully aware of all this and have consented to a life of service. That you willingly *sacrifice* your life so they are kept safe."

Lies, Romy thought. *All of it.* She stared at the floor, feeling utterly empty.

"Who did this to us?" Phobos whispered.

She looked up at Atlas and saw his hesitation before he answered.

"The Mandate orchestrated the deception of The Retreat and continued it as a way to control the rest of humanity through fear."

"What is the Mandate?" Thrym interjected.

The doctor answered from the door. "The world's government."

Not only had humans survived, they maintained a structured society too.

Atlas held up a commanding hand to quiet their protests. "I believe this is enough to process considering your current state." He faced Romy. "You will all have questions, and tomorrow I will answer them as best as I am able. But right now you need medical attention. You need to see your friend and you need to care for yourselves. The rest can wait."

First Romy trusted Atlas, and then she distrusted him, but now she was so confused she didn't know what to think. Romy put a hand to her head. The fog from whatever they'd knocked her out with was still slowing her down.

"Rosemary?" A hand tilted her chin. "You need help. You all do. I promise, it will make sense in the end."

She stared at him and hoped to hell he could see what she thought of that. Of him. Of him lying to her from the start.

His hand dropped to his side, but his gaze stayed where it was.

"Uh, Atlas," Houston called in a low voice. "The time. . . ."

Atlas looked at a gadget on his wrist and cursed under his breath. "Do the honours, would you?"

The shorter, lanky man wasn't given much of a choice as Atlas swept out of the room.

Houston looked from their group, to the door, and back, hovering in indecision. He held up one finger and wrenched open the door. "Just one sec," he said, and scrambled after Atlas.

The four immediately turned to each other. Romy saw her own weary bafflement reflected in her friends' expressions.

"But how did humankind survive?" Thrym asked, voice flat.

No one had an answer. *He* had all the answers.

Elara wrung her hands. "What other logical explanation is there? Why would he lie?"

"It just . . . can't be true," Phobos said.

Romy shook her head. She didn't know what she believed. The man had given them three damn sentences and expected them to swallow his story without question. But for some reason, that was exactly why she wanted to believe him.

How had the supposed government created a subterfuge of this scale? The Retreat was 150 years ago!

And then Elara asked a question Romy hadn't thought of. One that sent trickles of fear down her spine.

"If it's a lie . . . what will the Mandate do if they find us?"

A light lit in her mind. That was why Atlas didn't want them to say anything. But how would he explain their presence to all of the Earth humans outside? If the Mandate caught them. . . .

Well, Romy could only see two outcomes to that, and neither option—a memory wipe, or death—were good.

"If this government has kept this secret for over a century, I don't think they'll be happy to see us," Phobos said, echoing Romy's thoughts.

Thrym gave a tight nod. "Then we need to decide if we stay or go," he said.

Romy exchanged a look with Phobos.

"We have to stay. They have Deimos." He answered her unspoken question.

"We're too vulnerable at the moment," Romy said. "We'd need equipment, and, well, we need to know more about surviving here, too."

Elara pursed her lips. "We didn't pass any other camps on the way. Maybe we don't have to worry about being caught."

There was one massive flaw in that line of thought. "How many Earth humans do you think saw our battler enter Earth's atmosphere?" Romy asked.

The others returned her grim expression. The obvious answer was, a lot. And who knew what machines had registered the battler's entrance.

"The Mandate will search for the wreckage."

Just like Atlas had.

"And when they don't find our bodies?" Romy asked.

Thrym sighed. "Then they'll search for us."

"Find us." Elara's voice trembled.

"Probably kill us," Phobos added cheerfully. "Don't forget that."

Elara sniffed. Romy's fiery friend was at the very edge of her tolerance. "So, what? Stay. Wait while Deimos recovers. And then escape?"

It was a vague, uncertain plan. Stupid really, when the Mandate could show up without warning. But when the floor has just caved from underneath you, you hang on to whatever control you can to stay afloat.

Romy gazed at her knot with solemn eyes. "We learn all we can while we're here. We take anything that might help us survive," she said.

Three pairs of grave eyes met her own.

The door flew open, startling the group.

"Sorry, team," the doctor said. A grin covered his boyish, bespectacled face.

Romy frowned at his cheery façade. They'd just learned their entire existence was a lie. But the man with the curly, mousey hair was oblivious to their disapproval as he spun around to the hall, calling, "After me, aliens."

CHAPTER TEN

Eventually Romy stopped questioning everything Houston was doing.

After their visit to Deimos, he'd wasted no time in plugging her into medi-tech, which didn't concern her. It was a routine occurrence on the orbitos. But she knew that by doing so, he could alter the programming of her nanos.

He took a lot longer on her than he did on any of the others.

His answers to her questions included so many foreign words of Latin origin that she instead asked him, "Is it safe?" His reply of "yes" had somewhat reassured her. Which didn't make any sense, considering he was a bit strange.

The man took blood from Romy and the others, and injected them several times before programming the medi-tech to update their nanos for Earth diseases. Then, after what felt like hours, Houston finished jabbing and tinkering and led them to an isolated "bungalow," leaving the four members of the knot with instructions to clean and eat.

Knot 27 stood just inside the door, staring at the Earth house. It was made of dark wood. There was a table and chairs, four trundles and a separate bathroom. Houston had called them "aliens." But to Romy and her knot, everything here was alien. The textures, the materials, the tools. The contraptions were unfamiliar and the scents were strange.

Phobos dropped his bundle of new clothes onto the bed and turned to the knot, arms crossed. "Does anyone else get that feeling that you know less at the end of the day than you did at the start?"

Despite herself, Romy cracked a smile.

Thrym placed his bundle on a bed and sat down in one tired, drawn out movement. "At least we know one thing we didn't."

Deimos was alive.

Romy claimed her own bunk, atop Thrym's. She listened as Elara replied, "Dei will live."

It was the only good news they'd had since crashing.

Romy still couldn't believe how much better Deimos had appeared—though he was a shadow of his former self. All variety of tubes were helping to eradicate the pneumothorax he'd sustained in the crash and the ensuing blood poisoning, but they'd been told their friend would live.

That their knot would still be whole. That was all that mattered.

Any consequence that came after, or had happened because of Atlas and Romy's decision to follow him, was worth it.

She hoped.

* * *

The shower was glorious.

Once they figured it out.

What an unusual sensation to have water falling on you from above. The knot only ever had basin washes on board Orbito One. But this? This she could get used to.

Romy dried and put on the fresh underclothes they'd been provided. Hanging the towel to dry, she stepped back into the main part of the bungalow.

"Shower's free," she called to Phobos.

"Finally," he muttered. Romy frowned at him as he brushed past.

She raised her eyebrows at Thrym, who shrugged, face turning red as his eyes scanned her body. Romy wondered why he did it. It wasn't like her entire knot hadn't seen her in underwear before—a million times. The Earth underwear was a little different, she supposed.

She returned to her bed to find her bundle open and scattered everywhere. The pants and sleeveless shirt she'd seen before were gone.

Romy turned a glare to Elara, who lay on her stomach—wearing Romy's clothes.

"Sorry, Ro. I'm not wearing the thing they gave me," Elara said. She sat up and reached over, tossing a garment into Romy's face.

Blood rushed to her cheeks as anger swept through her. She pushed her temper down, turning away from Elara so the girl couldn't see. Her anger surprised her. It was only a bit of clothing, for comet's sake.

The garment was a shirt. But longer. A dress, Romy realised with a thrill, grinning at Thrym. It faded. He was sitting, casting furtive glances at her when he thought she wasn't looking. Was there something wrong with her? She tried not to fidget under his looks.

Slipping the dress over her head, she fastened the criss-crossing ties at the front and then twirled. Once she'd read a book called *Cinderella*. She felt exactly like the title character, except the dress Romy wore only hung to her knees, and had an orange floral print.

"Pretty," Thrym grunted.

She wasn't sure about not wearing pants. This was a completely new sensation for her. But it was exciting to be in Earth clothes. "Thanks." She smiled. Thrym blinked before spinning his chair the other way.

Elara and Romy shared a long glance.

Houston told the four they weren't to leave their bungalow before he came for them. Phobos was barely dressed when a loud booming knock sounded at the door. Thrym got up to open it. Houston charged through the door before her knot mate could get there.

"Good sleep, little aliens?" he asked.

Romy worked to keep her smile at bay. Everything that came out of his mouth was so offending, but for some reason she couldn't dislike him for it. Thrym, however, didn't look like he appreciated the digs.

Houston didn't wait for a response. "Atlas wants to talk again, now you've had a chance to scrub up." He slid his glasses down to the end of his nose, observing Elara. "You didn't like the dress? That's a shame."

The knot exchanged confused looks. This man had intended the dress to go to Elara? Elara's face turned Mars-red.

Houston coughed. "Before we go, cover story. You're a research team from the Orbitos. You are learning human behaviours to better integrate them into space life. Capisce?"

"Ca—peesh?" Phobos said slowly.

Houston blew out a slow breath. "It means, do you understand?"

Romy nodded in agreement. The plan worked to their advantage also. It meant the knot could ask questions without raising suspicions.

"Atlas told the settlement you had trouble adjusting to the ground." He spoke to Romy, waving them through the door.

His eyes rested on the dress Romy wore and he shook his head, casting doleful looks at Elara. The surge of anger she'd felt earlier reappeared. It was so intense it stopped her in her tracks, causing Phobos to smash into her.

"Watch it," he snarled.

His face melted into shock at his outburst. Was the same thing happening to him?

Houston observed them with sparkling eyes. "Can't wait to explain that. Come, come."

The doctor prattled on as he led them on a dancing walk through the buildings.

"So. 'Aliens' is hilarious and all, but originality points equal zero. I thought I'd run some names by you, if that's okay. . . ."

The response was silence and glares from the others, but Houston looked to the sky and held up one hand, screwing up his face.

"Vulcans," he said, scanning the knot.

Romy gave him a tentative smile.

"No?" he asked. "I quite liked that one." He ticked a finger off. "Hmm, what about The Force? I'm a big Star Wars fan."

Thrym began to simmer beside her.

"What about 'Stars'?" Elara offered quietly.

Houston stopped in his tracks and gave Romy's friend a small smile. "Stars, huh? I'm not sure about the others, but I think it suits you just fine."

It happened again. Elara went bright red: cheeks, ears, and all.

"And what about a name for you?" Phobos spoke up. The tone of his remark immediately alerted Romy he was about to erupt.

Thrym said, "How about Earthling?"

Romy squeezed her eyes shut.

"Ah, Thrym, originality points equal zero." Phobos shook his head. "I'm thinking 'Doesn't-Know-When-to-Shut-Up'." He circled Houston, leaning in to invade the doctor's personal space. "Or maybe 'Punched-in-the-Face'."

That certainly got the doctor's attention. Romy's mouth dropped open. Did Phobos just threaten to hurt someone? Over a harmless joke?

"Phobos. . . ," Elara interjected. She reached a hand out to him, which he brushed away.

"Leave me alone, *star*."

Houston's face lost its nervous edge, lighting up as his gaze flickered between Phobos and Elara. "Oh, I see." His grin was evil. "Ha! Well, that's gonna make for an awkward Christmas."

"Do you think he has frontal lobe damage?" Thrym whispered.

Romy didn't know, but if Houston didn't stop, Phobos was going to attack him. He wasn't himself. Something was off. And the vibes she was catching from him were stressing her out.

"Houston. Shut up," Atlas said, striding up to them. He was dressed in his black, pocketed pants and a white T-shirt.

Houston's laughter quickly faded to a soft snuffling sound.

"I expected you twenty minutes ago," Atlas shot at his friend.

"Well—"

Atlas cut him off. "And do us all a favour and keep the nicknames to yourself."

Romy couldn't help a giggle at Houston's surprised expression. He honestly hadn't noticed how angry Thrym and Phobos were getting?

"Come," Atlas said to the group.

They entered the tallest of the official-looking buildings in the semi-circle clearing. Houston led them to the same large room full of tables and chairs from the day before. Atlas didn't speak another word, just gestured to the doctor before taking the seat directly behind Romy. The hairs on the back of her neck rose.

"Atlas has some things to say to you, and as amusing as it would be to keep watching your knot, I really should explain why you're all going loco."

Romy straightened, listening with avid attention.

Houston closed his eyes briefly, utter bliss flittering over his face before he opened them once more. "Who here has heard of puberty?"

Puberty. Romy racked her brain for the answer. The term had a familiar ring to it, but she couldn't quite place it.

"The physical change from child to adult," Thrym said in a soft voice.

The reminder was all Romy needed to recall the reference. Houston's cheeks puffed out. Romy held true concern he might explode.

He recovered. "Correct. Started by the release of hormones from your brain to your junk."

"What does he mean by 'junk'?" Elara whispered.

"Houston, you're confusing them," Atlas reprimanded.

"All right, from the top," Houston said. "You..." He threw a glance at Atlas. "Space humans are harvested at twelve years old." He looked over his glasses and nodded when they affirmed the fact. "But when you're fished out of your tank, you're full-grown." He ran his eyes over Elara. "And the hormones in the brain that would trigger puberty are repressed with your nanotech and supplements in your food."

"This eliminates accidental reproduction," Thrym said.

Houston pointed at him, pacing in excitement. "It does. It also makes you emotionally stable. Creating the perfect soldier, unhindered by lust, infatuation, and the moods associated with fluctuations in hormone levels."

Romy could see no reason this was a problem. It made sense. She voiced her thoughts.

"Ah, Romy. It wouldn't be a problem at all—aside from the whole ethical immorality thing—except without the supplemented hormone repressors in orbito food, you would start to experience the first tickles of puberty." Houston clasped his hands together in front of his mouth, his eyes dancing as he observed them. "So I removed the suppressor nanos, too, so the process is short and *sweet.*"

Romy narrowed her eyes.

Phobos was fidgeting. "What would this make us feel?"

"Volatile anger, fatigue, attraction. Some are gender specific; males can experience rather interesting dreams, and regular thoughts of bow-chika-wow-wow, accompanied by—"

"Houston," Atlas's voice rumbled behind her. Romy jumped, having forgotten he was there.

"Sorry, *sexual intercourse*," Houston amended. "Does any of this sound familiar, Phobos?"

Romy shot her friend a look, only to find his face drained of all blood. Had he experienced something other than volatile anger?

"It will also affect some of your responses to external stimuli. You may feel emotions more strongly and your body will react to those emotions differently," Houston said.

"What about females?" Thrym asked.

Romy was grateful his question covered up Phobos's embarrassment. She grabbed Thrym's hand and squeezed it. Her knot mate tightened his hold, so their hands remained linked together.

Houston grinned evilly. "Oh, you know. They get periods and PMS."

Romy exchanged a look with Elara. "What is a period?" she asked.

She heard Atlas shifting behind her.

Houston's face deadpanned. "The shedding of the vaginal wall once a month."

Suddenly Romy didn't want to hold Thrym's hand anymore. She dropped it and fixed her gaze on the wall behind Houston.

She knew the anatomy of the human body. Her nose scrunched as she imagined the rest. An awkward silence descended upon the room, apart from the muffled snorts from Houston. He had to be the most unprofessional doctor she'd ever met. Or maybe all Earth doctors were like this.

"And what is PMS?" Elara asked.

Atlas chuckled behind her. Romy twisted in her seat, but his half-smirk had her facing forwards in a hurry. Why was her face getting hot? She'd never been embarrassed about her body in her life.

"Period Mood Swings, my star."

Romy watched in shock as Elara's eyes welled with tears. Phobos draped an arm around her and rubbed her back in circles.

Thrym kneaded his eyes. "This explains a few things."

Romy followed his gaze down to his lap and threw herself back into the chair when she realised what she'd done.

"Yep, explains the weird dream," Phobos muttered.

Elara wailed something unintelligible between sobs, her face blotchy and tear-streaked.

"At least you won't get periods," Houston added. "I've implanted a device in your arm to prevent pregnancy. It's illegal to have children without a permit on Earth. But it won't stop the real good stuff—the snapping, the crankiness, the crying."

Romy frowned at him. *Is that supposed to be good news?* She rubbed two fingers over the small lump in her arm Houston inserted yesterday.

"Space friends," Houston called over Elara's sobs. "Welcome to puberty at twenty-four years old!"

CHAPTER ELEVEN

"That's enough," Atlas commanded.

Elara's wailing quieted to an occasional sniffle.

Houston bowed and nodded at Atlas as he took the doctor's position.

Houston practically ran from the room. For some reason, Romy couldn't look him in the eye. But she didn't want to look at Thrym or the others, either. The puberty talk had weirded her out.

"I'll bet it's an involuntary thing," Phobos mused into the silence. "A male will be attracted to a female, no matter what."

She glanced up at Atlas and saw he was watching her. He broke off first this time, and answered Phobos, "We all have a certain type we prefer."

Thrym tensed beside her.

"There are more important things to discuss," Atlas said sternly.

Romy shook off her last bit of humiliation and refocused her attention on more important matters.

"I have spoken to my superior. Houston has given you the agreed alibi. Your knot is here on research. You are to stick to this for the entirety of your stay or face the consequences. Don't be fooled by the peaceful atmosphere here. Neighbour turns on neighbour at the drop of a hat."

No memory. Death. He didn't need to explain the consequences.

Romy raised her hand. Atlas nodded his permission. "The thing is, we don't understand why we've been lied to. We don't understand the reasons behind anything you've told us."

Atlas's jaw ticked. But he assessed her and gave a long sigh. "I will tell you what I can. But you need to accept that there are reasons I can't tell you everything. Very good reasons."

"Will you tell us one day?" she asked.

He didn't answer—not her actual question, anyway. "The Earth was changing at a rapid rate and the population was dwindling just as fast. Trillions of dollars were poured into technology to ensure humankind's survival. You have been told that when the Critamal were first spotted, all environmental research halted and all resources were then poured into nanotech. This wasn't true. By the time the Critamal arrived and began their siege, climate stabilisation had reached the final stages of testing."

Atlas stood in a relaxed pose, wide shoulders drawn back and hands hanging loosely at his sides.

Romy's mouth went dry. "Then why did they send us up?"

"The threat to Earth was doubled. The world faced attack from the inside, and attack from the outside. Earth couldn't abandon global cooling, but the threat from the Critamal was just as severe. After lengthy debate it was decided that there was too much risk in allowing the Critamal to reach Earth. It was a fragile time for the planet. The destruction of the climate stabilisers could have destroyed the balance we had only just achieved."

Elara interrupted. "But Earth had its own military. Its own astronauts!"

"The world was still in anarchy at this point; many countries no longer had communication in place. The military were occupied in calming the civilians across the globe and it was decided they could not be spared," Atlas said. "Make no mistake: global warming *did* happen. And only 10 per cent of the world's population survived."

Thrym's voice shook. "How many perished?"

Atlas's grey eyes clouded. "Just under 9.9 billion people."

She couldn't even visualise that number. *So many.* Of course, it was better than what they'd always been told—that all Earth humans were destroyed.

"But why continue to lie about it?" Romy asked. This was the part that made her want to follow Elara's example and give in to tears. The betrayal.

Atlas ran a hand through his hair. It reminded Romy of their time in the bush. It seemed so long ago, though it was merely days before. "That's not such a simple answer," he started.

Romy waited for him to go on.

He saw she wasn't going to let it slide and a shadow of laughter softened his face. It faded as he replied, "Have you never started a lie which you then wished to take back?" he asked.

Romy folded her arms. Was he making excuses for his own deceit?

His expression hardened. "The Mandate has deceived the world for so long that even if the opportunity arose to come clean, I doubt they would take it. Humankind was near extinction. They needed hope. And that hope came from the Heroes in the Sky. The soldiers of the orbitos. Your unknown 'sacrifice' is a continual reminder that Earth cannot be taken for granted. It is used to keep humankind focused. Humans are not content to remain in peace for long. Your presence in space is a queen on a political chessboard. The key to controlling Earth's population."

"They should have at least told *us!*" Elara accused, getting to her feet.

Atlas didn't move; he simply studied her. He didn't look at her the way Houston did. Atlas looked at Elara the way Romy had seen him looking at the poisonous milky myrtle plant—with distaste. It shouldn't have made her so happy.

"And with Earth dangling right in front of your eyes every day, would you have been content to stay in space? To protect a planet and people you'd never met?" he asked. "Playing the martyr could get old after a few years."

"You sound like you're justifying their lies," Thrym noted.

"I *understand* it," Atlas stressed. For the first time he appeared tense. "It doesn't mean I agree with it."

Something bothered Romy.

"Well, someone has to be up there," she said. "If we abandon our post, the Critamal will invade Earth."

"You know our technology has made large advancements." Atlas shook his head. "The Earth is completely carbon-neutral now. And has been for 157 years."

Excitement fluttered under Romy's sternum, despite the debris Atlas continued to dump on them. "Incredible," she murmured.

"What's your point?" Thrym asked.

Atlas stood and met the eyes of Knot 27. "I am trying to tell you that the technology to destroy the Critamal has been around for over a century."

Romy had done many space walks in her time, usually for maintenance. The silence in space was always eerie and daunting. . . .

And yet it did not compare to the silence of that moment.

She choked on the horrible words. "The war could have been over a *century* ago?"

Thousands aboard the orbitos had been lost in the war efforts over the last century and a half. Blown apart one second and callously replaced the next by the fresh cadets the orbitos had on tap. Each of them gave up living a full life, constantly putting their life on the line and submitting to the disgusting tanks at thirty-five. They accepted this out of necessity, persevering through each life cycle because it was the only way to earn the right to live on Earth again.

Except it wasn't a necessity at all.

The war was a farce—a cruel and twisted hoax used to strengthen this 'Mandate's' political position. Acid filled Romy's mouth as her stomach roiled. Her orbito comrades blown apart, *disintegrated* in Earth's atmosphere. All for what?

She looked around the group. Elara, Phobos, and Thrym's faces all reflected what she felt: like a fist had punched her in the stomach. Tears slid down her cheeks, but she wasn't ashamed. This was worthy of mourning. And anger. Definitely, anger.

Such a waste.

Atlas spoke softly. "You can imagine how much your presence in space must be worth to the Mandate leaders. They spend billions of dollars keeping you all where you are."

"But surely we are not the first to crash here," Thrym wondered aloud.

"No," Atlas agreed. "But no other knot has survived intact before. There are usually only one or two survivors. And . . . when they see their knot's remains. . . ."

"Orbito Four?" Phobos asked.

Atlas's face tightened, and he gave a curt nod.

Romy buried her face into Thrym's chest, feeling his arms wrap around her. She hoped it would drown out the terrible things Atlas was saying. It didn't mute his voice at all—and she just wished he would stop talking. Everything that came out of his mouth was raw and horrible.

"You cannot return to the orbitos. The High Command will hand you straight to their superiors. Understand this: You cannot leave and you cannot tell anyone the truth."

"But why?" Phobos exploded. "If the people knew the truth, the leaders could be overthrown."

Atlas's face turned to stone. "The Mandate has the technology to eradicate a warship seven hundred kilometres from Earth." His voice cut the air. It was the first time Romy had heard Atlas raise his voice. "They have the technology to *create* human life. Use your brains, boy. What do you think happens when Earth finds out?"

"They eradicate all human life and start again?" Elara whispered, staring at her knees.

The blood drained from Romy's face. Atlas didn't confirm or deny her friend's hushed words.

Thrym pushed to his feet, stepping towards the taller man. "And how do *you* know all of this? Tell us who you are. And who you work for. You might have already reported us to the Mandate. Why should we trust you? Why are you helping us?"

Careful, Thrym, she silently warned. They couldn't risk raising Atlas's suspicions if they truly intended to escape.

"I am attempting to cover your tracks," Atlas replied. His dark eyes were shuttered. "And I will either succeed, or fail. Whether you trust me is of no consequence. As for why I'm helping. . ." His eyes flickered. ". . . I have my reasons."

This wasn't the man who had shown her the sunrise on the beach, or who tossed her into the water.

One by one, the faces of the four knot members hardened.

Atlas must have read it in their faces. His expression contorted very slightly before his next stilted words. "If the orbitos collect you and you know too much. . . ." He stopped abruptly and clamped his lips shut, raking a hand through his dark hair. "If you value your lives, you'll do as I've said."

The brief explanation didn't appease Phobos in the slightest. "You make it sound like the Mandate could find us at any second."

Romy frowned. It did sound that way, like Atlas himself wasn't sure if he could help the knot. And what was the guarantee that Atlas was even helping in the first place? Only his words and the fact that he saved Deimos. He could be doing anything, telling anyone, and Knot 27 would have no idea.

He ignored Phobos's question. "You will keep your heads down and you will keep your mouths shut. That is the only way to survive now."

* * *

Atlas allowed them the rest of the day to become acquainted with the settlement. A tiny, fierce woman named Tina gave the knot a brief tour.

Romy's initial impression of the rectangular space cleared in the midst of the bush was correct. Rows of neat bungalows were situated in the middle, large sheds down one end—where she'd woken up, and the three large buildings down the other end—where they'd learned of the betrayal. And now she knew what the three official buildings were for. One was the Hull—an area where the Earth humans congregated to eat. The knot ate lunch in there and people stared so much they vowed to eat in their bungalow afterward and never return.

Another of the buildings, the middle one, contained the tiny hospital space where Deimos lay unconscious and where their nanos had been updated, as well as the meeting room from yesterday. It also contained four offices where Atlas, Houston, and Tina worked from. Romy got the impression that Tina ran the whole settlement. And clearly, Houston was the resident doctor. Romy didn't know who the fourth room was for, but she could surmise that only the important personnel of the camp got offices. Which begged the question of what exactly Atlas did. The question hovered on the tip of her tongue during Tina's tour. But Atlas's words echoed in her mind: *Don't trust anyone.* And honestly, Tina scared her a little bit.

"What's that screen for? Elara asked. She tilted her head at the hologram projection Romy watched the day before.

"Think of it as the Mandate's noticeboard," Tina replied. "It's a way for them to broadcast their announcements."

It seemed more like propaganda to Romy.

The last of the official buildings appeared utilitarian in comparison to the other two, though larger than the bungalows by ten times. Romy would have dismissed it, if not for the fact that only soldiers were scanning themselves in and out, and Tina seemed eager to move on from it, snapping that it was for "storage and supplies".

Romy didn't know if the village had a name, or even exactly where they were in Queensland, Australia. Tina wasn't forthcoming about this either.

Somehow Atlas had neglected to tell them the most basic information of all. Or maybe it was entirely on purpose.

"As soon as Dei is better, we need to leave," Thrym whispered in Romy's ear.

Romy turned to find his face right in front of hers. She knew the Mandate could find them here at any moment, but there was another undercurrent to Thrym's tone. "You think we're in immediate danger?" she asked.

He peered around the settlement. The people were bustling, going about their work. There was a rhythm to the camp; everyone had their place.

"You don't feel that?" he said, tilting his head at the Earth humans.

Romy's brows furrowed and she looked again, seeing the same thing.

Thrym smiled, taking her hand. "You only ever see the good in people, Ro."

"What do you see?"

"It's more a feeling," he admitted. "A threatening vibe. They're all watching each other." He shook his head, trying to find the words. "They're smiling, but . . . everyone is watching each other too closely."

She couldn't see anything like that. But then, she wasn't the most observant of the knot. That skill fell to Thrym. "You're not just seeing it there because of," she darted a glance at Tina, "what we've learned?"

His lips firmed in a straight line and he shrugged as though his shirt were too tight. "I don't know, Ro. I don't know."

The knot walked between the bungalows on their way to see Deimos. Romy was starting to get a feel for the area. She had to admit Earth wasn't what she expected. It didn't mean she disapproved; it was just different from the pictures and stories she remembered studying.

The settlement was contrasting.

Most of it was simple. The washhouse, the bungalows, the agriculture.

Yet the rest was incredibly high-tech: nuclear-powered electricity, machinery and vehicles, advanced medical and nanotechnology. And Romy suspected they also used brain transmission communication. She'd seen a transmitter in Atlas's ear this morning.

Atlas's words about self-sustainability echoed in her mind. Romy took a moment to let everything he had said sink in.

Earth was carbon-neutral. That meant the technology on this world no longer emitted more carbon dioxide than it used.

The planet was more stable now than ever before. And yet its rulers were endorsing genocide.

Maybe Houston was right to call the knot "aliens"—maybe they *were* different from the Earth humans. Romy kicked up a cloud of red dust, earning a disapproving glance from Elara. She ignored her and stomped after Tina.

The people were at once the same and different from what she'd always dreamed. They ranged in all colours, heights, and dress. Their skin was more weathered than any of the knot, but Romy guessed that was due to the harsh conditions and higher temperatures.

When they were going about their daily chores, the people weren't so bad. In time, Romy might consider approaching them. For the moment her "sacrifice" experience and the knot's uncomfortable lunch in the Hull was putting her off.

"Do you think Atlas is the leader here?" Romy asked the others when Tina dismissed them and left for her office.

"No idea," said Phobos. "I'm trying to figure it out. The dynamic between him and Tina doesn't add up.

Knot 27 made their way through the settlement towards their bungalow, doing their best to ignore the stares.

Romy's eyes widened as a large four-legged creature streaked past, obeying the whistle of a young boy.

"What *is* that?" she breathed. She'd never seen an animal like it. And it *wasn't* because Romy only liked cute animals. It was kind of like a dog, but much larger.

"Hybridization?" Thrym asked.

Romy covered her mouth with both hands. "Do you really think so?" She squealed and moved a little closer.

It was just one more effect of warming. As the temperature rose and the habitat changed, it allowed animals to widen their spread—into climates that were previously too cold or lacking in certain foods. Species previously unknown to one another came into contact and mated, forming a blend of the two. Where two weaker species could not endure, one stronger species might.

"What animals do you think survived?" Romy asked, not removing her eyes from the dog-wolf thing. "Just insects?"

Elara stood behind Thrym, not seeming too impressed with the hybrid.

"It would explain the 90 per cent drop in population." Romy brushed at the red dust on her trousers, hardly aware she was talking to herself.

"Warmer temperature, further spread of insects and therefore disease," Thrym added.

Romy wondered if he'd directly quoted that from one of their lectures on the space stations. "It must have been devastating. Imagine, 9.9 *billion* people."

Grim faces acknowledged her comment.

"And so is what they're doing to us," Thrym said.

"I feel so useless," Phobos said loudly. "I wish we could warn them somehow." He stared up at the blue sky.

Romy craned her neck to follow his gaze. They couldn't see the orbitos from here. Even if they wanted to warn the other space soldiers, how could they reach them? And if they did and were caught, would the knot's actions secure the death of the eight orbitos *and* the Earth humans?

Atlas's insinuation that the Mandate would simply wipe out all life from the face of the Earth and start again seemed like insanity.

But then, so did everything else that had happened since they crashed here.

"We stick to the plan." Elara's voice wavered. "Get our strength back, gather supplies. Get Dei back. And leave. It's not our problem. We can't do anything about it."

Romy noticed Phobos standing off to one side. She approached him, bumping his shoulder with hers.

"You all right?"

Phobos didn't take his eyes from the sky. "I miss him."

Romy's heart squeezed at his forlorn voice. "I know, Pho. We all miss Dei. But we'll have him back soon. Did you see how much better he was?"

The young man took a shuddering breath. "We nearly lost him."

Romy hugged Phobos around the waist as his shoulders began to shake.

Thrym and Elara walked a small distance away, knowing Phobos would hate the audience. Romy stroked his back gently as he'd done for Elara.

"This puberty thing sucks." Phobos dragged an arm across his eyes.

Romy grinned up at him. "Weren't the mood swings supposed to be a female thing?"

She laughed as he picked her up and tossed her over one shoulder.

"You shouldn't insult my manliness, little Rosemary. It provokes me to Neanderthal behaviour."

A few seconds passed, just a smidge too long. "How is that different from your normal behaviour?" she retorted.

Her short white hair swung as Romy stared at Phobos's back from her upside-down position.

"Did you guys hear that?" Phobos called ahead to the others. "Romy insulted me!"

Romy heard Elara giggle. "Oh yeah? How long did it take?"

Thrym's booming laugh joined the mix, and Romy grinned, heart lighter for hearing their amusement.

This is true strength, she thought. The ability to laugh when everything was crumbling to pieces around you.

CH/\PTER TWEL\/E

Romy sighed as she polished scalpels and arranged medi-tech programmes. While Houston's surgery had been in disarray when Atlas gave her this job, Romy had organised the whole room in half a day. For the last three days, she'd nearly gone out of her mind. Sure, there was a lot of downtime aboard the orbitos, but there were also her resources as well as four best friends to keep her company.

Deimos was just down the hall, but she could only spend so much time talking to him in his induced comatose state. And she felt like the others were working hard to earn their keep while she was twiddling her thumbs.

Houston sat at a white desk across the room, plugging notes from his latest patient into a nano. Romy estimated another two minutes would pass before he was out the door again.

"An open fracture of the femur which *didn't* cause artery rupture," he chuckled. "What are the odds?" Houston glanced up at Romy.

She exhaled loudly. "No idea, Houston. But I can assure you Thrym would know." Romy waved a scalpel in the air. "Can't you talk to Atlas?"

Houston returned to the tapping on his screen. "I have."

Romy sat up. "And?"

"And the answer was no."

Her eyebrows drew together. "You explained that I'm hopeless with all of this?"

"I believe I used the word 'clueless'."

She gave him a wry smile. "Thanks."

Houston stood and stretched back, his dirty lab coat falling open to reveal a stethoscope and medi-scanner stuffed in his pockets. "Maybe Atlas just likes having you around."

Atlas hadn't spoken a single word to her in the last few days. The only times they'd had any interaction was when he left his office. He would glance into Houston's room and nod to her on his way to Tina's office. There were no "hellos", not even a "how are you fitting in on this foreign world?".

"I doubt that," Romy said.

Romy wasn't sure what to think of Tina, the Earth woman who'd shown the knot around the camp. Unlike many of the settlement women who wore comfortable work clothing, Tina wore camo fatigues like the soldiers. The small woman walked as though she could take on any of the soldiers in the camp. Overall, Romy wanted to respect her.

But something held her back.

And it had to do with the way Tina draped herself all over Atlas. Somehow it made her angry at Atlas, instead of Tina. And that didn't seem fair.

"Doctor H?" a boy panted from the doorway. He held a floppy hat in one hand. "You're needed in the gardens. Martha's collapsed."

Romy watched as Houston snapped closed the clasp of his bag and swept out of the room.

Romy had gone with him on the first few occasions, after which Houston had kindly hinted that Romy might wish to remain behind. She huffed; it wasn't like she meant to black out. It had turned out she didn't like blood too much. They were *space soldiers*. Romy shot poachers from hundreds of metres away—and their blood was yellow.

She wouldn't mind shooting some poachers right about now.

Footsteps in the semi-circle entranceway had her looking up. Atlas. Returning to his room. *Probably from Tina's*, she thought darkly.

Romy's feet moved of their own accord. "Atlas," she called.

Atlas glanced over his shoulder, one hand on the door, the other on the frame halfway into his office. Romy knew what happened once he entered. The door slammed shut, and no one went in. Ever.

Grey eyes met her blue ones. "Rosemary. What do you need?" He reached up a hand and clicked the gadget in his ear.

She looked at the device curiously.

"Transmission device." He answered her unspoken question.

"That's a whole lot smaller than our transmission devices." The ones aboard orbitos were huge. They took up an entire room.

He smiled. "The limited space aboard the orbitos does not lend itself to much research."

Romy remembered what she was there to talk about and she felt a twinge of anger at what she coined the "bush smile". Otherwise known as the smile from before she knew he was lying to her.

Romy wanted answers. More personal answers. And considering he'd lied ever since they'd met, that fact was irritating to the extreme. Was he really forbidden from disclosing everything to them? Was it really unsafe?

His barebones explanation seemed like the convenient excuse of someone trying to take advantage of the situation.

With a start, Romy realised he was waiting for her reply. "I want to talk to you about this job," she said. "I know Houston spoke with you. And Atlas, he's not being cruel—I really suck at it."

A glint entered his gaze before winking out of sight. "Houston needs an assistant." Atlas continued into the room, gesturing Romy inside.

She swept past him, arms crossed. "Yes, he does. An assistant who *assists*. Thrym would be—"

"No."

Romy looked askance at the sudden anger on his face. "But . . . why?"

Atlas took her in, his soft grey eyes reading her face. She couldn't make out his thoughts at all when he stepped towards her, brushing one hand across her cheek. "Just no," he said.

"That's not an answer." But Romy was captivated by his mouth. It was directly in front of her. Usually she was fixated on his eyes, and she couldn't quite put her finger on why his mouth suddenly intrigued her so much.

His lips. They looked soft. What she wouldn't give to see what they felt like. Her fingers lifted of their own accord and she reached for Atlas's mouth, stuck in awe's thrall.

She was mere millimetres from connecting. She held her breath. Would they be as smooth as they looked? A warm hand encased hers, squeezing a little to stop her movement. With a jolt, Romy's eyes flew up to meet his and heat flooded her cheeks.

"That's why you're staying in here," Atlas said in a husky voice. He accompanied it with a single kiss to the back of her hand that somehow made her stomach flip.

Romy furtively looked back through the open door, thankful, for once, that no one was around. She remembered why she was talking to Atlas.

"But why does my knot get to work outside and I don't?"

Atlas broke away and retreated behind a large black desk. She rubbed her fingers together, feeling where his hand had been just moments before.

She glanced around his office. Apart from his desk, there were only two other seats. Everything was organised in neat piles, each document apparently having its place. His nano was set in the middle, emitting a pale blue light.

If it was like the one in Houston's room it would project multiple touch screens—much more advanced than anything on the orbitos.

"Because I said so," he replied. Atlas was now tapping on his device with a long pen, brow furrowed as he looked over something Romy couldn't see.

"Let's get this straight. Elara gets to tag after one of your mechanics." Romy raised her brow until he nodded.

"And Phobos is with the agriculturists."

No response.

Romy didn't mention Thrym's allocation to the washhouse. In her opinion his placement was just as bad as hers. It was infuriating that Atlas assigned Thrym there when her knot mate had such a good understanding of medicine. And it would have given them ideal access to materials needed to escape. Romy had no idea what to get.

He put down the pen with a sigh. Romy thought his face even softened. Atlas looked at her for a long beat before standing with a scrape of the chair.

He leaned forwards over the desk.

"You will stay here," he said firmly. "Every person has a role in this settlement. You are needed here. Everyone has to do jobs they don't like—that includes you."

Romy studied her feet, hands clasped behind her. He made her feel like she was twelve years old again.

"And," Atlas said, "if another position comes up, I will consider moving you. For now you will assist Houston with medical."

His grave expression never changed as he sat down and returned to his nano.

She had no idea what he was doing, and this, on top of his refusal to switch her and Thrym, only made her angrier. "What are you doing?" she asked.

He didn't spare her a glance. "You know I can't tell you that. . . . I have work to do."

With bitter surprise, Romy realised she was dismissed.

Burning with anger, she turned for the door. As she did there was a nearly imperceptible sigh. But when she glanced over at the mysterious man behind the tidy desk, Atlas had the same stone expression she remembered from when they first met.

Slamming the door made her feel better.

Romy pulled up sharply as Tina and an unknown soldier strode out of her office for the entranceway.

Romy smiled uncertainly at the woman who gave her a withering look in return, eyeing Atlas's door behind her. It gave Romy a certain degree of pleasure to know her presence in his room annoyed the put-together woman.

"Don't you have work to do?" Tina asked. Her tone was assertive, but fell shy of rudeness.

Romy shrugged. "Not really."

Tina rolled her eyes and swept out the door. The man accompanying her held back slightly. His features were pale, though his eyes were pitch black. An uncontrollable shiver trembled down Romy's spine at the lack of emotion on his angular face. He was dressed in the same patterned green clothing as the other soldiers. But none of the others had stared at her this way.

Tina's sharp voice echoed back into the building and the man cut their uncomfortable exchange off, ducking out of the doorway after Tina.

Romy returned to Houston's room for a mere five minutes before finally acknowledging she couldn't do anything else to help. Even if Houston came back, she wouldn't be needed.

Wandering down the hallway, right to the end, Romy peered at Deimos through the glass and expelled a shaky breath. It was still so close to the surface—how they nearly lost him. She understood how soldiers aboard the orbitos went insane after the death of their knot members. It didn't happen often, because usually the entire craft was blown to smithereens, but space walks failed, or sometimes surviving members were miraculously pulled to safety after evacuating the battlers. These soldiers—the insane soldiers—were sent to Orbito Four. It was the orbito no one wanted. Because if you went there, it was because everyone you'd ever loved in your short, controlled lifetime was dead.

Romy slid open the transparent door and stepped inside, closing it behind her.

Deimos's breath came evenly now. The ragged splutters of a few days ago were blissfully absent. There was colour in his cheeks and lips. And the long black lashes that matched his long wavy hair were spread out against his high cheekbones. Romy doubted Deimos could pull himself up with how weak he appeared. But this was an improvement, so she wasn't complaining.

She'd pulled up a chair and had just grabbed hold of Deimos's hand when the door slid open behind her. She was jerked from her thoughts as a blood-splattered Houston entered the room. Romy wrinkled her nose at the sight.

"Why aren't you polishing my scalpels for the tenth time?" he asked with a wink.

The young man approached the screen at the end of Deimos's bed and studied the information there over his glasses. It all looked like nonsense to Romy.

She shrugged, not answering. She was pissed off at Atlas and not in the mood to talk.

"Huh," was the bemused reply to her silence. "How 'bout we wake Frankenstein up?"

She knew her expression was utterly blank. "Who is—?"

Houston pushed a series of buttons on the screen. A single beep sounded, and the doctor pushed his glasses up, watching Deimos expectantly.

Deimos groaned and Romy flew out of her seat. She tore her gaze away from her knot mate, who was very clearly waking up.

Houston had both arms stretched outward, hands clawed. "It's alive!" he shouted.

Romy stepped back as the doctor erupted into manic cackles. The sound cut off abruptly and Houston rounded the table to Deimos's side.

He took in her shocked expression. "Haven't seen *Frankenstein*?"

Romy shook her head warily.

"Ah well," he replied. "You won't need to now. That was an Oscar-winning rendition."

He grinned at Romy, who turned her wide blue eyes instead to what the man was doing to her friend. The lanky doctor made sense most of the time, but Romy wondered if he walked close to the edge of madness. Then there was the fact that he wore his archaic glasses when the tech to restore his vision was ancient. Houston was a conundrum.

Deimos was moving his head side to side. Very slowly, as though floating in zero-gravity. It wasn't long before his eyes visibly moved under his eyelids. Romy held her breath, leaning in to kiss his forehead.

"Dei," she whispered, stroking his matted black hair. "Wake up, Dei."

"Ro—" His voiced cracked. His throat worked as he swallowed, painfully judging by the resulting wince on his unmarked face. "Ro?"

Tears burned her eyes, and she swallowed back emotion. "I'm here. You're okay." She kissed his forehead. "You're okay now."

She looked over Deimos's head at Houston, only to find the eccentric man's hazel eyes glistening with their own sheen of tears. The doctor smiled at Romy and bent to his work, racing between Deimos's side and the screen over and over again.

Deimos blinked his eyes open with clear difficulty. "Ro. The others? What happened?"

"All safe," she assured him. Romy gave him a quick account of what had happened to date, excluding the details of the Mandate's astronomic subterfuge, and puberty. Phobos or Thrym could have that honour.

Even her flash recount was too long. Deimos started to drift off less than a minute afterward. Romy darted a questioning look at Houston, who came around the bed to pat her hand.

"Just asleep, little skyling. Don't get your knickers in a twist."

Houston didn't take his eyes off of Deimos as he spoke and for the first time Romy detected a bit of relief beneath his charismatic façade.

"How close was he?"

Houston pushed up his ever-slipping glasses and gave her a serious look. It sat oddly on his face.

"Close."

* * *

Romy propped herself up on her elbows atop her bunk as her knot trailed in through the door.

Phobos grinned at her, covered in dirt from his day in the garden.

Elara had the intense focused look she got when processing information—she must have learned something interesting today. She muttered a "hello" to Romy and sat, tense, on her own bunk, brow furrowed.

Thrym entered last, pissed off and arms raw up to the elbows.

Romy rolled up to sit on her bed, a grin plastered on her face. "Deimos is awake."

Thrym's face cleared. Her knot erupted in whoops. Romy's breath caught at the blinding joy on Phobos's face. For the first time since colliding into Earth in their battler, he looked his normal boyish self. Like the space soldier who stole the extra chocolate cake.

Thrym caught her up in a hug, pulling her in to his chest and burying his face in her hair. She returned the hug, squeezing as tightly as she could.

"Houston said he'll be okay." Her words were muffled against Thrym's shoulder, but the others heard.

"Can we go see him?" Phobos said, prying Thrym away.

He wasn't too impressed when Romy told him to wait until morning.

"So how were your days?" she asked.

"Do you know they have permits for *everything* now," Phobos interrupted. "To have children, to cut down a tree, to burn rubbish. . . ."

"Really?" Romy asked. It kind of made sense to her, though.

Thrym nodded. "The penalties are pretty harsh from what I've heard. Apparently, a woman was taken from here a couple of years ago for littering. Like gone. Never to be seen again."

"Where was she taken?"

He shrugged. "Some island the Mandate controls."

"That's. . . ."

"Extreme?"

"Well, yeah. How did the Mandate find out?"

Phobos's green eyes grew murky. "One of her neighbours."

"Someone told on her?" Romy's eyes grew huge. She shared a look with Thrym, remembering his bad feeling from a few days back.

It seemed so harsh. To be taken from your family and friends for something so simple. But at the same time, one person littering wouldn't have an effect, but if the entire population littered, it would be global warming all over again in another two centuries.

Phobos drew a hand over his face. "It's going to make it hard to stockpile things so we can be ready to leave when Dei is discharged. I've never seen such strict accountability for everything. And we grew up on the *orbitos*."

"Can we get anything?" Romy asked.

The four sat steeped in thought for a while.

"I'll be able to get some of the smaller seeds," Phobos said with finality. "We'll want to grow crops eventually, and some of the tiny seeds won't be missed."

They looked to Thrym. He stretched his arms overhead and placed both hands on his head, a deep frown between his brows. Romy hated seeing it there; he took too much upon himself, cared too much for others.

"I need more time to assess the washhouse," he said. "There is a pile of damaged stuff that might not be missed. But I'd need help getting it out." He nodded at Romy.

She straightened. "That probably won't be a problem." Romy doubted she'd even be missed.

"Did you scope out the area on your trip?" Thrym asked Elara.

She'd spent her day in driving lessons after someone found out she was the knot's top pilot.

Elara shook her head. "Once we left the settlement the tracks all became a twisting mess. I'll try to make sense of it, but . . . you guys, we were driving out with men and guns, dropping them off around the settlement."

Romy frowned. "What were they doing?"

Elara sighed. "I think they're sentries."

"Sentries?" Thrym echoed.

The knot exchanged troubled looks.

It was Phobos who eventually said the words aloud. "What are they watching for?"

Romy shook her head. "More like, how do we get past them?"

Elara was trying to sit still on the bed, looking around the group expectantly.

Thrym laughed. "How was the driving?"

Elara bounced on her bed. "It's more about coordination with your arms and legs, and there are nowhere near as many switches or levers. You don't have to constantly stabilise the vehicle against acceleration. You know, because we're not in space."

Phobos groaned loudly.

Elara continued with a smirk. "And they have things called 'shocks' so you don't get thrown around quite so much. But then it's weird how the ground and wind can affect the steering. I went through a big puddle and we *aquaplaned*," Elara said proudly.

It sounded amazing. Romy felt a small twist of jealousy. Even Phobos had learned to grow food in vertical planters.

"Oh, the coolest thing?" she squealed. "They have 3D printers for everything. You can just be like, 'Hey, I need a radiator,' and just *print* one."

Romy shook her head. Honestly, that baffled her.

"Yeah, they print a lot of their food that way," Phobos interjected. "Except the fruit and veggies."

"Seriously?" Elara's face twisted.

Romy laughed. "I'd still take it over dehydrated orbito food any day."

Elara and Phobos snickered in response.

"Mine isn't as interesting," Thrym added. "But I learned there's no land ownership on Earth anymore." Thrym peeked sideways at Romy.

"Like no one buys a house?" Elara asked in confusion.

"Every settlement has everything necessary for survival, and the resources are communal. Everyone receives what they need to be healthy."

"I like the idea. It eliminates greed," Phobos said.

Romy found herself leaning towards Thrym, eager to hear more. He ignored her, sharing a look with Phobos.

Phobos glanced at Romy and grinned. "She's not as fidgety as Ellie when she wants to know something."

"Yeah, but my mouth doesn't hang open like that." Elara glared back at him.

Thrym's blue eyes twinkled and she blushed at being caught out. She couldn't help that this was the most interesting part of her day. She hadn't learned *anything* polishing Houston's medical instruments.

"Apparently, the big settlements are incredible. Huge circular structures with high buildings and transportation," Thrym continued.

Her eyes widened.

"And no one has jobs, really. They just help out with what they can, when they can."

Romy's thoughts drifted as the others continued their excited chatter. The settlement was more tightly run than they'd thought: sentries, strict accountability, and the loyalty of the Earth humans to the Mandate.

That was their biggest disadvantage—not knowing exactly how everything ran.

And if the Mandate could find out about a woman littering from another country . . .

. . . then how long would it take for the Mandate to learn of the sudden appearance of five space soldiers?

CHAPTER THIRTEEN

*D*eimos was washed and dressed in fresh clothing by the time his knot trailed in early the next day. He looked mildly more focused, though his cheeks still held that gaunt, near-death look.

Phobos carefully gathered his brother in an embrace. In a rather gruff tone, he simply said, "About time."

Romy visited Deimos a few times as the day moved on. As much as she wanted to see him, he was still exhausted and not up to talking too much.

Gathering her boredom was distracting Houston from his work, she moved to the wooden bench outside Atlas's office. It gave her a view of the entrance area where the four offices branched off. One was Houston's; one was Tina's. The third belonged to Atlas.

As the seconds ticked by, the unknown fourth office caught her attention. She assumed it was an office like the others, but in two days, not one person had entered or exited the room. At least not while she was there.

Romy swung her legs down and pushed her blonde hair behind one ear. Even a couple of weeks on Earth had seen her locks grow longer than ever before. Not that she would have ever told anyone, but she'd secretly wished for long tresses like a fairy-tale princess.

She approached the locked door, looking around to see if anyone lurked in the entranceway. No one had told her the office was "off limits", but instinct told her she shouldn't be opening that door.

But it was in plain sight. Unguarded. Romy reached out and turned the knob.

"It's locked."

Romy tensed at the sound of Atlas's voice. *Now* he chose to come out of hiding!

"What's in there?" she asked, heart galloping in her chest.

No answer came. Why didn't that surprise her? Romy crossed her arms. Annoyance bubbled up within her and she shoved it down to the best of her ability, knowing part of it was puberty.

Why couldn't he just give her one straight answer?

"Atlas. . . ." How did Romy begin to ask everything she wanted—no, *needed* to know? "What is going on?"

She felt such a rush when she looked at him, those loose strands of hair falling over his eyes. He was enigmatic and reserved. Romy couldn't decide if he was good or bad.

His eyes flickered away, darkening. "What's going on is your knot is supposed to be blending in."

Romy brushed aside his bogus answer. "Don't be obtuse. You know what I mean."

It came to her that, really, she understood everything she needed to about the orbitos, and the Mandate. All of her angst was from not knowing who *he* was.

She took a step closer. "Who are you?"

For the first time since their meeting, Romy picked up a flash of something in his eyes. A flicker of . . . uncertainty, perhaps? A crack in his broad-shouldered confidence.

He unclasped his hands from behind his back and approached her with coiled steps. It made Romy feel like she should run, but she forced her breath to stay even, straightening and levelling him with the same look. It was ruined by the fact that he was taller.

Atlas brushed her cheek with his thumb and her breath caught before resuming its staid pace. Why did he always do that? Before she could ask, he'd bent his mouth to her ear. Warm breath tickled her neck.

"The one person you should trust," he breathed.

Atlas inhaled deeply and Romy felt her legs shake beneath her. Her body thrummed at his nearness.

Gripping his shoulder, she looked up at him. "What's going on?"

A dramatic throat-clearing interrupted Atlas's reply. "That, little skyling, is your body telling you that Atlas would be a prime candidate for reproduction."

Romy shrieked, shaking legs forgotten as she whirled around, pressing her back against Atlas.

Houston stood, propped against the doorway in faux casualness.

"Reproduction?" she repeated dumbly. The word registered a split second later and Romy bit down on her lip, wincing in embarrassment. Atlas hadn't moved from behind her. At least he couldn't see her face right now.

"Yes. The act whereby a male inserts his—"

"How long have you been standing there?" Atlas cut in.

"—into the lady bits. Not long." Houston waved a hand in the air, a large grin splitting his face.

The man behind her hummed quietly. Romy wasn't sure she believed the doctor either.

Houston continued. "I could have told you the door was locked, my dear."

Romy narrowed her eyes. That was right at the start of their conversation!

The lanky man scuffed the floor with a shuffling foot. "Now that we both have your attention, Atlas, this has got to stop. I feel like I'm treating the entire campsite every day."

Romy jumped in. "Thrym is much better in this area than I am. He could actually help. I can switch places with him," she offered.

Houston pushed his glasses up, swinging his stethoscope. "Not to mention, it doesn't leave me much time to work on . . . other things."

Atlas grunted softly. Houston stared directly over Romy's head. It felt like the pair was having some kind of cryptic conversation. She turned to the side so she could inspect Atlas's grey eyes for herself. But the man behind her was an impassive mask.

"All right," Atlas ground out.

"What?" Romy exploded. After all her ignored heartfelt reasons yesterday, he was just going to agree?

Atlas glanced her way as he turned to his office. To lock himself away for comets knew how long again. "You will now be working in the storage room. Try to make some sense of it. Tina will show you. Tina!" he barked.

The door to Tina's office flew open. Romy peeked inside and saw maps and plans covering the walls. They could be useful. The thought of stealing from Tina was vaguely terrifying, however. Romy envisioned many broken bones if she were caught.

The redhead's scowl quickly turned to a saucy smile. "Yes, darling?"

Atlas frowned at Tina and, it seemed, avoided looking Romy's way. "I need you to show Rosemary how to use the scanner system in storage."

Tina's mouth dropped slightly for a long second before she snapped it shut. She glared at Romy. "I guess I can do that."

Houston walked to his room, gracing Romy with a dramatic wide-eyed expression at the tension between the other pair.

"That is all," Atlas commanded.

Who on Earth is he? Romy thought in exasperation. Atlas had mentioned a superior. Who did he defer to? It clearly wasn't Tina. Did his commander occupy the fourth room? If so, the person never ate, slept, or peed. Maybe they used diapers, too. She bit her lip to stop her laughter from bursting free.

"Rosemary," Atlas interrupted her musings. "Go with Tina. She will show you what to do."

It was an order.

She supposed she should respond quite well to orders. Or she had before, anyway. But now, with her hormones raging, Romy decided she didn't care who he was—no one spoke to her like that. Especially when they were lying through their butt. She tossed her short hair in his direction. "Whatever, Atlas."

Romy really needed to think up some better retorts. She left the entranceway in the wake of a furious Tina.

Her anger didn't stop her from straining to hear the voices behind her.

"Do you remember puberty, boss?" Houston asked.

"What's your point?"

"Rebellion would be the word that comes to mind."

"We need to keep her safe, H. You know we do."

"She's just in the next building. You can see the stairs from here. And I really do need more time to analyse. . . ."

Romy's feet slowed, but their voices were too faint to make out. Tina threw a sharp glance her way. A foreboding shiver worked its way down Romy's spine as she scrambled to catch up with the woman.

CHAPTER FOURTEEN

Gloves on, Romy skimmed over an age-thinned paper before scanning it with her portable device. She scrolled down the categories and directed the document to the right file: law. Organising the filing room—a muddle of towering papers and ruined books—was something Romy would love to drag out over a couple of months.

Especially when every second document caught her eye.

Endless information—on Australia, on life before global warming. On current technology.

After a week at her new job, she had to admit Atlas had given her exactly what she'd wished for. If he hadn't been so rude, she would have acted more grateful at the time.

The others in her knot were learning how to escape and survive in a post-global-warming world. And Romy finally felt like she could contribute to their efforts. She was going to be the informed knot member. The person up-to-date on modern Earth—not just fairy tales and fuzzy, *dangerous* animals.

The storage room was in one of the three official buildings. Or rather, this building was actually for the soldiers' supplies and these documents were stuffed in a back room as an afterthought.

None of the information was more recent than 2040, though the e-storage Romy had access to contained data dating back to 1000 BC. It was entirely tempting to read all day.

Soldiers filed in and out of the building throughout the day, never entering the secluded room where she worked. Through the always open door, Romy watched as they entered the room on the other side of the hall. They used a keycard to get in. And exited with weapons and combat gear.

Knot 27 would need guns. How to get them was another question. Romy doubted the soldiers left their keycards lying around. And missing weapons would be noticed quickly. Romy didn't want them to be caught before they'd even left . . . or anyone else at camp to take the rap for their theft.

She sighed, and returned to her work. Organising and arranging the multitudes of books and files gave her immense satisfaction. Romy wondered if she would have had a job like it back in pre-global-warming times.

She hadn't seen Atlas at all throughout the week. He'd disappeared somewhere and Houston wouldn't spill where he'd gone. The last conversation she'd overheard between Atlas and Houston troubled her greatly and she'd hovered on the edge of confronting the doctor about it several times. She was glad Atlas wanted to keep her safe. In fact, she'd replayed that statement over in her mind several times. But shouldn't he want to keep the entire knot from harm? So why was it that she was being kept close, but the others were allowed out? And did it have to do with whatever Houston was "analysing"?

It didn't make sense.

Neither did the moment between her and Atlas. Romy was attracted to him. She was in no doubt after Houston's unsubtle explanation. It was uncomfortable. To feel like that for someone who was nothing but a mystery.

"Why the frown, Ro?"

Romy smiled at the sound of Thrym's warm voice from the doorway. "Just thinking about all the things I don't know."

She peeked around a precariously tilted pile of boxes at her friend. The constant heat here had darkened his skin even more. And it might be Romy's imagination, but she thought he smiled a lot more on Earth.

Thrym whistled as he ambled through the room, sucking in to move around the littered chaos. "Bit of a job in here." He grinned over to her corner. "How much are you enjoying this? Be honest."

Hair tickled her nose and she scrunched it, tossing the hair back. Romy gave him a bored look. "It's okay."

Her knot mate eyed her with such disbelief that Romy's expression cracked and laughter burst from her lips.

"All right. I love it." She beamed.

Thrym pulled up short, gaping at her, his breath coming faster.

Romy frowned. "Thrym?" She squeezed between two piles. "Are you well?"

But he backed away from her in a hurry, throwing an arm out towards her. "I'm fine!" He swallowed, looking towards the floor. "I'm fine," he repeated. "I just saw Houston through the window. I think he needs me."

"O–kay," Romy drew out. What was up with him? He hadn't been facing the window; she was sure of it. Romy certainly knew him well enough to know when he was lying. Well, actually, Thrym didn't lie. He hadn't on the orbitos, anyway.

"See you for lunch." His voice cracked. Thrym dodged between piles, upsetting a stack, which hit the ground with a *slap*.

Hands on hips, Romy watched from the door as he ran across the very empty, Houston-free clearing, back to the surgery. She'd never seen him so flustered.

Thrym's odd behaviour receded to the back of her mind as Romy moved methodically through the archives. She was finally getting the hang of the e-storage system and noticed the information scanned here had the label "Jimboomba". Was this the name of the settlement? It was a strange word to get her mouth around. "Jim-boom-bah." She grimaced. She'd ask Houston what it meant later.

Scrolling down through the list, Romy could see there were many other uploaded scans from other places: Wagga Wagga, Christchurch, Colorado, Edinburgh, Nepal, Reykjavík. She looked at the dusty room. It made sense there would be more information to scan than what was in this room. But her mind boggled as she continued her search. There were hundreds and hundreds of location tags. Just how much information did Earth contain? And how could she ever read it all?

A finger tapped on the window. Elara stood outside in her work overalls. "Lunchtime," came her muted voice.

Romy giggled as her friend danced outside the window. After a glance around, Romy did her own wacky move.

Romy left the scanner and documents and jogged out of the storage room and down the steps to her friend. The pair shoved each other as they raced back to their cabin to eat. They still hadn't returned to the Hull. Funny how twenty people watching you chew could put you off food. Like, thirty centimetres from your face, staring. Not cool. They took turns collecting food for the entire group.

The others said it wasn't as bad when they were out with just a few camp individuals. Elara said the guys she worked with got over their fascination pretty fast. They mainly wanted to hear about spaceships and the Critamal and seemed disappointed the knot weren't ninjas.

Romy crunched on some celery—as Phobos had called it. She rather liked the burst of flavour and the texture. Nothing on the orbitos ever had texture. Or such freshness. All space food was mushy, rehydrated slop. This stuff was amazing. Everything in the Hull was served from heated cabinets. Quantities were controlled, though the portion sizes were larger than what the space soldiers had ever received.

"Where's Thrym?" Phobos asked.

Romy glanced out the window from where they all sat around the small table in the bungalow. "Not sure. Probably somewhere with Houston. He was acting a little odd this morning."

Elara's fine eyebrows drew together. "Odd how?"

Romy stabbed at a chickpea with her fork. "We were just joking around, then he got all flustered and ran out the door."

Phobos choked on his water.

Elara frowned at her, her food paused halfway to her pinched mouth. "Is he sick?" She leaned over to pat Phobos on the back.

Romy glanced at Phobos's scarlet face, then back at Elara. "I really don't know."

The girl shrugged and went back to her meal.

"Did you go visit Dei?" Elara asked her.

Romy shook her head. "Didn't have a chance."

"I did," Phobos offered. "He sat on the side of the bed for ten minutes or so. But his blood pressure is weird from lying down too long. He spewed everywhere. Carrots and all."

Elara grimaced, dropping her roll.

Romy grinned, mouth full. The old Phobos was back. "So how long before he's discharged?"

Phobos stretched his arms up in a shrug. Romy saw Elara watching the movement. She gave the other girl a questioning look and Elara quickly looked away.

"Thrym may have an idea," Phobos said. "But Dei was saying he hopes to be out in a week."

"You think we still need to leave?" Elara asked.

Romy's brows rose. "You don't?"

"Don't know. I'm starting to get comfortable, you know?"

Phobos scowled. "It still doesn't change the fact that we don't know how secure we are."

Romy collected their dishes and tipped them into the sink. "Well, even if we change our minds, it doesn't hurt to be prepared, does it?"

She heard a thudding noise and a grunt. Glancing back she saw Elara had kicked Phobos in the shin. There was a crash and Phobos tackled her to the ground.

Thrym chose that moment to walk in the door. He hardly cast a glance at the other two—this wasn't unusual for them. Instead, he kicked the door closed and reached under his T-shirt to drag out some stolen goods.

Romy took them from him. "From the damaged bin?" she asked.

He nodded, leaning past her to grab a roll. "I snuck in after last bell. Everyone is at the Hull."

There was a jacket and a pair of warm pants.

She took them to her mattress and stuffed them in through the slit they'd made there last week.

No, she thought. It never did hurt to be prepared.

CHAPTER FIFTEEN

The orbito was clinical white and rigid efficiency; Earth was none of that. Even if something began as white here, it would soon be coated in the red dust swirling in the air.

Romy sat on the steps of the weaponry building watching the Earth humans go about their jobs.

There was no strict order to the business of the day. You woke with the early bell. Started work with the mid-morning bell. You ate three times. And you finished work with the final bell. Everyone had their individual roles. Everyone pulled their weight. Everyone knew what was acceptable. There was no obvious greed.

Romy couldn't sense the disquiet like Thrym had. But she trusted it was there, knowing she tended to overlook these kinds of things. She *did* notice that the gaze of the settlement's people was often drawn to the Mandate's ever-playing hologram. It showed the same images as the first time Romy saw it; the happy family, the happy children, the happy elderly. It was blatant mind-washing poacher poop, but the people here didn't seem to see that. Often as not they'd smile as they passed it, pausing to appreciate the pictures.

The Mandate used the flickering projection to maintain a presence in Jimboomba. But they were only silly pictures, weren't they? The more time that passed, the less she thought about the threat of the Mandate lurking over them. Maybe Knot 27 could stay here and become part of the settlement.

"'Scuse me, lady."

Romy turned to see a gaggle of small children. A largely toothless, pigtailed girl stepped apart from the others.

"Yes, little one?" She smiled. Children. She'd never spoken to a child before! The cadets developed in space were all born with pre-set maturity and intelligence. But she'd watched the other Earth humans interact with their young. Romy knew she should smile a lot.

"Do you kill heaps o' aliens?" the girl asked.

The group waited suspiciously for Romy's response.

There seemed to be some division amongst them. She worked to hide her grin. "Why yes, I've killed many of the Critamal." She didn't mention that Knot 27 was only called to the largest battles. The battles where the commanders needed all their numbers. That they tended to pick up space rubbish on most days. *That* could remain unsaid.

The girl's pigtails whipped around as she stink-eyed a tiny boy. "I *tol'* you," she withered.

The freckled boy's face went bright with embarrassment. "How d'ya know she's not lying, *Tessy*?"

It seemed like a good question to the others.

Romy spread her hands either side of her. "I could tell you how I do it?"

* * *

Atlas's groan was audible as a fuming Tina slammed the door to his office behind her. She really lived up to the colour of her hair.

"How exactly did you make the children cry?" he asked.

Romy ran her eyes over him. Layers of dust coated him from head to toe. The hard gleam often present was gone, and a bone-deep weariness was there in its stead.

She cleared her throat. "I didn't know they would react that way. They were asking about the Critamal." Romy shuffled her feet. It was awful. One at a time, the young people's eyes had welled with tears until they were all sobbing their little hearts out. "They seemed interested, so I went into more depth."

A flash moved through Atlas's eyes. "Tina said the kids were screaming about yellow blood and brain mush."

Guilt made her unable to meet his gaze, though she stood to attention. "Yes. That seemed to be the beginning of the end." Romy finally looked at him. "I feel terrible, Atlas."

Booming laughter filled her ears.

Her mouth dropped open as Atlas lost it. Dust flew up from his muscled shoulders. He hunched forwards in his desk chair, going silent in patches with the strength of his laughter.

A few giggles rose unbidden in her throat as the sound went on. She'd never seen him laugh so hard . . . not since the beach.

Atlas pushed back a few dark strands of his hair, which had flopped over his eyes. He surveyed Romy over clasped hands. "Thank you. I needed that."

Worry had her edging towards him. "Are you all right, Atlas?" she asked. Where had he been during the last week? He didn't just seem tired. He seemed a little downhearted, too.

Romy crept closer.

Atlas appeared amused at her question. But on second thought, the mask slipped ever so slightly. Was he trying to fool her?

"I don't think you are," she said softly.

Atlas watched her, laughter gone as she rounded the table. He wasn't frowning, and he wasn't barking orders. It was like their time in the bush, alone. And now they were alone again. . . .

The air thrummed between them. At least it did for Romy. Could he feel it too? Could attraction be only one-sided?

"Do you need help, Atlas?" She would help him if he needed it. She could take a break from scanning and reading for a couple of days.

Grey eyes flashed at her approach and a low hum escaped his lips. But he didn't say a word.

Romy didn't quite know what to do once she rounded the table. Instinctively, she laid her hand on his, which was resting palm up on his desk. His warm fingers curled around hers.

His hand was nearly double the size of her own, though he was only a head taller when standing. She met his eyes, hoping he wasn't seeing a young girl when he looked at her.

"I mean it, Atlas. Are you okay?"

He leaned forwards, the chair tilting with the shift of his weight. She barely knew anything about him, other than he was an excellent crocodile hunter. But his fingers curled about hers and for the first time since she woke on Earth, dangling in her harness, Romy felt secure.

Atlas studied her face. His grey eyes were soft for a change. "Yes, Rosemary. I'm okay. You don't need to worry about me."

Romy knew he wasn't telling the truth, but it seemed important to him that she believe the lie.

Something bothered her.

"Would you tell me if something was wrong?"

He untangled their entwined fingers, and lifted his hand to her face. Romy tilted her head into the fingers that grazed her jaw.

She peeked up at him through veiled lashes.

He didn't shift his eyes. "Your skin is so soft."

He hadn't answered her question. But she took in his slouched shoulders and let it go.

Romy bent forwards and gave Atlas a whisper of a kiss on his cheek. His unshaven skin scratched at her lips. It wasn't unpleasant at all.

What she really wanted to do was press her lips against his mouth. She hadn't been able to stop thinking about it. But Romy wasn't quite brave enough. His cheek seemed safe for now.

Turning away from his sharp intake of breath, she made for the door.

"You should get some rest," she ordered.

A quiet chuckle reached her ears. "I promise to rest, if you promise not to make any more children cry."

Romy didn't believe that dignified an answer and she left the room.

CHAPTER SIXTEEN

Knot 27 cheered as Deimos took wobbling steps.

Phobos hovered close by, face pinched in worry. The simple movement had the sick member of their group sweating and pale.

Romy caught Thrym's eye; he gave a subtle shake of his head. Deimos's hospital stay was now at two weeks and counting.

More than anything, she wanted Dei back with them. Things weren't the same without him. In fact, the dynamics within the knot were a little . . . weird.

Since that day in the storage room, Thrym had been acting odd around her. Different. He touched her just as often; a held hand, a ruffling of the hair. But some barrier lay between them. Her best friend was closed off and felt inaccessible most of the time. Deep down, Romy had an inkling of what his problem might be. However, thinking about Thrym being attracted to her on top of everything else was just too much.

If he was, then attraction could certainly be one-sided.

Thank goodness her relationship with Phobos and Elara hadn't changed. Though she couldn't say the same for the relationship between *them.*

"What's wrong, Ro? You look constipated," Deimos joked.

She shook her head as the others laughed, a witty response eluding her.

"Phobos has filled me in on the plan," Deimos continued.

Elara clucked her tongue. "Really? If anyone hears us talking, they'll figure out what's up."

"Listen to you, sounding all Earth human," Phobos teased. His smile fell as she glared at him.

Elara hadn't been as bad lately, but she was still prone to flashes of PMS. Romy actually felt like she'd gotten a handle on the puberty business now. Elara's prickly fury made her glad this was the case.

"What should we call it then?" Thrym asked.

"Catheter," Deimos offered.

The group groaned in unison.

"That's sick, Dei." Romy grimaced.

"Exactly," he stated proudly. "No one likes to hear about catheters."

Romy giggled at the look on Elara's face, which showed baffled agreement mixed with sheer disgust.

Phobos raised his hand in a fist-pump. Deimos weakly pressed his knuckles to his twin's.

Romy waited.

And ended up cracking first. "So don't you want to hear about the catheter?"

Thrym's composure cracked. The hospital room was too small for their laughter.

"Shh," Elara hushed them. Tears streamed down her face. "Someone will come."

Deimos looked around the isolation room. "The way I'm going, it will take me a while to regain strength. I don't want to slow you down." He hesitated. "If something happens—if *they* find us—you need to leave without me."

Phobos stood up from his perch beside Deimos. "Did you really just say something that stupid?"

Deimos rubbed a hand over his face. *Is that stubble?* Romy wondered.

"I mean it. It's been a while, but if the Orbitos or the Mandate find out we're still alive, they'll kill us to protect their secret. You have to leave at the first hint of danger."

Elara's voice cracked. "We almost lost you once. We can't lose you again."

Deimos studied their faces and shrugged. "No one likes ripping a catheter out."

It lightened the mood marginally, though not for Phobos, who slid open the door and stormed out, slamming the door behind him.

Deimos turned to the rest of the knot, eyebrows raised.

Thrym clasped the recovering man's shoulder. "Don't worry. It's just puberty." His face went red as he glanced behind him at the girls. "It's knocking us all around."

Consternation lit Deimos's face. "What's puberty?"

Romy and Elara shared a panicked look and scrambled for the door. That was their cue to leave. Thrym sighed as they rushed out.

Elara pulled on Romy's hand to make her stop when they were just out of the door. Muffling a laugh, Romy crouched down, listening at the crack left in the sliding door.

"Man, where do I start," groaned Thrym. "It sucks. The girls don't really seem affected."

Elara scoffed under her breath.

"But Phobos and I have had it bad."

Romy and Elara both tensed at Thrym's words. Suddenly, Romy didn't want to be listening at the door.

"Any reason you two are blocking the hallway?" A whisper sounded in Romy's ear.

She stifled a scream as she fell backwards.

"Houston," she hissed.

He crouched next to Elara, who looked like she'd suffered a heart attack.

"You know," he said, "you shouldn't listen in on people's conversations about puberty. It's a very trying time."

Romy blushed. "You're right, we—"

Houston waved a hand at her. "Shh. I can't hear."

Elara fisted her hand in front of her mouth, her giggle still making it around the sides.

Against her better judgement, Romy crouched down again, thinking Houston was the most unethical doctor she'd ever met.

Thrym was still explaining. "Phobos said he had some luck thinking of Critamal females. He said it seemed to help it go down."

Houston pushed his glasses up, shaking his head. "I prefer dead puppies, myself."

Romy caught Elara's alarmed look.

"Houston!" a voice screeched.

The crouched trio jumped at the piercing sound.

Heavy shoes stomped down the hallway towards them. Romy rose as she saw Tina strutting their way in combat boots. Houston placed a palm on her and Elara's backs to press them forwards. Romy swore he muttered "Tina the Terrifying" under his breath.

But his smile was blinding. "Tina, what can I do you for?"

The petite woman snapped her fingers in his face. "Don't give me that. There's a medical emergency in the orchards. We need you there, not acting like a child in the halls."

Houston snapped to attention. "Yes, sir!" he said before sprinting down to his surgery.

Tina's gaze softened as she looked at Elara. "Elara, dear. How are you settling in? Mr James has said you're catching on very quickly."

Elara beamed under the praise, while Romy inwardly gaped.

"Thank you, Miss Lyons. I find it all fascinating."

Tina's laugh tinkled. "Please, call me Tina."

Seriously?

Pink with pride, Elara grabbed Romy's hand to go. As though with great effort, Tina turned her fierce green gaze to Romy.

"Yes, Rosemary. Run along to the archives now."

Romy sarcastically mimicked Houston's salute. "At once, Miss Lyons." She wasn't quite brave enough to call the woman "sir".

Tina's eyes narrowed at the motion and Romy's insides shuddered a little. Trust her snarkiness to decide to show up at the worst time.

Elara squeezed Romy's hand. She broke away from Tina's perusal.

"Just try not to make any innocent children cry."

Romy ground her teeth as she strode away, hand in hand with her knot mate.

They pair got outside into the fresh air. Fresh was not entirely accurate; it was muggy, similar to the weather before the storm on the beach. Romy hoped there wouldn't be a repeat of the three-day onslaught of rain.

"So, Tina doesn't like *you* very much," Elara started.

Romy looked back. "Yeah. Can't say I feel any differently."

"Because of Atlas?"

Romy turned to stare at her friend.

Elara winked. "He's always staring at you."

It was Romy's turn to go pink. "No. I don't think that's why."

But Elara continued. "Well, Tristan, one of the sentries, said Atlas and her get it on."

She felt her eyes widen in response. "Reproduce?"

Elara snorted. "Well, kinda. But without the kid. But yeah, they sleep together."

Sleep together. Present tense. Romy felt like she'd been punched in the stomach. She swallowed her reaction with difficulty. Elara continued on, oblivious to the injury she'd dealt her friend.

"I mean, she's welcome to him, right? He's scary."

Romy echoed her empty agreement.

* * *

At some level Romy had known there was history there. Why else did Tina touch Atlas so much? But it hurt that she was so attracted to Atlas, only to find out he liked someone else.

She found herself overanalysing the kiss on the cheek. Did he take a breath because he was shocked? Or worse, did he see her advances as childlike? He didn't look all that much older than Romy, though he was always so confident and self-assured. Did he view her as someone too young to be attracted to?

She was proudly embarrassed, and a little excited about the kiss before today. Now she was mortified. Avoiding Atlas sounded like a good idea.

No wonder Tina didn't like her. Romy felt guilty for overstepping the boundaries. She'd read enough Earth material to understand relationships were mostly monogamous. And from her observations, the people in the settlement seemed to stick to one person.

Romy scanned a document on tidal measurements in the 2020s. Every piece of information she'd read from 2020 to 2040 documented the same trends—rising water level, increase in temperature, spread of disease, loss of animal species, and the inevitable, astronomic loss of human life. A piece of paper she'd scanned yesterday detailed the death toll. Most were from low socioeconomic areas. Many died from disease, most from malnourishment.

Placing a book titled *Marketing for Dummies* to one side, Romy's eyes landed on a squashed poster below it.

The rubber band snapped as soon as she touched it, cracked and dried from age. The poster unfurled and excitement burst within her as she saw what it was.

A map!

A swishing collapse sounded behind her. Romy turned, expecting to see another toppled column. But her heart raced at the soldier dressed in camo holding a gun in the doorway.

She dropped the map, purposefully clumsy, so it floated down out of view.

Romy recognised the soldier. It was the pale, black-eyed man who had looked at her strangely in the entranceway that day Atlas refused to give her another task. The man had been following Tina somewhere. The only reason Romy remembered was because he was looking at her in the same creepy way right now.

"You scared me," she said, smile firmly in place.

The man had the kind of wiriness that could either be weak or incredibly strong. As his black gaze swept over her from head to toe, her instincts screamed it was the latter; that this man was not someone to be messed with.

The gun dangling within easy grasp did nothing to dispel her uneasiness.

"I was told you were in here," he said.

Romy said nothing. Did Tina tell him? Was that why he was here? Was Tina laying down the law?

She waited for him to get to the point.

"I have a few questions for you."

Romy smiled again, deciding to play the fool. "You need a reference? I'm afraid I might not be much help until I've got this mess sorted."

The man smirked, sauntering closer. "No. Not a reference." He tilted his head to the side and settled on her chest. She wore a white T-shirt today. She'd been self-conscious putting it on because it was made for a child. His look made heat fill her cheeks.

He circled even closer and she resisted the urge to run for the door. The way he stared and the way he was invading her personal space made the bile rise in her throat, burning its way to her mouth.

"Now you've got it." He congratulated her.

Trying to be circumspect, Romy scoped out the storage room. After a week here, she knew the place back to front—literally. There was one way in and one way out. And it was on the other side of this man. Unfortunately, the room was long and narrow. It would be hard to get past the soldier.

She decided to take the Critamal by the pincers. "What do you want?" Romy said flatly, arms crossed over her chest.

The soldier rushed at her. Before she had time to scream, he was right in front of her. Romy couldn't help stumbling backwards in fright.

"I wouldn't mind a few things from you, darlin'. Pretty sheila like yourself. But for now, you'll be telling me all about how you came to land here on Earth."

A deep, consuming beat drummed in her ears. He was under Tina's orders. Did Tina work for the Mandate? Atlas's warning never to reveal the truth echoed in her ears.

"We're here on research," she said. The monotone reply sounded like a lie even to her.

The man reached for a strand of her hair and she swatted his hand away, moving along the wall to put distance between them. She was loath to step on top of any of the papers. These were historic documents. *Easily damaged* historical documents.

"We both know that's a lie, darlin'," he said. The man rested his finger on the trigger of his weapon. The message was clear.

"Surely Tina told you why we're here," she pressed. There were other consequences the soldier couldn't understand. By telling him, Romy would betray her knot. And that was something she was physically incapable of doing.

"You better get out of here right now, or Atlas will be hearing about this," she said calmly.

The man laughed and Romy faltered. "You think Atlas will listen to you? He's shoved you in this junk pit for a reason, you stupid bitch." He kicked over a pile of books, which thudded onto the floor, spines contorting in a splayed sprawl.

For the first time Romy felt more anger than fear. But she knew showing her anger was a grade-A bad idea.

Atlas hadn't placed her here because he disliked her. That she was sure of. But doubt nipped as she wondered if this soldier was right on one count. Would Atlas *listen* to her? He always brushed off her questions.

And he thinks I'm a child.

"One way or another you'll tell me the whole truth." He leaned towards her, glancing over her body once more. "And the sooner you tell me, the more pleasant it will be for you." He leaned away, smiling. "But tell you what. I'm feeling charitable. How 'bout I give you some time to think it over?"

Terror held her still. She didn't trust that smile for a second.

The camouflaged solider strolled for the door, thumbs hooked in his belt.

"I've already told you why we are here. There's nothing more to tell," she choked out.

The man didn't break his strutting walk. "Anyone finds out I was here and I'll slaughter your knot."

Romy gasped.

His black eyes turned back to her, framed with white lashes. "Same time tomorrow, darlin'?"

CHAPTER SEVENTEEN

"I'm getting a handle on the tracks around camp," Elara said to Thrym just as Romy kicked the door of their bungalow shut behind her.

Romy took in the scene. Phobos sat at the small round table watching Elara with a perplexed furrow between his brows. Elara looked back with slight disgust as she disappeared into the bathroom to change. Since when did any of them leave the room to hide their bodies?

Meanwhile, Thrym stared at *her*. And Romy tried not to stare at anyone. Especially now that she knew about the thing between Tina and Atlas. When did things start getting so complicated within their group? More than ever, she needed something solid to hold on to with both hands, and it wasn't there.

"I got some more seeds," Phobos added, digging into his pocket. "I'd like to take some seedlings if possible."

"Good," Thrym said. "Add them to the stash."

Romy already had a collection of tiny seeds in her pillowcase, and the large slit in her mattress hid some of their other collected supplies. She got the job for looking the most innocent.

"We'll have to watch pack size," Elara warned.

Romy asked, "What packs?" They only had a bunch of seeds and some clothing full of holes.

The group ignored her.

Thrym nodded. "On second thought, it might need to just be seeds, Pho. There are too many necessities we'll have to take: clothing, blankets, medicine. Now, about that. We obviously won't be able to take the tech, so I'll have to rely on old medicine. Houston keeps stocks."

"Ro, have you been able to get into the soldiers' supplies?" Elara asked.

The word "soldier" froze Romy to the spot for a few seconds as memories of the soldier in her office assaulted her. She exhaled a shaky breath.

Elara awaited her reply, cute nose wrinkled.

Romy recalled the question and drew out the folded map from inside her light jacket. She hadn't wanted to damage the document, but it was the only way to sneak it from storage without anyone noticing. "There aren't any windows to the supply room. The only way in is a keycard. I really don't know how we'll be able to get in," she reported. "But I did find *this*."

Romy spread the map on the floor, since the table was full of plates and food. The knot put their heads together over the document, staring down.

"It's from 2021," Phobos noted.

Thrym traced a finger over the date. "Pretty ancient."

Elara sighed. "And a lot has probably happened since that time. How much do you think global warming changed Australia?"

The group looked at Romy.

She blinked, sitting back on her knees. "Modern Australia contains the largest inland water body in the world. I remember how excited I was when the researchers brought back the news."

They looked down at the map. The map of Australia below them showed a mass of desert land in the centre. According to Romy's information, a good portion of this was now a lake.

"A map isn't much help if we don't even know where we are," Thrym said in frustration.

She knew that one. "Jimboomba!" Romy exclaimed.

Phobos leant away, covering the ear closest to Romy.

She grinned at him, unabashed. "We're in Jimboomba."

Thrym put his nose close to the map, blue eyes squinting. "Jimboomba. . . ."

It took them several minutes of searching to find Jimboomba on the map.

Phobos eventually located it. "Jimboomba," he drew out. "Am I saying that right? What kind of word is it?"

Romy inspected the map. "Aboriginal, I think."

"Well, they certainly live up to the 'original' part."

Elara snorted. "Lame."

"You are."

"Queensland, Australia," Romy breathed.

Elara stared at the map. "Did you say here?" She pointed at the east coast of Australia.

Thrym nodded.

Elara was already shaking her head. "I don't think we're that far inland. Pass me a fork or something," she said to Phobos. "Where's the scale on the map?"

Elara measured the distance based on the map scale, and tapped the fork against her thigh. "Three days ago we took a patrol to the beach," she thought aloud. "We covered a hundred kilometres in two hours to get there. This map says the route is only fifty kilometres."

"But the route could have changed time and time again," Thrym said. "Maybe you didn't go directly to the coast."

"Or the location is just different altogether," Elara countered.

"Regardless, Atlas told me we're in Queensland, Australia," Romy said, "so it's safe to assume we're on the East Coast. That means . . ." She looked up at Thrym.

He raised his eyebrows. ". . . That if we trek west, we come across the lake in the middle."

There were many holes in the theory. After lengthy discussion it seemed likely the lake was situated further south. A large water inlet—Murray's River—was already present in 2021. As water levels rose, it made sense that existing waterways would simply grow larger.

Romy walked over and sat on her bunk, staring at the wall opposite her. The soldier was going to come again tomorrow.

What was she going to do?

A gentle hand brushed back her hair. "What's up? You've been acting weird all night."

She gazed into Thrym's blue eyes. Eyes she trusted. And eyes she'd do anything to protect.

If the soldier found out Romy told her knot, he could make good on his threat. She doubted any one of her knot would be able to keep their cool if they knew.

She wasn't willing to risk their lives.

"Nothing." She smiled. "Just tired. Nothing a good sleep won't fix."

"I grabbed dinner from the Hull on the way. Sure you don't want to eat?"

She shook her head, dislodging his hand, which was still stroking her hair. "No. I'm not hungry." The memory of the slimy man still made her insides twist. Food wasn't an option right now.

"You sure?" Thrym bobbed his head down to catch her eye.

Romy hesitated before tightening her resolve. She flashed him a quick smile, turning away to enter the bathroom. Maybe she shouldn't judge Elara for escaping here.

Everything was just so out of control. And it was compounded by the fact that she simply didn't know the rules down here. How could she protect herself against a soldier? Against someone with more power than herself?

. . . What was more powerful than the soldier?

The corners of Romy's mouth flipped up in a smile.

CH/PTER EIGHTEEN

It was Phobos's turn to brave the Hull to get the knot breakfast. But Romy offered to take his place, leaving much earlier than she needed to.

Romy grabbed a bread roll for herself. She'd come back for the others' food in a few minutes.

She dodged a couple of gawking Earth humans, mumbling rushed apologies as they attempted to engage her in conversation. Even if you were only speaking to one person, fifty others were listening and repeating your every response in whispers, until everyone was discussing what you'd said. It was unnerving.

Chewing on the bread, she made for the exit. But something stopped her in her tracks. The soldier from yesterday, he was in the clearing outside, by the Mandate's hologram screen. Romy backed away from the exit so he wouldn't see her.

She watched as he crossed the clearing to enter the storage and supplies building. *Crud.* There went her plans to barricade the door from the inside. Was he going to the supply room, or was he going to wait for her in the archives? She slid onto a bench to watch through the wide window. She'd only go in if he came out.

"What are you looking at?" a blunt voice asked.

Romy jumped and glanced around at a girl who looked to be in her late teens. She had orange hair, freckles, and the most amazing violet eyes.

The hull didn't have long tables and benches like the orbito. Instead, there were smaller circular tables, each of which held around ten of the Earth humans. There were eight others at this table . . . who she'd somehow missed while focusing on the soldier.

"Uh. . . ." Romy stalled. Throwing caution to the stars, she decided to be honest. "I was wondering what that soldier's name is." She pointed out the window. The soldier was disappearing inside, but the girl who'd first spoken answered anyway.

Romy was relieved to see her face screw up. "That's Lucas. Or, as we like to say, Mucus. Officer Cayne."

A laugh burst from Romy's lips. Mucus. She nodded. "Suits him."

The girl eyed her intently. "You're not half as snobby as you appear to be."

Romy bit into her roll again, wondering how to take the backhanded remark. She wasn't really surprised at the girl's statement. She and her friends simply grabbed food and left, making no effort to fit in. At least the others worked alongside the people of the settlement. Romy didn't. She stayed inside all day, dashing in and out of the Hull every second or third day to get food.

Romy shrugged, meeting the girl's remark in kind. "You guys are pretty full-on with all the staring and questions."

The orange-haired girl pursed her lips, observing the surrounding crowds. Most of the people gathered were grinning at Romy like she'd shared a secret with them.

"You could be right about that," the girl decided. She jerked her head in the direction of a woman who was trying to catch Romy's attention by bobbing her head from side to side. "I reckon that one would combust if you spoke a single word to her."

The table erupted into hooting hilarity. Romy found herself giggling, too.

The girl pulled her arm across her mouth to dislodge a few crumbs. She wiped her hand on her faded trousers. "So, what's your name?"

A boy to Romy's left snorted. "Don't act like you don't know."

"I'm Romy," she said, holding out a hand.

The girl, blushing faintly from the boy's remark, shook Romy's hand with three decisive pumps. "I'm Nancy. Don't wear it out."

The same boy groaned. "You're so lame sometimes."

"You'll *be* lame if you don't shut up." The girl neither looked angry nor sounded angry as she retorted.

Nancy focused on Romy again. Her eyes flicked to the left and Romy glanced over her shoulder to see the soldier, *Mucus,* bee-lining for the Hull.

Romy met the girl's eyes and something passed between them.

Nancy pushed up from the table. "You travelling with us today, space monster?"

What was with the name calling here? "What does that involve?" she asked.

"It involves stealing a car and guns, sneaking past the sentries, and target shooting."

For a long beat she thought Nancy was joking. But no one laughed. Romy chewed her lip. "I don't think Atlas would like that," she hedged.

The teen crossed her arms. "You always do as you're told, little sky girl?"

The answer was yes. That was just how life on the orbitos was. But . . . she was on Earth now. A slow grin spread over her face.

"No," she replied. "Not anymore."

A thrill raced through Romy as a table-full of teens grinned back at her. What they were about to do was against the rules, and the danger of it sent adrenaline straight to her fingertips.

In twos and threes the table dispersed—in different directions. Romy walked beside Nancy, trying to rein in her excitement.

Nancy moaned. "Everyone's gonna suspect us if you keep that up."

"Keep what up?" Romy's steps slowed.

"You're supposed to be going to sort papers. It's not your bloody birthday. Slump your shoulders or something."

Romy attempted to slouch.

Nancy moaned once again. "Just, never mind. Have you ever slouched in your life? Pick up the pace. Everyone's staring."

The two girls took a weaving path through the settlement. Nancy glanced casually around before pulling Romy down an alleyway. They ran to what Romy thought was a dead end, but as they got there, the violet-eyed girl slid a propped board to the side and squeezed through the gap.

The other teens were already on the other side. Two were dragging a large leaf-covered net from a vehicle wedged between the fence and an abandoned-looking bungalow.

"No one knows this is here," Nancy said quietly. "Took us ages to get all the parts. But Eddie is a fair-dinkum mechanic." She slapped a small boy on the back, who stammered his thanks.

Romy stood aside as Eddie jumped in the car and six others began to roll the car out of the wedged space. Nancy and Romy trailed after the rolling vehicle.

The others kept up their pushing for five minutes. Then, without warning, they all abandoned their shoving and ran to the vehicle doors as the car rolled to a stop.

"This is the pinch," Nancy said. "The ride's only really big enough for five people."

A quick head count told her there were nine present, including herself.

"Shotgun not boot," one yelled. The cry was quickly echoed by all. The group stared at Romy.

"I don't know that she'll actually fit in the boot, though," a tall, lean girl said.

Romy looked at the boot and had to agree. She was the tallest there by far. "Uh, I can try?"

Nancy crossed her arms. "No. It's your first time. And you didn't know shotgun rules. Hannah, mate, you take the boot this time."

The girl, Hannah, appeared mutinous for a moment, but a few pushes from the others had her grumbling and trudging to the boot.

After a few minutes of squeezing, everyone else managed to cram into the car. Eddie drove and two others crowded into the front beside him; a smaller girl stuffed into the area in front of the passenger seat. With five in the back, Romy ended up on Nancy's lap, head bend forwards at an uncomfortable angle. It would have made more sense for Romy to be on the bottom, but she kept the observation to herself.

"The door won't close!"

Romy couldn't see who was speaking.

Nancy grunted from under Romy. No wonder; she was smothering the poor girl in her armpit. "Just hold on to it, then. We're only driving twenty minutes!"

Eddie started the engine, and the vehicle lurched into motion.

Laughter bubbled in Romy's throat. "This is ridiculous," she burst out. Giggles erupted from her, muffled by the shoulder her face was smooshed into.

Nancy was snorting and hiccupping beneath her.

The car bumped along for what seemed like an age. And Romy realised this was a chance to find out more information.

"I thought there were soldiers watching the settlement," she started. "Don't they notice you going in and out?"

"There's a section they don't bother with because they reckon sheer cliffs block anyone from entering. But me and Eddie found a way beneath them," Nancy said with a grin. "Awesome, huh?"

"Very awesome," Romy agreed, deep in thought.

However funny the predicament was, not moving her legs for that long turned out to be unpleasant. And it was possible her neck would never straighten again.

After falling out of the car, closely followed by the violet-eyed Nancy, Romy stretched tall, looking around her. Nancy wasted no time before dashing off into the bush, orange hair bobbing like a torch against the dry leaves.

The area where Eddie stopped was similar to the forest Romy had hiked through after they crashed. Eucalyptus trees rose high and extended as far as she could see into the bush. Any ground not covered by grass and wiry shrubs was red dirt. The only difference to this area was the random array of target boards hanging from the trees.

Nancy was returning to the clearing, carrying weapons. Romy smiled as she realised the girl had been retrieving the guns from a hiding spot. She handed Romy a small one, calling it a "baby gun".

She passed another small gun to the others, who began squabbling over it. Nancy kept the largest for herself.

Romy studied the weapon and quickly found the safety. She slid the magazine out and pointed it into the bush while she pumped the rack a few times to empty any forgotten rounds. She snapped the magazine back into place and raised the weapon, staring down the front sight. It was foreign to the battler guns and a *lot* tinier, but had the same parts overall.

She looked up and found Nancy and the crew gaping at her. "What?" she asked.

Nancy held out her own gun. "Jeez, looks like you should use the AK-103 instead."

Romy shook her head as she studied the much larger weapon. "I'll begin with this baby arm. Shooting battler guns in space and shooting on Earth will be very different. I imagine the wind and light will take a little getting used to. Not to mention the pressure and temperature." She looked around, studying the environment with interest.

"Did you just calmly insert 'battler guns in space' into a sentence?" a boy asked. He didn't wait for an answer. "That is freakin' cool." The boy slammed a fist in the air, making Romy smile.

They couldn't understand that the opposite was true. Everything *here* was "freakin' cool".

"Yeah?" grunted Nancy. "I'm just thinking about 'baby arms' and feeling freaked out."

The freckled girl guided Romy in front of the tree with the closest target.

"I don't really know how weird this will be to adjust to. So I guess you should just give it a go." The girl shrugged.

Romy held the gun out with two hands and let Nancy adjust her grip. The battler guns were gripped on both sides; the shooter sat in a rotating chair, which allowed them to swing the weapon and follow the Critamal ships. It was odd to have her hands encircling the weapon—awkward. But Nancy was adamant it would get better.

Romy studied the target. There was a slight breeze, and she had no idea what gravity would do to the bullet's trajectory. But there was no point in trying to guess what would happen. She squeezed the trigger.

Laughter trickled behind her.

Nancy was grinning. "Hey, at least you got the same tree . . . or maybe the roots."

Romy gave her a sheepish look. Her shot had gone straight to the bottom of the tree. She pumped the rack and raised the gun again, tilting it upwards.

She pulled the trigger.

"You got the board," Nancy said. "Hey, not bad!" She turned to the others, who were cheering. "You see that? I taught the sky girl everything I know."

"You can't claim that," another girl called.

"Just watch her, Freya," Eddie stammered. Nancy threw him a look. There was no missing the fondness sparkling in her purple eyes.

For the next hour Romy practised with the baby gun. She hadn't missed the target since the second shot, and had even hit the bulls-eye several times.

She clicked the safety on and dangled the weapon at her side.

"I wanna see the sky girl shoot the AK-103," a larger boy called. His name was Fred, and he was the one who'd gotten so excited by her "battler" comment.

A chorus of "me too's" chimed from the others. Nancy approached with her gun—the largest gun. A challenging gleam lit her eye. Romy had watched the girl shoot it. She was good. Hadn't missed once.

"You game?" she asked.

Romy wasn't sure. But she didn't want to lose face in front of the young Earth humans. "Sure."

Whoops and shouts followed Romy as she made her way to the rightmost area, where Nancy had practised. She could barely see the target in the distance. It was much farther than the few she'd practised on.

"Now this one's gonna kick. Make sure you prop it on your chest. And brace yourself or you'll end up flat on your back. Not that that wouldn't be funny and all, but I don't want to have to explain a broken nose to Dr H. or Tina."

"I don't think she'd care," Romy muttered.

Nancy sniggered. "Probably not. I've seen her look at scorpions with more fondness. All right, you've got the target. Pretend it's a poacher, or something."

Romy chose the "or something" as she peered through the front sight of the much longer weapon. The gun was heavy. If she held it too long, her arms would begin to tremble. She inhaled slowly, thinking of the Orbito soldiers hundreds of kilometres above her, fighting for a useless cause. Fighting because of greed and politics.

In other words, fighting for the exact same reasons global warming had occurred in the first place.

Whatever happened to her knot, Romy knew she'd never blindly follow anyone ever again.

She squeezed the trigger. And the target exploded down the way.

Silence greeted her ears as she replaced the safety and pointed the rifle to the ground, absently rubbing her shoulder.

Nancy had her mouth open. "Holy shite. You just blew up the target. On your first try."

Romy shrugged a shoulder up and rubbed the back of her neck. "Well, I'd already practised for a while with the other gun."

Nancy grabbed the rifle. "You did not just seriously compare a Glock to an AK-103?"

Romy flexed her fingers, studying the target. "I think I prefer the big one."

"A woman after my own heart." Nancy sighed dramatically. "But hands off. This one is mine."

* * *

The eight teens and Romy crammed back into the car for the return journey. Romy's stomach twisted nervously as she tried to memorise the path they took. She'd avoided the soldier for one day, but what was to prevent him from coming back at any time? And what if her absence had been noticed? Romy couldn't help but feel Atlas might have something to say about her disappearing with a bunch of teenagers—even if it was the most fun she'd had on Earth yet.

Romy hadn't really considered the consequences before going.

"C-can you tell us about the Critamal?" Eddie asked shyly.

The low muttering of the young group halted at his question. None of them could move, but Romy had a feeling that if the others could, they'd be turning to stare.

"Sure," Romy said. "What do you want to know?"

Eddie's eyes went wide in excitement. She could see his expression in the cracked mirror in the middle of the windscreen.

"It must be amazing, living up there. *In space*," he sighed, stutter disappearing.

Wriggling in place, she tried to mask her amusement. "I guess," she replied. "It's all I've ever known, just like your homes here, I imagine. It's the same with the Critamal. They've always been a part of my life—I don't really find the Critamal all that interesting, to be honest. Though battle against them can be an exhilarating change to daily life, and the way their brains stay intact after their body explodes gives me shivers. They're just something to kill. Something to survive. Something not to get caught by. They want Earth, and we want to stop them. If global warming had destroyed Earth, it could have just as easily been us trying to take their home."

Nancy hummed. "I never thought of the poachers that way."

A muffled response came from the opposite seat. "That's so badass."

Romy flushed. She didn't want it to sound like she was bragging. "To my knot, being on the orbitos, it's the same as . . . feeding the chickens. You get used to it, and it's just a job you do because you have to." Romy wasn't entirely successful at keeping the bitterness from her voice.

"The grass is always greener?" Eddie asked.

"I don't know." Romy frowned. "Is it?"

The car rocked with the sound of laughter from the eight teens while Romy went bright red.

Nancy snorted into Romy's side. "It means, you always think something far away is more exciting than your life."

Romy wondered if she'd find feeding the chickens more exciting. *Probably,* she thought.

"Yes, I suppose that's true."

Nancy was shaking her head. "That's messed up."

The same muffled voice came from the other side. She assumed it was the boy, Fred. "I say we make her tell us about the aliens and guns! It's the least she can do after we broke her out today."

This was how, when his suggestion was met with wild agreement, that Romy found herself talking about space soldier life—in what she hoped was a voice void of sourness—for the entire drive back.

* * *

"I was pretty hungry after the person meant to bring breakfast skipped out on us." Phobos glared at Romy over Elara's head as she walked into the bungalow.

She covered her mouth with both hands.

Romy looked over the three of them. Phobos was angry, Elara suspicious, and Thrym—well, he seemed a little peeved as well. "I'm so sorry. I completely forgot!"

"Forgot? How, Rosemary?" Thrym stood up in an angry movement. "I went by the storage room *five times* today. You weren't there at all. I was beginning to think the Mandate had captured you!"

He was using her full name. Definitely annoyed.

Earth wasn't like space, where if you couldn't find someone, you knew they'd only be minutes away, available at the touch of a button. If the others disappeared on Earth, they could be anywhere in the world, never to be found. If Romy couldn't find one of the others, she would be upset, too.

She sat down on her bunk. "I'm sorry. I went off target shooting with some humans today. I didn't even think to let you guys know where I was going." Her relief at escaping the soldier, Lucas, for the day had taken first priority.

Thrym regained his seat, still tense. Phobos came to sit next to her.

"Next time, let us know, okay?" Phobos said, pulling her in for a hug.

"I will," Romy sniffed. She hated when they were mad at her. "Were you hungry all day?"

Phobos leant in to whisper loudly, "Thrym won't want you to know that we left twenty minutes after you did to get our own food."

Romy smiled, and they fell into an awkward silence.

Elara was looking around the group, a bewildered look upon her face. "How about the bit about the target shooting? You guys don't want to know about that?"

Romy gave a quick recount of her day with the Earth teens. Phobos was up and pacing the room as she finished. Thrym sat, arms folded, one finger tapping on his elbow. A small smile graced his face.

"Of course you hit the target." Thrym winked.

She exhaled in relief. He'd forgiven her.

"Yeah, yeah. You're proud of her," Phobos interrupted. He sat backwards on his chair. "I'm more interested in the fact that Romy knows the location of a car full of weapons."

Romy shook her head. "Nancy has a hiding spot for the guns at the clearing. I don't think anyone else knows where it is."

"But you know where the car is."

She grew still at his statement.

Elara squealed and danced on the spot. Phobos watched his knot mate's willowy movements in consternation.

Romy folded her arms, lost in deep thought. The group had always planned to steal a car, courtesy of Elara, and ditch it somewhere along the road. It would be easier for a recovering Deimos and would get them a reasonable head start on Tina's force if they could get their hands on the unknown car right away.

The teenagers' car provided the knot with an easy solution to a difficult problem.

But Romy felt uneasy at the betrayal of Nancy's trust. The bluntly-spoken girl had saved her from Lucas, if only for a day. Her brow furrowed at the thought of the young people meeting at the car one day, only to find it gone, stolen by the space soldiers they looked up to.

But protecting her knot trumped any others, any day. And since crashing on Earth, that included making decisions to protect them that she didn't necessarily like.

She looked up to Phobos, returning his wink. "I guess I'm forgiven for forgetting breakfast?"

CHAPTER NINETEEN

"**A**re you sure this is a good idea?" Elara eyed the Hull in mistrust.

Romy didn't blame her. There was a person pressed up against the glass staring at them.

"What's the plan?" Phobos muttered.

Thrym bent his head towards the group. "Elara and I get the food. You guys circle back from opposite sides. They won't know where to look. Meet at the girl's table."

"Nancy," Romy supplied.

The knot looked at the building, and Elara exhaled loudly.

Phobos stepped forwards, determination on his face. "Let's do this."

The Hull wasn't so bad when they split everyone's attention four ways. Nancy eyed Romy as she approached the earth girl's table. Her same friends from yesterday surrounded her today.

"The whole knot is braving the Hull today," she said.

Nancy acted blasé, but it was at times like this, when she used Orbito terms, that Romy wondered just how much the other girl knew about the space stations.

Romy caught the twinkling of Nancy's teasing violet eyes. "It helps when we can sit at a table with people that don't stare."

"That *don't* stare, Fred," Nancy hissed at her friend.

Romy followed Nancy's gaze and caught Fred's open-mouthed expression. Looking to see what he was starting at, she held back a grin. Thrym was approaching, arms laden with plates. Fred was obviously in awe of her knot mate. And why not? Thrym was the perfect image of a space soldier: muscled, tall, strong. She jerked her thoughts to a halt.

Thrym slid a plate in front of her. Romy gave a blissful moan at the sight of eggs. Fresh eggs. Not dehydrated, synthetic yuckiness.

"Hate to hear what you sound like on Christmas Day," Nancy muttered.

Fred winked at her. "Don't think I'd mind the sound."

Thrym stiffened.

Romy shoved some eggs into her mouth. "Everyone, this is Thrym."

She gathered from the snorts around the table that the group was aware of just who *Thrym* was. So when Elara and Phobos warily took their seats, Romy didn't bother to introduce them.

The eight teens had smooshed together on the bench to accommodate their four alien guests.

Hushed whispers caught her attention from across the table.

"But they're all at our table."

"And they won't stay if you don't play it cool."

Romy smiled behind her fork and peeked at Phobos when he kicked her. His green eyes were solemn, but she knew the look meant trouble. She narrowed her eyes as he cleared his throat.

"Thrym, did you happen to retrieve my Critamal tooth from the battler?"

Elara choked on her bacon.

Romy tuned him out as Phobos had his fun. Her mind turned to the storage room. She didn't feel safe there anymore, but she didn't want the soldier to win. Leaving meant he would know he'd scared her. If he knew she was scared, his suspicion that she had something to hide would be confirmed.

If he knew she had something to hide, then their alibi would come into question, which was dangerous for her knot.

Not happening.

But it wasn't within Romy to be a complete fool.

Houston was sitting with Tina at the front of the room. She watched as he made to leave, no doubt to begin another long day. Mumbling a quick goodbye, she grabbed her plate and moved to intercept the doctor.

What was more powerful than Lucas? Only one thing that Romy could think of.

Damn, he moved quickly.

"Houston," she called as he reached a cleaning station by the doors

The doctor whirled around on one foot, coat swirling behind him. He stamped his front foot, like it was a dance, and spread his arms wide.

Romy smiled at his oddness. She scraped her plate into the compost bins and slid the dish on top of the dirty pile beside it. "I have a question for you."

"Which I'm happy to answer. But you'll need to walk and talk. Got a dislocated knee to tend to. They always scream so much, half of the time I only snap it back in so they'll shut up." Houston grinned manically at her.

"I think the other half of you does it because you care."

He swung open the door to the Hull. "Perhaps, little skyling, but don't tell anyone. I'll be laughed out of Jimboomba."

"What does that mean?" she puffed. His legs were about the same length as hers, but she nearly had to run to keep up with his stride.

"Jimboomba? Paradise on Earth. Ironic, huh?"

Romy thought of the rivers and ocean, of the red dust and the peaceful vibe. "I don't think it is far off."

"I estimate you have one minute and thirteen seconds to spit out your question."

This wasn't a conversation Romy particularly wanted to be huffing about out in the middle of the settlement. There weren't many people milling around, though, so she dove in with both feet.

"It is a little bit delicate. Could you not repeat this to anyone?"

"I'm a doctor," he replied. "Fifty-one seconds."

That did little to reassure her, considering her knowledge of his past actions. "Uh—okay. Are there any rules here about touching people?" she blurted.

His pace slowed. Romy held a stitch in her side, thankful for the more reasonable pace.

"You will need to be more specific, skyling," Houston said.

She peeked sideways at him, but couldn't tell anything from his expression.

"Well, say if someone wants to touch you. And you don't want them to. But they still want to. And it makes you . . . uncomfortable. Is there a rule against that?"

Houston jerked to a stop. "Romy, there isn't just a rule against that. There's a law."

I knew it, she thought. There was a reason she'd felt so dirty and creeped out when Lucas touched her. It was wrong.

Romy brightened; there wasn't just a rule, there was a law. That would stop the soldier. "Like a Mandate law?" she asked.

"The Mandate is the only law."

"Great!" Everyone here seemed afraid of stepping out of line. "And what is it called? That law?"

"Sexual harassment, or sexual assault," he answered quietly.

She smiled. It made her feel a lot better, having something to use against the man if he returned. "Thanks, Houston." Romy ran up the steps to the archive room.

He called to her, "Wait! Romy!"

She looked back from the top of the stairs. "Yeah?"

"Has someone . . . done something to you?"

Her smile dimmed as she took in Houston's solemn face. But the same thought process whipped through her mind: Houston talking to the

162

soldier; the soldier knowing there was something to hide. Danger for her knot.

She shook her head, recovering a grin.

"No, doctor. Just curious."

* * *

An unusual thing had just happened.

Scanner in one hand, Romy stared down at the document spread over her partially cleared desk. The e-storage hadn't given her any choice in cataloguing the material. Instead, the screen now flashed "CLASSIFIED".

The scrunched paper didn't look like anything special. It was a permit denying a reproduction request from a man called Tony Debranc. Debranc . . . it was a funny name. Romy wondered what country it was from.

She tapped the screen to exit out of the classified tab, but the shining device was frozen. She tapped harder.

Loud footsteps sounded on the three small wooden steps into the building.

Romy stood to attention as three soldiers burst into the room.

"Where is it?" the front man demanded.

Wordlessly, Romy pointed to the table, to the unassuming failed permit. The second soldier stepped to one side. Her mouth dried as she saw the third soldier was Lucas.

"It is scanned?" the same man asked.

She nodded.

The second soldier snatched the document from the table while Lucas moved forwards to Romy's side at the computer. She sucked in a breath. Surely he wouldn't do anything in front of the other soldiers.

She remained coiled as he turned to the device and ran a tag over the screen. Romy peered at the screen from the corner of her eye.

It was only brief. A new screen flashed.

It had categories just like the normal screen. But instead of the usual—construction, legal, environmental options—it read: sentry rosters, posts, weaponry.

She swallowed as Lucas brought up a screen reading, "Authorised to Continue?"

His dark gaze moved over her. "Wouldn't want you reading anything you're not supposed to." The soldier flicked a glance to the two others. One had produced a box, and the document was now incinerating inside.

A hand brushed her chest.

Romy knocked his arm away with gritted teeth, and instead of stepping away, she leant in. His breath was foul, like his teeth were decayed. It suited his personality.

"Don't touch me," she hissed. "I know the law. You can't touch me if I don't want you to. It's sexual assault. So. Back. Off."

He laughed. And Romy rocked back at the genuine, sardonically amused sound.

"Officer Lawry, Officer Meaker. Kindly wait outside while I ask Ms Rosemary a few questions." Lucas spoke over his shoulder without taking his eyes from her.

How could someone so dangerous speak with such politeness?

They left without a word, closing the door of the storage room behind them, and cold sweat ran down her spine.

She gasped as Lucas clutched a fist of her hair so tightly her eyes watered. "Let go!" She reached back and took hold of his hand, attempting to free the strands from the agony of his grasp.

"Sexual assault?" he snarled. "You don't know anything about *sexual* assault." He smirked down at her. "Not yet."

She tried to turn her face away, but his grip in her hair was too firm. She brought her hand down and struck out blindly, connecting with something bony. Pain shot through her wrist.

Lucas grunted and reached for her wildly striking hand. He caught her hand and wound it behind her back. Romy cried out from the pain in her shoulder.

And then the soldier crushed his lips down onto hers. She stood completely trapped, trying to find air to scream. The two officers were just outside the door!

The force was bruising, almost to the degree of drawing blood. Romy screamed into his mouth as he bit hard on her lower lip. The sound was muted. She thrust her head to the side, hearing the snap of her hair ripping free.

It was no use. She was immobilised in his painful grasp.

She couldn't do a thing.

He swept her legs from underneath her, and she landed on her back, with a cry, on the hard wooden floor. The relentless pull on her hair was gone, but he hadn't let go of her arm until the last second and now it was trapped underneath her body. The shoulder shrieked at her to get the limb free and she rolled with a groan, easing her arm from behind her.

The brittle casing of her fear snapped and her breath came fast, eyes wide and trained on him as he lowered himself atop her, trapping both of her wrists with bruising force and pushing them above her head, pinning them to the floor with one hand.

She bucked side to side.

"Mmm," he said. "I like that."

She barely heard the words through her terror. His hand was working the button on the front of her shorts. It was something unlearnt, something in her makeup that told her the worst was coming. Because she had no experience, no idea what Lucas could truly do. But Romy's instincts were telling her that she had to get out of there. She opened her mouth to scream—the sound never made it past the stinging slap from the soldier. Her head lolled to the side and his hand continued its downwards movement. He paused to study her, and Romy hated, *hated* that she was gasping in fear, *hated* that she couldn't move. But at the same time there was nothing she could do to stop it. Her body was reacting beyond her control, fear holding the reins.

"I work outside of the law," Lucas whispered into her chest. "If I want to 'sexually assault' you, no one will stop me."

Horror flooded through her as she realised her grievous mistake. Lucas didn't work for Tina. He worked for someone higher. Lucas worked for the Mandate!

He licked up the side of her face and bile threatened to spill from her mouth.

"We got incoming," one of the officers called from the door.

They know what he's doing and they aren't doing anything to help, she realised.

Lucas's expression was triumphant as he ran a finger across Romy's collarbone, the sensation nearly painful. "You can make this go away if you tell me why you're here. I don't *want* to do these things. But I get a little . . . angry . . . when I don't get answers."

Romy stared straight ahead at his chest, determined that he would not see her cry. Even if her knot had been standing at gunpoint right then, she didn't think she'd be able to meet his gaze. Romy's reply was wooden. She was surprised when her voice didn't betray her panic. "Our knot is here on a research trip."

He gripped her upper arm in a vice-like grip. She yelped in pain.

"Officer Cayne?" came a questioning call.

Romy's eyes filled with shameful, humiliated tears. But they wouldn't fall. Not in front of him.

The grip on her arm disappeared and she whimpered as blood rushed back into the limb.

Lucas strode to the door, gun swinging over his shoulder. He smiled at her demeaned state. "That was your last warning. Next time, I'll follow through on my promise."

Romy twisted away as soon as he disappeared from view. She pressed a fist against her mouth, squeezing her eyes shut. No sobbing. Not until he was gone. Rising on tip-toes, she watched the three soldiers march away. Tears tracked down her face as she finally let out her terror. Dry gasps shook her body in torrents.

Wave after wave passed. And she felt filthy. As though she should wash for days. It took her ten attempts to do up the button of her shorts with fumbling hands.

She just sat there. Sat there until the last bell chimed. And Romy felt calm.

Calm and empty.

Lucas was right about one thing: she hadn't known what sexual assault really was.

The thought of what that man might do to her made Romy sick to her stomach. She looked around the room and stood on shaking legs. Romy was less of a fool than she'd been this morning. Lucas had no qualms about breaking the law.

She sighed. She couldn't stay in this room by herself. It wasn't safe. The matter had gone past the point Romy could deal with. Self-preservation had kicked in.

Lucas would think he'd scared her off with his physical advances. And he had. He was also arrogant enough that he wouldn't expect her to tell anyone.

And she wasn't going to because she suspected his orders came from the top.

But she wasn't going to stick around for him to hurt her, either.

CHAPTER TWENTY

"Are you sure there's nothing I can do here?" Romy asked. The question took on a whining quality. If Houston had no work for her to pretend to do, she didn't know where else to go.

Houston looked between her and Thrym with a baffled expression. "I'm sure," he said slowly. A frown lingered on his brow.

"Is there a problem?"

Romy whirled to find Atlas in the doorway. Did he have some kind of damned Romy radar?

Houston waved a hand at Romy. "Blonde skyling is bored with filing and has crawled back to her first job."

That sounded bad. But it was the gist of what she'd said.

Atlas's eyes darkened. "No."

"You say that a lot," she muttered.

Atlas watched her, grey eyes flicking over her face in consternation. Romy didn't miss the shared glance between Houston and himself.

"You can't keep swapping roles, Rosemary."

She'd had about enough of that. "It's Romy," she snapped. "Use it."

Thrym walked up behind her and rubbed her back. "Ro, what's wrong?"

"What makes you think something is wrong?" Her voice shook. "I'm just bored from being alone in that room."

"The job isn't there to be entertaining. It's there to be done." Atlas's jaw clenched.

Romy hated that he thought her lazy.

His glare was met with her own. She folded her arms.

"Well, can I pick someone to help me at least?" *Safety in numbers*, she thought.

The tall man in front of her was noticeably confused. The urge to tell him was overwhelming. But Lucas's words haunted her. He was above the law. And she could only guess that meant he worked for the Mandate. Atlas and Houston stood no chance against them. Getting them involved would put *them* in danger, as well as Knot 27. Romy's head throbbed painfully.

Atlas was watching her, not answering her question.

"Well?" she repeated in a weak voice.

Houston cleared his throat and Atlas jerked. He clasped his hands behind his back. "I'll see who might be suitable to join you in storage. But it will take me a few days."

Romy's heart sank. Atlas's face flickered at her reaction. A few days? What might Lucas do to her in that time?

Romy didn't uncross her arms as she moved around Atlas to the doorway. She was disappointed she hadn't gotten what she came for: an escape from Lucas. Part of her knew it was unreasonable to be mad at Atlas when he didn't know all of the facts, but the rest of her was deathly afraid for her knot.

And she was learning fear could make you act in ways you never thought possible. She walked out of the room without another word.

Her feet dragged as she approached the storage room. She darted looks around the clearing, hopeless in the knowledge that Lucas wouldn't show his face until she was inside and trapped.

Orange hair caught her attention. *Nancy!*

The girl walked casually across the clearing. Too casually, in Romy's opinion. And she was all alone. Romy knew what that meant.

She raced after her young friend.

Nancy was nearly through the hidden panel in the alleyway when Romy skidded to a halt behind her. Nancy jumped at the sound, hitting her head on the fence.

"Jeez, you flamin' Galah, why'dya do that?"

Romy bent in half. "Can I come?"

Nancy winked. "Got a taste for the guns, right?"

"Right."

Nancy pulled her through the fence. "The others are already rolling. Took me a while to get the dishes done. Come on."

She took off through the trees, and Romy skimmed over the grass, which had been flattened by the car moments before.

Salvation.

At least for another day.

* * *

Romy lay back on the ground after checking for bull ants. She wasn't eager to encounter them after Freya had been bitten five minutes before.

"Does Earth still have koalas?" she asked.

Eddie shook his head, blushing. "N-no, they were classified as extinct last century. Before genetic staples were created."

Romy went blank. "What?"

"You know, they take a staple of the species DNA to clone," Nancy said, rolling her eyes.

"I see." Humans had not only survived global warming, they'd saved some of the at-risk species. Romy tried to keep her face in suitably bored lines, but really the information amazed her.

"They're g-gone for good," Eddie explained.

Nancy laid back and placed an arm over her eyes to shield them from the glaring sun. "They all had chlamydia anyway."

The group laughed. Romy smiled uncertainly.

"What's chlamydia?"

Nancy wrenched upright. "What?" She laughed. "Don't tell me—space soldiers don't get STDs?"

Her mind rang empty. She was unfamiliar with the term. "Not to my knowledge."

Hannah was the first capable of speech. She wiped a tear from her eye. "That's bleepin' priceless."

Romy shrugged, not in the loop whatsoever. It was something she was getting used to. "What other animals were lost?"

"All the cool ones," Freya said. "Elephants, tigers, pandas, emus, lemurs, hippos." She pursed her lips in thought. "Penguins, whales, and dolphins."

"I liked the lemurs." Romy frowned. "But you have some new species too, don't you?"

Nancy scrunched her nose. "Mainly insects. But there are wingos." She caught Romy's expression. "Wolf dingos. Not too weird. The dingo is a wolf anyway."

"There's mutterflies. Moth butterflies. Quite beautiful, but deadly," added Eddie.

Romy's mouth dropped.

"The crows and seagulls have mated with every single bird they can."

"Polar bears are gone. But not before they did the deed with the grizzly bear."

Romy wracked her brain for the name. "Pizzly?"

Freya laughed. "Grolar bear. Pizzly is lame."

It was about as lame as "grolar", but Romy didn't argue the point. She shook her head at the information. "That's amazing." She couldn't wait to tell Phobos.

The others didn't seem impressed.

Nancy brushed away a speck of dirt. "Yeah, whatever, sky girl. I just wish we had a chance to see the other animals before our ancestors killed them off."

"*Yours* didn't," Eddie said to Nancy. Romy wondered what that meant.

"Doesn't matter, in the end," Nancy said brusquely. "They still died like everybody else."

The playful mood was torn away, settling into a heavy glumness. Romy opened and closed her mouth before finally asking, "Was it . . . bad? After The Retreat?"

Nancy turned her head away. They couldn't have been alive 150 years before. But it was still raw, judging from the sudden closing of the group.

Her whole life Romy had blamed the Earth humans—for not appreciating what they'd had, for being greedy and selfish, and careless. She'd even thought that they deserved what they got. She glanced around the circle of teens. Romy could tell from the sole tear trickling down Nancy's face that, no matter the Earth humans' crimes against nature, they had paid for their mistake time and time again.

"Are you guys coming to the settlement festival tomorrow night?" Freya asked shyly, after several minutes of tense silence.

Fred scoffed as he crawled into the car. "Of course they are. Right, Ro?"

Apparently Romy and Fred were on nickname basis now. Romy smiled. "I hadn't heard about it until now."

"We have a celebration for the coming of each new season," Nancy explained.

"Has the season changed?" Romy inquired, looking at the trees.

Nancy answered with a barking laugh. "You can't feel it, but technically the season ends tomorrow. Plus, what Freya really wants to know is if Thrym will be there."

Romy's eyes widened as the other girl punched Nancy hard.

Something dropped inside her. "If our knot goes, I'm sure he'll be there," she said in a hollow voice.

"Would you introduce me?" the red-faced girl asked.

Nancy groaned. "Ugh, stop thinking with your pants, Freya. I swear you're all about boys these days."

"Just because you still want to climb trees like a child, doesn't mean I do!" Freya shot back.

The girls sulked as Romy kept up an awkward conversation with the boys.

"How old are you guys?" she asked Eddie.

"Nancy and me are nineteen," he replied. "The others are seventeen and eighteen. Except—"

"Me." Fred's chest stuck out proudly. "I'm twenty-three. But mentally, I'm thirteen."

A grin played on Romy's lips. When she was out here, it was easy to forget all of her troubles.

"What are you guys doing tomorrow?" she asked carefully.

"Dishes, dishes, dishes," Nancy groaned, coming out of her mood. She whacked her head on her forearms.

"We only get away maybe once a week, if that. Sometimes, in winter, it's once a month." Hannah pouted.

There went her escape plans for tomorrow. Maybe she could go and sit with Deimos. There was no way she was going to that room. And as far as she was concerned, Atlas couldn't make her.

Romy picked some grass. "Tell me more about Earth."

Nancy turned on her side. "What do you wanna hear about?"

She could be subtle about it. Or. . . . "Tell me about the Mandate."

"Take less than you need!" the others chorused before falling into laughing heaps.

Romy smiled. "I've seen that flashing on the screen. What does it mean?"

Freya answered, rolling her eyes. "It's the Mandate's mantra."

"It doesn't even make sense," Nancy grumbled. "Less than you need," she scoffed.

Romy thought about it. It really didn't.

"It was designed to erase our ancestors' mindset that a want was a need," Eddie began. "It's not supposed to make sense. It reminds us that needs like food and water shouldn't be taken for granted, or expected."

Fred pushed Eddie to the ground. "Blah, blah, blah."

That signalled the end of the discussion and the group piled into the car.

Romy didn't talk much on the return. When they got close to the settlement, Eddie cut the engine, and the group hopped out to push the car the rest of the way.

"Why don't you guys just leave the car here?" she asked.

"Patrols would find it," Nancy puffed, straining against the vehicle. "Gotta get it in and out during the middle half hour. They lurk about fifty metres into the tree line. And occasionally fleece the area outside of camp."

She hadn't known there were camp patrols, and Thrym and the others hadn't mentioned them. Their knot could have left, only to be caught in the first few steps!

Sweat rolled down her neck. *Season changing, my butt—it's as hot as ever.* Romy tore off her overshirt to reveal the tight black tank underneath. She wished she hadn't made the last-minute decision to wear three-quarter camo pants instead of shorts.

Eddie and Freya concealed the vehicle with the net. It really did look like a pile of leaves had built up between the fence and the abandoned bungalow. Fred peeked over the fence and one by one they all squeezed out. Romy couldn't help noticing how much easier it was for the three other girls. Her tall frame barely made it through.

Romy pulled away from the others as they reached the clearing. She'd decided to sit on the steps of the storage building to give the illusion she'd been there working all day.

It wasn't to be.

"Where have you been?" A furious voice spoke from her left.

Romy blanched at the six feet, six inches of angry Atlas bearing down on her. Angry was an understatement. He was livid. How long had he been looking for her? Her eyes flicked to Nancy and the others who were stalling, watching her exchange with Atlas.

"I was . . . walking."

His face showed disbelief and contempt. "Walking? All day?" he asked sarcastically.

"Well, I wouldn't say all day," she hedged.

He was wearing a singlet, tucked into black camo pants. The skin on his arms glistened from the unrelenting heat.

"That would have to be the case." His eyes sparked dangerously. "Being as I left in search of you five minutes after our conversation and couldn't find you until now."

He grabbed her shoulder. "I've had everyone out looking for you. Where have you been?"

Romy set her jaw. "I was walking," she repeated. She knew he could tell she was lying. It was her typical weak Romy-lie.

She must have looked Nancy's way one too many times because suspicion lit Atlas's eyes, and he began to turn. She held her breath as the group began to scatter.

Romy waved her hand in front of Atlas's face. "Why were you looking for me?"

He faced her, but blinked at her arm and very slowly grew still. His eyes locked on something. Romy glanced down and couldn't help the loud inhale she took. She stared at the blue-black finger mark bruises surrounding her upper arm.

She shrank, staring at the marks that were quite clearly from a large hand. Dreading what she would see, Romy raised her eyes to Atlas's. Grey eyes were on her, watching. His calloused hand made for her elbow and she flinched away. Hurt flickered in his dark eyes and Atlas's hand fell back to his side.

He regarded her silently and Romy felt like he was just as out of his depth as she was in hers.

"Come with me," he said.

It was nearly dinnertime. Maybe. . . . Her eyes slid to the Hull.

"Now," he ordered.

Romy jumped and glared at him. She glanced around. The settlement was on their way to dinner and she and Atlas had drawn a crowd. With a huff, she strode after the demanding man.

She stormed past Atlas into his office. Romy saw Tina's shocked face for a split second before Atlas slammed the door. She wondered what the woman would make of this conversation.

"Who gave you those bruises?"

Romy untied her shirt and shrugged it back on. "No one."

Atlas wasn't looking her way. His hands were clasped loosely behind his back. He stood like a soldier. Lucas was a soldier. The politics of this place made no sense to her. She didn't know what move to make.

"Do you think covering them makes them go away?" His eyes were like flint. The angriest she'd seen them. "Tell me, or I'll find out myself."

Romy was silent in the wake of his fury. He couldn't help her—not if Lucas worked for the Mandate. She wouldn't dump him in trouble, too.

"Was it Thrym?"

Her mouth dropped open. "What? No!"

Atlas turned on the spot and she was trapped under his gaze. "Then who are you protecting?"

My knot! she wanted to scream. Always her knot. *And you, you fool.*

His frustration grew as she remained mute. "I don't understand, Rosemary. If someone's hurting you, I can help."

Romy swallowed and remained mute. Lucas had more power at his back than the small camp of Jimboomba. Though maybe she should say something, she thought. Maybe Atlas could help her? Her head throbbed; she just wasn't sure about anything.

He circled his desk. "Houston told me about your conversation yesterday."

Hurt rocked through Romy. Houston told Atlas? "He did?" Mortification stung her, but anger quickly overrode it.

Atlas looked a little regretful at revealing the information. "He did. Because he was worried as to why you'd ask those questions in the first place. If anyone has touched you like that . . . I need a name, Rosemary."

She could feel something building in response to the rawness of his voice. Romy tried to choke it back. But all at once, everything—crashing, the changing dynamic of their knot, the soldier, Houston telling Atlas—it was *too much*. "My name is Romy," she shouted.

To her horror, tears began to slide down her cheeks. Thick, childish, stupid tears that made her look like a thick, childish, stupid girl. Why did this have to happen in front of *him*? Romy covered her face—as though that would hide her breakdown.

Atlas approached. His hands hesitantly brushed up her arms. When she didn't move, he enclosed her in his embrace. She'd like nothing more than to tilt her head up. But the knowledge that Atlas was with Tina stopped her.

"Why won't you tell me?" he said hoarsely.

This Atlas she could care for. The one who worried for her, and allowed himself to smile that smile. She could get used to the sight of him in his singlet and camos, hair tousled from where he ran his hands through too often. She could get used to the way his grey eyes clouded over when his worries melted away. She could care for this man and his wry sense of humour. But she couldn't like the other cold man, who ignored her and treated her like a child. The one who hid the truth from her and pushed her away. Which man was he? Romy lingered far too long in his arms before she pulled away. She dropped her hands from her damp face.

"Because I am protecting the people I love," she whispered back.

"I can protect them for you." His earnest eyes tore at her heart.

She shook her head. And realised he wasn't going to let her leave. Romy took two steps back and wiped her tears.

She intended her next words to be harsh, to put him off, but in some ways she meant every word.

"Why would I let you?" she asked. "When I don't know who you really are. . . ."

* * *

174

She'd gone straight to bed after relaying the information about the hourly sentry patrols to Phobos. She heard the others whispering about her once they thought she was asleep. Apparently, even Thrym had been sent out looking for her. Thrym had guessed Romy was with Nancy and the others, but guilt swamped her as she listened to his concerns over her behaviour that morning in Houston's office.

In typical knot fashion, they knew Romy would speak when she was ready. And Romy resolved to do so once they were clear of the settlement. More than ever, she wanted to be away from Jimboomba. Away from Lucas and Atlas, and the gorgeous Tina.

She stomped beside Phobos on the way to breakfast the next morning. Sleep had been elusive and fitful last night. Sensing her disquiet, Phobos grabbed her hand and squeezed it tightly, questioning her with his eyes. Romy shook her head, and he gave her a small smile.

If only Atlas would take a simple hint like that.

Romy gave his hand a quick squeeze and untangled her fingers, seeing that Elara was watching with a small frown. That was all she needed—for the others to think her and Pho were attracted to each other. Honestly, Romy's stomach rolled at the thought, as handsome as Phobos was.

"Deimos said he would meet us at breakfast," Thrym said. "Cover story: he was injured during landing. Shouldn't be hard to stick to, being as it's true."

If anything could have salvaged Romy's day it was this news. It almost made her burst into tears again. This *had* to be hormonal. She'd never cried so much in her life.

Romy skimmed across the floor when she spotted Deimos already sitting at their table.

"Dei!" She kissed his cheek and threw her arms around him. He wrapped his arms around her tightly.

"You all right, lovely?"

Like she was going to spill the plasma to a man just healed from the brink of death. She nodded with a beaming smile. "I am now that you're better."

Deimos suffered through hugs from the rest of the knot. "'Better' would be a comparative term. But I'm out of bed and I've been worse."

Nancy was watching from the table where they usually sat. Excusing herself, Romy approached them.

"We're just eating together today, but I promise we'll be back tomorrow. It's only because Dei is out of hospital," she explained.

Freya's eyes were huge. "I *see* that."

Eddie smiled. "W-what about Thrym?" he asked the girl.

"What about him? Deimos is drop-dead man stuff."

Romy felt the same drop in her stomach as she had when Freya mentioned Thrym yesterday. It made her feel better. For a moment, Romy had thought she might have felt something in return for Thrym. But maybe she just didn't like anyone showing interest in her knot.

Nancy was stabbing at her plate. "Did I ever tell you, you need acting lessons?" She glanced up with raised brows over her violet eyes.

Fred was more obvious. "You told Atlas you were out *'walking'*. Are you serious?"

Romy's cheeks warmed. "I'm not good at lying."

"Is that an enhancement thing?" Freya asked.

Romy shrugged. "Could be." Though Phobos and Deimos never had any problem with it. But then, they were unlike many aboard the orbitos.

Someone was calling her name. She turned to see Houston jogging towards her.

"Romy. Glad I caught you." Houston waved her over to one side.

Anger flared within Romy. She hadn't forgotten Atlas's slip. Houston had told on her, plain and simple.

"How could you tell him?" she asked when they were out of the Hull.

Houston sighed, taking off his glasses. For the first time since she'd met him, the lively doctor appeared as weary as his long hours should make him. It made her irritation grow.

"I trusted you." She frowned.

The man looked at his feet. "I'm sorry. But my duty as a doctor is to keep people safe. Even from themselves. You were asking questions about sexual harassment. For all I knew, you'd been *raped.*"

Finally a word for what Lucas threatened her with. Rape. The word was just as disgusting as the man himself.

"Was I supposed to ignore that? Would you have wanted me to ignore it if, say, Elara, had come to me?"

Romy looked into his tired eyes, deflating with the mention of Elara.

"No. But I wish you would have gone to someone else, Houston. Now Atlas thinks I'm an idiot."

Long, thin fingers tilted her chin upwards. "I can assure you he doesn't."

Romy fell silent.

Houston replaced his glasses. "And seeing as you won't tell anyone who the dog is, I need to ask you an uncomfortable question."

Romy nodded and swallowed.

"Have you been raped?"

She avoided his gaze. Her knot was watching through the window of the Hull. Why had Houston decided to have this conversation here? Away from Atlas? Away from Tina? Or was it just coincidence?

"No."

Houston continued. "Whatever it is you won't tell me about, I want you to know none of it is your fault. It is theirs, not yours. *Never* yours."

She blinked rapidly and cleared her throat. She didn't trust her voice not to crack.

"If you wish to talk more about this, my door is always open." Houston's tone was decisive. "And Atlas has found other tasks for you to do, to assist him. Away from the storage room."

Joy and confusion simultaneously competed for first place.

"Why?"

Houston smiled. "You're asking me why Atlas does the things he does?"

Romy laughed louder than she normally would at such a statement. A by-product of the tense nature of the conversation.

Houston dipped his head down to catch her attention. "And I *am* sorry."

Romy reached across and squeezed his shoulder. "I know."

She forgave him. But she wouldn't forget.

The doctor nodded. And somehow Romy gathered that he knew she wouldn't be telling him any more secrets.

"Then Atlas expects you directly after breakfast. You will go directly to jail, you will not pass GO, and you will not collect two hundred dollars."

Romy gave him a puzzled glance.

Houston let out a manic cackle and strolled away.

CHAPTER TWENTY-ONE

"You have things for me to do?" Romy asked quietly.

The door to Atlas's secluded office was sitting open for the first time in weeks. Romy hovered by the entrance.

Atlas took a few seconds to answer, wiping his hands across the projections in front of him. What in all of space was he doing?

"Rosemary."

Romy ground her teeth together. Top on her agenda was keeping her temper in check with the elusive man for as long as possible. She would not ask him questions, she would not kiss him, and she would not cry in front of him. Romy was going to be civil.

"You requested my presence, sir." Romy stood to attention. Two could play that game.

He narrowed his eyes at her reply and stood from his desk.

"Has anyone ever told you, you can be fiercely stubborn?"

She pressed her lips together, refusing to voice a sarcastic response. Why was he so infuriating?

"I have a job for you," he continued. "You may have noticed the extra bustle today. It's because there's a festival tonight."

"Yes, N— Uh, yes, I heard." Mentioning Nancy's name wasn't a good idea.

A half-smile graced his face for a fleeting moment.

"You can sort out the seating arrangements for the meal."

Romy wrinkled her nose. "What? Why? Can't people just sit anywhere?"

Atlas ran his hand through his dark hair. "You would think. However, there are politics in any place. Everyone gets on, but no one gets on."

"That makes no sense."

His lips quirked.

She approached and took a pile of papers from him. "Is this what you do in here all day?" she asked doubtfully. "Worry about festivals and guest lists?"

Another smile curved his full lips. "No. Not quite. Tina supplied this as I had nothing for you to do."

"Then what do you do?" The question hung between them and she winced as his eyes turned away. An awkward silence strained between them.

Romy glanced down at the pile in her hands, blurting, "Wouldn't a list suffice?"

"Tina thought not." Atlas turned back to his desk space. "I'll need you to work down the hall, in the debrief room."

That must be the room with all the tables and chairs, she realised. *Translation: I don't want you to see what I'm doing.*

Her anxiety immediately spiked. She knew Lucas was in and out of this building with Tina all the time. And if Tina had given Atlas the papers, Lucas might know where Romy was working for the day.

Romy still wasn't sure about Tina's involvement. But Lucas Cayne might not be working alone.

"I'll be leaving my door open."

She looked up. "Huh?"

Atlas watched her closely. "I said, my door will be open. You can keep your door open, too. I'll hear if you call for me."

I will hear if you scream. "Okay."

He circled back around the desk, drawing near until he was close enough to reach out and brush a thumb across her cheek. "Will you call for me if anything is wrong?"

Would she call for Atlas if Lucas touched her again?

"Yes." Romy doubted there would be a choice. Lucas had told her he was done with threats.

He twirled a piece of her white-blonde hair around his fingers. "Your hair has grown."

A folder slid off the stack she held. Paper erupted across the floor. Atlas crouched down and studied one of the documents.

"It looks like you'll be having an exciting day." He snorted. "Just don't sit me next to Mrs Stewart."

"Who's she?"

Atlas shuddered. "You don't want to know."

* * *

Hours later, Romy stared at the wall. It had to be midday, but there was no way she was going to lunch. How was it possible that seating arrangements were so hard? She certainly wouldn't have thought it. But then she started on the pile—after reading Tina's note.

Read these.
Put the names on the tables.
Don't screw it up.
— Tina

Thomas Maloney had ruined Maurice Lawrence's best shirt last year.

Sandra Gates had been engaged to Roger Downs, who then got married to Rita Sheppard.

How much drama can one settlement have?

Every time Romy arranged the names in a particular order, she would find a table that simply didn't work.

She slumped in her chair and groaned dramatically.

"Hmm, that won't do."

Romy yelped and darted from her chair. She held a hand to her chest. "Houston, you scared me."

Houston was studying the arrangement of names she had spread out on the floor. "Griffins don't like Slats, and Stewarts don't like Maloneys."

Heart rate returning to normal, Romy found she actually appreciated his advice. She switched a few of the names and awaited approval.

"That would be nice, but the Maloneys don't like Griffins."

"Really?" she exploded. "Is there no way to keep everyone happy?"

Houston held his glasses in place. "Ah . . . probably not. But I would say that's the point."

Romy frowned. "What?"

"Toodles," he called out. "Oh, and don't sit me next to Tina."

Returning to her slumped sitting, Romy wondered if Tina had given her this task because she deemed it impossible. Romy would have understood Tina simply passing on the task because it sucked. But now Romy had something to prove.

* * *

A gentle shaking drew her from sleep. She moaned and blinked the blurriness from her vision. A familiar chuckle sounded. Romy bolted upright, brushing off a paper that was stuck to her cheek.

Thrym stood in front of her.

"Tiring work?" he asked.

Romy glared at him and then at the unfinished seating arrangements. "I challenge you to do this stuff without falling asleep."

Thrym held up his hands.

"What's the time?" She yawned with a crack of her jaw.

180

"Four o'clock."

Romy jumped up. "Comets! What time does the festival start?"

"In an hour," he replied calmly.

She circled the names on the floor, ignoring Thrym's sniggers. "It's not funny! The Griffins don't like the . . . Slats. And I don't think the Maloneys like *anyone*."

"It's kind of funny," Thrym said.

Romy marched up to him, and he backed away behind a table.

"Easy, Ro. All I know is someone is going to be unhappy. Just accept it and move on. You can't please everyone. Plus, Nancy wants you to find her once you're done. You and Elara are getting ready with her, Freya, and Hannah."

"But I don't want anyone to be unhappy."

"I know. You're literally the worst person for this job."

She glared murder at him. "Thanks." Maybe she could just add another table. Tina's words—*Don't screw it up*—echoed in her mind.

But Houston and Thrym had both said that someone would be unhappy. To achieve the task, did she have to admit that the task was unachievable? On some petty level, was Tina just toying with her?

Romy's eyes alighted on Houston's name, next to Atlas's. A mischievous thought entered her mind. And as she rearranged names, Romy didn't notice Thrym watching her sadly for a long moment before he left.

Furiously scribbling down the names on the backside of a paper, she collected the cards and ran out of the room.

Atlas may have called her as she ran past, but Romy ignored him and she ran down the steps.

And stopped.

Because the clearing had been transformed.

Lanterns hung from ropes, surrounding the dusty clearing and criss-crossing overhead. It wasn't dark enough for them to be lit, but their bright colours were beautiful. Some of the Hull tables had been dragged out for the occasion and bright tablecloths decorated them, along with candles and rustic decorations.

How did this all happen in the space of a day?

"I've been looking all over for you!" A scowl marred Nancy's face, and she stomped towards Romy, flanked by Freya and Elara.

"Don't ask. Just help." Romy spread out the cards and her list. "I need these names put in this exact order on the tables. *Exactly*."

"Ooo, stern Ro. I likey." Elara picked up the top cards and scrutinised the list.

With four of them it didn't take long to get the names in position. It took Romy a further ten minutes to double check. She'd done what she could. Romy would have to hope the Griffins didn't mind the Stewarts. Or whatever.

Elara came to her side. "It looks like your day was even worse than mine."

Romy frowned at her friend. "What happened?"

She looked around and bowed her head. "I think the head engineer caught me checking out his nanopad."

"Why were you looking at it in the first place?"

"I'm trying to understand the sentry rotations. It's hard because I only work during the day, and they switch up the one we drive out to every shift."

Her friend was freaking out.

"Ellie," Romy said calmly, "we'll figure it out. The main thing is laying low. Do you think the engineer is suspicious?"

Elara nodded. "He's keeping an eye on me now."

Poacher poop. This was bad. "You need to do everything right until he backs off. Don't ask any more questions."

Elara scrunched her delicate nose and rolled her eyes. "Well, duh."

Freya stamped up to them. "Seriously. We have like twenty minutes to get ready."

The girls ran to a homestead down the way, and Romy tried to draw Elara away from the worry that pinched her eyebrows and mouth.

Nancy's abode was close to the garage where the knot had first awoken. And it was tiny. It looked like it was only one room.

"Don't you live with your family?" Elara asked.

Nancy was digging through her closet, but Romy could see her body stiffen from where she sat on the unmade bed.

"They're all dead," she said shortly.

Elara's mouth formed an O and she shot Romy a panicked look.

Romy spoke quietly. "That's terrible, Nancy. I'm so sorry."

Elara echoed her sentiments.

Freya barged in with an armful of clothing, Hannah trailing behind her. "There!" she declared proudly.

The five girls looked down at the pile of nondescript dresses.

"I dunno," Nancy said dubiously.

Freya tossed her long silken hair. "Nancy, no offence, but your clothes suck kookaburra droppings."

"Probably because I'm not trying to attract the whole settlement."

"You act like you're not interested, but you totally are."

"Where do we start?" Elara asked loudly.

Romy exhaled, throwing her knot mate a thankful glance.

Freya tapped her bottom lip in thought, surveying the pile and the girls on either side of her. Suddenly she clapped her hands in glee.

". . .I've got it."

CHAPTER TWENTY-TWO

Romy tugged down the dress as it rode up *again*.

Tight and white.

Her dress fit both bills.

After several wasted attempts at argument, the four girls submitted to Freya's every whim. As a result, Romy's bob-length hair was braided into a wispy arrangement encircling her head. She'd been handed a razor and was rudely told to "deal with her bush-pig legs".

Elara found this hilarious until she was told to do the same.

Romy estimated she had six cuts on her legs, but she couldn't stop touching the smoothness. The short amount of time she'd spent on Earth had given her skin a golden hue, and dare she say it, Romy thought the colour contrasted nicely with the bright whiteness of her borrowed dress. She felt pretty. And even though she knew she shouldn't wish it because of Tina, Romy hoped Atlas was impressed.

Elara, Freya, Hannah, and Nancy were all in white dresses too. Freya was adamant that having a theme was the "in" thing. Nancy's orange hair was swept back in a high ponytail and the bottom of her mid-thigh dress waved out in pleats. Elara's hair was out, but Freya had added a clip on one side. Romy though her friend was always beautiful, but the sleeveless white stretchy dress Elara wore hugged the soft curves of her body. Tonight, her friend was a willowy goddess.

Romy was excited to be dressed up with her new friends and knot mate, but each step she took towards the decorated clearing in her slip-on shoes had her chest tightening.

A small hand slipped into hers. "Don't worry about the seating plan." Elara rolled her eyes. "So like you to fret over something stupid like that."

The seating plan! Romy had forgotten all about that. She grinned, remembering the change she'd made so everyone would be happy. Well, *nearly* everyone.

"Dei!" Elara squealed.

Romy spun around and saw the rest of her knot getting drinks. They were all there. All the people she loved, safe and together for the moment.

She skipped over to Deimos and reached up to put her arms around his neck. "Dei, you're out?"

"For a while. Until I get tired. Had to practically sell my soul before Dr H. would let me come."

Romy felt fingers at her thighs and glanced at Phobos, who was trying to tug her dress down to cover her legs.

"Where's the rest of your dress?" he demanded.

Elara burst out laughing and Romy joined in. She noticed that while Phobos seemed concerned with how high *her* dress was, he didn't mention Elara's.

And Elara certainly found the short-sleeved, navy shirt Phobos was wearing interesting, especially where it pulled over his biceps, though she didn't spare a glance at Deimos.

Deimos was looking between Elara and Phobos. He arched a dark brow at Romy. She shrugged.

He turned to scrutinise the pair a bit more, a grimace on his face. Romy sighed in relief, glad she wasn't the only one weirded out by how they were acting.

Thrym held out a drink to her. She took it with a smile.

"Ro, you look. . . ."

"Ridiculous?" she supplied, sipping from her cup.

"Stunning," he breathed.

Her cheeks grew warm at his reverent tone. And she felt Deimos's eyes on *them*. Romy cleared her throat, wiping the back of her palm against her lips. "Thanks." No way was she going to look at Thrym right now.

"Rosemary, my flower, would you care for a stroll amongst the lanterns?" Deimos bowed before her and she giggled as he dragged her away.

He waited approximately five seconds. "What the hell is going on?"

It was like a dam burst inside of her. The burning in her chest was almost painful as she realised how much she'd missed Deimos. "You know those pesky things called hormones?" she started.

Deimos spun her to face him. Romy's eyes flicked down. A white bandage stuck up over the neckline of his woven shirt. His intelligent green eyes sparkled. "Yes," he said in a low voice. "They're . . . hormonal for each other?"

Romy tucked away her smile. "Well, I don't know really. They alternate between being angry and confused. I'm not sure if it's attraction, or just a change in their relationship."

Deimos's face screwed up, reflecting exactly how Romy felt about the matter. "Sick!" he yelled.

Romy covered his mouth with her hand, laughter hovering on the edge of her lips. "Shh."

Deimos was shaking his head in denial. "Uh-uh, there's no way."

A lump formed in her throat. "Dei?" she said. The handsome man she deemed a brother peered down at her. "I'm so glad you're back."

He pulled her in for another tight hug. "No doubt. Especially with the way Thrym is looking at you."

Romy winced. "That bad?"

"Kind of like you're chocolate cake."

Romy gripped his arm. "What do I do about it?"

The pair looked at each other in bafflement.

"I'm pulling up blank," Deimos admitted, "but I'll put my mind to it. Don't know why he's so fixated on you, with all the pretty girls around. I mean you're hot, Ro—no doubt. But you're hot in a 'touch my sister and I end your life' kind of way."

Romy's eyes lit with mirth. "Thanks. I think."

"Who is *that*?" he breathed. Romy followed his line of sight to Tina.

"That's Tina. She doesn't like me."

Deimos immediately turned his eyes to an exotic dark-skinned girl in an orange dress.

Romy rolled her eyes and pushed him towards the woman, turning back to her friends as others from the settlement began to take their seats. Phobos held out her chair, and she focused on tugging down her dress. She scanned the tables and couldn't notice any discontent. *Take that, Tina.*

"Don't worry so much." Thrym smiled, patting her hand.

Romy saw Houston moving to take his seat. "Oh, I'm not worried," she mumbled.

She exploded with laughter as the doctor sat down next to Tina.

"That's just cruel." Elara winked at Romy nevertheless.

Romy laughed even harder when Houston picked up the card on his other side and blanched.

The food and drink were the same as usual. But eating outside with the lanterns and open air made it seem special somehow. Romy sighed.

"This is what I thought Earth would be like," she whispered to Thrym. She placed her napkin on her cleared plate.

Thrym nodded thoughtfully. "I don't think I ever had any expectations. It never crossed my mind that we'd get here in this life cycle. So I didn't think about it."

Such a Thrym thing to say. She smiled. "I can understand that. It's wonderful, but . . ."

". . . Bitter?"

Romy smiled. "Yes. Bittersweet. Better now that Dei is back. I didn't realise how much his absence has affected me."

Music was starting up from the stairs of the offices. She glanced up and spotted Atlas shifting tables away to clear space for dancing. Romy knew about dancing. She'd read about it in fairy tales.

She played with a strand of hair as she watched Atlas. He was so. . . . Romy wasn't sure of the word to use. Appealing? She wanted to run her hands across his shoulders—which were currently covered by a crisp white shirt. The sleeves were rolled up, and he wore black trousers, without the multitude of pockets for once. His hair was the same tousled mess. It was obvious he didn't care one iota about his appearance. It looked like he'd paused long enough to exchange one set of clothing for another—and the result was entirely distracting.

A finger closed her mouth. Romy blinked sideways into Thrym's impassive face. His blue eyes were icy. She looked past him and saw Houston heading towards their table.

"Gotta go. Delay Houston for me." She whipped out of her chair and headed in the opposite direction, drawn towards the dancing.

There didn't seem to be any form to it. Young and old alike moved in the space, throwing out their arms, twirling, and stamping their feet in random order. She smiled as she caught sight of Freya shaking her butt in the air.

"That wasn't nice of you."

Romy shivered as a low voice brushed close by. She craned her neck to the left to confirm it was Atlas.

It was. And he was entirely too close for her peace of mind.

"W-what?" She licked her lips.

"Seating Houston between Tina and Mrs Stewart."

"No. It wasn't nice!" Houston stamped up beside Atlas.

Romy held back her grin, with effort. "I believe it was you who told me I couldn't please everyone." She shrugged. "I just took your advice."

Houston was dressed in a bright-coloured shirt with an unusual print. "I specifically told you I didn't want to be next to dragon bitch."

Romy squeaked in the effort to restrain her laughter in front of Atlas. She had to say he didn't seem too upset with the doctor insulting Tina. "You did mention that. It was very helpful."

"But how did you know to put Mrs Stewart on my other side?" he asked.

Romy peeked between her lashes at the man beside her.

Houston stabbed Atlas in the chest. "You?" He rubbed his finger after.

Atlas grinned. "I just told Rosemary I didn't want to be next to her," he said, with a glance at Romy. She lifted a brow.

"Why did you listen to him and not to me?" Houston exploded.

Romy laughed. He really was worked up over this. "Well, you were already in my bad books. And—"

"And Atlas is a prime mating partner," he finished.

"No, that's not—" Her face flamed. She avoided looking anywhere near Atlas.

Houston's eyes glinted in the growing moonlight. "Payback, little skyling. Gotta go. Enjoy."

"I don't know what he's talking about." Romy turned to Atlas, still not looking straight at him.

Atlas's brows rose high. "You don't think I'm a prime mating partner?"

His half-smile was back. She eyed him suspiciously and sniffed. "No. I don't."

Atlas laughed. "Feisty."

She secretly savoured the sound, her heart stopping as Atlas reached a hand around her waist and drew her in to his side. She leant in to him, hesitantly, inhaling his eucalyptus smell.

"I've decided I'm not leaving you alone tonight," he said conversationally.

Romy frowned. "As if that were your choice."

The kitchen workers were lighting the lanterns now that the last rays of daylight were fading. The lantern above them illuminated Atlas's grin. His eyes were the gentlest she'd ever seen them.

"Seeing as most of the men in this camp are staring at you, I think it best."

She tugged on her dress. "No they're not." She reached a hand up to her hair.

Atlas stopped the motion with his own hand. "Yes. They are. You look surreal." His eyes burned into hers. He touched her hair as though afraid to mess it up. "It looks like you're wearing a halo with the light above you."

Warmth flowed in her chest. She smiled shyly up at him. He returned it, not embarrassed in the slightest, and straightened after a long beat. The distance pulled a nagging thought to the fore. He was still holding her hand. She held up their clasped hands.

"Won't Tina mind this?" she asked.

Surprise lit his face. "Why would she?"

Romy stared at the dancers. "Someone told me you two were involved. I don't want to cause a rift." She desperately wanted to cause a rift. Her feelings were now involved well past the point of decency. She was a horrible person, she'd decided.

"We were involved. It's over. It was never anything serious," he explained.

Jealousy flared. So there *was* history there. She knew it. And despite his assurances, she didn't believe Tina was as okay with the end of the relationship as he was. After listening to Nancy and her gang gossip, Romy was aware of the type of relationships that occurred in the settlement.

"And what about Thrym?" Atlas asked, drawing her back.

Romy stiffened as she realised what he'd said.

"What? You can ask about mine, but I can't ask about yours?"

She fidgeted. "That's because there hasn't been anyone. And . . . Thrym. He's just my friend. My best friend."

"He wants more than that."

"I know. It's just a phase."

Atlas hummed, and she didn't know what to make of the sound.

"I don't feel that way about him," she added, turning towards the band.

Phobos was on the dance floor, jabbing his elbows in jerky motions.

"And what about Deimos?"

Romy crossed her arms. "No. And not Phobos either. They're like my brothers, Atlas." She stepped out of his embrace. "I don't want to talk about this anymore."

The mysterious man reached out and uncrossed her arms. Romy let him. *Damn his handsome face.*

His eyes slid to the dance area and he raised an eyebrow in question.

She looked at the dance floor and felt the drumming beat of the music. Smiling in permission, she followed Atlas into the throng of Earth humans.

CHAPTER TWENTY-THREE

$\bigwedge$ few swaying couples remained on the dance floor, but the majority of the settlement was drifting off to their bungalows, worn out from hours of eating and talking. Knot 27 sat at their table along with Nancy and Eddie, not making much conversation, just relaxing in that stupor between wake and sleep.

A loud honking noise disrupted the peace. Thrym groaned, blinking sleepily.

"He does this every festival," Nancy grumbled.

Romy winced at another squeaking shrill in the air.

Houston had his mouth to a long wooden instrument. The band had actually trailed to a stop behind him, but the doctor didn't seem to care. Romy giggled, watching as Atlas made his way to intercept the drunken doctor. Though the rest of them looked half asleep, Atlas remained alert and upright.

"What is that awful sound?" mumbled Deimos. Romy was surprised how long he'd lasted tonight. If Houston wasn't so intoxicated he would have given the twin his marching orders hours ago.

Nancy chuckled sleepily. "The didgeridoo sounds beautiful when it's played properly. Houston just sucks."

"He's had too much to drink." Eddie shifted.

"No," Nancy disagreed. "He sucks when he's sober, too."

Eddie rubbed his eyes. "I a-actually think h-he's a little better when he's pissed."

Elara snorted, wiping away a few tears of mirth.

"How long have they been here? Atlas and Houston?" Deimos asked the teens.

Nancy shrugged. "They come and go. Usually they only stay a couple of weeks. But with you guys here I guess they've extended it."

Her knot was silent.

Deimos continued. "And what is it Atlas actually does?" He jerked as Phobos kicked him under the table.

"T-Tina says it's classified and we're better not to notice it if we know what's good for us," Eddie said.

So Knot 27 weren't the only ones in the dark.

Romy still had her eyes on Atlas. Before she knew what she was doing, her chair was pushed back and her feet were leading her to the stage. To him.

He was glaring at Houston.

"You don't like his playing?" Romy asked.

Atlas quirked an eyebrow at her obvious amusement. "Would you rather he continued?"

She pretended to think hard before smiling up into his grey eyes.

The lanterns still burned overhead. And past their dim light, the stars twinkled far above. There were so many of them. It was one thing Romy loved down here—the stars. They were lost when you lived among them. Stars didn't look so good through high-powered telescopes—not pretty and sparkling like they did from here.

A woman was screaming with laughter from the dance floor.

Dragging her eyes to the sound, Romy was surprised to see who the noise came from.

Tina appeared to be nearly as drunk as Houston.

The drop-dead gorgeous woman wavered on her little feet. Why did she have to be so tiny?

Atlas called to two nearby soldiers. "Officers, please escort Ms. Lyons to her room."

That was when Romy found out that although the woman was small, she was not weak. Tina planted her feet, barking at the two soldiers when they neared her. The dancers weaving on the floor halted to watch the ruckus. This was one of their camp leaders. Romy could see their shocked looks.

Atlas searched for and held her gaze. "I need to sort that out." He sighed.

Romy realised it was funny how she could laugh like she meant it, even as her stomach fell to her feet. "Okay," she forced out. *There isn't anyone else who can do it?*

"You sure?"

"I'm sure. It's probably best." She wished he'd see through her words.

Atlas kissed her cheek and Romy stopped breathing as his warm breath blew over her skin. "I'll be back soon. Stay here."

He strode across the dance floor, rolling up his sleeves. Romy's eyes devoured the simple motion.

Tina stopped screaming immediately and the two soldiers stepped aside, relief evident on their faces.

"You'll need to carry me, At-a-lus," Tina drawled.

Romy ground her teeth together. Atlas sighed and gripped the mahogany beauty by the arm. For a few steps, it worked. But after two near-faceplants Atlas swept her up, trudging off through the bungalows.

Holding Tina in his arms.

Romy returned to the table with her friends.

Disquiet settled in her stomach and made her regret making it easy for him to leave. Romy didn't even know where Atlas slept. How would she know if he kissed Tina or something?

She rested her head against the back of the chair and stared up to where she knew the orbitos sat high in space. A part of her wished to be up there, oblivious, sniggering while Deimos and Phobos got in trouble, and Thrym yelled at them, or exchanging an exasperated look with Thrym as Elara took too long to get ready for a debris clean-up. Earth was causing her to feel so much all at once. It was overwhelming, and a lot of it wasn't pleasant and simple like the life she'd led before.

Deimos was first to leave. He stumbled over to awaken Houston from where he'd fallen asleep sitting forwards with his face smooshed into the didgeridoo.

Elara and Phobos stood to leave next and Romy made to stand with them, but Thrym gripped her hand, warning in his eyes. Swallowing, she looked at the pair, noticing the tension between them for the first time. *Oh.*

"They need to talk." Thrym whispered low in her ear, causing a shiver to work its way down her spine.

"Night," Elara yawned.

She swept down to give Romy a kiss on the cheek, and Romy concealed her relief at Thrym's timely warning. That would've been an awkward-ass walk to the bungalow while the two were fighting, or ignoring each other, or watching each other. Romy didn't want to know.

Until. . . .

"And so do we." Thrym's soft voice washed over her.

Her spine snapped into place as trepidation eliminated any trace of fatigue. "What?" she stalled weakly.

Thrym watched her intently, fingers thrumming on the table.

"I'm actually pretty tired," she hedged, moving to rise. Walking with Phobos and Elara was looking less awkward by the second.

"I think I love you." The words were levelled at her, delivered in Thrym's straightforward way.

All the tension drained away as dismay took its place. Romy froze, staring into his blue eyes, which were focused on her. Waiting for her to answer. The words rang in her mind, echoing through her.

"I love you too, Thrym," she said kindly, wincing horribly on the inside.

"Thank you. But you know that's not what I mean."

Romy slid back into her seat. "I don't—"

Thrym's hand clenched on the table. "And part of me hates it because I know it weirds you out. I know when I stare at you and want you, you're creeped out because you can't see me as anything but a brother."

"Thrym, that's not true."

His blue eyes softened. "It is. And I wish I could make you see me as something else. That you could love me in return, the way I love you."

She opened and closed her mouth, unsure of what to say.

"And what's more, you're *infatuated* with a man you don't even know."

Irritation bubbled. "I do know him," she retorted.

"What's his last name? Where is he from? How did he get here? What does he do? Why does he disappear into that locked room three times a day?"

Her mouth dried. "He does?" Atlas was going into the fourth office that often?

Thrym shook his head. His black hair—usually shaved—was the longest Romy had ever seen it. "Yes. And that just proves my point."

A lump formed in Romy's throat. She squeezed her eyes shut. "No," she whispered. "It doesn't." She struggled to find the words to voice her true sentiment. "I can't help the way I feel about him. Even if it is a mistake that I may regret. But I know that right now, I don't feel that way about you. I only see him."

He winced.

"And even if I didn't, I couldn't see you in that way."

It sounded like a garbled mess of words to Romy.

Thrym looked up at the night sky, his dark skin illuminated by the moonlight. He truly was handsome. Just not for her.

"Do you understand that I think you are so beautiful it breaks my heart to look at you?" he whispered.

Her breath caught and unbidden tears sparked her eyes.

He continued. "And it's because when I look at you, I see *you*: the Romy I have always known. The one I would share anything with." He looked down at his hands. "The one I respect. I didn't feel this for you on Orbito One; I couldn't. But relationships change. You might not want this now.

But soon, when we are away from here, from him, you could change your mind."

Romy shook her head. But Thrym stopped her with a finger on her lips. The action alone shocked her enough to stop whatever she was saying.

"I don't want you to say anything more. My feelings will not change. So if yours do. . . ." He trailed off, his meaning evident.

He licked his lips. "But there's one thing I want to ask you."

Foreboding sank into Romy's bones.

"If nothing ever happens between us, then that's your choice. But, I just want to kiss you once. Just one time."

During their conversation, Thrym had already moved closer. His face was still directly in front of hers.

Romy didn't think it was a good idea. But guilt twisted her gut, side by side with annoyance that Thrym had asked her in the first place, knowing it would make her uncomfortable. Her knot mate moved closer, and she shook her head as he tilted her chin.

"No—"

It was a quick kiss—long enough, though, that Romy had time to analyse the taste and texture of him. Something she hadn't ever wanted to do. And for some reason, she felt like it was her fault. Maybe she should have said no straightaway . . . but she'd been thinking! He hadn't given her time to answer.

Was silence an answer? Romy didn't think so.

She stood slowly and glared down at Thrym.

He was gasping. "Ro. I'm sorry. I just had to. Just once. You have no idea how much I've dreamed of that moment."

She stepped away from him, trembling with rage, regret, hurt—all balled up in one confusing mess. "I'm glad you got what you wanted."

Romy strode off, leaving Thrym alone in the empty clearing.

CHAPTER TWENTY-FOUR

Romy didn't want to go back to their bungalow—Thrym would go there. Screaming was what she really wanted to do. In reality, though, she paced in front of some random house, hoping she wasn't disturbing the people inside.

It wasn't just the kiss with Thrym. It was that Atlas never came back.

Thrym said he wanted Romy because of who she was. Was he implying that Atlas just wanted her because of . . . what? She kicked up some red dust. It just made her angrier—not satisfying enough to relieve her fury. Nor her doubt.

Romy pulled up short with a sigh. The night had become chilly and she rubbed her arms for warmth.

She was wide awake now, reliving that perfect moment before Atlas left the festival. Why couldn't the night have ended there? After staring up at the stars for a long beat, Romy decided there was no chance of sleep for her tonight. She had to see Atlas. Maybe it was pathetic, but she needed him. Because—and this was the main source of her misery—she might have just lost her best friend.

She crept back to the clearing, grateful to find Thrym gone. The dance floor and tables were abandoned. Most of the lanterns had gone out. She had no idea where Atlas slept, but there was one place she could check. If he wasn't there, then she'd go to Nancy's and sleep on the ground.

She wasn't going back to her knot tonight. It was the first time she'd ever contemplated sleeping without them.

As she weaved between the tables, Romy saw Atlas's office door was ajar, and a thin stream of light filtered outside into the darkness of the entranceway. She could just glimpse the door to the surgery, and to Tina's room, while the locked room was shrouded in shadows.

Her heart beat loudly in her ears and she placed a palm on his door. It opened with a soft creak and she saw him at the window, his face expressionless.

He'd watched her cross the clearing.

"It's not safe to wander around at night." His tone was bland.

"I wanted to see you."

He didn't turn from the window. "I wonder at your self-preservation sometimes." He was angry.

"Should a space soldier possess self-preservation?"

A ghost of a smile hinted on his face. Then it faded. "You're no longer a space soldier."

"No." She rested her head against the frame. "I guess not." She didn't know if she even had a knot anymore.

Atlas didn't respond. She didn't know if he'd heard.

"Is Tina okay?" she asked.

Atlas finally turned to her. "Right now, she's fine. Tomorrow she'll have the hangover of her life."

"Oh."

His lips curled. "Oh? And should I ask if things were resolved between you and the boy?"

She frowned. "Don't called Thrym a boy. And . . . I'm not sure."

Atlas halted. "And that means?"

Romy looked at her shoes. "It means he told me a few things. And then . . . kissed me. And I'm not sure if we're friends anymore."

"Ah." A thumb brushed across her cheek, catching an escaped tear. "I saw."

Heat stole through her face. "You did?" He'd seen the whole thing? And after she'd been so adamant nothing was happening between her and Thrym.

His jaw ticked. "These things happen to us all. Unrequited love. He's young; he'll get over it. And you will be friends still."

Romy sighed and stepped forwards into his warmth. "I hope so."

His arms enclosed her. "And you are beyond tired. Things will present more clearly after you rest."

She shivered as his hot skin brushed against hers. "Wise Atlas?" she murmured.

"More-Earth-experience Atlas," he said. "I've, uh, had a few relationships. And someone close to me always says sleep makes things better."

"A friend?" She pressed closer still, wrapping her arms around him, feeling the firmness of the muscles in his back as she did so.

". . . My mother."

She pulled back and saw his mouth had pressed into a thin line. Her curiosity would drive her mad, but the look on Atlas's face told her he wouldn't open up any more. "I don't want to go back to my bungalow," Romy said instead.

Atlas relaxed. "The longer you leave these things, the worse they fester."

"I know. Just not tonight. C-could I stay with you?"

He gazed at her for a while, smoothing a wispy piece of her hair back in place, before nodding. "Do you need me to carry you, too?"

Romy laughed and shoved him.

He echoed the sound and grabbed her by the hand, leading her through the back of the offices. They passed out of the building down the hospital end. Romy didn't know anyone lived out back here and she said as much to him.

"Just me and Houston," was the short reply.

It made her nervous for some reason, or perhaps it was the fact she'd just realised she'd be alone with Atlas for an entire night.

Atlas paused at the door. "Nothing will be happening here except sleep."

Something inside Romy relaxed. "Good."

Atlas grimaced at the relief in her voice. "That could make a lesser man doubt himself."

She grinned. "Sorry."

The inside of the small bungalow was as tidy as his office. Nothing like their knot bungalow, which had clothing strewn everywhere—thanks to Elara. It was nondescript. A single bunk. A basin. A set of drawers and a closet. All encased in the log cabin.

The bed didn't look very big. "Will we both fit in that?" she asked, slipping off her shoes.

Atlas was digging through his drawers.

"I can sleep on the floor."

Romy eyed the floorboards. "You want to?"

"That would be a no."

"Then why suggest it?"

Atlas tossed her a T-shirt. "My mistake." The half-smile appeared and remained as they looked at each other.

He pointed at the shirt in her hands. "I'll leave while you change. I can't sleep next to you in that dress."

Romy looked down at Freya's dress. She didn't see that much difference between the dress and the shirt. Maybe Atlas's clothing would be a little looser.

Atlas stepped outside and she tore the dress over her head, replacing it with the T-shirt—heart racing in case he came back inside.

He entered as she was placing the folded garment on top of his drawers. A muffled sound drew her attention. Atlas was staring at her as though he'd never seen Romy in his life.

"What is it?"

He closed his eyes and dragged in a breath. "It's worse, that's what it is."

Romy concealed her smile.

Though it slipped off her face a second later when Atlas reached an arm up and drew his shirt over his head. Taut muscles hardened as he twisted to get the shirt off. He was sculpted, the kind that only came from vigorous training. It didn't correlate with how often he was at his desk. His skin was smooth and there was so much of it to look at, her eyes didn't know where to start. Warmth flushed through her.

She whipped around to face the bed when she realised she was staring and drew back the covers. Where did he want to sleep? Against the wall?

"I like to put my feet out of the covers," he said from behind. He sounded a bit sheepish about it.

The wall it was.

She squeezed over as far as was possible. It might have worked if his shoulders didn't take up all the space. He lifted the arm closest to her, and she snuggled into his side as he dropped the limb around her shoulders.

Romy listened to his heart pound in his chest. Eventually the sound lulled to a slow, even beat and despite the fact that the most attractive man she'd ever seen in her life lay next to her, she was drawn down towards sleep.

Warm lips brushed her forehead.

Maybe the night hadn't ended so badly.

* * *

Atlas was gone when she woke at the crack of dawn. Did the man ever sleep? Oddly, instead of disappointment, she enjoyed the moment, snuggled in the blanket that smelled like him, at liberty to take in his room at her leisure.

Romy walked as fast as she could through the campsite not long after. For some reason she was embarrassed to be seen wearing her white dress from last night. Her relief at reaching the bungalow was immediately overridden when she creaked the door closed behind her and turned around with a yelp.

Her knot mates.

All four of them.

"Why are you here?" Romy asked Deimos to evade their questions. The best defence was a good offence.

Elara and Phobos sat at opposite ends of the room, not looking at each other. It seemed their talk went about as well as her and Thrym's had. Romy snuck a look at Thrym and saw him glowering at the object in her hand.

She'd stolen Atlas's T-shirt.

"Houston kicked me out of my room so he could use the medi-tech to cure his hangover," Deimos answered.

Romy giggled as she crossed the room to place Atlas's T-shirt in her bag.

"Don't have to ask where *you've* been," Elara said.

Phobos and Deimos both stood. "Does he need to be hurt?" Phobos said.

Honestly, Romy thought. Deimos was barely capable of standing right now.

She held up both hands. "Whoa. Whoa. No. No one needs to be hurt. Nothing happened."

"Except you spent the night in a stranger's room." Thrym's voice was cool and detached.

Romy ground her teeth together so hard they nearly snapped. He'd said his piece. She'd said hers. As far as she was concerned, the matter was done. Closed.

"Yes, I did," she snapped. Grabbing a random assortment of clothes she escaped to the bathroom, slamming the door behind her.

A shower did nothing to soothe her frayed temper.

When she exited, everyone was gone—except Thrym.

Great.

"Romy. . . ."

Romy shoved her toiletries away. "Not *again*."

"Look," he said, standing. "I was out of line. . . . Ro. This is really hard for me."

She turned to give him a piece of her mind. Hard for him? How about hard for her to be comfortable around him anymore? Why did he have to go and ruin everything?

But her anger deflated when she saw the hurt in his blue eyes.

"I don't want you to feel strange around me. Like you can't talk to me, or be yourself," he whispered.

She returned his honesty. "And I don't know how not to feel strange about it."

He pondered it, thrumming his fingers on the table. "We could . . . go back to just being friends?"

The tightness in her chest lightened. "Could you do that?"

The skin around his eyes was red. He probably hadn't slept at all, and her heart broke for him. Why did this have to happen to someone so important to her?

"I can try." He exhaled heavily.

Puberty was hell. Reproduction just wasn't worth it.

She blew out a long breath. "All right."

Romy held out her hand.

He chuckled and grabbed it, pulling her into his arms. "Since when have we ever shaken hands?"

"Since never."

"Friends?"

"Friends," she echoed, untangling herself. "Catch you at lunch?"

She pulled the door closed behind her, heart sinking at the soft "Always" from the other side.

CHΛPTER TWENTY-FIVE

"**D**id you see Tina yesterday?" Thrym was grinning over the table at Nancy. "An absolute mess."

Nancy snorted into her watercress soup.

Thrym tore a chunk from his roll. "Houston told her the medi-comp was broken so she couldn't get rid of her hangover."

Phobos chuckled. "That's evil. Especially after he used it on himself."

"I like that man," Deimos agreed. Deimos had been discharged that morning. Romy didn't want to think about what this meant for Knot 27.

Freya was drooling over the "twins". She seemed to change her mind as to her favourite on a daily basis. It no longer bothered Romy. Freya was just a young girl, looking for attention from the coolest males in camp. Not that the green-eyed bandits needed a boost to their confidence.

"What's your job now that you're out?" Elara asked Deimos.

Deimos nodded towards Romy. "I'm helping Ro in storage. Houston said it will be relaxed enough to not wear me out. And apparently you could use the help." He directed the last sentence towards her.

This was news to her. And it confirmed her suspicions that Atlas was avoiding her. He hadn't made any effort to speak to her since the night in his bungalow. She'd glimpsed him numerous times at a distance, and he hadn't acknowledged her existence once.

Her feelings for him took on a wary edge. There was something about his actions that sparked a warning inside of her. Romy liked to think she was in tune with her instincts. When you were facing a horde of Critamal warcrafts, you didn't really think as you shot the gun. At some point, it just came down to feel.

She watched him all day yesterday.

. . . Thrym was right. Atlas disappeared three times into the locked room, always making sure no one was near.

He didn't open the door wide like he did with his office door. No, he *slipped* inside, not opening it more than necessary to squeeze his six-foot-six frame through.

Romy's instincts told her that the locked room held something she didn't want to know about.

The room bothered her.

Romy simultaneously wanted to know what was in there, and didn't. She'd never experienced anything like what she felt for Atlas. She wanted to explore whatever was between them, and find out where it might lead.

For the first time in her lifespan, Romy cared for someone outside of her knot. It was fresh, and exciting, and . . .

. . . a mess.

There was Tina.

And Lucas.

Thrym.

And she wouldn't put it past Phobos and Deimos to deal with Atlas should she spend any more time alone in his bungalow.

Not to mention there was the constant threat of the Mandate discovering them. Though, with each passing day Romy worried less and less about this and more about the pressing issues, like Lucas, and Tina, and Thrym. It seemed an endless cycle of worry.

Romy sighed.

Maybe Thrym was right, and they needed to regroup away from the Earth humans for a time. Perhaps the knot shouldn't stay. Three weeks ago, Romy felt ill-equipped to deal with Earth's mysteries. Now she was confident their team could pull the plan off.

The real issue was, Romy didn't *want* to leave anymore. Even knowing Atlas had his secrets.

Knot 27 still came first.

But if she allowed herself to grow any closer to Atlas, would that still hold true?

When they were alone together everything was simple—she trusted him. As soon as they were apart, she began to wonder about all the other things that *should* matter: who he was, who he worked for, what his plans were for their knot. Maybe she didn't have any right to this knowledge. They'd only known each other for a few weeks, after all.

But this distance didn't mesh with the comfort she felt alone in his presence.

At least with Deimos in the storage room, there was no way Lucas would attempt anything.

One way or another, the matter would settle itself. Preferably before Romy lost her mind.

* * *

The two knot mates chatted as they worked that day. Well, Romy did the work. She refused to let Deimos lift more than a finger, not convinced he had the strength. She monopolised the single scanner and asked him to read through some dusty material to keep him busy.

This was the first time she'd been back in this room since Lucas attacked her. It was the first chance she'd had to look for the "classified" listings she'd spied over the soldier's shoulder. After scrolling through the categories on the device over the last hour, Romy hadn't found anything to do with a "classified" section. She didn't expect it to be so easy. Lucas had used a key card.

She needed one of those cards.

If she had one, Romy could get the answers to everything—everything Atlas refused to tell her—and she could finally decide whether he was trustworthy. And if she found the answers here, he'd never know that she'd doubted him. It was a win-win.

Deimos had been nearly as disappointed as Romy at not finding the classified category, for more altruistic reasons.

Romy sighed. "I'm starting to feel like I don't want to leave, Dei."

Maybe if their knot remained prepared. If they kept their supplies packed to leave at a moment's notice if they were ever discovered. . . .

Then maybe they could stay until there was an actual sign of danger.

"I can't wait to be gone." Deimos shook his head.

She was leaning over, trying to pry a box free. She looked under her armpit at him. "Reason?"

"Because I feel sick when I look at the Earth humans."

Romy abandoned her efforts to face him. "What do you mean?"

Deimos picked his way closer. "Every time I look at them I'm reminded of the four thousand soldiers dying needlessly, over and over again. *For nothing.* And each time the Mandate's lies flash across the screen in the clearing, it takes everything I have not to smash the thing to pieces."

Romy hated the screen, too. "I can understand that. I wish we could tell them."

He clenched his fists. "When I was in the hospital, I spent the first few days just staring out the window at night. All I could think about was the orbitos, constantly circling in and out of danger. All for nothing. I don't think I've ever felt so much hate."

"Why didn't you say something?"

He lifted a shoulder. "Have you ever been too angry to speak?"

Romy thought about it. "Perhaps."

His eyes widened in horror. "Our gentle Romy? Angry? Must be those hormones."

Anger, fear, attraction—she'd felt it all. "Don't talk to me about hormones."

Deimos laughed, and they settled into companionable silence. It wasn't until the final siren sounded and they made to leave the room that he spoke again.

"I'm going to kill them one day. The Mandate."

She could barely make out his green eyes from where he stood in the shadows. She swallowed thickly. Romy had never heard him speak like this, not even about the Critamal. How had she missed the disappearance of her light-hearted friend? In his place was a darker man. A man changed by near-death and betrayal.

He stood and turned his back to her.

"I'm going to kill them all."

They exited the storage room, sharing a confused look at the large influx of Earth humans entering the clearing. The dinner bell had rung, yet they weren't heading into the Hull, instead gathering around the Mandate's ever-present projection next to the office building.

"What's going on?" Romy asked.

Deimos glared at the screen. "No idea."

"The Mandate has a scheduled announcement," a low voice whispered between the knot mates.

It was Atlas. Romy tensed and didn't turn.

"Great," Deimos muttered.

Atlas gripped his shoulder tightly. "There will be eyes on you. Don't be a fool."

Deimos returned Atlas's harsh expression with murderous eyes. The two men stared at each other. Romy laid a hand on her knot mate's arm.

"Dei . . . the others."

With a slow blink, Deimos broke away. "Got it."

Romy refused to look directly at Atlas. He'd been ignoring her and she wanted to return the favour. Unfortunately, her curiosity was running rampant. "What is the announcement?"

The low voice came after a short moment. "It is a trial. For a woman who once lived in this settlement. She was found stealing."

Romy recalled Phobos speaking of this a while ago. "They make the settlement watch the conviction of their own friends?"

"No," came the quiet reply. "They make the entire world watch it."

Deimos's words were scathing. "A display of power."

There was no answer from the man behind her, yet Atlas didn't contradict Deimos. Was it possible he disapproved of this power display? That was what she didn't understand. Atlas surely had to be an underling for the Mandate in some capacity. The soldiers obeyed him, Tina obeyed him, and Romy assumed the work he was doing all day was classified. But why did he work for them if he didn't agree with their laws and punishments?

Unable to help herself, she met his grey eyes and wondered if there was a vulnerability in them she'd somehow missed. Was Atlas trapped? Did the man before her want more than a life under the lies of the Mandate? Was helping Knot 27 a silent rebellion against the world leaders?

Disjointed words blasted through the clearing's speakers and Romy broke away from his intense stare.

The words smoothed out and a picture flickered into view on the pixelated hologram: a woman dressed in filthy rags, kneeling on whitewashed stone. There were gasps among the Jimboomba crowd and Romy could gather that this woman looked nothing like the person they remembered.

"Silence," Atlas barked.

Everyone stilled, and Romy's eyes widened. She shared a sideways look with Deimos. Shouldn't that be Tina's role?

It seemed no one else dared to make a sound when the picture zoomed out to show a line of hard-faced men and women filing up onto raised seating. There were seven of them. And each wore stark white to match their pristine surroundings.

"Who are they?" she asked.

"The current Mandate," Atlas replied.

These were the people responsible? Each member of the Mandate lowered themselves with poise onto their own white throne-like seat, spaced evenly across the length of the trial area. It was hard to tell from the picture, but Romy got the impression the trial was outdoors; she could see the bedraggled woman's hair waving slightly in a breeze. She looked filthy against the white and slouched at the foot of the seven thrones. Romy ground her teeth; the contrast was purposeful, no doubt. Deimos was breathing hard, and Romy stretched out to grip his hand, hushing him under her breath. She was unable to tear her eyes from the screen as the cowering woman's trial began.

It was a sham.

Each of the seven took a turn condemning the Earth human, and then, when she was finally given permission to speak, her voice was so weak it barely carried through the speakers, her legs shaking as she neared collapse.

And the Jimboomba crowd watched in silence. Most in the settlement were nodding, booing the person who used to be their neighbour and friend. Was the Mandate's hold so tight? Could they have brainwashed the world so absolutely? To Romy, the trial was a clear setup, designed to consolidate the Mandate's lies. But then, she knew about the biggest lie of all, forewarned of the leader's capacity for manipulation and deceit, and she probably looked at the streaming image before her with different eyes.

The warmth grew at her back. "I don't know why they're doing this now," Atlas breathed.

Deimos froze. "Our presence?"

"It could be coincidence," Romy added.

There was a hum behind her. "I don't like coincidences. You all need to lay low."

"I don't see how we can lay lower than we already are," Deimos snapped.

Romy watched the projector with unseeing eyes as the convicted woman was dragged away. A picture of an island took up the screen; it was a stronghold. Could this be the prison she'd heard of? Image after image flashed on the screen: kind prison guards, evil and hulking prisoners, even a prisoner beating a young woman.

Peaceful music filled the Jimboomba clearing and the camera zoomed in on a woman's face—one of the Mandate. She was petite and smiling. "The Mandate will always take care of you. May peace be with you all, and remember," she winked, "take less than what you need."

"Are you saying they're watching this camp?" Deimos said in alarm.

Romy looked the twin's way, and jerked as the black eyes of Lucas glinted at her through the crowd. Had he been watching them the entire time? For a reaction?

"It would appear so," Atlas said grimly. "Unfortunately, thievery wasn't the woman's only crime. She was conspiring against the Mandate. I think I have a way to get your knot to safety, but I need a little more time."

"You've had three weeks already," Deimos accused. "And we're no further from the Mandate than we were at the start."

Romy pinched the hand she still held in warning, swallowing nervously as she tore away from Lucas's gaze. They shouldn't be talking about this here.

What had her expression been like as she watched the woman's trial? Or more importantly, had Officer Cayne glimpsed the tense exchange between Atlas and Deimos? Her mind was in chaos. She couldn't think clearly.

The Earth humans were breaking off and heading into the Hull. Lucas slung his arm over another soldier and sauntered away to get food, but Romy stayed close to Deimos, scared about what she'd seen in Lucas's eyes.

Atlas glanced around them before leaning close. "You still think I'm not on your side?"

Romy twisted and found him staring straight at her. His question caught her off-guard. "I-I'm—"

Hurt lit the grey eyes before her and his head reared back.

Deimos scoffed. "Can you blame her?"

Atlas's jaw clenched and unclenched several times. "After everything I've done, *am* doing for you. You can't trust me."

A lump rose in Romy's throat, but she couldn't give him an empty reassurance, despite the fact he so clearly believed she should trust him. "Maybe I would know whether I should trust you if I knew what you were doing. Telling someone they should trust you . . . with no actions to support it. . . ."

His eyes blazed. "Saving you, showing you to your friends . . . those weren't actions?"

They glared at each other, noses almost touching as they argued in whispers. Romy's chest heaved. Anger swelled within her and she ignored Deimos, who was darting looks between them. "Lying to me from the moment we met, you mean."

Atlas blanched and he stepped back. He looked between her and Deimos; both of them had their arms closed. With a weary sigh, Atlas ran a hand through his hair, casting a worried glance towards the Hull. "And that is what you think of me?" he asked.

Romy's eyes burned with unshed tears. "I don't know what to think."

He stared down at her, eyes flickering over her face as his expression slowly hardened. Without another word, Atlas strode away.

* * *

"That doesn't sound good." Phobos shook his head as Deimos and Romy finished relating what had happened in the clearing. Elara, Thrym, and Deimos had watched the trial from the other side.

Romy was storing more of the seeds Phobos had "borrowed" in her pillowcase. Doing so after watching the trial made her nervous.

"I don't like it," muttered Thrym. "Like Atlas said, it's too coincidental. The Mandate just chose to screen that trial weeks after we landed here? There's something else happening."

Phobos paced in the bungalow's small space. "Dei is out of hospital. We have the means to grow food, we have a car, Elara knows where the sentry posts are and how to drive, and Romy knows when the patrols pass and the route to get out of here. Thrym's watched Houston treat people. I'm confident we can find shelter. I feel like we're out of our depth here now."

Deimos stood beside his twin. "It's become too dangerous. We're trusting an entire camp to remain quiet. Do you know how stupid that is?"

That was what puzzled Romy. How wouldn't the Mandate find out about Knot 27? A crashed battler couldn't be an easy thing to miss.

"Tina, Atlas, and Houston are the only ones with transmitters," Elara objected. "Unless they tell, the Mandate won't find out."

Romy didn't know that. She'd seen the blue devices in Atlas and Houston's ears, but assumed many would have the transmitters.

Phobos folded his arms, shaking his head. "How do we know there aren't more?"

"Tina said so," Elara withered back.

If Lucas worked for the Mandate, surely he'd have some means of contacting them. But if he had a device, why hadn't the Mandate turned up to cart the knot off already? Her head ached from trying to puzzle it out.

"Tina, Atlas, and Houston," Thrym said, lifting his head. "They're tense. I've heard them arguing a lot lately. They seem . . . on edge."

"You think it's to do with us?" Romy asked, mouth dry.

He shrugged. "I've heard our names, but that's as much as I got. Actually," he stared at Romy, "they mention *your* name . . . like, a lot."

She blanched. "Me? Why?"

"I figured maybe it was about you and Atlas," he said, looking away. "But then I heard them mention the rest of us."

Elara circled to Romy's side. "You think it's bad?"

He shook his head. "I have absolutely no idea. It could be nothing. A bad feeling I'm giving too much attention to." Thrym flitted a look towards Romy.

Phobos clapped Thrym on the shoulder. "It's not just you. I feel it, too. I know you all think I'm just a pretty face."

Elara snorted.

He ignored her. "Romy . . . I think Thrym's right. Houston barely stops watching you to eat."

She looked around the knot with wide eyes. "I don't know what it means."

Deimos grimaced. "If it were a good thing, wouldn't they tell you?" He stood and paced the room, a heaviness in his shoulders. Romy didn't know if it was because he was still weak, or if it was his newfound hatred.

"And that's the thing," Thrym said. "We were told not to ask questions. And we haven't because we were told it could make things worse. But Atlas also implied this situation would be short term. It's been three weeks and we're still clueless. There's something going on I don't like." A determined gleam lit his blue eyes.

Romy was more concerned about Lucas's presence, which she had yet to tell anyone about. Indecision tugged her as she wondered if she should confess her suspicions.

"I say we collect food over the next few days and then go," Deimos said from behind her.

Romy's heart lurched as she turned. "So soon?"

Thrym nodded. "A few days is good. We have most of what we need. Ro, will the car be ready?"

Misery stamped on her again. "Well, yes." She felt terrible to be doing this to Nancy, Eddie, and the others. "But I—"

"Can't it be longer?" Elara asked. "I don't think we should leave until we need to. This could all be nothing. Or the Mandate could even be trying to flush us out."

"I don't want to be here any longer than I have to. I want it just to be us again. We can regroup and figure out our next move once we're away from here," Deimos argued.

"What do you think, Ro?" Phobos asked, watching her flounder.

"I. . . ," she started. She thought about Lucas, and the trial. Phobos was right; everything was in place for them to go. But Romy desperately wanted to give Atlas a chance to prove himself. It shouldn't make sense that she would delay leaving for him, but the yearning to do just that overwhelmed everything else. "I'm with Ellie."

Thrym's expression darkened for a second. Just a fleeting second before it cleared. And Phobos's face told her he saw right to the heart of her reasons to stay.

She tilted her face in the other direction.

"A vote, then," Deimos suggested. "Those in favour of staying?"

Elara and Romy raised their hands.

The boys' hands stayed down.

"We need to be ready to leave at any moment," Deimos said. "We have three days to get everything we need."

Romy stopped listening as her chest squeezed painfully. Leaving the others to discuss their escape plans, she made for her bunk. She stared at the blank wall.

Knot 27 was leaving in three days.

Atlas was angry at her. Houston was watching her. They were talking about her, and Knot 27.

Atlas thought she hated him.

And somehow she had to say goodbye.

* * *

There were two things the knot needed to do before they left: Get medicine and as much food as possible.

Stealing food would be the trickiest as most of the Hull food was perishable. They would have to kill animals in the wild for meat, which wouldn't be too difficult if they had weapons. But they didn't. No matter how much Deimos and Romy stared at the soldiers' supply room for the answer. And no matter how long Thrym and Phobos discussed plans to break in.

Atlas was avoiding her yet again, except this time, she knew why. It was clear he wasn't going to tell her the truth in time.

But the locked room might.

Romy needed to see what he was up to in there. Maybe it could help her decide whether or not to tell the grey-eyed man of the knot's departure. She couldn't do so without proof Atlas was on their side, and she remained unconvinced he didn't have another agenda.

She took to testing the doorknob whenever she passed, which was often because she was trying to bump into Atlas to say sorry.

The two days passed and Romy only saw him in the Hull, and it was getting to the dire stage, with only one more day left that she would have to approach him there. How did you strike up conversation with someone who you'd told you didn't trust? And what if he ignored her in front of Tina? She grimaced at the thought of being embarrassed in front of the other woman, and Deimos gave her a sideways look.

What would she even say to him? She couldn't just say, "Sorry, goodbye". If he grew suspicious after she spoke to him, it could put the entire knot at risk. But Romy couldn't bear to leave without talking to him one last time.

She felt like a small piece of her would be torn off when they left. It occupied her every thought. As she stashed stolen clothing into her doona cover—each of their blankets now held a variety of seeds, food, and clothing; as she pocketed a piece of fruit after every meal with the others; and even as she agonised over stealing Nancy's car, she thought about never seeing Atlas again. Of the hurt that would be in his eyes when he discovered they were gone.

They would leave Jimboomba and never see any of these people ever again—if they were successful. It seemed a cruel reward.

Romy watched Atlas as he left the Hull that night, ignoring the talk around her.

The light in Atlas's office flicked on. Excusing herself and avoiding Thrym's suspicious gaze, she left in the direction of their bungalow.

Once out of sight, she retraced her steps, keeping close to the buildings. She glanced towards the window where her knot was seated, laughing with the teen humans. And guilt churned her stomach because she knew she might be risking the entire knot. Perhaps it was pathetic and selfish, but she would rather not look back on this moment and regret not reaching out one last time. He'd held her in his arms for an entire night. It had to mean something.

Romy crept up the steps, avoiding the flickering light from the projector screen at one side. The smiling face of a Mandate member—the petite female again—flashed across, followed by the usual brainwashing words. A thin stream of light illuminated the centre of the entranceway. It came from Atlas's office and cast the other offices into shadow.

His door was ajar. As Romy drew near, her ears picked up the sound of a voice inside his office. Not his own.

And not just any voice.

Hers.

"It's time, Atlas," she said.

Romy ground her teeth together and raised her hand to knock.

"You know how to address me," he replied.

The coldness in his voice was what stilled her hand. Lowering her arm, Romy pressed her eye to the crack and had to muffle her gasp. Tina was dressed in her usual combat gear, looking just as put together as always. Except her palms were splayed out over Atlas's stomach.

An ugly red anger pulsed through Romy before settling in her gut.

"I know how to address you when we're alone," she purred. Romy squeezed her eyes shut and rolled sideways onto the wall, still listening.

"It's time," Tina pressed. "Why delay any further?"

Atlas paced the room. He was agitated for some reason, and she needed to know what it was. This was her last chance. Romy leant closer, with a quick look over her shoulder for Houston. The building was empty and dark.

"You're right. It has to be done. I'll make the call in the morning," he said, voice hollow. "The Mandate will send a team down to collect the bodies."

Horror riveted through Romy in a slow, vibrating tide. At first all she understood was that he was calling the enemy. Then the rest of what he'd said hit her. Atlas was alerting the Mandate. . . . Her mouth dried and she swayed on the spot. He couldn't be reporting *them*, could he?

There was no way his words could mean what she thought they meant.

Cold fear trickled down her spine as she tried not to leap to conclusions.

"Will it be so hard to say goodbye to her?" Tina simpered.

Romy's head spun as the woman confirmed her terrified misgivings.

"No," he said. "It won't."

Hurt stabbed its way through her. It couldn't be.

He. . . .

He wouldn't do that to her. She ran through the conversation again, searching for any loophole, studying it from all angles.

But Tina's words had confirmed it.

The Mandate was coming for the bodies of Romy and her friends.

Atlas was betraying Knot 27.

He was betraying *her*. He meant to kill them all.

Had the trio planned this from the beginning? Atlas, Houston, and Tina. Anger built inside of her and she longed to throw the door open and scream at the pair.

Why hadn't they just killed the knot at the start? Why mess with them? Make the knot think they had a chance?

It was cruel.

And he hadn't just played with her heart.

Atlas had toyed with the lives of her family. Romy's face hardened.

"I'll go finalise the details," Tina said.

Her voice jerked Romy back to the present. Footsteps were drawing closer. Romy whirled, looking around her, and skimmed as quietly as possible to Houston's door, testing the handle.

Locked.

Not bothering to check the other two doors—because one belonged to Tina, and Tina might be going there and the other was always locked—she twisted, dashing for the only furniture in sight: the bench outside Atlas's office. Romy pressed herself into the corner's shadows, sliding down behind the bench.

She held her breath as Atlas and Tina exited his office. Tina went straight into her workspace, but Atlas veered off, heading for the locked room. He jammed a key in the lock and flung the door open. He'd never opened it so wide, nor so carelessly, but to her utter frustration she couldn't see inside from her vantage point. Romy didn't dare move a muscle to sneak a peek.

Atlas rushed inside, and she listened to the frantic rustling of papers for a minute before he reappeared in the doorway. He balanced the armload of papers as he reached back, clicking a button on the inside of the door before giving it a soft pull.

The door to the secret area creaked as it began to slowly swing closed.

Atlas quickly disappeared into Tina's room and shut the door. Their voices were just a murmur on the other side.

. . . But the door to the *locked room* was still open, swinging towards a close. It was three-quarters of the way there.

Pushing her warning instinct aside, Romy darted forwards on silent feet, shoving her fingers into the gap just in time. She paused in this position, tensed just outside the locked room, listening to Atlas and Tina, but there was no interruption in the low hum next door. No sounds of discovery. Romy eased the door open and slid inside. Inside the locked room at last.

Her heart stopped as the door to Tina's office creaked.

"Hold on. They're in my bunker," Atlas said.

Romy fumbled desperately on the inside of the handle for the button she'd seen Atlas push. The automatic lock sprang off with a soft click. No way was she getting trapped inside.

Romy gently closed the entry, palms slick with fear. Atlas marched past where she stood on the opposite side of the door only seconds later.

Her breath was bated as she strained to hear through the wood.

If Atlas found this room unlocked. . . . Romy breathed a sigh of relief when the footsteps moved off down the hall. Two sets, she realised. Tina and Atlas were both going to his bungalow.

She can have him. Romy waited until their voices had faded.

And when silence returned to the building, *that* was when she stared blankly at her knees and tried to absorb the enormous lie of her time on Earth.

Why was he reporting them to the Mandate? Why now?

Was he protecting the settlement? Had he always planned to do this? She couldn't understand any of it, or rather, only one part.

Atlas meant to kill them. His reasoning for doing so wasn't of immediate concern.

The word "bodies" implied Knot 27 wouldn't be receiving a simple memory wipe upon collection.

Thrym was right, and she never saw it. Atlas was the enemy.

And Romy was the fool.

Romy pressed shaking fingers to her mouth in an attempt to keep her humiliated *hurt* inside. To think she'd been so torn at having to say goodbye. That she'd been on her way to confess her feelings and put her knot's entire plan at risk.

Gentle Romy, who never saw the bad in people. Gentle Romy, who was a silly, naïve little girl.

The burning loathing she felt seared away her tears. Romy used the desk to pull herself up and looked around the locked room for the first time.

A platform sat in the middle of the room. A control panel sat on a slanted desk at the end of the platform. On the far side, in the middle of the raised stage, was a screen.

The setup was familiar. It was a transmission dock.

This was what Atlas had been hiding, she thought in confusion. It didn't make sense. Why was this here? Earth used *brain* transmission now—the blue transmitters Tina, Houston, and Atlas wore in their ears.

The transmission dock was just a way to communicate . . . a bit old, but hardly any reason to be so secretive.

Romy made to leave, but a flashing blue light from the control desk caught her eye. Her instincts were screaming at her.

. . . He'd hidden this for a reason. She hesitated, eyeing the platform.

Who did Atlas talk to in this room, three times a day, every day? Why was he so eager that no one see? If it was just a transmission dock, why did he hide it?

Romy pushed the flashing blue button on the slanted desk and stood to one side of the screen. The receiver would only see the empty platform, but she wasn't taking any chances.

The screen went red. Romy tensed on the balls of her feet.

And then the red flickered.

And a face filled the screen.

214

CHAPTER TWENTY-SIX

The thing about new technology was that it often wasn't compatible with old technology.

For instance, the orbitos possessed old technology, like this dock. The transmission docks even took up an entire room, just like this one.

But Earth used the newer tech.

The small brain transmission devices were useless for communication with space. It made sense that to talk to the oribitos, you would need to match their outdated technology.

"What is the reason behind this unscheduled call?"

She'd always admired the calm leadership in his voice.

The Orbito One commander looked the same; he had the same age lines on his forehead and around his mouth. Romy used to attribute these to stress because he was trying to save the lives of so many and bore the burden of hundreds. *Liar.* Crew cut, greying hair—not grey because he was exempted from the shorter life cycle to command. It must be stressful work, lying to hundreds of sacrificial soldiers each day.

Romy stood, physically hunched over from the hurt she felt as she stared at the person Atlas was betraying her to.

"Commander?" Cronus barked.

Commander! She nearly staggered in disbelief. Atlas wasn't just a soldier, not just a betrayer—he . . . was in the Mandate's high command?

Her disbelief was quickly replaced by seething anger. She finally understood Deimos's murderous promises. Face-to-face with the person responsible for the mass murder of thousands, a fury consumed her, burning through her body like acid.

She'd looked up to this man her whole life; respected him. Trusted him. *Pitied him.* Been thankful for his sacrifice. That he chose to bear the loneliness of retaining his memory longer than any soldier.

Liar!

The bodies of space soldiers strewn through the war zone flashed in front of her eyes. They didn't wipe memories to be merciful—they did it to cover their damn tracks. Bile rose in her throat.

They did it so their little political game could continue on.

A soldier went into battle against the Critamal knowing every breath could be their last.

Fury wasn't a strong enough word for what she felt. Unadulterated hatred squeezed out of her pores. And she knew, like Deimos, that if she could reach through the transmission screen and choke this man to death, she'd do so gladly.

Her stomach rolled at the disgusting sight of him, irritated and impatient in front of her.

What she wouldn't give to walk onto that platform and announce her intention to tell everyone the truth. It was tempting. . . . Romy shuffled one foot forwards.

But the second foot refused to follow.

Atlas had warned them about the Mandate's weaponry . . . whether that was true or it was a lie to control them was debatable. He'd lied about everything else! Regardless, she couldn't bring harm to her friends. For the first time she saw the knot's bond for what it was—a weakness; a method to control them. If it were just her, she would climb onto the platform, just to see the fear on this cruel man's face for an instant.

Romy gasped and quickly muffled the sound.

"Who's there?" Cronus demanded, his eyes squinting at the platform.

No wonder Tina answered to Atlas. He was further up the Mandate chain than she was. And no wonder the trio had purposely kept the information from the knot. They would have run for their lives, dragging Deimos behind them.

"Commander!" The sharpness of Cronus's voice jerked her to the present.

Her knot.

Romy squeezed her eyes shut and stepped back. She pressed the blue button and the monster on the screen disappeared.

She stared at the dock long after it fell blank. Drawing an arm across her face, she was surprised when it came back wet with tears. Her knot had to be told. Taking a shuddering breath, she forced her gaze away from the platform.

They had to leave.

Tonight.

She locked the door as she left. Maybe their group's absence would go unnoticed for a little longer. The entrance was empty, and she dodged back between the bungalows before reaching their quarters.

She didn't turn on the lights.

"Get up," she ordered.

Romy couldn't see a thing, but heard shuffling.

"Ro, what is it?" croaked Phobos.

She relented and turned on the bathroom light, closing the door most of the way so only a crack appeared. It was enough to illuminate the room. Enough to see all the boys sitting upright, eyes barely open. Elara was still asleep and Romy went over and shook her roughly.

"Elara. Up. Now."

She caught a shared glance between the twins.

"I *dislike* you," Elara muttered.

Crouching in the middle of the bunks, Romy didn't wait for Elara to sit before reporting. "The Orbitos are coming for us tomorrow. Atlas has betrayed us. He works for the Mandate."

Elara wrenched upright. That got them moving.

The others crouched around her in a circle on the bungalow floor. Romy's hands were balled in tight fists. She couldn't believe she'd gone there just to speak to him like a stupid fool!

"Tell us." Thrym held her gaze.

And for a heartbeat, all Romy could think was how he'd been so right about Atlas. How all along she should have believed her best friend.

She lowered her voice to a hush. "I was going to talk to Atlas," she admitted, voice vibrating with anger. "He and Tina were talking about making a call in the morning for the Orbitos to come and collect us. To collect our bodies."

Deimos sat back. "They have contact with the Orbitos?"

Romy laughed darkly. "You know the locked room? I got in. There's a transmission platform in there. And guess who was on the other end?"

Elara's soft brown eyes were huge.

"Commander Cronus."

The others stared at Romy in disbelief. Fully awake by now.

"And he addressed Atlas as 'Commander'," she grated out.

Thrym punched the floor with a fist. "I knew he was filth."

Romy's insides twisted.

"But why now?" Elara was frowning. "It's been weeks."

She'd been asking herself the same thing. Why didn't Atlas report them straightaway? Or had it all been a game? What could he possibly gain from keeping them alive?

Deimos was pacing the small space. "Could it be our isolated location?"

"I'm not sure." Thrym shook his head. "Maybe—"

"Maybe doesn't matter right now," Romy burst out. "The Mandate's forces are coming. We need to leave. Now."

There was a soft squeeze on her shoulder. She turned.

Thrym was looking at her. "Ro's right," he decided. "Escaping is our priority."

Her mind was already well into the process of their escape. "We need to get medicine. And weapons."

"We don't have enough time," Elara said.

Romy glared at her. "We make time. It's dangerous out there, and none of us have combat training. We don't stand a chance without guns."

"I'm with Ro," Deimos said.

They all looked at Romy. She stared at Thrym with hard eyes.

He sighed. "The weapons are locked away. Keycards, remember?"

"Yeah, how are we supposed to get them?" Elara leaped on board.

Romy set her resolve. "It's not a matter of how. It's a matter of who."

* * *

Her visit to Nancy served two purposes. The main reason: to get Lucas's location. The second: to ask if Romy could take the teen's vehicle. She really couldn't bear the thought that Nancy and her friends would think of them as thieves and criminals. And Nancy had lost her family. Romy didn't want to let her down.

Romy knocked quietly on the door. She shook her head at Phobos and Deimos, who were with her. They shrank back into the shadows of the neighbouring bungalow.

The door cracked open and Romy pushed it the rest of the way.

"Hey," Nancy exclaimed. "What the hell?"

"Shh," Romy said. She checked out the window and listened carefully for signs Nancy had been heard.

The other girl picked up something was wrong immediately.

"What's happened?" She closed the door and turned to Romy, arms crossed.

Romy left the window. "Nancy, our knot needs your help."

The young Earth human's eyes went wide. Mouth ajar, she asked, "Why?"

It was a debate Romy had on the way here. She didn't want to endanger Nancy by telling her too much, but she knew if she didn't give her enough information the plan could explode in their faces.

"The Orbitos are coming to kill us," she explained quietly. "I can't tell you much. But you need to know that everything is not as it seems. They

218

want to silence us because we uncovered something we were never meant to."

Nancy sat down at the table, expression unchanging.

Leaning down, Romy gripped the girl's shoulders. "You know me. You *know* I wouldn't ask you if there were any other choice. Please, Nancy. We need your help."

The girl from space and the girl from Earth looked at each other for a long beat before Nancy swallowed.

"H-how?" her voice cracked. "How do I help?"

* * *

Romy crept out of Nancy's bungalow. Her last warning—"Don't breathe a word to anyone. Trust no one"—lingered on her lips.

"Where's Lucas?" Phobos asked.

"He's in a room just off the clearing." It explained how the soldier was somehow able to know exactly when Romy arrived at the storage building and when she was alone.

The twins led the way, with Romy following on quiet feet.

In the darkness, the sound of their footsteps and breathing seemed to carry forever. Phobos motioned for them to hide in the shadows as they reached the front of Lucas's bungalow.

"I don't like it," Deimos decided. "He's too close to the clearing. There are lights on in Atlas's office. What if Atlas or Tina are in there?"

Their roughly assembled plan consisted of breaking in and overpowering him. But he was too close to the offices and other houses.

The three shared helpless looks. But a quiet thought nudged Romy.

Her heart took off in a gallop at the mere thought of doing it, but she knew it was the only way.

"I ... might have an idea."

* * *

Romy knocked on the door, wiping her sweaty palms on her beige cotton shorts. She couldn't believe she was about to do this. Flashes of Lucas's hands down her shorts made her swallow back bile. It was the worst plan ever—*a desperate plan*. She'd lied to the twins and sent them to retrieve a book from the archives that "Lucas was searching for yesterday" while she "practised what she'd say". They didn't expect the lie from her, so they didn't hear a lie. They would be back in a couple of minutes.

All she had to do was get in and incapacitate Lucas. Incapacitate a trained soldier. . . . Suddenly she realised what a terrible plan that was.

The door swung wide, and she blinked into the barrel of a gun.

Romy looked down the weapon to its owner: Officer Lucas Cayne.

The safety was clicked back on and Romy exhaled in relief.

"What are you doing here?" the soldier asked suspiciously.

This was it. Romy was about to put on the performance of her life. "My knot," she started. At least she didn't have to fake the trembling in her voice. "I'm ready to tell you."

The soldier grabbed her upper arm and dragged her into his room. Romy scrunched her nose at the smell and disarray of his quarters.

"Tell me." His eyes gleamed.

Romy frowned. "Don't you already know?"

She caught the hasty rearrangement of his features.

She'd forgotten how tall he was. What was she thinking?!

"I want to hear it from your own lips," he hedged.

Romy squeezed her eyes together, both to perform and to collect her wits. "We didn't come here for research."

He circled her, his eyes glinting.

Keep him talking. Where should she aim? The jaw? She saw a solid-looking object weighing down some papers on his desk next to a knife.

"You're wasting my time, darlin'." The soldier advanced on her, hand raised to strike her.

She used the opportunity to step closer to the desk. "We crashed here," she blurted. "Weeks ago, after a battle with the Critamal."

She relaxed a second later when the blow didn't connect.

Oil dripped from the expression on Lucas's face. Romy tried to contain her shiver, but couldn't. If anything, his eyes lit at the sight of her shuddering.

He was close.

"You'll tell me everything you know," he said. "And I want something else, too . . . since you kept me waiting."

Romy widened her eyes. It wasn't hard—fear gripped her tightly in its claws. "Wh-what do you mean?"

Lucas turned away and she blindly searched behind her for the weight, brushing over papers. Her breath halted in her throat as her fingers closed on the cool surface. Romy brought it behind her back, wrist brushing against the hilt of the knife there.

The Mandate's spy faced her.

She met his gaze. "I'll do anything to save my knot."

He circled towards her slowly. Nearly close enough. "Yes. You will." Lucas wet his lips without breaking his stare for a second. "A virgin, I bet."

He spoke from behind her. "I want payment now. The first payment. I can assure you there will have to be many to keep a secret of this size."

Phobos and Deimos should have returned by now. She hoped they guessed she was in here. Though if Romy screamed for help, they were all dead anyway.

Just one more step.

She turned her face away, adopting a scared voice. "Okay. B-but you won't tell anyone? You won't tell the Mandate?"

It was a slip. And she saw his eyes flash. Horror froze her on the spot. He hadn't known she'd guessed who he worked for! Lucas rushed her, and without thinking, she brought the weight in her hand around, throwing her entire body into the blow.

There was a crunch as it connected with his mouth. The spy staggered back, clutching at his face before falling to the ground with a soft thud. His fall was softened by the dirty clothing littering the floor.

Romy stood for a few precious seconds, her whole body trembling. The knife! She grabbed it and skirted around him for the door. Lucas wasn't unconscious. She needed the twins.

An arm jerked her back, and she was whirled back the way she came. The back of a hand met her face in a strike so hard Romy was blinded as she fell to the floor with a small cry, the knife hitting the ground with a clatter.

She could barely see through the pain.

By the time she blinked the hurt away, he was astride her.

Her T-shirt tore in two as his hands clawed at her.

Next was the front of her shorts.

The knife lay to her right. She had to get the knife.

"I'm sorry!" she sobbed without tears.

"How did you know who I work for?" He gripped her throat and she choked, scratching at his hand.

"You . . . you said you were above the law," she gasped. "I g-guessed."

He pulled her up to sitting so they were eye to eye. Romy had both hands at her neck, pulling at his fingers. Black dotted her vision as Lucas's eyes filled the space in front of her.

It was the unhinged streak in them that told Romy he didn't intend to stop.

And she couldn't let him continue.

Lolling her head to the side, she let her right arm hang limply. His hands didn't abate their cruel pressure.

She inched her hand outwards, desperately reaching for the knife. Her fingertips touch polished wood and she fumbled to grip the weapon, terrified it might slip, terrified because even if she wanted to scream for the twins, she no longer had the breath to do it.

If she couldn't reach the knife, she would die.

Romy twisted and stretched her arm forwards, enclosing the knife in her grip. With the last of her strength, she threw herself to one side, dragging the knife across his throat.

A pain thrust through her mind. So sharply, she forgot all about Lucas, about the room, about her knot as she writhed, clutching at her head. There was only white. Nothing. She clawed at her scalp trying to get to the source of the agony inside her skull.

What was happening?

Moaning, Romy cracked her eyes open, realising she'd fallen to the ground. Lucas was swaying above her. Blood poured out in a sheet down his throat and onto his naked chest. But it was as though once his body registered the mortal wound, a dam burst: blood spurted, covering the ground, covering him, and covering her.

Romy lay on the floor, too weak to move, gasping as the red wave poured over her. She couldn't shift her eyes from his widened gaze.

For the first time he looked afraid. He'd intended to rape her. Had made her weeks in Jimboomba hell. But it didn't mean she couldn't see his humanity when all else was stripped away.

The soldier toppled forwards, no longer in control of his actions. She spat his blood out of her mouth, struggling for air as he slid his hands over her in desperate movements, still trying to kill her in the time he had left.

The slippery movement of his hands became weaker.

And weaker.

Until his death rattled within him like a loose bolt in a broken engine.

A high-pitched noise rang in her head, a tinnitus of excruciating levels. She pushed the heels of her palms into her temples as the ringing intensified, building to overwhelming degrees within seconds. Had Lucas damaged her brain when he choked her?

Someone was shaking the door. The edges of Romy's sight began to blur as she stared at the dead officer on top of her.

Knocking.

The twins, she realised in a daze. Pulling herself from underneath the dead man, Romy approached the door, slipping twice in the large puddle of blood.

Phobos and Deimos gasped when they saw her.

Anger stirred deep inside her, a defensive mechanism at what she'd done, but she could barely feel it through the thick numbness encasing her.

Deimos gripped her arm as she swayed. "Where did he get you?"

Romy looked down. *Blood.* The ringing sound restarted with resounding force. Nausea swam upwards at the thought of how Lucas's blood was covering her. "Not mine," she choked out. "Not mine. Not mine. Not mine."

Her voice was high-pitched. Hysterical. She knew it, but couldn't stop. She wasn't in control anymore.

Phobos pushed past her as Deimos remained where he was—glued to her side.

Phobos returned with the keycard. The reason she'd killed a man. "A rapist," she corrected herself. She didn't mean to kill him. Kill him. Kill him.

Deimos looked at her strangely. "Who was a rapist, Ro?"

Romy stumbled out of the bungalow and into the tree line, emptying the contents of her stomach. Every time she thought of the blood on her hands she was wracked with another bout of gagging. Why wouldn't the ringing stop? *The blood was red. Bright red.*

"Ro . . . we need to get the weapons." Deimos stroked her hair back, whispering. "No one's gotten up, but we can't be sure they didn't hear. There was a bit of noise."

The weapons. More killing. The thought echoed to her through a long, dark tunnel. "Y-yes." Her lips formed the word. She heard the sound from spectator seats.

Phobos shrugged out of his shirt and pulled it over her numb body. "She's in shock," he said to Deimos.

This wasn't shock. Romy felt like she was hovering outside of herself. This had never happened when she killed the Critamal. What was it? Because she'd killed with her own hands?

"Maybe we should take her back first?" Deimos said to Phobos.

A fresh shot of adrenaline helped to push the blurriness back. Her friends needed her. They didn't have time for her to freak out. The clanging in her mind didn't recede, and she had to work to move her mouth around it.

"No." Romy managed to speak. "N-no. I'm okay." She lifted wooden arms and pushed her hair back, wet with Lucas's blood. She looked up at the doubtful members of her knot. "Let's do this," she repeated in a hollow voice.

Not waiting for an answer, she led the way. Her feet dragging with each step, she retreated behind a couple of rows of houses as they moved around the clearing. Atlas couldn't find them. Not when they were so close to escape. She wondered if he was sitting in his office. Or laying awake in his bed. The bed they'd *shared* as he plotted to betray everyone she loved.

It was easy to move around the camp. No patrols worked within the settlement. She crept up to the storage building steps, Phobos and Deimos behind her.

The e-storage screen was shining in the room to the left, and the keypad to the weapons room, a tiny red flashing circle at its base, was to their right. Phobos passed the keycard into her outstretched hand and Romy waved it under the keypad.

The red light flashed green and the door clicked open.

She waved the twins through. "Go, get the . . . the supplies. I n-need something from the e-scanner."

Her grip on the keycard was slippery. She staggered under the weight of the ringing in her head to the illuminated machine in the far corner.

Rocking with pain, it took her three attempts to push the keycard through.

Red files loaded on the screen in front of her disjointed vision. They needed to put as much ground between themselves and this camp by the first siren tomorrow morning.

Romy scrolled through the documents, blinking often to refocus. Rosters, incident reports, weapons registry.

One section caught her eye: HIGHLY CLASSIFIED.

She clicked on the heading.

Nothing happened. Lucas worked for the Mandate, but clearly wasn't high in the ranks. Not like Atlas. That she'd been worried about telling Atlas about Lucas in case he got hurt made her want to pull her hair out in handfuls.

Deimos and Phobos approached behind her, five large stuffed packs in tow and arms full of weapons.

"We found camp gear in there." Phobos grinned in the dark.

It was a good find, she knew that. She just couldn't bring herself to care.

Romy's eyes flicked across the screen. So much of this could be useful: Long-term settlement forecast, transmission codes. But there was one thing they needed.

New World: Australia (Settlements: 2198 census)

Got it.

She clicked on the heading, and held her breath as the file opened. A map was loading.

"Where's the map I gave you?" she ordered.

Phobos swung his backpack to the ground and rifled through the contents.

The screen loaded in front of them. And for the first time, the knot saw where on Earth they were.

"Jimboomba" was spelled out in red capitals halfway up the Queensland state, inland. Elara was right. They weren't as close to the beach as the old map told them. This settlement was entirely different from the old Jimboomba.

Deimos and Phobos flattened the 2017 map on the floor. They needed to mark the other settlements on the page. They needed to avoid them. Romy pulled up short. They had nothing to mark the page with.

Blood dropped from her hair to the ground. The red on her hand caught her eye in front of the shining screen. The bells in her head started afresh … but … there was nothing else.

Romy squeezed her hand in her hair, looked at the screen and pressed her forefinger onto the map. A bloody fingerprint was left north-west of Jimboomba over another settlement's location.

"That is—"

"Shut it, Pho."

Romy worked quickly, translating the locations. She ignored the little island below the main island of Australia, expecting there was no way they would ever get there with the strip of sea in between.

Nine of the locations had thick red rings around them. Romy took that to mean they were major bases. Wetting her forefinger, she made the circles over these locations bigger. Two of them, New Brisbane and New Cairns, were close to Jimboomba.

Job done, she returned to the screen, scrolling.

"We've gotta go, Ro. It's midnight. We have six hours to get a safe distance away from here."

The words "Mandate Operatives" blared at her from the e-storage screen.

"You know we need that time," Phobos insisted.

With an aggravated growl, Romy turned from the screen and glared up at her friends.

Deimos was tucking the map back inside the rucksack. "We have plenty of information for now."

She nodded stiffly.

Phobos pocketed the keycard. He eyed the others, taking two packs and swinging three guns over his shoulder.

She reached for a bag, but Deimos tugged it from her, eyeing her with concern. He already had a heavy pack on each shoulder and carried her one in his arms.

"Let's go," he said softly. "Ellie and Thrym will be waiting."

* * *

Knot 27 sat waiting in the shadows of the short alleyway. Five bulging packs were arranged in a row, the objects within them the only chance they had to survive the wilderness.

Ellie and Thrym had managed to get basic medicine, but none of the anti-venom and antibiotics they'd planned to steal.

Her heart thumped wildly in her chest as they waited for the patrol to pass.

The ringing was still there, lessened, but not gone; muted enough to allow Romy to think coherently for the time being. She should be entirely focused on the escape, but something happened to her when she killed Lucas.

Something terrible. Something felt off, as though she were a shadow of herself.

She jumped as Phobos shuffled beside her. He reached out an arm and rubbed her back. Romy usually liked it, but at that moment it felt like he was grinding gravel into her skin. Her brows drew tight and she pushed his arm away, turning to stare at the fence. Bile rose in her throat for the umpteenth time as she remembered the blood spurting from Lucas's throat. Romy whimpered, rocking a little in place as the ringing intensified.

Thrym held his finger against his lips. The moonlight shined off his dark skin.

Soft voices drifted towards them from the other side. The voices sounded just a few metres away in the silent night, but Romy knew from

Eddie that the patrols moved fifty metres or so inside the tree line. On the hour.

As agreed, the group waited a further ten minutes once the patrol had passed.

Romy was first to stand.

She had to move. If she didn't move, she'd scream.

She approached the fence and slid the hidden panel aside. "Packs over the top," she murmured through stiff lips.

"What happened to her?" the whisper came from behind.

Romy ignored the question. Ducking through, she quickly surveyed the area for signs of life.

All was quiet.

Romy winced at the grating noise as Phobos forced his body to move through the fence. Leaving the others to deal with the packs, Romy crept to the vehicle and in rustling increments drew the leafy cover to the ground.

On second thought, she rolled the material up into a bundle and shoved it into a corner of the car boot.

"This is a heap of junk," Elara hissed.

Phobos snorted. "Feel free to go get us the most recent model, princess."

"Quiet," Romy snapped. "Elara, go take off the stopper so we can roll it."

"*Handbrake,*" was her muttered reply.

Thrym pushed in the fourth pack. The fifth wouldn't fit.

"It can go on our laps." Romy took the supplies from him and laid it inside the car.

She leant over and pointed to one side of the trees. "See that gap there?" She pointed. "That's how we normally get out."

Elara squinted. "Right. Got it."

Romy went around the back and the others followed her cue as she put the side of her body to the car and began to push. This was it. The moment where they were most likely to be caught. Tension held her body like a trigger.

They pushed for over half an hour, losing their way twice. Even then, nerves jolted through Romy when Elara turned over the engine.

The vehicle coughed to life.

"Thank the comets for that," Phobos puffed. He wiped a forearm across his face.

"Everyone in," Romy said.

She took the front to guide. It also meant she didn't have to touch anyone. The three men piled into the back, the fifth pack on their laps. Ironically, it was just as crowded in the car as the daytrips with Nancy had been, though they had just over half the number of people.

They turned the lights on dim after Elara nearly rolled them into a ditch.

"Watch out for the big ditch around the corner," Romy instructed.

Elara drove much slower than Eddie. Instead of the usual twenty minutes, another hour passed before the vehicle ambled into the target area.

"Where to now?" Elara asked. "I'd guess we're moving west of Jimboomba at the moment. But it's hard to tell."

Thrym stuck his head out of the window and looked up at the stars.

Elara's mouth snapped shut.

Deimos cleared his throat. "I'm sure if it weren't so obvious we would have thought of it."

Phobos chuckled.

"Southern cross is that way." Thrym pointed to the left. "We're travelling west."

"West will take us away from the other settlements," Romy said. The map was still vivid in her memory.

"It will also take us to water," Deimos said.

Romy twisted to look at him in the backseat.

He answered her silent question drily. "Not all of us were focused on the settlements. The updated map had other things on it. Like water."

"There's a mother of all lakes in the middle of this continent," Phobos added. "Towards the lower half, as we suspected."

"How far?" Thrym asked.

"No idea," Phobos replied cheerfully.

Elara pursed her lips and looked at Romy. "Away from the camps and towards a water supply."

Romy breathed heavily through the ringing. "Sounds like a good place to get our bearings."

"Westward," Dei cried.

Romy flinched horribly at the noise, and saw Phobos scowling at his twin in the rear-view mirror.

"Where to now?" Elara asked.

Romy shook her head. "I've never been past this point."

It was then Romy realised she had led her knot down an unknown path.

Elara shook her head, glimpsing Romy's terror. "Ro, if we'd taken another road, we would have had to abandon the car by now to avoid a sentry point. You did well."

She tried to smile at her friend's reassurance.

Thrym leant over. "Ro, are you okay? You. . . . You're acting a little strange." He was talking to her, but avoiding her gaze. He'd been doing it ever since he'd seen her covered in blood and continued to do so although she'd wiped off most of the blood in the bungalow.

Dizziness assaulted her and she squeezed her eyes closed.

The boys were whispering, but she could hear every word.

"She's been like that since she killed him."

Killed him. Killed him. Killed him.

"Uh, you guys?" Elara threw a worried look at Romy.

Romy realised she was rocking and stopped.

Deimos reached forwards and squeezed her shoulder. She shrugged him off.

Thrym was staring out the front window, deep in thought. "I think we can assume it's a little surprise from the Orbitos."

"What are you thinking?" Elara whispered to him, still casting furtive looks Romy's way.

"I'm not sure, yet." Thrym met Romy's gaze for a fleeting moment.

This time she turned away. "We shouldn't be wasting time sitting here." They were talking about her like she wasn't there. "Keep driving. We take the vehicle as far as we can to save Deimos's energy."

Elara's eyes lifted to the mirror, exchanging a look with the boys. Whatever she saw there had her shifting the middle stick into position. "Roger that, Ro."

The car lurched forwards into the unknown.

CHAPTER TWENTY-SEVEN

They walked through dense bush, only stopping for a couple of hours at a time. Hardly enough time to generate the energy to continue, and definitely not enough time to think about Atlas. So Romy wasn't complaining. Knot 27 had ditched the car three days ago, covering it with the leaf netting, after emptying it of their supplies.

An AK-103 now bounced against Romy's side.

There was only one thought on their minds: the people on their trail. Through Atlas, the Mandate and the Oribitos would be well aware of their escape by now.

Deimos held up an arm. "I need to rest."

His usual olive complexion was haggard and white. Deimos had looked near collapse all morning. Already, the night breaks had extended to three hours to give his nanos time to ready his body for the next day. Romy guessed burning hatred was the only thing keeping her knot mate going.

Phobos leaped forwards and guided the swaying man to the ground.

Elara was watching her. They hadn't stopped watching her since the car. She wished they wouldn't. It made her feel as though they were planning something behind her back.

"How are you feeling?" Elara asked.

Romy's mouth spoke the word, "Fine," before she turned away from Elara. How could she tell them that the ringing was still there? That the only time it lessened was when she moved, or ran.

They thought she was losing her mind.

She thought she was losing her mind.

And it happened when she killed Lucas. When she let her mind slip back to the sound of the knife slicing across his throat, an odd floating feeling came over her. With every passing second, she had to fight the urge to slip away in nothingness.

She was deathly afraid.

Thrym looked up at the sky through a patch of the dense bush they were trekking through. The sun was low on the horizon. "I say we stop for the night."

"No, I can keep going," Dei objected.

A surge of anger came over her. Romy dropped her pack in the shrubs and forced Deimos back to the ground. Defiant green eyes blinked up at her.

"If you collapse in two days when we're being chased, because you didn't take the offer of rest when it was given, I will feed you to a crocodile," she snarled.

Romy glared at the others. Thrym instantly looked away and Romy bit down on a fresh rush of irritation.

Blood. Bright red blood. Romy squeezed her eyes shut.

"You heard her, Dei." Phobos tried to cover the awkwardness with a joke.

Deimos relaxed underneath her. Romy forced her eyelids apart and found his green eyes were already falling into slow blinks. Shaking ever so slightly, Romy rose and picked up her pack, laying it to one side.

Elara was rolling out her lightweight swag. It was a mix between a sleeping bag and a tent. Deimos and Phobos had found them in the soldiers' supply room.

"You guys sleep. I'll take first watch," Romy offered.

The others shared a look. But she turned away before they could object.

Romy wedged her back against a tree and watched as her knot mates slipped into their swags and sank into an exhausted sleep. This was when the ringing was the worst. When she stopped moving; when her heart rate slowed. When it was quiet.

Romy climbed to her feet, opting to pace around the campsite instead. She knew her body could only be pushed so far, even with the nanotech, but until that happened she'd do anything to keep the ringing at bay.

Hours later, she rustled Elara's swag to wake her. It wasn't that Romy was tired; no, she just didn't want the knot to become warier of her than they'd already become.

"I went walking," she whispered to the half-asleep girl. "There's a waterfall a couple of hundred metres away."

Elara groaned and Phobos's swag shifted. "I'm having a bath tomorrow morning, I don't care who's chasing us."

The knot hadn't dared to stop at either of the two rivers they'd passed. Her white-blonde hair was still red at the tips with blood. Romy felt *sure* the ringing would go if she could get rid of the rest. She swore the smell of the blood's stench was still there, reaching her in the heat of the day.

And how could her knot forget what she'd done when Romy was still drenched in the evidence?

Every one of them had killed. But, it seemed, killing a human was different.

* * *

Phobos woke her at first light the next morning. He thought he did, anyway. Romy hadn't slept. Just closed her eyes and attempted to hold herself together.

"You and Elara go wash," he said. "We'll go after."

The promise of being clean was the brightest point of the last four days.

Elara stood on the bank next to her ten minutes later

Instead of a deep pool, the waterfall emptied into a shallow area dotted with boulders and stones. At most, the water looked knee deep, the bottom clearly visible and crocodile-free.

Elara shed her clothes in excitement and with a soft yelp, splashed her way into the small pool. Hesitation tugged in Romy's system. The bloody strands of her hair were a red blur in her peripherals.

In a few minutes, a dripping Elara climbed back up the bank, frowning at the fully-clothed Romy.

"What's the matter?" she asked.

How did Romy tell her that she didn't want Elara to see the water running red? That she was worried she was about to lose it? Romy didn't know if she could control her reaction to the sight.

"I . . . ," she started. "Would you give me a moment?"

She avoided Elara's heavy stare.

Romy scratched at her forearm where small dried flecks of blood dotted her tanned skin. "I need a moment."

A small hand lay on her arm. Romy surprised both of them by jerking away. But she couldn't help it. The sensation was like splinters of wood shoved under her fingernails.

Sad, sparkling hazel eyes met her own. "I'll see you back at camp," Elara said hoarsely.

Romy waited until Elara was out of sight before peeling off her grimy garments. She'd changed her clothing at Jimboomba, too. This wasn't the stickiness of blood; it was the stale sweat of walking eighteen hours a day in the savage heat.

She picked her way across the boulders, neck hairs rising at the cold spray from the waterfall.

Starting with her feet, she used her balled-up T-shirt to scrub at her skin. When that didn't prove good enough, she grabbed a handful of gravel from the riverbed and scoured the skin, relishing in the sharp pain. She sobbed as she worked upwards to her waist—kneeling in the shallow water, spending the most time on her hands, and her face where the warm blood had poured onto her. She closed her eyes briefly and Lucas's glassy eyes flashed across her vision.

Hiccupping, Romy waited for the water to run clear before submerging her head. She did it ten times, scratching at her scalp in the cool water. She had to get rid of it all. She keened as she scrubbed at her scalp harder and harder.

Occupied with the crazed, frantic scrubbing of her head, she didn't notice the person behind her until a shadow fell across the rock in front of her.

The person said something, but it was lost in her terror as her muscles tensed to bolt. But she didn't have time to move before she was encased in iron arms—a man's. One arm under her breasts, and the other firm across her mouth. Recovering, Romy screamed into the hand and threw herself backwards.

The tall man grunted and fell back, but otherwise didn't budge.

Romy kicked her legs, trying to dislodge the person's hold. Water was erupting everywhere, and the muffled yells she made seemed loud to her own ears, but she knew the sound would never travel the two hundred metres to her knot.

Why did she make Elara leave?

On second thought, Romy had never been happier that she did. Maybe her knot would make it out alive.

"Rosemary. Stop."

That voice!

Romy wrenched her head to one side to confirm it. Grey eyes stared down at her. Angry eyes.

Atlas.

Anger gave her strength she never knew she had. Romy ripped her head to the other side, dislodging the hand from her mouth. Then she bit down on his forearm. Hard.

She took a huge breath, ready to let out an almighty scream as he yelled in pain.

"Really, Atlas," another voice reprimanded.

A sharp sensation stabbed into her shoulder.

Romy's vision blurred. Her head lolled against the arms of a man she *loathed*. She hated that her death was in his arms.

Shining spectacles twinkled in front of her.

Houston.
Everyone on Earth was a lying traitor.

CHAPTER TWENTY-EIGHT

Her mind was slamming against her skull.

Romy groaned, lifting a hand to her temple. Her stomach rolled as the ground lurched beneath her.

"Rise and shhhhhine."

It spoke for how terrible she felt that Romy didn't react to Houston's voice by clawing his eyes out. Forcing her eyes open, she took stock.

Her knot members sat in a circle, tied to a tree. Blood trickled down Thrym's face, and their supplies were strewn all over the clearing. There had been a fight. And her knot lost. Dread fell like a rock into her stomach. She groaned again, this time because of a different pain. Atlas was going to hurt her family. He'd caught them.

But how?

She locked eyes with Deimos.

"The catheter has a kink," he said.

Romy tried to sit. And that was when she realised just how naked she was. Blushing, Romy pulled up the blanket wrapped around her so it was just under her chin.

"Bit late for that, little skyling," Houston sang. "Your breasts are divine, by the way. You wouldn't think it from outside the clothing, but believe me—"

A fist flew out of nowhere and smacked into the back of the doctor's head.

"Ow!"

Tilting her head, Romy unleashed the full power of her loathing on *him*. Atlas's expression flickered with some kind of emotion before he turned away.

He chucked some clothing at her. "Go, put these on."

Romy glanced at the clothing, not moving.

"And don't think of running. I have your knot."

Anger bubbling, Romy snatched up the clothing with one hand, clutching the blanket with the other.

Once in the tree line, she thought rapidly. Did the pair have backup? It seemed unlikely they came alone. Romy jerked a white T-shirt on and stormed back into the clearing. As she did, her eyes fell on a streamlined, two-wheeled vehicle that Houston was rolling into their strewn camp.

That explained how the pair caught up. But not how they found them so easily. Romy still didn't know if there were others.

Atlas turned as she approached. He didn't move as Romy pulled back her left hand and slapped him as hard as she possibly could across the face. His head rocked to the side, his feet unmoving. She heard Elara gasp behind her.

"You traitor," she said in a shaking voice.

He turned to face forwards, red handprint bright on his cheek. "You *idiot*," he countered. "Do you have any idea what you've done?"

Whatever response she'd expected, it wasn't that. Romy folded her arms, taking a step backwards. When in doubt, remain silent.

Atlas invaded the space she'd just established. "You were nearly safe," he yelled.

Romy's eyes widened, despite her own fury as Atlas lost his temper. She shook her head. "I heard you, Atlas! I heard you talking to Tina, saying how the Orbitos were coming to get us. Our *bodies*."

Atlas opened his mouth.

"Atlas," Houston said quietly.

"How did you find us?" snapped Romy, turning to the less-confusing doctor.

Houston rubbed the back of his head. "Uh, well, I put trackers in each of you."

Why was it Houston kept failing her? He grew pale under the force of her withering glare.

Romy looked between them as Atlas ran a hand through his hair. It looked like he'd been doing it constantly for the last several days. "Houston, they need to be told something."

Houston stared at the larger man. "You know the risk?"

Atlas gave a curt nod and turned to Romy. "What you *think* you heard, was not what you think at all."

She crossed her arms. "Okay, let's hear it, then."

His jaw clenched at the sarcasm in her voice. He inhaled heavily. "That's all I can tell you, right now."

"You have got to be joking!" Deimos shouted.

Atlas whirled on her knot. "I want you to listen closely. And I want you to think about what I'm saying, and what it might mean."

It was like the ground she was standing on was shaking. Because she desperately wanted there to be a valid reason for his lies. He still affected her in the best possible way, and she hated it.

Houston had grabbed Atlas's arm. "You need to be careful," he muttered. "Until we get to the bunker."

She wasn't sure if that had been meant for her ears.

Atlas faced their knot. "Did any of you ever consider that if you were caught, your memories will be studied? That everything you've heard will be noted. And to a small degree, what you have seen will be watched."

Romy squeezed her eyes shut. What was he saying? How was that possible?

Houston stepped in. "Genetically enhanced soldiers are each fitted with extensive memory nano-wear. It is most accurate with recording what you hear, for lack of a better layman's term."

Thrym spoke behind her. "So we weren't told anything in case we were caught."

Houston and Atlas nodded, staying silent.

Her brows drew together. "Why didn't you just tell us that was the reason?"

"Because the information is only known to a select few. It would have narrowed their list of suspects considerably," Atlas replied.

Houston had said audio was the particular thing they had to watch for. "What about visual?" she asked. Should they be more worried Knot 27 had seen their faces?

Houston shook his head. "Too subjective. Clouded by judgements, light, and emotion—just to name a few."

But Atlas spoke to Commander Cronus daily.

. . .Was Atlas playing both sides? She darted a look at him. Was that even a thing? Was there another side to be *on*?

"Unfortunately, your actions alerted the Mandate to something being amiss," Atlas said flatly, staring at her.

Was it the call? Or killing Lucas? She ground her teeth. "Are you seriously blaming me, *Commander*?"

Houston cursed under his breath. "Shit, Atlas. They know too much already. The Mandate can't get ahold of them with the information they know. It will lead straight to you."

Atlas placed his hands behind his back and approached Knot 27. "I need you to come with us. Right now. Once Houston has a chance to remove your memory chips, then I can tell you all you wish to know."

"Why didn't you take them out when we first arrived?" Elara burst out, struggling against her bindings.

Both Houston and Atlas kept their lips closed.

Romy's heart beat wildly in her chest. Could there be a chance she'd been wrong about it all? Devastation pulled her downwards. Lucas. If Atlas was innocent, then she'd killed a man for nothing.

"I can tell you everything once we reach the bunker."

One thing was bothering her.

Phobos beat her to it. "I hope you're not implying we take your word for it?" He eyed Atlas with distrust.

Romy's head gave a painful throb. "Ro?" Elara asked.

She wrung her hands together. "I don't know whether to trust what they say. I won't trust him until he tells me everything."

They were still looking at her expectantly.

"I can't make this decision."

"I'm afraid it doesn't matter whether you believe me or not. If you don't follow me, you'll all die. Your entire knot." Atlas's eyes were hard. "They're behind us. They're hunting you."

Shock coursed through her and she welcomed the mental clarity it brought.

"As I said, you can either stay put and get caught by the Mandate in just over twenty-four hours. Or you can follow me to the safe house."

"I say we do it," a deep voice said. Thrym?

Romy couldn't help the sound of surprise that left her. Out of everyone, Thrym trusted him?

Thrym was staring at her from where he sat tied to the tree. Sure. Now that the blood was washed off he could look at her.

"We need more information. . . ." He trailed off, and Romy could see he was thinking hard. Thrym had another reason for wanting to go with the two men. He had a plan. Elara and Phobos were watching him. They nodded at the same time.

"I say we go to this safe house," Phobos said.

"We'll come with you," Thrym said again. "But you will tell us one more thing before we leave."

Atlas remained silent.

Thrym licked his lips, glancing at Romy.

And Romy understood what he was going to ask. Whipping around, she turned to repack her swag, unable to stand their stares. But her ears strained to hear every word.

"What's happening to Ro?" Thrym asked softly.

Houston interrupted immediately. "We can't—"

"No, H," Atlas said.

"Are *you* insane?" Houston whispered. "If they ever found out. . . ."

Footsteps approached behind her. She clenched the swag in a death grip as she rolled it.

His voice spoke only to her, though everyone could hear.

"The Orbitos creators knew that if the four thousand ever found out about the betrayal, they'd need protection from you."

Romy stared at her pack with unseeing eyes.

"And so each of the four thousand has a built-in safety . . . which triggers when killing a human being."

"Enough!" Houston shouted. "You've told them too much, Atlas! Don't be a fool. We've worked too hard and too long for this."

And what was the safety, Romy wondered. To go insane? That was how she felt. To die from lack of sleep? Or to stop functioning altogether? She wanted to lie down, right here, and stare at nothing. Was that what it did?

Her eyes closed as the terrible truth settled upon her. Something inside her *was* broken.

Everyone was shouting at each other. Houston was screaming at her knot. And Romy was just too tired to deal with it all.

"It was him?"

She jumped at the words, glancing over her shoulder at Atlas.

He studied her intently. It reminded her of his expression when they first met. He'd looked at her like she was an experiment.

She didn't answer.

"If he hurt you, he got everything he deserved," Atlas said in a low voice.

Did one unwilling kiss, a forced caress, a few pushes, and threats justify killing a man? Romy looked up at Atlas, who watched her still.

You didn't mean to kill him, his expression seemed to say.

But she had.

She should feel remorse.

But she only felt terror at the memory of his blood.

CHAPTER TWENTY-NINE

Romy walked at the back. She couldn't be near Atlas until she knew he was telling the truth.

The ringing had disappeared just before daybreak this morning.

Instinctually, Romy knew its replacement was worse.

A block had descended on her mind that she couldn't push through. It was as if the denial had made her stronger before. But now that she had confirmation something was wrong, her defence was stripped away.

A fog clouded her judgement, keeping her slightly to the side of reality. It filled her with every breath, but didn't leave her lungs on the breath out. It was filling her mind, slowly taking over her actions. The floating sensation was back. Romy had become a shadow of herself.

Worse was the glass. That was the only way she could describe it. It felt like Romy's sanity was encased in a glass cabinet. And she stood paralysed, scared to move for fear the glass would break.

There were cracks in the glass already, in her mind's eye. The largest was right under her feet—from killing Lucas—with the other cracks branching out in ugly splinters all around her.

One was from Atlas's betrayal.

Another from the thought of Knot 27 perishing.

Washing the blood from her hair.

Thrym's avoidance.

Her knot's wary glances.

"You all right, little skyling?"

Romy blinked into Houston's face. She looked around and saw she'd wandered quite far from the rest of them. She was heading in an entirely different direction. Her eyes met Houston's once more. She expected to see amusement in his features at her wandering off the path. But it wasn't there. There was concern. And something else she couldn't grasp. Excitement?

Romy swallowed. "Of course. Just tired."

He stared at her until he caught sight of her perplexed expression, and straightened with a sniff.

"Don't wander off. There are drop bears everywhere." He looked up into the trees with apprehension as he shifted back to the group.

240

Romy peered into the trees also.

She brushed through the knee-high, grass-like shrubs and looked up, noticing Houston was now up by Atlas, their heads together in deep discussion.

Thrym searched her face as Romy neared. She kept her features blank.

He shied away as she came close and Romy jolted, seized in fear as the glass in her mind cracked just a little more.

* * *

Every so often Houston would fall back to Deimos's side and give him a shot of something. Whatever it was, it kept the twin going long past what he would otherwise have been capable of. Romy walked into Elara.

"We're stopping for the rest of the night," Elara explained.

It didn't look like Houston was on the same page. "We should keep going," he was insisting.

The moon was bright. Bright enough to see Atlas flick a dark look her way.

"No," he said.

Romy shucked her pack and rested her back against a tree. She wanted to keep moving, to ensure her knot was safe before she fell through the glass in her mind. Romy didn't expect she'd come back if that happened.

Heavy steps halted in front of her. Romy's chest squeezed as Atlas approached. But the man simply righted her pack from where she had dumped it, opened the top, and removed her swag with a sharp tug.

Romy peeked under her lashes as he rolled the swag out onto a clear patch of ground. Atlas stared down at the bedding afterward and then turned his head to meet her gaze.

Anger, worry, arrogance, compassion, deceit. It was possible every one of those emotions were present. But without knowing which it was, Romy wasn't going to trust those gorgeous grey eyes. She'd trusted them once before. And if he broke her trust again, that would be the end.

The tall man folded his long frame to sit down next to her. Not touching. Somehow he knew not to touch her. He sat near enough that she could feel the added warmth of his body.

"Hey. Look what I found!" Houston exclaimed. He was plucking something off his body.

He ran over to Romy and held out his hand. In between his thumb and forefinger was a small, wriggling insect.

She gave him a doubtful look, too tired to care. "What is it?"

A wooden sound reached her ears. Was that her voice?

His glasses glinted in the moonlight, giving the doctor's face a creepy luminous quality. "It's a *leech*, little skyling. They suck blood from human bodies."

Romy froze at the mention of blood. Why was he showing this to her?

Houston pinched his fingers together firmly. The bug exploded. Red trickled down over the doctor's hand. The leech writhed in jerking swirls and time slowed as Houston threw the bloody insect to the ground, droplets of blood flying from his hand.

To land at her feet.

It was all over her! Spurting blood! Everywhere! The floating unreal sensation had been present ever since killing Lucas. But this time she didn't just float. Romy was flung out of herself. A drumming noise bounced everywhere, the noise doubling back on itself in an escalating clamour. And above it, a high keening. Romy looked down to the ground and reeled back.

She was high above the ground now, floating there. Below her, side by side with only a thin wall between them, sat two apparitions. Her eyes fixated on the left side of the partition.

The person there had the same blonde hair as Romy.

It *was* her, she realised. But this Romy's hair hung in greasy clumps, blue eyes popping wildly from her face. This version writhed in agonised spasms, screaming and twisting, trying to escape the box she'd been squeezed into.

On the other side, the second Romy sat on a rock, frozen in the moonlight, staring at the dirt by her feet. In this scene, the Romy was musing that the dust wasn't *really* red here after all; more an orange. When it was put next to human blood, the difference in hue was obvious.

Romy hovered over the two scenes. She could go to either, but not both. She merely had to choose which one to land in. She felt the choice should be obvious, but couldn't recall why that should be. She looked from the serene Romy to the demented Romy once more.

Then, squeezing her eyes closed from high above, she chose.

* * *

The scene was wildly different from when she left.

Atlas had one hand wrapped around Houston's throat, the other hand raised to deliver a hammering blow. Thrym was sprinting at the larger man. Atlas roared and threw him back with a powerful swipe of his arm.

What was going on?

Atlas had let go of Houston to get rid of Thrym, but he now resumed his stranglehold.

Romy could see he was going to slam his fist down onto Houston's face. *Blood*.

Romy was up and had a hold on Atlas's arm as it descended. She pulled back with all her strength. Atlas turned on her in a blur.

There was a small instant where she saw the murder in his eyes. But then. . . .

The doctor was dropped with a thud.

Romy winced as his head bounced on rock. Houston gasped for breath, too weak to roll out from the dangerous space Atlas occupied.

Atlas was staring at her in amazement. Like he could barely believe his eyes. What had he witnessed in those first few seconds?

"You?" he breathed.

"What?" Romy snapped. What the hell was going on?

"You're still here."

He was trying to conceal his reaction, with obvious difficulty. And for the first time, Romy came to understand there must be something unusual in her behaviour—to how she'd reacted to Lucas's death.

"Why wouldn't I be?"

Romy waited, but the answer didn't come. *Not until the safe house*, she thought bitterly.

Atlas's look of amazement didn't quite make sense, and it was making her paranoid.

Romy ignored the hushed silence and slipped into her sleeping bag where no one could see her. It quickly grew unbearably warm in the space as her breath heated the inside. But she stayed there, hanging on to herself with her fingertips. What would have happened if she'd chosen the wild Romy? She stared at the dark material centimetres from her face.

Gradually, the others quietened.

It was possibly hours later when someone finally spoke.

Houston was whispering. "I told you. She's the key. I think we've finally found it, Atlas."

The bespectacled man was always cheerful, often excited, and always glib. Which was why Romy held her breath at the desperation in his tone. The anguish. And the longing.

A sharp order to "shut his mouth" came from Atlas.

Several long beats passed and Romy was just about to emerge from the sauna-like temperature in her swag, when the doctor spoke again.

"We need her, Atlas. You know we do."

Romy strained her ears, shutting her eyes and holding every muscle tight as though if any other sense were open, it would make hearing Atlas's reply impossible.

Atlas's words slipped through the dead-calm of night towards her with ease.

"I know."

CHAPTER THIRTY

It might make her a terrible person, but right then she would have chosen to return to the lie, to the Orbitos. Romy remembered the chocolate cake; she remembered her nanopad and the cadets' lectures. And if given the choice, in that moment, she would have given up her memory.

Her knot hardly spoke to her as they continued their blind trek through the forest after Atlas. They didn't know how she'd react. *She* didn't either.

There was one change.

When she rose from her swag after another sleepless night, she'd noticed a difference in the glass case around her mind. One of the tiny cracks had healed. A miniscule change. Romy could only put it down to her "floating experience" yesterday. She wondered if maybe it had healed because she chose the right path. The fog was still thick in her mind. But as the knot and two men marched ahead of her, Romy clung to this infinitesimal difference. The crack had healed. It had to mean something.

It gave her hope that whatever was broken could be fixed.

"I heard them talking last night." She spoke to Thrym as they paused either side of a eucalyptus tree. Romy could tell by the direction of the sun they weren't heading towards the middle of Australia anymore. They were moving north, keeping up a fast walk with barely any stops. If the sun hadn't been there, Romy would have no idea. The bush repeated over and over, only interrupted by the occasional dip and crest. Atlas and Houston seemed to know exactly where they were going, she thought darkly.

Thrym jerked in surprise. She didn't blame him. This might be the first time she'd spoken to him in days and her voice sounded like she'd screamed into a pillow for a week straight.

He looked ahead after a moment. "What were they saying?"

"That I was the key. The answer to their problem."

Her friend took a long time to mull this over. Too long. "You don't believe me," she whispered. The realisation made her want to vomit.

He was quick to reply. "Romy. No. Don't think that. It's just . . . well, you've been a bit paranoid. And—"

A bitter taste flooded her mouth. "You don't believe your own knot mate?" Some friend he was.

Thrym grabbed her arm and swung her around. She wrenched her arm free, her right fist curled tightly.

His brows drew together as he struggled to form the words.

"What is it?" Her voice could lash bark from a tree.

He looked her square in the eyes. "That," he said. "That's 'it'."

She gave him a flat look.

"You're unstable, Ro. And I couldn't care less if you're the key, or that this could be a trap. Houston is the only person who may be able to fix you and that's all that matters right now."

Romy stared at him in disbelief. "*That's* your reason for following them?" she said, her voice growing in strength. "I thought you had an actual plan, Thrym." A sharp pain lanced through her and Romy gathered from Thrym's startled expression that its cruel passage had flashed on her face.

"I only agreed because I thought you had a plan," she scoffed before turning away.

Slowly, with grating fractures, the tiny crack in the glass she'd been so relieved to find gone this morning reappeared.

* * *

Thrym spread word to the others. Her knot now watched Romy like the Critamal and Orbitos watched each other—with both eyes.

The shift was blatant. But her knot hadn't told Atlas or Houston what had transpired between her and Thrym. Nevertheless, the pair could sense the tension and wariness the others now treated her with.

Her knot thought she was dangerous.

Romy wanted to throw her head back and scream that they were all idiots. She was still here. In control for the moment. Waiting for the fragile something to shatter and the bubbling insanity underneath to splinter forth and consume her.

Or did they think she'd run?

They should be worried about her staying. Who knew what would happen once Romy became the woman on the other side of the wall—the feral version of herself.

Sleep was impossible. She lay down anyway, just so Phobos, the one charged with first Ro-watch for the night, would be able to carry out Romy-duty in relative comfort.

But she lay awake and stared into the dark.

Soon only the creaking of crickets and the occasional scramble of fighting animals in the distance could be heard. There was no ocean, no breeze. Just dead stillness.

Until a tiny rustling alerted her to Atlas creeping from his swag. She stared, unblinking, as he took a tentative step just inside the tree line. He had one hand to his ear. When he turned she saw the expression on his face.

It was as though a hand had reached inside her and gripped her stomach in a tight fist.

Fear. His face was slack with it. Eyes wild, pacing now jerky and uncontrolled.

Romy slid soundlessly from her bedding, grabbing the knife next to her. Phobos didn't move—he always was a useless sentry.

She glided up behind Atlas and watched him a little longer. He had a hand to his ear. The transmitter, she realised. He still had it with him. What was he doing with it?

Romy adjusted her grip on the knife by her side. The hilt was slippery in her sweating hand.

"Something wrong?" she asked.

Atlas whirled towards her, thunderous scowl in place. But then two things happened.

The man in front of her held a finger to his lips, and shut his eyes while listening to the transmission device in his ear.

Then he looked up at her in horror, face half-cloaked in shadow.

"They're coming."

CHAPTER THIRTY-ONE

She stuffed her bedding into her pack after jostling the others awake.

She shoved the knife in after it. What had she intended to do with it anyway? She couldn't stomach killing someone she hated—how could Romy even consider hurting someone she used to care about?

The camp was in disarray.

Houston injected Deimos with the unknown substance. Romy wondered how much he had. She wouldn't mind some to keep her awake another couple of nights.

"We'll be moving fast. Keep up, or die," Atlas said.

He wasn't exaggerating about the pace. It was closer to a run than a walk. Her pack bounced up and down in a heavy beat, dragging at her shoulders.

Even with the injection, a few hours later, Deimos began to flag.

If Romy had never gone to Atlas's office that night, then Deimos wouldn't be pushing himself to the edge of exhaustion. A long, thin crack appeared in the glass of her mind. She stumbled over a tree root in the physical world, scrambling to regain her feet.

"Leave the bags," Atlas ordered.

Romy's mouth dried. They needed their supplies. The others had shirked theirs and Atlas shoved them into the brush, out of sight.

Her hands hovered above the straps.

"We don't have time for this." Atlas pushed the straps from her shoulders.

"Wait!" she cried, quickly retrieving something. He threw the bag into the bush, eyeing the map clutched in her hand.

Next, he reached for her AK-103. She turned that side of her body away and scowled at him.

He conceded and reached for her hand before stopping himself. "I'll come back for the packs once it's safe."

She swallowed her disbelief, flashing a placated smile.

His eyes narrowed as he began jogging, pulling her along. "I want you to stay up front with me."

Before, they'd jogged. Now they ran. The sun rose, the looming trunks turning a haunting grey in the dim light of dawn. A tension filled the air and Romy couldn't be sure if it was generated from their group of seven, or because some sixth sense told her hunters were close.

They didn't stop.

A glance over her shoulder told Romy that the others were taking turns helping Deimos. But their pace was dropping further and further to accommodate his gasping weakness. Romy could almost feel Atlas's frustration. Could interpret from it that if their speed didn't pick up they would have problems.

Elara yelled from the back as Deimos tumbled forwards and crashed to the ground.

The rest of the knot rushed forwards, but Romy stayed where she was, watching Atlas's face. Furrows of worry riveted his brow.

Atlas spoke softly. "He has to be left behind."

Whatever she'd expected, it wasn't that. "No."

He looked up, surprised to see her there.

"We have to." He gestured to his ear. "We're two hours away from the bunker. They can't find us there. But we have to get there first." Atlas grabbed her shoulders and turned her to the right.

"That hill," he said. "We need to get over that hill."

Romy noticed he didn't specify the direction. Even now he worried more about the audio chip in Romy's brain than giving her tangible details.

Obviously the memory card still worked if the space soldiers were dead. Which they were going to be, because a meteor shower couldn't stop her from bringing Deimos with them.

"No," she repeated.

"Don't be a fool." He shook her. "We can save the rest of them. Deimos will be okay. Houston will stabilise him. We cover him. I'll come back for him once you're safe."

A protectiveness she hadn't felt in a week surged to the fore. "No! Not happening."

Atlas ran both hands through his black hair and surveyed her, gripping what he could of the short locks.

He brushed past her and barked at Houston to stand back. Picking up one of Deimos's limp arms, Atlas hauled Deimos—not small by any means—across his shoulders.

He moved back to the front of the group as Romy tried to withhold her surprise.

They resumed their pace. It was quicker than before, though Atlas carried the unconscious Deimos. Romy couldn't help casting frequent darting looks at the towering man beside her. He continued to alter her perception of him every time she thought she might finally understand him.

He was carrying Deimos on his back.

But you've been wrong once before, a voice reminded her. Romy brushed it aside.

Did he do it for selfish reasons, because Romy was "the key"—whatever that meant—or because he cared?

The one good thing about their gruelling pace? Romy felt stronger than she had in days. Like the adrenaline surge had placed a temporary welding over the worst of the cracked glass, holding her strong until her knot was safe. Even the fog was gone.

Romy swung the rifle higher on her shoulder and looked behind to check everyone was there. Elara had her head bowed, clearly near her limit. Romy's dedication to her exercise routines on the orbito had paid off, and Elara's laziness hadn't.

Atlas gave her a glance as she started dropping back. A light frown shone under the glisten of sweat.

"Elara needs help," Romy explained.

He nodded, grunting as he hoisted Deimos into a better position.

Romy let Phobos, Houston, and Thrym pass by to jog beside Elara.

"You can say it," the pixie-haired girl puffed.

"You should've done more cardio," Romy said immediately.

Elara let out a breathless laugh. "You . . . suck."

Romy pointed upwards. "Atlas said it's just over that hill."

Elara looked up. And up. And groaned with what breath she could spare. "Shoot. Okay. But there better be some kind of massage lined up when we arrive."

A tight smile played on Romy's lips as she jogged just behind the girl, gun bouncing at her side. When the going got tough, Elara became a comedian.

The ground beneath her feet began to slope upwards, and the burning in her calf muscles grew with each step. It seemed like the hill was too much for even Atlas to maintain a jog. He slowed to a walk, ignoring Thrym, who offered to take Dei.

"Do you think Dei is faking it so he doesn't have to run?" Phobos called back.

Elara chuckled, holding her side.

Romy moved up to ask Atlas how much longer.

The man stopped at her query, breathing hard. He looked up the hill. They were about halfway there. As he looked back the way they had come, his features contorted.

Romy spun to see what had startled him.

At first she couldn't see anything. But there. . . . Romy's eyes widened. A glint flashed not far from the base of the hill.

Atlas cursed under his breath and turned away without answering.

They'd found Knot 27. Their pursuers were here.

"How did they find us?" Thrym asked Atlas.

Romy fell back again to walk beside Elara. She strained to hear the reply.

"The Mandate has many ways of finding those they hunt. And we have few ways to hide from their hunters," Houston said quietly.

They reached the top of the hill in the next half hour. Atlas sat on a rock and studied them, panting.

"We need to move downhill like the Critamal are up our arse," he said.

He didn't have to expand on his statement. The Mandate's forces had to be hot on their trail.

That meant . . . when their group reached the bottom of the other side . . . the enemy soldiers would be at the top. With their guns. It would be like picking up space debris. Her group would be powerless, unable to stop the jaws from closing around and crushing them.

"Graphic," grunted Phobos.

Atlas nodded, standing once more. Romy couldn't believe he was still going. She remembered reading about Trojans once. Atlas was like one of those mythical beings.

"Rosemary," he called back. "I want you up beside me."

He hoisted Deimos into a better position. "You don't stop running for anything," he told her. "Now, go!"

CHAPTER THIRTY-TWO

It quickly became apparent that Atlas couldn't safely navigate the slope with Deimos over his shoulder. Phobos and Thrym became his shadows, helping Atlas to pass Deimos down the steeper sections and supporting what they could of his weight. They ran down the hill in a barely controlled stampede.

Blood pumped through her body, and Romy smiled as she sprinted. This was the best she'd felt in a week. Adrenaline coursed through her veins.

Romy could feel the ground under her feet, and was tethered to *herself*—not her shadow—for the first time since Houston squished the leech.

She stayed close in front of Atlas down the hill. It bothered her that they were leading the Mandate straight to the bunker.

But Atlas and Houston must have taken that into consideration, she realised.

It took them much less time to get down the hill.

Getting down the hill wasn't the hard part.

The sparse bush was their enemy now—the lack of cover.

Atlas's breath was laboured as he kept up a fast clip beside her. Sweat streamed from every part of him, drenching the tight black T-shirt he wore. He stared resolutely at the ground in front of him.

"How far?" Elara gasped, holding her side.

"Nearly there," Houston called.

The doctor looked over this shoulder, back at the hill. And his face drained of blood. "Take cover!" he shouted, diving for Romy.

He threw himself in front of her, shoving her back as a gunshot ricocheted, embedding into a tree right where Houston's head had been.

Romy stared at Houston, who was frantically searching her for . . . a wound? The others had scattered, but were torn between watching the doctor and trying to guess where the next gunshot would be.

"What are you all staring at?" Atlas bellowed. "Move!"

Elara screamed as she ran, dragged along by a merciless Phobos.

Houston darted into a thicker patch of bush and dropped to his knees, fumbling in his pocket.

"What are you doing?" Thrym puffed.

"Stand back!" Houston shouted. He clicked on the contraption he'd pulled from his pocket. Romy and the others watched as, with a loud groan, the forest floor opened beneath them.

Atlas signalled to Thrym. "Take him." He deposited Deimos unceremoniously into Thrym's arms. And then turned, sprinting onward through the bush.

Romy took a running step after him. A hand gripped her arm.

"No, Romy," Houston said. "He's leading them astray."

The ground was still receding beneath them like a series of sliding doors gliding open, except the sliding doors were two-metre-deep slabs of rock. Layer after layer opened until Romy could no longer see into the depths. There were no stairs, no ladder, and the tunnel was completely vertical. How were they supposed to get down?

Atlas returned, wet, and relief coursed through her.

A whirring sound came from the vertical tunnel. A grating. Something within the tunnel was rising. How long did they have before the soldiers got down the hill? Could they see them from here? The bush had thickened once more, but they'd know Knot 27 disappeared somewhere in the area.

She squinted as a caged platform rose into view from the tunnel's depths. Houston waved them all on board.

"Quickly." Atlas gripped her elbow and she was forced to leap onto the platform, or be dragged.

She helped Thrym with Deimos, laying him down on the platform as the others jumped after her. There was another click, and they began their descent. The rocky layers closed above them as they dropped deep into the earth.

* * *

"My point is," pressed Thrym, "that the Mandate knows exactly where we are."

Atlas looked exhausted and Romy wanted to tell Thrym to stop. But her friend was right.

Maybe they'd fall for the trail that Atlas had created, leading to a river close by. Maybe they would follow the river, thinking the knot had jumped in. *Maybe.*

"This bunker has five different exits. Regardless of whether they know where we are or not, they won't be able to get *in*. Not even by dropping a bomb directly on top of us," he replied.

Romy blinked the ringing away. It was just starting to come back. "So . . . we're trapped."

He swung his tired eyes to her. "They might find the one entrance, but there are four others that we can leave through. We're not trapped."

"But we're not safe." Thrym folded his arms. "You promised us safety."

Atlas stood toe-to-toe with him, the taller of the two. "You would currently be dead without me. Compared to that, you are safe."

Thrym snorted, refusing to budge.

Atlas didn't break the stare. "Houston," he barked.

"What can I do ya for, boss?"

Phobos snorted.

"I want Rosemary's memory card out, now."

"She doesn't *like* being called Rosemary," Thrym ground out.

Houston pushed his glasses upwards. "Well . . . ideally, I'd like to study—"

"Now!" Atlas shouted, breaking away from Thrym.

Atlas grabbed Romy's arm and pulled her with him. She tore her arm away and jogged to keep up.

They'd descended for well over a hundred metres before arriving at the bottom where a horizontal tunnel greeted them. They'd walked for an hour, doing their best to drag Deimos along, before arriving in this cavern—the bunker, a multi-roomed facility carved from the stone.

There were rooms, beds, medical equipment, printers—everything they'd need to survive.

They entered into a room filled with screens and medi-tech. There were five screens, each showing a different picture of the bush. *Cameras*, she realised. Watching the entrances.

Atlas pushed her gently down onto the hospital bed beside Deimos's bed.

"How long did this place take to make?" she asked.

"Ten years, five months, and twenty-seven days," he answered without emotion.

Houston instructed her to lie down, and busied himself connecting her to what felt like a hundred different machines.

"We followed you here. We've held up our end of the bargain. Now talk," she ordered. Her hands fisted in the sheets on the bed as she stared at Atlas.

The three conscious members of the knot had filtered into the room behind Romy. Elara had large rings around her eyes, and immediately collapsed into a chair. Phobos and Thrym both looked wired. Phobos paced in front of the door, while Thrym stood to attention, hands gripped too tightly behind his back.

Houston broke away from Romy to stab something into Deimos.

Everyone jumped as Deimos sat bolt upright, drawing in a huge breath.

"Gets me every time," Houston chuckled.

Phobos crossed to his twin's side. "We made it to the bunker, Dei. You're okay. We're safe."

Atlas approached Romy's bed. She shifted her feet to allow him space, and he sat. Weariness slumped his shoulders.

"I'm not sure where to start," he said, running his hand through his hair.

"I think you should start in the middle, and then do flashbacks to the start," Houston offered. "Or, *Or!* Start at the end and work back."

Romy winced as the doctor yanked down the front of her top to slap some electrodes below her clavicle.

"That guy never shuts up," Phobos muttered, now at Deimos's side.

Atlas stared at Romy for a long, long moment. She was unsure what he was searching for. Something shifted in his gaze the longer he kept his eyes on her. His handsome face settled into softer lines.

He inhaled sharply. "From age eighteen, I've been commander of Orbito Four. I was placed there as a cadet at seventeen."

Romy and the others stared at him. Thrym rounded to her side, dodging around a focused Houston. The doctor pushed a needle under her skin, and she barely felt it. *Commander of Orbito Four.*

"How did you become commander?" she croaked.

He shifted uncomfortably. "I have some high-profile family members . . . and I'm not the commander anymore. Not after the events of the last few days."

The knot sat in frozen silence as they absorbed that.

Elara licked her lips. "Wouldn't your absence be noticed?"

"Orbito Four is full of. . . ." Atlas glanced at Romy. "All the people who have lost their knot."

Her gaze fell to her fisted hands. What he meant was, Orbito Four was for soldiers who had lost their minds. Everyone knew what Orbito Four was for.

He shrugged. "They do not register my absence. Orbito Four is a research vessel first and foremost. The unstable soldiers are studied and we send teams out to Earth."

"The research teams," Romy said.

Atlas looked at her. "Yes," he said. "Except the teams don't research. They are orbito representatives at Mandate meetings. The teams are doctors, strategists, psychiatrists, engineers, geneticists. All those aboard Orbito Four are in the employ of the organisation I work for. It has taken us over a century to infiltrate to this extent. It was our greatest achievement."

And he'd thrown this away to help them. Romy could see the sadness in his eyes; over ten years for his people to build this bunker, over a century to infiltrate a space station. Yet he'd chosen to help the knot and risk it all, at great danger to himself.

Understanding dawned. "That's why you had the transmission dock set up. So Commander Cronus would think you were on the orbito!"

Atlas nodded.

Her eyes were unblinking. Atlas was commander of Orbito Four? This whole time?

Houston rolled Romy onto her side. She jerked as a long needle slid between the vertebrae in her neck.

"Be careful!" Atlas snapped.

Houston ignored him, going about his work.

"You're setting up a rebellion," Romy whispered.

The knot and Atlas stared at her in stunned silence. She winced as Houston's hand jolted.

"Ha!" Houston exclaimed. "Told you she would figure it out, shit-for-brains."

"Jesus, H, try to show some damn respect."

"I've been with you for too long for that."

Atlas mumbled, "I don't think you showed any at the start either."

Houston smiled. "And I probably won't at the end."

Something passed between the two—a camaraderie that ran deep.

Atlas stood from the hospital bed and turned to Romy. "Yes, as you have obviously worked it out, there are . . . efforts . . . to counter the Mandate's rule." His eyes landed on Romy. "Though it was created well before my *birth*."

She knew he was born, not made. But an unwelcome thought occurred to her as he stressed the word "birth". Did it matter to him that she was made?

"Our network is vast."

That's why he's a little too tall.

"But how is that kind of thing faked?" Elara asked around a yawn.

Atlas's eyes shifted to Houston. "Once we transport you to the main base I'll tell you more about our organisation; our vision, our plans. But we work against the Mandate. That much you've probably guessed."

256

Houston was flicking the machines to life. They started with a whir, and Romy closed her eyes. The ringing had grown to a bell clamour.

"What are you doing to me?" she asked.

"Removing your memory card; taking some snaps of your brain. Turn those on, will ya?" He pointed Thrym to the screens behind the bed.

Atlas continued. "When I first found you, Rosemary, I immediately noticed how . . . together you were. You'd potentially lost your knot. Yet, you were still caring for yourself, eating and drinking."

Romy blushed. He made it sound like a selfish thing.

"It is nothing to be ashamed of," he reassured her. "Just rare to the point of . . . you being the first I'd seen acting this way. And I spent ten years on Orbito Four."

"You kept asking me questions," she said through numb lips. "Asking me what I'd do if they were dead."

"And you grew hysterical each time, but still didn't stop functioning."

Anger churned in her chest. Even then, he'd been testing her.

"But why did you leave when Thrym came? Why did you lead me to my friends?"

He avoided her gaze and didn't answer.

The clamouring grew unbearable. She cried out, clutching her head.

"Shh, Ro, you're okay." Thrym hovered by her side.

"It hurts, Thrym," she whimpered.

His eyes burned with unshed tears. "I know, I know. But I'm here. I won't let anything hurt you."

The right words. From the wrong person.

"I led you off-course at first, following a branch of the river." Atlas's voice broke through, rushing. "I could easily fake one space soldier's death, and leave the rest of your knot to be found by the Mandate."

Of course he did, Romy thought bitterly.

"But then, I . . . ," he trailed off, almost sounding nervous. "I woke one day, and I just couldn't do that anymore . . . so I led you to your friends," he finished.

And disappeared.

"I meant to wait until Deimos died," Atlas admitted. "One less body to fake."

Silence occupied the cavern, aside from the steady typing from Houston.

"Well . . . that's . . . shitty," Deimos said.

"I was going to get rid of Rosemary's part of the ship with a team, and then collect the rest of you, and bring you straight here. But then . . . I couldn't do that either."

He sounded angry about it, not apologetic. Some of his decisions seemed callous and ruthless, but with this insight into the weight he bore, it was no wonder he'd made them.

"Thank the stars you wanted to have sex with Romy," Deimos muttered sarcastically.

Houston laughed and Atlas glared at him.

The doctor shrugged. "Everyone's thinkin' it."

A slight red tinged Atlas's cheeks. *Her* face was burning. Thrym's face hovering directly in front of her wasn't helping. She cleared her throat, sweat breaking out on her forehead.

"We told you to tell the others you were there on research," Atlas said. "But what we didn't tell you is that we told the Mandate all of this. An edited version. But they were aware of where you were the whole time."

"They *knew?*" Phobos said, stupefied.

Atlas nodded. "I contacted them and reported that my people found you; that you were mentally impaired from the crash and my psychiatrists wished to observe you on Earth. The insane space soldiers cost the Mandate billions and billions of dollars every month. The Mandate agreed to let us study your transition."

Elara whistled low. "That was the biggest bluff of The Retreat."

A flicker of amusement crossed Atlas's face. "Yes, it was. They gave us a month. We had a month to find your body replacements."

Thrym's eyes looked over her head, watching Houston. That was the "other stuff" he'd been working on.

Phobos's voice was adamant. "The bodies never would have passed inspection."

Houston rounded in front of Romy, checking the placement of a cable. "Not if we didn't have people in the right places."

The knot was quiet. Could it have worked? Had this organisation infiltrated that far into the Mandate and the Orbitos?

Romy spoke stiffly, not wanting to jostle anything. She was covered in cables and tubes. "You were going to make the switch the next morning. . . ."

Atlas crossed his arms. "I was."

She blinked hard. "And I ruined everything."

He crouched by her side. Thrym refused to budge. Romy didn't want to look at Atlas with Thrym so close.

"I wanted to tell you everything, Rosemary. But I couldn't. The Mandate maintains their presence in each settlement. I knew someone would be watching us, monitoring, reporting back. It could have all fallen apart. Now we know Lucas was their ear."

"How is it that Lucas didn't report you were on Earth?" Phobos asked.

He shrugged. "Atlas is not the name I use aboard the orbitos. As far as Commander Cronus and the Mandate know, Atlas is my top psychiatrist. I have a number of different aliases."

For some reason, Romy hated that his name wasn't Atlas. "Atlas . . . isn't your real name?" She frowned.

He brushed a thumb over her cheek. "Atlas is my real name, Rosemary."

"Why did you even take us back to Jimboomba?" Deimos asked. "Why not bring us straight to the bunker?"

Atlas stood. She wished he'd come back. "Because you wouldn't have made it here alive, Deimos. They would have searched the immediate area and closest settlements until they found you. We had to prepare your body doubles at our main base. This was simple enough; we used 3D printers to alter the appearance of five of our recently deceased soldiers. Houston created your faked results from the samples he took upon your arrival at Jimboomba. The transportation of the bodies to Jimboomba took the longest. Our main base isn't close on foot, and air travel is strictly monitored by the Mandate. We only use it in emergencies and never if we mean to keep a secret. The body doubles had to be transported via the ground, skirting around the settlements on the way. They arrived a week ago. All I needed to do was make the call that you'd discovered the subterfuge and I had to put you down. The fake bodies would be analysed by our own men in the system, leaving the simple matter of getting you to the bunker."

He'd disappeared for a full week. This is where he'd gone? "You came here when you left for that week," whispered Romy.

"There was still equipment we needed here. Once here, we wouldn't be able to leave for some time, until the Mandate turned their eyes elsewhere."

"I can't believe you were going to leave me to die," Deimos exploded.

"He carried you," Phobos said quietly. "All the way here when you lost consciousness. Over the hill, on his back."

Deimos snapped his mouth shut.

One of the machines was whirring faster and faster, the sound building. Romy tried to look back, but was held in place.

"This will fix her?" Thrym asked Houston.

He surveyed Romy with tight lips. "I'm not sure. There's never been anyone like her. No one has ever come through what she has . . . mentally intact."

"How many of the space soldiers have killed a human, though?"

"Many, unfortunately," Houston said sadly. "Twenty years after The Retreat, when our organisation was young, they revolted against the Mandate. It was before anyone knew what happened when a space soldier took a human life. The battle was quickly lost when the bulk of our force lost their minds. There hasn't been another one since."

Her mind was boggled by the fact there had even been a rebellion she wasn't aware of. But of course, the memory wipe would have erased all traces of that, if she'd been alive then. "Wouldn't Earth humans remember that?"

"Settlements are few and far between," he reminded her. "And the Mandate controls all communication. We only see what they wish us to see."

Houston clicked a button and peered up at the screens. Romy could just see one screen by straining her eyes upwards. You couldn't see the five exits anymore; instead, images of two brains flickered into view.

"This is the brain of one of the soldiers aboard Orbito Four." It was a brain full of reds, yellows, and oranges. *A brain full of pain*, she thought.

"And this is little skyling's brain." He clicked again.

Romy couldn't see the rest of the other screen.

There was a long pause. ". . . I don't see the difference," Elara said.

"Exactly!" Houston rounded the bed, eyes flicking over the two pictures as though he was staring at a secret the rest of the world couldn't see. "Then why is she still sane?"

"Get the card out, H." Atlas settled on the foot of the bed once more.

Romy stared at him. There was so much she wanted to say.

But she settled for the words, "I'm so sorry, Atlas. I messed everything up. I . . . I should have trusted you."

His stone eyes softened, framed by black lashes. He half-smiled at her. "I'm sorry you couldn't. I knew you could sense there was something going on, but my hands were tied. You're not to blame for this."

She smiled back.

"All right," Houston said. "Everyone stand back and *brace*."

Thrym took a large step back, and the others held their arms in front of their faces. Elara gripped onto the side of her chair with one hand.

Atlas didn't move.

Romy tensed, ready for the pain.

Houston cracked his knuckles. "In three, two. . . ."

Click.

Seconds ticked by.

And nothing happened.

"It's done," Atlas said gently.

"But I. . . ." She frowned. "It didn't hurt." For some reason she'd expected pain.

Houston was ripping the cables from her, laughing like a madman after his dramatic display.

Then Romy realised.

The ringing was gone! She closed her eyes, searching.

The glass.

It was fixed.

The cracks had disappeared. Romy sobbed, and pressed a trembling hand to her mouth. The cracks were gone. She wasn't broken anymore.

Experimentally, she let go of the sheets.

There was no floating sensation.

No feeling that she could be ripped from Earth in an instant.

She gasped, opening her eyes to stare at Houston. He winked at her, squeezing her hand, which was frozen like the rest of her.

"How did you know that would work?" she asked.

"I didn't," Houston answered.

Thrym interrupted. "*Why* did it work?"

"I've tried it before, with poor results. But for whatever reason—that I will most assuredly be getting to the bottom of—it worked on the little skyling." The excitement in his voice was clear. Houston glanced sideways at her. "I would expect you wouldn't remember much outside of this cave?"

"I. . . ." Romy frowned. "I remember from the time Atlas found me, uh. . . ." Her face heated.

"Gloriously naked under the waterfall?"

She turned away, blushing. "I remember how much it hurt. The thoughts I had." She covered her eyes. "I had some terrible thoughts about you all. . . . You have no idea how grateful I am that you made that go away, Houston." Romy dropped her hands. "*Thank you.*"

"Do you remember why you were in pain, little skyling?"

She picked up the short strands of her hair. They were still pink. "I . . . hurt someone." Her eyes met Atlas's. She tried to reach back, but there was nothing there. "I think."

"And what do you remember about each of us?" he asked. "What do you remember about Atlas, for instance?"

A beautiful ocean was drawn from somewhere in her mind. "A sunset at the ocean," she said, puzzled. "His office. The . . . the locked room. And your bungalow." Her eyes met his once more. "I know you're commander of Orbito Four."

Concern etched Atlas's handsome face. A face she trusted. "How do you feel?" he croaked.

She flexed her fingers, swinging her legs down as the last of the electrodes were removed. Romy stood, wobbling ever so slightly. Her body was exhausted, severely fatigued. They said she'd been functioning and taking care of herself, but she hadn't really.

She was filthy for a start, filthier than any of the others. Her mouth was completely dry; she hadn't been drinking water.

And she was ravenously hungry. Her stomach rumbled, echoing through the cavern.

"Did you just fart?" Phobos asked.

Her face flamed anew. "That was my stomach!"

"Sure."

"Shut up, Phobos." Elara rolled her eyes. Romy threw her a grateful look.

Her legs trembled from holding her weight.

"Ro, honey," Deimos said gently.

She started. The twins came round from the other bed. She looked to her other side where Elara and Thrym had neared.

The knot enclosed her in their arms.

And she held tightly to them, tears falling silently to the floor as she said, "I'm okay. I'm okay."

Deimos shifted to hold her closer, and she met Atlas's eyes through a small gap.

He stood with Houston, who was wiping his eyes beneath his glasses.

Atlas looked sideways at Houston, and quirked his lips when he met her eyes again.

She grinned, her heart swelling in her chest.

Knot 27 was together, and alive. And that was all that mattered.

Or . . . it used to be. Romy studied the man she had alternately trusted and distrusted for weeks. She was glad it turned out she could do the former. Glad for him, but also for herself. Romy could trust in her instincts again.

It was all okay now.

Atlas was turning from the room. Romy attempted to untangle herself.

"Where are you going?" She stared after the towering man over Elara's arm.

He turned in the doorway. "I need to contact the main base and have them send a force to retrieve us."

She eyed her friends, who stood as a barrier between her and Atlas and sent him an exasperated smile. "I don't think I'm going anywhere."

And those were the last honest words she ever spoke to him.

CHAPTER THIRTY-THREE

Pain shot through Romy as she was slammed against the Mandate vehicle.

It was only two hours ago that Atlas made the call for his organisation to collect Knot 27 from the bunker.

That was when Houston had turned the screens back from Romy's brain to the security cameras at the bunker's five exits.

All five cameras had shown Mandate soldiers. They were surrounded. Houston had raced for Atlas, who had already seen on another set of screens in the control room. For a while everything was chaos.

And all they could say was how they shouldn't have been found.

. . . Until Atlas figured it out.

"They caught Tina," he said.

Tina was part of the rebellion. She'd known everything about the bunker. About the knot. About Atlas. She'd tried to run, knowing with Lucas dead and the knot gone, she'd be targeted. Obviously, Tina didn't make it far.

Romy cried out, her hands twisted behind her back and contained with a sharp binding. There was gunfire everywhere, all of it aimed at the object in the sky. The flying contraption containing all of her friends—her knot, Houston, and Atlas.

The man behind her gripped her neck and marched her to another vehicle. But she didn't—*couldn't*—take her eyes off her friends in the sky. They weren't supposed to come back for her, she screamed inside. But she should have known they would. Being part of a knot was a life sentence.

The gunfire was lessening.

The Mandate was realising the flying machine was too far away to hit. Romy closed her eyes with a smile.

The vehicle door opened and Romy was shoved through it, hitting her head hard against the top of the car. The Mandate's hunters were yelling at her in a wall of noise.

But she couldn't stop herself from smiling, even as a syringe plunged into her neck and black flooded her vision.

They got away.

* * *

"We open this door; it has the least amount of soldiers on the other side. We rush them," Atlas decided.

One of the exits only had seven soldiers at it.

Even odds.

If the knot were combat trained.

Which they weren't. The odds weren't remotely even.

"We open all the doors."

She looked up to find them all staring at her. It was she who spoke.

Romy stared at the screens. "If we open one they'll rush to that exit."

"The exits are at least five hundred metres apart," Atlas said. "They won't know which one to cover."

"Exactly," she said. But Romy had another plan.

Houston was busy wiping the medi-tech of information, transferring and destroying all evidence of Romy's body.

The knot had none of their packs. Only the old map that Romy purposefully gave to Elara for safekeeping. It seemed pointless now, knowing Atlas was part of an uprising, but she didn't want to leave it behind for the Mandate to see. Banging and crashing made her jump. Houston was smashing the machines. Thrym was helping him while Deimos looked on, swaying on his feet. The shot Houston gave Deimos earlier was beginning to wear off. How much more could he take? Apparently yet another shot of the energy-boosting substance; Houston administered it while Phobos joined in the smashing.

"Okay." The doctor nodded to Atlas. "I'm ready."

Romy had never seen him so serious. And she knew it was a bad sign.

"How far away are your friends?" she asked, rushing after Atlas as he left the room and entered a different one. One full of controls.

"Nearly two hours," he answered tersely. "It will take us most of that time to reach the surface." He shouted to Houston, who shouted back.

They were ready to leave.

Atlas closed his eyes, wiping at a sheen of sweat. Romy watched his actions carefully. There was a red button in front of each entrance's camera. It seemed simple enough.

"What's this one for?" Romy asked. There was another green button off to one side.

"It seals off the internal rooms from the tunnels."

Atlas moved down the line, pushing on all of the red buttons. Red lights began to flash in the cavern, noiselessly alerting them that the bunker was open to attack.

Atlas grabbed her arm. "Come on. You're up front so I can keep an eye on you."

They ran for the exit with the least number of soldiers. Atlas pulled Romy along by the hand. They ran for half an hour, Deimos keeping up for now.

Romy looked back at Elara, who was flagging.

"Atlas," she called. "I'm going back to help Ellie."

He gave her a hard look.

"Or I can stay up here with you and we won't notice when Ellie collapses," she said harshly.

Atlas opened his mouth.

"Atlas," panted Houston. "We need to move. We don't have time."

Romy looked pointedly at him and moved back so the others could pass. "Keep going." She whispered encouragement to them. Phobos patted her back as he passed. Deimos gave her a smile. Thrym asked her if she was all right.

She fell into step behind Elara and grabbed her hand, dragging her, aware that Atlas was turning back to watch her movements from the front.

"Atlas," called Thrym. "We need your help with Dei."

Atlas threw one last look Romy's way before bending underneath one of Deimos's arms to support him.

"Keep your eyes on the ground in front of you, Ellie. Just focus on that. You'll be there soon," she encouraged her friend.

Elara whimpered and did as her lying knot mate asked.

And that was when Romy turned back.

She flew down the tunnel. And she knew that despite not having enough time to return for her, that they would. Because that was what a knot did.

They protected each other until the end.

So she ran, surpassing speeds she'd ever run before. Flying over rock in the flashing red light of the cavern. Romy always thought she'd be running through trees on Earth. Leaping over logs. Leaves brushing her face. Not to be, it seemed.

She skidded into the control room, unable to tell how much time had passed. It didn't matter because she couldn't hear her friends in pursuit so they were too late.

Romy sprinted for the green button and pushed it.

She ran back out to the main chamber and watched the doors come down. Her eyes widened as she spotted Atlas hurtling around the corner.

"Rosemary!" he shouted. "Don't do it! Open the doors."

She studied the doors' descent. He wouldn't make it. "Atlas, please take care of them," she called. "Go now, and make sure you all survive. I'll help from down here."

"Please," he shouted. Romy faltered at the utter despair in his next words. "I need you."

The doors were nearly closed. "You have my memory card. Houston will figure it out. Thank you for trying, Atlas. Thank you so much," she called back, her voice breaking.

She steeled herself. "Take care of them, Atlas. Promise me!"

The bunker sealed with a resounding boom.

Romy watched him for ten minutes as Atlas threw his fists against the bunker wall. He knew how futile his efforts to break in were. He was shouting, but she couldn't hear anything, until he turned to the camera and then she could read his lips.

"Please open the door," he said.

She couldn't look away, even as she refused to listen to his plea.

Ten more minutes passed before he gave up and sprinted away.

She deflated. Even though it was her last wish that he keep them safe, it was also the last time she'd ever see Atlas and his half-smile.

Her eyes fell on the cameras in front of her.

The fools, she thought.

The Mandate's forces had split in half. Half were entering the tunnels, while half stayed outside. Romy smiled and pushed the red buttons, walking down the row of them as Atlas had over an hour earlier.

She looked at the clock on the wall. Eleven-fifteen shined back at her. The ETA for pickup was midnight.

It took the soldiers outside a few moments to understand what was happening. And by then it was too late. The flashing red lights in the bunker calmed. Romy knew they would have stopped in the tunnels, too. Atlas would understand her plan.

That she'd sealed the outside doors. The Mandate's forces were now halved.

The odds were even.

Romy swallowed as she watched the impassive faces of the Mandate soldiers through the cameras. It took them thirty minutes to arrive outside the sealed bunker.

But there was one tunnel they didn't arrive through.

The one by which her knot left. It gave her hope.

Romy looked at the clock. It was now 11:47 p.m.

She walked back along the row of red buttons, pressing each one. The flashing red lights resumed in the bunker. And Romy smiled again.

The soldiers outside stayed put. They'd learnt. What a shame.

The soldiers in the tunnel outside the bunker scrambled back, raising their guns, wondering if the red light signified attack.

And that's when she saw them.

Her knot and Atlas. Outside.

She pressed her face to the screen. Phobos was unconscious; Elara was clutching her side. But they were alive! Atlas shot the three guards outside with eerie precision. He'd done as she asked. Tears streamed down her face. He was looking after her family.

Romy watched until the knot was out of sight.

And walked slowly to the green button. It would open the bunker, and seal her fate.

It needed to be her. She was the only knot member without a memory card. The Mandate couldn't glean anything from her. Houston was needed; Atlas was needed. Her knot would take her loss hard, but Houston now had the information from Romy needed to help them. Knot 27 had each other. They'd be fine, as long as they got away from here.

Romy had to keep them safe.

That was her job all along.

CH/\PTER THIRTY-FOUR

F*lames, smoke, burning.*

The first sensation Romy registered was the reek of smoke on her clothing. Her pupils moved beneath her eyelids as she took stock.

There was a beeping noise. A bunch of beeping noises. And an incessant ringing in her ears. For some reason the sound tickled something deep within her. A forgotten terror.

Romy's head lay flopped to one side. Her feet were bare. She twitched her toes. *What happened?*

The smoky smell brought a rush of images to the surface. Her breath quickened and the beeping on the machine grew faster and faster.

A door slid open and Romy focused on the rise and fall of her chest, attempting to calm her breathing.

"Which one's playing up and making all the racket?" someone asked in bored tones.

Romy inhaled and then went limp, keeping the movement of her ribs shallow and even.

Footsteps approached. "This one," another voice answered.

"You wouldn't think it, would ya?"

"What?" the second man grunted.

The man whacked Romy in the leg.

"That this one could cause so much trouble. Don't know why they just don't put her down. It's not like there ain't three thousand, nine hundred and ninety-nine others, ya know?"

The second made an exasperated sigh. "How about because they cost three billion dollars to make?"

"Yeah, I know. But they can afford it, right?"

Romy's mind raced beneath her motionless state. *She'd been shoved in the vehicle; they'd knocked her out.* The Mandate were going to keep her alive? What for?

"Guess so. But waste not, want not. That's New Earth," the second man joked.

"Take less than you need!" the two choroused, then chuckled.

"Plus," the man continued, "I heard they're not sure whether this one'll make it, anyhow. Said she might've gone loop-the-loop."

Romy felt twin pinpricks where the men stared at her. She desperately wanted to wrench upwards and take them by surprise. But she had no idea where she was. A lab, maybe? Or a hospital? They'd said, "Which one's playing up?". She took that to mean there were others in here.

Please not my knot.

The sound of swishing water caught her attention.

Where on Earth was she?

The more intelligent of the two made an awed sound. "I never met a crazy one before."

"Bert from Collections said he's heard they keep the bonkers ones on Orbito Four. That's the research orbito, you know."

"They'd do better to just use their parts to make useful soldiers."

"Expensive times. Expensive times. More cost effective long-term to observe and study them to try and eliminate the fault in future batches."

"Did Bert say that, too?"

"Why do you always say that? Maybe I thought up those words my own self," the man said angrily. He sighed. "Anyways, I think it's right they try to get rid of the nutter gene. That's all we need, looney soldiers protecting our kids."

"You don't have a kid. The Mandate won't let you reproduce. You're too dumb."

The answering voice was indignant. "I told you, the results were wrong! I was sick on the day of the I.Q. test."

"Yeah, yeah. Well, I'm just not sure about all this nonsense. Seems too tricky to me."

"*Obviously*, the top people know more about space stuff than you do."

"And a lot more about everything than you."

A clanging came from underneath her. The table Romy was on began to roll forwards. The two men held a disgruntled silence for a time as they pushed. Romy cracked an eye open and couldn't help the small jerk when she saw where she was.

There was a reason knots were called knots. She stared at the chaos of tubes and tanks gathered in clusters. She was in a cultivation room. Romy barely withheld her gasp as she realised what was happening. They were putting her back in a tank!

The endless room was covered in tanks, gathered in clusters of five. Unsuspecting, genetically enhanced space soldiers, raised for the slaughter. Bile seared her throat. It made her want to burn the whole building to the ground. It made her want to drown each and every

Mandate operative in these same tanks. The tanks they used for nothing other than self-gain.

"How long does she have to swim for?" Number One asked.

"Pretty long, I reckon."

Loathing split through her and Romy couldn't bear it any longer.

With a cry she rolled from the trundle bed. Cords ripped free from her neck and arms and she'd smashed a fist into Number Two's face before she could think.

She wavered on her feet, but was drawn to the sound of the other man running. It was the smartest thing he'd done. Romy crouched down and searched the groaning man for a card. She found it attached to his shirt pocket.

Alarms wailed and Romy grimaced. A sinking feeling rushed through her gut. Soldiers were pouring into the hanger as she searched frantically for an escape.

The soldiers sprinted in from all sides. And Romy stood in the middle of the knots, dressed in a hospital gown.

She deflated. There was no escape.

Romy glanced away, down to a tank by her side. A tiny girl floated there. Her eyelids flickered rapidly, expression otherwise serene. It would remain so until she was blown to smithereens by the Critamal on the Mandate's orders.

She backed away from the soldiers as they edged closer, locking her in.

Romy blinked at the tank behind her. It was open, full of translucent gel. She didn't have to guess who it was intended for. It was a cultivation tank, just for her.

The phrases "Pretty long" and "Not sure whether she'll make it" echoed through her mind.

A sharp sting bit between her shoulder blades. By now, she'd been the victim of a tranquiliser often enough to know what it was.

Not a bullet. A sedative.

Romy took two faltering steps as the air around her took on a rushing quality. She reached forwards for the lip of the tank to push herself away. She wasn't going in there willingly. If she went in, who knew how she'd come out. Part of a new knot? An empty shell? She'd forget everyone and everything.

Who knew what they would do to her? She'd *prefer* a bullet.

But that was when she looked at the human-sized tank neighbouring her own. A young boy floated inside. She looked to her other side, where a woman, nearly ready for cultivation, floated in the gel.

She looked every which way, and in every direction it was the same. Her comrades were being developed, unaware of the betrayal. Ignorant of what their lives were to be.

Her grip on the tank tightened, though she didn't push away.

How many space soldiers were in this room? A hundred or more? The tank was the only chance that Romy might one day make it back to help them. That one day, she may remember and help the rebellion.

That one day, she would make the Mandate pay for the longest genocide in Earth's history.

Romy released her grip and tipped forwards, eyes closing against her will. Gel flowed over her as she splashed into her tank. It muted the yelling from outside as the soldiers closed in.

The superficial calm spread quickly. She wondered, peacefully, if she'd ever come out.

Deimos and Phobos's green eyes flashed. She smiled as the hazel eyes of Elara, and the blue eyes of Thrym joined the twins. She called out a greeting to them, frowning when only thick bubbles came forth.

She looked back, and the frown eased. Because a fifth set of eyes had joined her knot.

And they were grey.

Romy blinked at the grey eyes as she descended.

Down.

Down.

Down.

Glossary

Fair Dinkum—*genuine*

Flamin' Galah—*bit of a fool*

Jimboomba—*paradise on earth*

Darl—*term of endearment*

Swag—*a combination of a sleeping bag and tent*

Doona—*duvet cover/blanket*

About the Author

When Kelly is not reading or writing, she is lost in her latest reverie. Books have always been magical and mysterious to her. One day she decided to start unravelling this mystery and began writing.

The Tainted Accords was her debut series. The fourth title in this series releases October 2016. The After Trilogy is her latest work.

A New Zealander in origin and in heart, Kelly currently resides in Australia with her ginger-haired husband, a great group of friends, and some huntsman spiders who love to come inside when it rains. Their love is not returned.

Sign up to her newsletter to receive once monthly emails with release information at www.kellystclare.com

And receive these gifts FREE:

Chapter extras from Jovan's point of view

The Tainted Accords mini coloring book

Translucents (a short story) by Kelly St. Clare

THE RETURN
(The After Trilogy, Book Two)

Three months ago, Romy emerged from the cultivation tanks after a year
floating inside.

Body intact. Mind broken. Memory gone.

Now she undergoes regular testing as doctors work to find out . . . well,
she's not exactly sure what.
The tests must have something to do with the reason she can't remember
her knot--the single lucid memory the other insane soldiers on Orbito
Four still possess. Whatever the researchers are searching for, if it aids the
soldiers in the deathly war against the lethal alien invaders--the Critamal--
the excruciating pain is worth it.

But a grey-eyed man has other plans.

Boxed in and caught, Romy is taken hostage by people who shouldn't
exist! They dress in black and carry weapons she's never seen in her
genetically enhanced life.

Reunited with Knot 27. Memories returned.
Fifteen months have passed since her world shattered into bright red,
ringing chaos. Things have changed--people have changed. How long until
what was once as familiar as breathing is familiar once more?

276

Kelly St. Clare

Friendships. Love. Freedom.

Can the new Romy reconcile with the old, or will the two halves of herself remain locked in an internal battle?
And if a victor should arise from this silent war . . . will it be the part of her that kills without hesitation, without mercy?

All it takes is for the cracks to join and blood will pour.

NOW AVAILABLE

Fantasy of Frost
(The Tainted Accords, #1)

I know many things. What I am capable of, what I will change, what I will become. But there is one thing I will never know.

The veil I've worn from birth carries with it a terrible loneliness; a suppression I cannot imagine ever being free of.

Some things never change…

My mother will always hate me. Her court will always shun me.

…Until they do.

When the peace delegation arrives from the savage world of Glacium, my life is shoved wildly out of control by the handsome Prince Kedrick, who for unfathomable reasons shows her kindness.

And the harshest lessons are learned.

Sometimes it takes the world bringing you to your knees to find that spark you thought forever lost.

Sometimes it takes death to show you how to live.

COMPLETE SERIES NOW AVAILABLE

Kelly St. Clare

Made in the USA
Middletown, DE
24 January 2020